Getting to Lamma

Copyright © 2002 Jan Alexander

All Rights Reserved

ISBN 1-59113-144-8

1st edition published 1997 by Asia 2000, Hong Kong. Revised edition published by Iscandria Press, New York, NY 10023, U.S.A. ©2002 Jan Alexander. All rights reserved. No part of this publication may be reproduced, stored in a retrieval system, or transmitted in any form or by any means, electronic, mechanical, recording or otherwise, without the prior written permission of the author.

MANUFACTURED IN THE UNITED STATES OF AMERICA.

The characters and events in this book are fictitious. Any similarity to real persons, living or dead, is coincidental and not intended by the author.

Booklocker.com, Inc. 2002

Getting to Lamma

Jan Alexander

Getting to Lamma

Dedication

*For Elizabeth Evans Wroton Alexander and James Carlisle Wroton III.
In loving memory.*

Acknowledgements

Special thanks for this edition to Delorys Welch-Tyson, and to Jean-Marc for being there. Others who made this book possible include my editor, Mike Morrow; Moveable Feast in Hong Kong; my teachers Bob Shacochis and Lynn Freed and the Bennington Writing Workshop, and the friends and family members whose guidance and encouragement pointed The Way.

Cover illustration and design by Julie Tam.

Feng Shui for Our Times

The ancient sages of China believed that in the beginning, a great vital force, or qi, thundered forth from the infinite space they called the universe. Qi landed in a frenzy and created yang, or male life force. Afterward it rested and gave birth to yin, or female life force.

From the yin and yang sprang the seasons, and the metaphysical elements that reigned over one another in a circle without hierarchy.

Each element had a governor. Wood was the agent of the Minister of Agriculture. If this minister became corrupt, the Minister of the Interior, in charge of metal, would set things right.

Metal overcomes wood.

If the Minister of the Interior became corrupt, the Minister of War, governor of fire, would punish him.

Fire overcomes metal.

If the Minister of War became corrupt, the Minister of Justice, governor of water, would put a stop to his evil deeds.

Water overcomes fire.

If the Minister of Justice became corrupt, the Minister of Works, governor of earth, would execute him.

Earth overcomes water.

Earth was the agent of the Minister of Works. If he became corrupt, the people of the land would rebel, led by the Minister of Agriculture.

Wood overcomes earth.

Just as the seasons cancel one another, justice cancels corruption and corruption cancels justice. Yang conquers yin and binds her feet, but yin still refuses to stay in place.

There is no final resolution, but there is always a new season.

Chapter 1

My plane careened into Hong Kong's neon skyline and hit the ground with no loss of speed. I heard a whoosh as the cabin door opened, letting in a blast of heat that reeked of noxious chemicals. Intoxicating truth. I stood up, swaying a little.

I was running from Tim and his cocaine madness. I'd lived with the razor-scratched mirrors, with our bank accounts drained, with the fear he'd be waiting every time I went outside. If he'd known where I was going he'd really do some damage. "I suppose you're thinking of running off to Asia with your scrawny little boyfriend," he'd screamed often enough. It was true, I was dreaming of exotic places, and Steve happened to be in Asia. Out of the frying pan into the hot wok.

Steve might be here to meet me. He'd said he would, though he wasn't always reliable. But I wasn't here just to see him. Hong Kong was a quick stop on my way to Shanghai. "Why don't you teach English in China?" Steve had made the suggestion years ago, right after we first met, while grazing my hand and insisting he wasn't just another married man after my then-young body. The perfect solution, I decided when we became lovers. I could leave the country and get out of this foolish entanglement as the victor. Instead I married Tim. Okay, so Steve staked a claim to this continent while I was caught up in a mess of a marriage. No matter. I was here to be an explorer in my own right, even though, on this night in July, 1990 I was at least a hundred years too late to discover something new in the land mass that was Asia. I filled out my entry card while standing in the immigration line.

"Occupation," the card requested. There should, I decided, be enough space to write "Disillusioned Westerner, not a believer in any opium-clouded myths of the Orient, seeking nonetheless to discover what's on the other side." Surely there were enough of us coming through this airport every day. I shook my pen and squeezed in "Journalist and teacher."

Past immigration and customs, I carried my heavy equipment — cameras and a laptop — and light suitcase down a long hallway, pushing my way into the greeting area. It was a vast room, air-conditioned close to the freezing point in spite of the hordes of people — stooped old women in Mandarin jackets, young men and women in trendy fashions, their bodies slim and swaying like bamboo reeds, a few British-looking faces here and there, voices shouting into mobile phones. Everyone greeting someone. In my fantasy scenarios — and there had been many fantasy scenarios – Steven West had always been at the foot of the gangplank as I caught my first whiff of Asian air.

In my fantasy, I always floated down to his rapturous embrace. At last I saw him, a head of wiry dark hair amidst many heads. Neither-of-us-believed-I'd-ever-follow-my-heart-and-join-him-and-now-what-do-we-do, I realized in a flash, and considered fleeing, except how do you flee from flight?

Steve threw his arms around me, bags and all.

"You're here! You're actually here!" He sounded amazed.

"You... look wonderful," I said. He still knew just how to disarm me. In his gaze I was a goddess just beyond his reach. Funny, in my twenties I'd loved him partly because he made me feel unattainable, when actually he was the one who couldn't be had.

His face was florid, warm against mine. For a moment our lips and tongues moved like a random collision, until they found the old rhythm and tangoed together long enough for another plane to land.

Steve was still wiry all over, with deep-amber eyes that sunk into half-moon shapes when he brooded. Even his chin, which was long with a slight cleft, had a way of twisting to the right when we argued, to the left when he relaxed. He had never been drop-dead handsome, but he had a cocky half-smile and a confident stride that were, I think, what women noticed first about him. That and the way his hair was always disheveled from the way he ran his hands through it while lost in thought.

But now, in spite of the half-smile, he looked wilted, his hair sprinkled with gray. Now that he was not-quite forty, he looked as if he'd been wrestling with life and spending more time traipsing through jungles than keeping his college-swim-team muscles toned. I liked that about him, that his vanity was more cerebral than physical. He still smelled like sandalwood soap, but it didn't mask a tropical dampness that clung to him.

"Soooo... show me Hong Kong," I said. His chin drew back in a way that suddenly made me feel as if we'd disconnected.

"You haven't changed a bit," he said.

Seven years ago, on the morning of my wedding day, Steve had called and said, "Come run away with me to a tropical island." His voice choked just enough that I thought he might be acting.

"Too late," I said.

"Will you still be Madeleine Fox?"

"Of course." I couldn't imagine signing my name as Mrs. Tim Donnelly, or Madeleine Donnelly, like some middle-aged hausfrau. I was only twenty-seven

and I was marrying Tim because he'd promised we'd be free but together — my life with him to lean on, always faithful, unlike Steve.
"Did you like the present?" Steve asked.
"I opened it and had a sense of craziness. Does that make sense?"
"Sure. That's because you're marrying a man you don't love."
"I *do* love him."
The present, which he'd had delivered to my parents' apartment, was a large globe with white oceans, on a shiny brass pedestal. The card said, "You can always find me. Love, Persona Non Grata."

Steve was a reporter for *Worldweek* magazine. Around the time I agreed to marry Tim, Steve received word that he was finally getting an Asian posting. While I was planning my wedding, he was planning his move to Bangkok. Two years later, it was Hong Kong. I looked longingly at the globe whenever I visited my parents. I read everything I could find about Zen and authoritarian governments, ancient ruins at Angkor Wat, gamelin music, capitalism with Chinese characteristics. I imagined him moving on and growing world-weary, never quite clean, never without a notebook. Something squirmed. I imagined scenarios in which my husband's objections didn't exist, and I'd catch up with Steve on the Eastern Hemisphere and we'd talk about the things we'd seen. That was when the future hovered over me like a vast euphoric cloud in which anything was possible, when I was so young that the future seemed light years away from the moment of confrontation. But here I was, breathing Hong Kong's steamy air, realizing that eventually you have to get there.

Steve and I stood in the taxi line, touching each other like objects with intriguing textures, talking about the heat and what we might do with the time we had tonight. We got to the front of the line and he opened the door for me. Instantly the air turned frigid. In the cold back seat we brushed hands, stroked thighs, kissed, explored. His hands had bony knuckles and a leathery feel. "I love your untamable hair," he said.

The driver, a skinny young man in a white shirt, jerked his head back in my direction from time to time. He wasn't watching us; it was a tick that made him jerk back that way, each time revealing one glazed, lizard-like eye. He was driving like a maniac the whole time, changing lanes every time he got a few yards behind another car.

"Slow down," Steve shouted.
The driver shrugged and muttered something.
"*Qing man yi diar,*" I said.
"Don't bother showing off your Mandarin," Steve said. "They don't speak it here."

I knew that, of course — but Miss Hong, who'd been my tutor the past year, had said sometimes Mandarin worked in Hong Kong. Steve had always had an abrasive streak. It had come out at odd moments in the past, always followed by a worshipful apology and assurance that the rough-edged comments flew out of his mouth because he was a flawed guy, much too preoccupied with himself, but he'd try in the future to be more deserving of me.

I shivered. Steve put his arm around me, an apologetic gesture. I smelled manly, tropical sweat.

"Do you remember the story of the man who bought exactly one hundred and six bricks to build a house, to perfectly detailed blueprints? Then when he finished building the house, he found he had one brick left, which made him so furious he hurled the brick up into the air and out of sight?" Steve asked, his long chin, so cleanly shaven it glistened, grazing my shoulder.

"Is there a moral to this story?"

"And then there was a fat old dowager who was sitting on an airplane, next to a man with a big cigar."

"Why wasn't the man the fat one?"

"Oh okay, he was fat. She was aging in a graceful way, and had far more substance than she'd had in her youth. Anyway, she had an obnoxious little yipyap dog in her lap."

"Right," I said. "And she said I can't stand your cigar and he said I can't stand your dog. So they agreed they'd throw both out the window."

"You have heard it?"

I groaned and pinched his cheek. "So the dog landed on his feet, since he'd been to some New Age guru who'd taught him to believe he was a cat in a previous life, and guess what was in his mouth when he landed, the brick."

"A body rises in space, a body falls in space. Infinite combinations can come together, as a matter of chance. One event miles away changes another."

"We're not miles away anymore," I pointed out.

"Not in theory. Things will happen to you."

I kissed him.

"Kowloon," Steve said.

Our driver had plowed into a snarl of traffic. The slower we moved the faster his head twitched. Light rain steamed off the cars. Faces seemed to be peering down at us from double-decker buses, as if we were being watched. This wasn't a good thing to be doing, groping with Steve in the back seat of a cab while his wife and son were at home. Anne was not the enemy. Anne was sort of a saint – too all-good for him. They had a convenient but distant marriage, rushed into when he was only twenty-three, when *Worldweek* Magazine hired him and he dragged her from New Orleans to New York. She went with him and didn't like

New York, didn't like Asia. I assumed they both made an impulsive decision when they were too young, and now they had a child. I didn't want to be another woman's nemesis, yet it seemed so unfair, that I'd loved him partly because he wanted to take me to exotic places while she just wanted to go home. I was going to have to move on soon.

I looked out at Hong Kong. It was a place slapped together with fast money. Apartments churned out by the hundreds, laundry hanging on every balcony, shopping malls connected by steel beams to bigger, brighter shopping malls, lights blazing on night shift. I had seen pictures but still imagined, for no logical reason, that there would be a few willow trees.

The driver let us off on a jumbled street.

"It's so packed we might as well walk it," Steve said. "And if you think this is bad wait 'til you get to Shanghai."

He paid the driver, and slung my bags over his shoulders. The heat fell over us again.

"You're traveling light, considering," he said. I'd shipped my books and winter coat to Shanghai. Clothes can be washed by hand every few days and worn so often people remember you by a color; this I had learned from my job as an associate editor at a travel magazine. I was wearing an ensemble I'd selected to make me look like the traveler-without-itinerary that I was: pale blue jeans, ivory linen jacket, beige designer sandals and leather knapsack.

"I hope I'm not more baggage," he added.

We crept through a pedestrian traffic jam, past hawkers' carts spewing out rancid smoke. My jeans clung to the backs of my knees and my head felt foggy.

"People are always horrified by that smell the first time," he said.

"What is it?"

"Dried squid."

The moderate-priced hotel I'd found through a guidebook — Steve had tried one place that was booked, warned me that the backpacker haven called the Chung King Mansions was also a flophouse for drug dealers and cockroaches, and left the rest to me — had a garish but clean lobby. The desk clerks and the guests milling about were Indian, the men in turbans and women in saris. The efforts at decor stopped in the elevator, which had bare painted walls.

My room had no windows. There were two twin beds with threadbare chenille spreads.

Steve stared at my surroundings, frowning. I turned on the air conditioner, which was perched in a hole in the wall. It made vicious whirring sounds as it blew out freon.

"I'm used to staying either in luxury hotels or native huts," he said.

"I'm here to see the city, and you, not a hotel," I said. We stood swaying against each other.

"Want to go out?" he asked.

"MMMmmmm... eventually." I'm not a morning person, and I love staying out all night in a new place, as long as I have a friend to stay out with. There was anxiety in his breathing, in the twist of his chin. He was thinking of what time it was, I could tell. I tried kissing him.

"Do you want to sit on the bed?" he asked. Why didn't he just glide me over there? What if I didn't excite him anymore? I still had wild copper hair and an angular face that people considered pretty in a pronounced, sharp-featured way. I was thirty-four. How much longer would I enjoy the sight of my own lean legs, stretching out inviting him to peel off my jeans?

He laughed a little. The room was musty, the air conditioner circulating dust. I fondled the dark hairs on his arm.

"I should take a shower," I said.

"I like you earthy." He sat next to me on the bed, still tentative at first, warming up as he told me I had the body of a sapling, with lips like ripe berries, then slowly peeling off my tee shirt and jeans. His hands lingered here and there, as if he were looking for something.

There had been a few other men since I'd left Tim — indeed even before we'd split up, there had been that time in New York with Steve, when he'd talked in bed for hours about how exciting it was to be a reporter in Asia and something had stirred in me that wouldn't go away. His body had felt unfamiliar then, as it did now. He was waiting, lying fully dressed beside me, his eyes dark crescents in the light from a cheap gooseneck lamp overhead, and I saw that he was improvising the scenario just as I was. Hold back a little, I decided. Talk and get familiar all over again.

"What made you want to go to Asia in the first place?" I asked him, letting him keep me warm since I was stripped down to my bra and panties, but unbuttoning his shirt only to stroke him in a studious way, memorizing contours and hairs and the rosy amber hue of his skin.

He remained in the same position, only squeezing me a little tighter.

"You love tempting me and pulling back, don't you?" he said, with affection. "You love being pursued and I love pursuing you."

I shrugged. "Actually, I don't know how to pursue..."

"No, you've never had to..." That was how he made me feel like a goddess again. "Anyway, in answer to your question, I read about Edgar Snow. In high school. But even before that I had some idea I couldn't spell out in my mind about being in places where there were insurrections going on that would change things for the better, and being part of it, even if it meant being out in freezing

weather with no shoes. No, especially if it meant being right there in the middle of hardship. Nobody I knew understood what I was talking about, then I heard about Mao and Snow marching through China with him and really believing that this was a great thing. Boy, was I born too late."
I laughed, mostly because I also wanted to march through China with no shoes. "Do you want to know why I came here?"
"If you want to tell me." He kissed parts of my neck.
"You got me intrigued of course, but only because you answered something that had been there a long time. Did I tell you..." I pulled the chenille over us. "Did I tell you that my father enlisted in World War II as soon as he was eighteen, and he wrote for an Army newspaper in Asia and had lots of grand adventures, including of course fucking Asian women left and right?"
"Are you ever going to forgive men for your womanizing father?"

I was here because of things that got started long before I met Steve. It's funny what childhood memories we hang onto. Do we become what we are because of the scenes we remember, or do we remember certain moments because they fit a view of life that's forming even before we're aware of it? I have a recollection of a time, for instance, when I was six or so and had something big on my mind. I went up to my father, sitting in his leather reclining chair as he did in the evenings if he didn't have something more important to do. He would sit there enveloped in his newspapers and cigarettes, and I was pretty sure he didn't really want to be there, living in suburbia with my mother and my sister, Katie, and me. He'd been all over the world.

"What happens when you die?" I asked my father — actually I called him by his name, Walter, or sometimes Walrus like in the Walrus and the Carpenter. Saying "Daddy" felt too much like touching him. I was always nervous, asking him anything. Walrus was handsome, though he was putting on weight around his chin, and his middle, which hung in a paunch over his belt when his starched white shirt was unbuttoned. He always sat in his chair that way — tie on the coffee table, his shoes on the floor, his shirt unbuttoned. He would scratch the bare part of his chest as if it fascinated him. He had very thick brown hair and eyes that were called hazel, like mine, and a face that reminded me of square, flat puzzle parts, except for his long formidable nose that held his horn-rimmed glasses up like a shield to ward off stupid comments from people who didn't know as much as he did. I cleared my throat, and he glared at me. It irritated him when I made coughing and throat-clearing noises. Only years later did I connect it to the cigarettes.
"You become nothing," my father said.
I shivered.

He put his paper down and sighed impatiently, but said, in his booming voice, "Sit here," gesturing to the arm of his chair. I always felt terrified when I got too close to him, terrified of something in the way his breath was always heavy, with a little whistle when he sucked in air, even when he was sitting down, and smelled of tobacco. I thought he liked the sound of his own breath and the way stale cigarettes tasted in his mouth, not caring that it didn't sound nice, or smell nice, to me. And there was his mouth, and the way he would moisten his lips with his tongue. I was afraid his tongue might try to stretch out like a snake and pull me in, just for his own amusement. He could do anything he wanted.

"Maybe," said Walrus, "when people die they just go to San Francisco. Or to the Orient. When someone you know goes far away, you don't see them, right?"

I nodded obediently.

"When they die you don't see them either. So maybe they're just on a long, long trip."

I giggled because I knew he wanted me to. "You're being silly. What really happens?"

"I'm busy. I give you silly answers because you ask silly questions," he said, lifting me off the chair.

Walrus had an album full of pictures that were black-and-white and kind of crumpled. As I eventually pieced together, he had worked for an Army newspaper called *Roundup* in the last years of World War II, and then for a wire service as a reporter for a few years. He went to India, Hong Kong, China, Thailand. He had pictures of himself, looking younger and slimmer and like an old-fashioned movie star, always in a short-sleeved shirt that was a dull color and had a lot of pockets. In some he was seated cross-legged beside a dark man in a strange headpiece. An Indian guru, he said the man was.

"He never has to eat food. He breathes in air and it nourishes him," my father said.

"I want to see a goo-roo," said Katie.

"I'll take you to India someday," he told her. "You'll appreciate it."

He liked Katie better than me because she didn't ask silly questions. She was eight then, two years older than I was, and taller, with sensible hair that mother kept cut just below her chin. My parents said I was the pretty one, but that only meant I didn't count for much. Katie and Mother and I all looked a lot alike, really — we were all kind of lanky, with green eyes and bronze colored hair and sharp features, but the two of them wore their hair chopped off, and wore any old thing from the closet. Katie had just composed her first violin sonata and played it at a school assembly. She thought all of her teachers were stupid.

"I don't wanna go anyway," I said, but I didn't mean it.

"Wouldn't you like to go to China?" he asked me. "They have men there who can make mountains move."

"How do they do that?"

"With their minds."

I didn't ask him to take me, because I knew he'd say no. It was strange that my father wanted to disappear into the big void that I imagined such a trip to be, like actually diving down through a hole in the mud after a rain on the slim hope that you might slither through the center of the earth all the way to China. I tried to picture being swallowed up and becoming nothing. There was something terribly scary about it. Yet there was also something irresistible about whatever was there, on that opposite side of real life. The more I thought about it, I began to believe I could escape to some other side when I grew up, and Walrus wouldn't be in charge of things there.

"So you came in the footsteps of your father?" Steve asked, quite solemnly.

"Yeah... but then there was my mother's infatuation, too. Not that she'd ever been."

The clock radio beside the bed had luminescent numbers. When Steve said, "I want to make love to you," I realized he was thinking of the time and his other obligations. What else could I have expected? A tropical island that was ours alone?

I pretended we were on that island, for a little while, and remembered all the reasons I'd loved him. He understood why I had to discover truths, he listened even when I was being moody because he had promised to immortalize me when he had the time and inspiration to write his novel. He told me my skin was silky, my body a garden of peach blossoms. I told him we were two volcanoes. Later, when we were both damp and relaxed, his legs entangled with mine and it began to feel natural. Yet I could tell, just by his shallow breathing against my heart, that he was calculating how soon he'd have to pull away.

I used to get an urge to fly out the window when Tim said, "it's hard to tell where I end and you begin," which wasn't even true; Tim was a master of overkill, as in the way he convinced me — along with himself — that our grunting groaning acrobatics in bed added up to a reason for getting married. I preferred the idea of partial borders, like *guo*, the Chinese character for country, which has an opening only at the bottom. I always ran to the bathroom right after Tim and I made love, and took my time, enjoying his scent on my body in diluted form, not wanting to merge too closely with him.

Steve said, "You're better than ever," but he liked having borders too. I was good at gyrations and kisses and touching men in the right places, but I wondered if it was possible to lie there afterward and lose myself in some transcendent way that has nothing to do with being swallowed up.

"So... the first night of your grand adventure," Steve said. "We should all get to start over. Why would you look sad at a moment like this?"

"Nothing. Not because of this." I had black spells sometimes that made me feel frozen.

"Tim called just a day before I left," I said.

"You didn't tell him where you were going, did you?"

I shook my head. "He'll find my phone disconnected, and I've left the magazine, and everyone has instructions to tell him I'm traveling somewhere in South America."

He laughed a bit viciously. "A cokehead combing South America..."

I shuddered. "And how's your family?"

"The same."

"Come run away with me." The moment I said it I wished I hadn't. That had been his line.

He stroked a strand of my hair. "You know I would if I could. "

"I was joking."

"Don't worry, you're never alone for long."

"I'm just looking for a handsome intelligent Mr. Wrong to have a baby with," I said.

He didn't know this was an incantation to ward off what I feared might happen. When I was very young I thought men would want to marry me because I made a great show of wanting to be free of binding commitments. You play the game the way men do and time begins to run out. I'd just begun to understand that happy marriage was probably a myth for me. A myth, though, gives comfort. A myth requires sacrifices to the gods, hence my ritual involving Mr. Wrong and the baby, uttered with a swagger I wished was real.

"That'll put a damper on your traveling days," he said.

I pointed out that he had a child and still managed to get around.

"Is that fair? I have pressures too, you know. Listen, we can talk about this tomorrow, but the last ferry is at midnight."

"The guidebook says there's a tunnel."

"I have to go," he said. "Will you be okay?"

I kissed him goodnight at a door with peeling paint and a lock I had to unbolt.

"I don't need a man for this," I said out loud.

In the night I felt his body, reached for a phantom that I could inhale on the sheets, for warm flesh that wasn't there. I need to do this on my own, I reminded myself. In the morning he called and woke me.

"I don't know if I can see you tonight. I'll call you later, okay?" he said.

"Yeah, sure."
"Sorry. Don't let the bastards get you down. I guess I'm one of them."

* * *

I did have a job to do in Hong Kong. I was supposed to write an article for the magazine I'd just left. Work, I thought, is a wonderful thing. As long as someone was counting on me, there was no time to drown in the black hole. I went out and walked alone, down Nathan Road, the main thoroughfare of this people-infested little tail of the Chinese continent, the Kowloon Peninsula. My camera bag swung against my hip as I took my first look at Asia in the daylight. The heat was languid, a heat that owned the land and mocked all efforts to muzzle it, even the icy blasts of air conditioning that blew out of doorways, smelling metallic and destructible. Yet everywhere, people were at work. Men did move mountains here, with cranes. Every inch of Nathan Road was covered with concrete and metal, yet drills whirred everywhere, building buildings on buildings. Man conquers nature and has to keep fighting for his claim.

"Buy cheap Rolex?" a teenage boy asked me. He spoke my language as if it were a salty pill. I pushed past the crowd, sweating. I bought a cold bottle of mineral water from a small stand, and paid for it with huge, heavy coins. I was supposed to look at pearls, and real designer watches, and all of those things that people buy because they think they'll look better or feel better with them while all around the masses feel rotten because they barely have enough to eat. If only I could be really absorbed, like Steve, in articles about politics and business and the things that make the world spin, then maybe it would be easy to place him aside as he'd just done to me. Instead I looked at pearls, in shops that were so cold inside I thought my bones would crack. I watched the beatific look on a woman's face as she walked out with a shiny bag.

"I give you good price," said the man behind the counter. He held up pinkish pearls. They practically glowed, iridescent, so many nuances of color and light. What if my mother had done a painting inspired by pearls?

My mother, who was happiest in old trousers and tennis shoes, carrying a sketchbook in a small backpack in case something inspired her. She would have said give one pearl to every worker crouched down drilling the street, every beggar out there, so that everyone can have an object of beauty. Maybe she'd paint just one pearl, one for every member of the population, or else she'd paint a strand of them in colors as cold as death. Not that she had ever painted material things. She painted people, and bowls of fruit, and trees. There were those times, when I was in high school, those two years that Walrus was gone, running around the world with that other woman, when my mother was always coming home with junk. A china ashtray that was painted in mother-of-pearl colors and had a little mermaid stretched out on one side, smiling. A soapdish, plastic, shaped like an indented turtle shell, with the head and legs sticking out. A small cream pitcher in the shape of a black-and-white cow, with udders. She'd giggled and told me she'd swiped them from the store.

"Why such yucky stuff?" I'd asked.

"I figured I was doing the store a favor getting rid of it." She'd hide the things after she showed them to me, or maybe throw them out.

I fled the jewelry store while the man still held his pearls pointed at me. I walked to Salisbury Road and the harbor, and watched freighters lumber along. I'd never seen a container ship before. Huge boxes, green, red and blue crayon colors, everything inside worth heavenly dollars to someone. Machines for new factories, Dior suits, carburetors, dried potatoes. On the Star Ferry, top deck, I sat by the window and watched Big Mac cartons and a plastic garbage bag bob along the waves like ducks.

I wandered the streets on the Hong Kong side, heading toward Western, up into the mid-levels. The air became hotter as I climbed each section of hill. Heavy air, smelling of glue and spoiled meat. My feet sloshed in my sandals. I bought a barrette to pull my hair up, but tendrils clung to my neck and face, soaked in sweat. On the narrower streets were outdoor stalls, filled with gnarled old men and women selling live chickens, dried fish and toadstool-shaped medicinal herbs, and brilliant arrays of tropical fruit that should have smelled like honey nectar but didn't. The old Chinese people yelled at me to go away when I tried to shoot them. A teenage girl passed by in a shirt that said "The wildest love is double suicide." Against every building was a tiny altar to the ancestors, some made of red lacquer blocks, some just strips of red paper wedged between iron gates. Oranges, apples and mangoes sat on trays beside some of the altars, and incense smoke curled into the air.

Steve had told me once that he was never homesick, but surely all of this had seemed alien to him, too, at least at the beginning. I'd left behind a Manhattan summer, with red and purple petunias blooming in window boxes all over the Upper West Side. I inhaled incense from a little street altar, and felt like a fugitive. I'd left behind a job I liked fairly well, and friends I'd known for years. Yet for so long, I'd been telling everyone who'd listen that I wanted to escape and run around the world. Ever since the day Steve came to town and I agreed to see him, against my husband's wishes. I'd even told Tim I wanted to leave America long enough to let the exotic become familiar, and instead of agreeing to travel with me he'd escaped deeper into his cocaine cloud.

I ate quick, greasy noodles at a small stand, in the daylight. To go into a nice restaurant by myself would make me feel very much alone. I got back to my room about 6:30. The red light on the room phone was lit up. "Mister Steev-a called. And same name, Mister Steev-a called." said the operator. I tried calling his office. No answer. I didn't want to call him at home, although he'd said I could. I felt heavy all over. I lay back on the worn chenille and succumbed to jet lag.

When I first met Steve I was twenty-three, and an affair with a married man was hardly what I had in mind. I didn't especially want to fall in love with anyone, though the idea of romance was alluring. I was living in a West Village walkup with my friend Sandy and a steady stream of visitors. I had a job as a fact-checker with a magazine. The editors treated the fact-checkers like their personal lackeys and the salary was low, yet all of this was satisfying because it felt so very temporary. I felt gloriously free, knowing that one chance encounter might cause me to walk away with a dashing lover, or a great job offer, or a chance to ride the rapids of some tropical river.

Steve came to a party at my apartment one Friday night. I already knew of Steve, who came from New Orleans. I also knew he had a wife. They were a few years older than I was and he was supposedly a rising star at *Worldweek* and planning to be a correspondent in Asia eventually. My ears had perked up when I heard that, and I thought too bad he's married. I started talking to him that night only because I saw him brooding over his whisky glass, gazing outside the circle of people chattering. Anne was not with him. I offered him a refill. "Don't get lost in thought without plenty of this," I said. I had nothing in mind. I was just trying to make my guests feel comfortable. Sure manners are bourgeois, but it's good to make other people feel comfortable, my mother had told me a million times.

"You're not from the South are you?" he asked.

"A little bit. My mother is."

He said there was something in my manner that made him think that. I was well equipped with young-single-woman radar, and I sensed yet another married man trying to come on to me.

"Too bad your wife couldn't make it tonight," I said.

He shrugged. "We don't especially like each other's friends."

We talked and he said he was just biding time in New York, waiting to get sent abroad. "If it doesn't happen soon I'm going to have to think about moving on," he said.

"Moving on. Sounds like a country song," I said. "I'm going to say that one of these days... to my boss, and whoever I'm going out with at the time... I've got to be moving on. Do you move on often?"

I poured a bit of whiskey into my own glass and sipped it straight without wincing too much.

"You could just say you're going to lunch one day and get on a plane with a backpack and never go back to the office," he said.

"Good idea. I'll do it," I said. I meant it. Someday in the distant infinite time I had.

He called the next morning and asked if we could have a drink that afternoon.

"He's on the make," Sandy, my roommate, warned me.

"Pity," I said. "He was nice to talk to." And I met him for a drink because I'd enjoyed talking to him. Was I supposed to deny myself an interesting friend just because he was married?

We sat on barstools in a place full of pale varnished wood and hanging ferns.

"Lots of married men are after my body," I told him halfway through my first bloody Mary. "I came to ask you for suggestions where I could go when I make my grand escape."

"It's tough to be a beautiful woman," he said. He smiled charitably, as if he understood why I needed to be so obnoxious.

"I hope we could be friends," I said. I gazed at him wistfully, pouting. It was an expression I'd perfected.

"We can. But I guess I should admit I'm wildly attracted to everything about you, not just your body."

He would make a nice photo, I thought, his eyes golden-glinted and lusty, his hair tousled. "By the way," he went on, "in answer to your question, lots of people get jobs teaching English in Asia. Anywhere. If I were you I'd try China."

"China?" I rolled the word around in my mind that afternoon in 1979, my elbow resting on the blond-wood bar, downing my second drink. "It must be hard to get into and even harder to get out of."

"Would you be up for an adventure?" he asked.

"That kind, yes."

We became good friends of a sort. He called every day. We had drinks and lunch, not particularly discreetly but nothing was going on anyway, and talked about all kinds of things, especially about going to Asia about the fact that I wasn't willing to sleep with him. He said Anne was a wonderful person. She came from a prominent family in New Orleans, but she'd decided early on to go into social work and counsel troubled teenagers. But she was stressed out by her job in New York, and homesick for her family and lifelong friends. He was cheating, at least in his mind if not officially, on a wife who was a saint. It bothered him but he didn't stop. I said their lives didn't seem to be very compatible.

"Maybe you're the one who needs an anchor while you roam around the world," I said.
"Don't you know it's rude to psyche people out?" He said that teasingly. One evening when his wife had gone home for a couple of weeks, we drank an entire bottle of Beaujolais. Working stiffs' wine and barely ripe, I knew from my father, but like the fruit of knowledge going down. I had no excuse. I wasn't drunk. I just watched him talk and wanted him to be kissing my breasts. Behind my madras cloth, we made love for hours. Four times in a row, I counted. Then another. It was like walking a plank. Tinkerbell was safe walking the plank, I thought. I would have to learn to sprinkle pixie dust and fly. The sun came up while we were groping, still frenzied.

I sent for the application to teach in China, knowing that the best thing to do was exit. I'd enjoyed watching Steve look unhappy while agreeing that I should go. The kind of stories he was doing then involved things like trailing the President's visit to New York, stories that he hoped would impress the *Worldweek's* editors enough that eventually they'd trust him in an overseas bureau. The men I went out with then, including Steve, said I seemed like a woman who did whatever I wanted. Yes, there were other men. The only way to cope with such uncontrollable desire seemed to be to slice it into quarters, into eighths, and share it with friends like the richest chocolate truffle.

I would tell the various other men about my plan to go to China, and they would say things like, "that's fascinating," looking into my eyes with new appreciation. I'll miss you I'd say back. I was perfectly capable of looking men in the eyes and telling them the same stories that they seemed so good at telling women, although it was more fun to say such things when you meant them. I almost meant it when I said, "I'll miss you," to Tim — at least, I thought, I'd miss the way he was stroking my jeans at that moment. He was a struggling actor with dark gold hair and baby blue eyes. I liked his hard jawline and the way he kissed. He was handsome in a faintly working-class way, but he'd told me, more than once, that he was too intelligent to be a product of his upbringing. "Come visit," I'd added. Anything to get that look out of his eyes and purge the way it made me feel evil.

"I can't afford to travel right now," Tim said. A few nights later we were in a restaurant neither of us could afford, and he sulked. "Does Steve West have so much power over you that you have to go all the way to China in hopes that he'll join you? He's as much of a shit as your father was. Some men can be trusted, you know. I've even gone to demonstrations for women's rights." The therapist I'd been seeing recently in New York had said I gave in to Tim because I had a confidence problem, which I used sex appeal to hide. At the time, though, I convinced myself that Tim was right, that my urge to go to China was just a tie to Steve. For the first few years of my marriage I believed I was happy. Tim and I planned a little girl we'd have. We gave her Tim's stone-chisel profile and an explosive talent that we'd nurture from a very early age. We would deny her nothing. Of course, we would have her sometime in the distant future, when we got over our chronic shortage of both time and money. We went out to clubs and parties almost every night and spent all the money we had.

When he got the soap opera role he thought we'd be happy forever. "You shouldn't waste your talent fact-checking other people's stories. Stay home and write," he told me. I concentrated on writing short stories, some of which were published in literary magazines that paid almost nothing. I had a small exhibition of abstract photographs, but I put my cameras away afterward, tired of trying to see something essential in the scenes before me. Let's go traveling, I said to Tim.

"We'll go this summer," he said. "We can't afford plane tickets right now." Summer came and we were still short of cash.

I believed I was happy until the winter that Steve called just after New Year's, when he was passing through town on his way back to Asia.

"I'd love to see you. Couldn't we have lunch?" he asked. We hadn't seen each other in five years.

"It's crazy not to," I agreed.

I dressed carefully for the occasion, in black onyx earrings, black stretch pants and black boots with a blue tunic sweater. It was a day of pale-yellow sunshine and a crisp breeze. I waited outside a restaurant, glad that Steve was a little late, giving me time to change my mind and run. But I kept waiting, and when a taxi screeched up to the curb, I watched him climb out, smiling at me with no sign of fear, exactly twelve minutes late by my watch.

He moved toward me, arms outstretched. Dangerous. My hands were still trembling. He was wearing only a trenchcoat. He'd never learned to dress for Northern winters. The first words that came out of my mouth, after so many years, were "Aren't you cold?"

He smiled. "No," he said. "It's great to see you." I felt him gazing at me, and saw that the golden tint in his eyes had begun to fade.

Sitting down, with a bottle of wine on the way, I let my mouth babble with a life of its own.

"So," I said, "how do you like Asia?"

"I love it," he said. "I have everything I wanted careerwise."

The waiter brought wine and poured it into our glasses.

"How," I began, feeling a little twist of malice curling the right side of my lips, "is your novel coming along?"

"Haven't had time for it in years." He shrugged unconcernedly, as if the thought had been dredged out, no longer useful, from a drawerful of battered pencils and long-crumpled shopping lists.

We ordered food. He said he was hungry. The wine stem teetered in my hand.

"So, how's your marriage?" he asked.

"Fine... I still have your wedding present. At my parents' apartment of course. Funny, Tim knows about it anyway. Not long after our wedding he saw it and came home furious at me, saying he touched it and could tell it came from you. So I asked my mother to keep it hidden."

He looked at me strangely, which I figured was appropriate. I still found Tim's mysterious bursts of ESP creepy. "I guess he still hates me?"

"You're sort of a... a potential death sentence that hangs over an otherwise perfect marriage."

"Perfect? And monogamous?"

"Yes. Although, he'll never forgive me..."

"What's to forgive or not forgive? You know what I've always said. There's love fucking, there's recreational fucking, there's revenge fucking and just plain curiosity fucking. And I suppose there's even utilitarian fucking, if your main goal is to procreate. How can you deny someone a range of experiences?"

Steve could be so juvenile, talking like that. Definitely, I told myself, Tim's faults were less detrimental than his. Yet I toyed with the food that had arrived, trying to look down, away from his eyes.

"I can't believe we're arguing about this," I said.

"Sorry. I didn't want to turn this into an argument."

I nodded and took a bite of bread and butter. "So, how's your marriage?"

"Same as always. We have a two-and-a-half year old boy."

A sliver of bread dropped from my hand.

"You haven't had kids, have you?"

"We plan to. When we have more money."

"I thought Tim was making a bundle from television."

I shrugged, toying again with the same piece of bread. "It slips through your pockets here, you know that."

He looked at me curiously. "I wish you could come and work with me."

"I'm not a political reporter."

"It's not too late. Or you could do other things. I still want to show you the world."

He touched my hand, twisting my wedding ring.

The next day I went up to his hotel room, but we only kissed. Technically, I wasn't seduced; that didn't happen until his next trip to New York, six months later. By then, I'd left Tim. Steve wasn't responsible for what happened in those intervening months. Certainly it wasn't his fault that Tim woke me up in the middle of the night, shaking me and saying "You saw your boyfriend. It came to me. You want to be in Asia with him."

It was Katie, who always knew everything, who said, "Dummy. Where is your diary?" On her suggestion, I went through the spiral notebooks that I used as diaries. I'd trusted Tim, who'd said he'd never read anything without my permission, and kept the notebooks in the bottom drawer of my desk. Katie was right. Everything Tim knew about Steve was written there.

I hid my diaries and thought about exotic escapes. Tim dragged himself in from the studio exhausted almost every day. I nagged him to see a doctor. "How much cocaine is he doing?" asked know-it-all Katie. I went to a couple of Al Anon meetings, and began making phone calls to drug clinics, couples therapists, anything to pin down the problem. He got mad every time I suggested help. We ran out of money; there was nothing left in our checking account, even in the overdraft. We had over $50,000 in credit card bills. We did go to a bankruptcy lawyer together.

One night I half-dreamed of a knife at my throat and found him close to me, grabbing me up from my nest of pillows.

"You're such a jerk," he shouted. "You spend so much money on clothes you've driven us to bankruptcy."

For just a moment I thought I'd done something wrong. Then I saw his madness. It wasn't until that night that I saw just how far gone he was.

"You're crazy!" I spat out at him. "Let me go." He had shackled my arm in his strong hand, his burning sweat pouring down the crook of my elbow.

I tried to grab the telephone.

"Who do you want to call at this time of night? Your globe trotting boyfriend? Here..." He had the receiver in his hand. He swung it at me. Then something exploded. That was the way it felt. The thunderous, splitting pain against the right side of my face, but more than that the terror, the realization that a demon stood over me. One split-second, one savage blow with the telephone as a weapon. In the instant it took to sever my marriage, I understood that power is a potion, one-third brute strength and two-thirds hypnotism. You can shatter your oppressor's hold if you stop believing in him, though you still must make a physical escape. The oppressor hypnotizes himself too. He pummels your psyche with verbal cruelties to mold you, like clay, into a winecup that waits for him to pour forth the bouquet of his knowledge, but the bouquet turns to stench the moment you stop believing.

"You're hysterical. I had to calm you down," Tim said.

My right eyelids had already swollen shut, so I could see him through one eye, all iron fists and fear — a potentially fatal combination. My jawbones throbbed too much to move. I whistled words through my lips. "I have to go to the bathroom," I muttered. It hurt more to stand.
"No you don't."
"I do... let me go..."
Survival, I thought. I stood and stumbled.
"You're weak. Get back in bed..." He sounded almost tender.
I learned something about survival that night, willing myself to ignore the pain and run. I tore into the little room I used as an office, locked the door and managed to dial 911 before he kicked the door open.
"Calm down," I said. He followed me into the living room, breathing behind me.
"Sit down. Let's talk about this," I said.
"You've hurt yourself," he said. "You're hysterical. Come back to bed with me," he said. He reached for me, trying to put his arms around me. His sweat had turned cold. I let him hold me in a frigid arm lock, small tears sparkling on each of his cheeks, his heart pounding in baroque rhythm.
"Kiss me," he said. "I'm dying, you know."
I sat with him, suspended in slow motion until two police officers arrived.
"Do you have somewhere you can go?" one of the cops, the younger one, asked. They waited with him while I packed a small suitcase. I kept the keys to my parents' apartment in my desk. It would be the fastest escape, faster than waking a friend up.
"Does your husband have a drug problem?" the same cop asked when I was safely outside.
I stayed with my parents for several nights, and they surprised me.
"You have to get away from him. I'll help you," said Marian. "Whatever the deposit is on an apartment, I'll give you the money. I'd say go traveling, but wait till I'm not here."
"Don't talk that way."
"Madeleine, I've been to the doctor again. There are cancerous cells in my bones."
"But you'll recover."
Walrus stuck closer to her than he ever had before. At night he set up wires and plugs on her back. When he turned them on they created electrical impulses that were supposed to tap into vital energies, like acupuncture.
"She says it doesn't help. But she wants to try everything," he told me somberly one night after she had gone to sleep. "She's finally agreed to start chemotherapy. Of course, she'll lose her hair and be sick all the time."

I had the strangest feeling that he liked her better sick. They'd had dinner delivered from a nearby restaurant and gone through most of a bottle of wine. I was on pain pills and could open my mouth only enough to slide oatmeal down. My father seemed tipsy. I could tell by the way he was sprawled on the couch, in much the same position my mother had painted him. He belched.

In the dim light, I sat with an ice pack against my face. I could see my father looking straight ahead, not at me, not at anything in particular.

"I made your childhood unhappy," he observed.

"What brought that up?" I asked, still whistling out my words.

"I think you should know what was going on. Marian and I used to fight a lot. I took a lot out on you because I was fighting with her."

"I know."

"We fought about sex."

"I don't want to hear about it," I said.

"Marian had a puritanical upbringing," he went on, as if he were answering a dare. "I'd been in Asia, and met girls who knew the Kama Sutra. But Marian said anything but the missionary position is improper. We fought about it."

I was numb from pain pills and words sputtered through my mind. You selfish scum. Why didn't you act kind and loving, and reassure her that you held her in high esteem? Then maybe she would have felt more comfortable with a little variety. At length I said, "You should have been patient and loving."

"Men are selfish," he said.

As the swelling on my face went down, a found myself jolted into a simple survival instinct. It was a glorious feeling that I wished my mother could experience, the adrenaline rush that helped me find a friend of a friend who was going out of town and eager to have an apartment sitter, talk my way into a job, and wake up early each morning to comb apartment listings until I found an affordable and sunny one-bedroom apartment of my own. I didn't eat or sleep much and I asked friends to come and sleep on my couch, because Tim was hounding me on the phone at work and might find where I lived. The bruises went away, but I had a permanent dent in my cheekbone.

"What an awful thing to have to go through," my mother said.

"It's better than being with him," I said.

"Don't you feel anything for him? Ambivalence, even? Pity? Men aren't aliens, you know. Maybe I've taught you that."

"Loathing, pity..." I said. "You know, when I save up some money, I'd like to go traveling. I'm right back to where I was ages ago. Maybe I'll even apply to teach in China. Why don't you come with me?"

"You know it's too late for me," she said.

"Don't say that."
"Please, promise me you won't go away just yet." She sighed. My mother had died in February, leaving me plenty of time to send for a new application to teach in China.

Since my room at the hotel had no windows, morning announced itself through voices in the hallway and a beam of silver dust from beneath my door. Outside, however, sun had washed the pewter sky. Dutifully, I went to the Hong Kong side and rode the cable car that clattered up a mountainside that was nearly vertical, to Victoria Peak. Huge palm and rubber leaves brushed the windows on the way up. The guidebook said all of Hong Kong was once rock and scrub, but the British came and planted tropical vegetation.

On the mountaintop I breathed, as if for the first time in days, and found the path that led across a rocky expanse of the island. How typical of Hong Kong, that even the green part would be carved with a path, marked with signs telling how far you'd walked, with name tags in English but not Chinese on the trees, cinnamon, bamboo, plantain. I heard steps behind me and stiffened a moment. I turned and faced two Chinese teenage boys in hiking boots. They nodded as they passed me. I stopped on the path. I didn't have to run from anything, I realized, the way I might in New York. Birds shrieked and twittered over the distant sound of drills and hammers. The northern side of Hong Kong Island stretched in snake-like curves, the buildings a blanket of shapes that looked easy to pick up and toss aside. The horizon stretched into the blue harbor, then a sharp-edged skyline of white and gray buildings, then jungle green hills, dotted with buildings and more construction, stretching into an infinite haze. Somewhere beyond the haze was China.

The air was much cleaner up above the city. I continued down the path. The southern side meandered through a jungle, with huge banana leaves for shelter. There were no panoramic views, just occasional glimpses of low-lying islands off to the south, and three smokestacks growing incongruously out of a dark green hillside.

I wish I'd discovered this before Steve, I thought. Then I'd show it all to him as if it were my land. Then I'd feel like the victor.

In my room that evening, the red light again. "Mr. Steev-a," said the operator. "And Mr. Steev-a again."

No answer at his office. I wasn't tired.

I found a bar in a luxury hotel nearby. I'd never been to a bar alone before. I ordered soda water, because I couldn't imagine drinking alone. I would never have done this at home, deign to speak to the German businessman who sidled up to me. The German was not much older than I was. He was tall, with gold-

and-silver hair coifed too perfectly, so that I couldn't help but imagine him in a uniform in spite of his casual white polo shirt and white woven leather shoes. Objectively speaking, he was not unattractive, but his eyes were steel blue, Nazi eyes. I told myself not to make hasty judgments.

"Do you vant to hear some music?" the German asked.

We went to a club that was in another hotel. It was a huge room with silver wallpaper and small round tables. There was a small dance floor, but no one was dancing. A singer there stood there, fixed in one spot, a young Chinese woman in a gold dress that fit her curves like paint. Her full red lips caressed the microphone. The place smelled like stale alcohol.

I watched the singer, who was warbling what sounded like a syrupy love song in Cantonese. The high notes stuck in her throat. "Can't sing, not that I can either, but she's beautiful," I said.

The German shrugged. "I don't find Asian women much to my liking. I only like Filipino women, because they have some European blood."

I felt my skin crawl.

"My father's grandparents came to America from Germany. They were Jewish," I said.

"The holocaust was a shameful episode." He sounded sincere.

I wondered if I was being too hard on him." You weren't even born yet," I said, but wondered if my father had ever wandered into a bar in this part of the world, and in midst of pretending to love some Asian girl found himself facing the enemy.

The German called the next morning, and asked if I was free for dinner. I said yes just to keep from sitting around waiting to hear if Steve would be available. And I decided to take some action. I asked the desk clerk at my hotel to recommend a travel agent.

Trying to make conversation that night, simply looking at the German across a candlelit table, I drank my wine too fast and felt as if I were in someone else's skin.

"How is your article coming?" he asked. He wore a big pinky ring with an oval-shaped sapphire in it. I'd never gone out with a man who wore jewelry before.

I shrugged. "Actually, I'm on a mission."

"Mission?" he looked puzzled.

"I'm a spy."

The German insisted on paying the tab. I watched him pull out his credit card and an expensive fountain pen. He signed his name with a sweeping stroke that looked like a question mark. In my own wallet I had empty pockets where credit cards had been until Tim's drug habit drove us into bankruptcy. Don't compromise yourself with the wrong man, Grandfather had said. My mother had grown up almost rich — that was why she had the luxury of denouncing capitalism, because she knew her own Daddy would always come to her rescue, and he'd left money in trust that was to be divided between Katie and me when my mother died. He'd even told me, one peaceful afternoon at the country club, about how he'd made sure the money would be safe from my parents and their crazy schemes. That was after Walrus had come back and bought the farm where the guru stayed. Of course, I'd be crazy to blow my modest inheritance away on dinners.

"Vould you like to come to my room?" the German asked pleasantly when we were standing outside the restaurant.

"No, thanks," I said. "I... really feel tired... I'm going out on a hike with my friends here early tomorrow. But thanks for dinner..."

He must have known the friends I'd mentioned several times were imaginary. Why would I be staying in a seedy hotel and going out with him if I had friends? I ran away from him and didn't look back to see if he was glaring at me and thinking what a liar and a pricktease this woman is.

I'd just dozed off when Steve called.

"Where have you been?" he asked.

"Out seeing Hong Kong."

"I'm working at home... I've got five stories to file in the next few days and I've been working every night, otherwise I would have taken you out."

"It's okay. A German filled in for you."

"Oh..." I was thrilled that he sounded disappointed. I wanted him to feel a knife in his chest while he sat surrounded by his work and his family.

"Do you have a hot date tomorrow?" he asked. "I'll play hooky for a few hours if you want to meet in the afternoon."

He told me to meet him at the Foreign Correspondents Club. I rolled the name around in my mind. It made me think of pith helmets and elephants, and British gentleman adventurers drinking gin with lime.

Go to the top of a hill the next day, to the intersection of Ice House Street and Lower Albert, he said. Such colonial sounding names. I took the Star Ferry to the Hong Kong side and pushed through crowds on an elevated walkway, elbows getting in the way when I tried to pass. Lots of stylish Chinese women and men in summer suits. I noticed a tall Western woman with light brown hair pulled back with a chiffon band. She was dressed in a nondescript denim skirt and tee-shirt, and she had an adorable little boy with dark hair. She was carrying him, though he looked a bit big to be carried. My eyes and hers met as we passed. I smiled at her, wanting to be a messenger of cheer. She didn't smile back. How could her life be so joyless? Is she unhappy with her husband?

An awful thought hit me.

I didn't tell Steve about the woman right away. I couldn't, not there in the crowded FCC, as everyone called it. You could inhale the air-controlled stale beer and pink-body aroma of it from the street, a building of reddish brick with Band-Aid style white striping across it. Inside, the lobby was nothing fancy, just an official-looking space where two young Chinese secretaries sat behind a desk, but just beyond the lobby, muffled streams of chatter gave the place a feel of expectation. I might see Somerset Maugham, I imagined. Something in the stucco walls, in the settled look of the wooden horseshoe bar, in the clinking of glasses, gave off a feeling that everyone who'd ever passed through here had a story to tell.

"I like this," I said to Steve, after I'd settled into a barstool and ordered a beer. He stood behind me, leaning his arm across the back of the stool. He had purple circles around his eyes. He smiled at me tiredly and stroked my shoulder.

"It's a safe haven for drunken hacks and lawyers," he said. "It's not what you came to Asia for." His voice had a faraway echo. Maybe it was the way the acoustics muffled everything, as if the bar were awash in foam.

"So," a paunchy guy said to Steve, "are they going to de-list?"

"If I knew you think I'd tell you?" Steve said. "Madeleine, this is Neil. Madeleine's a travel writer and photographer from New York." Neil was British, with a resonant voice and a doughy face that would have seemed right at home under a pith helmet.

"Do you work in radio?" I asked Neil.

"Why, did you hear the speech that got me sued?"

"He's a business reporter for Radio TV Hong Kong and he just wishes someone would listen," said Steve. "See what keeps me working fourteen hours a day? The big news is some old established companies in these parts might pull out of the Hong Kong Stock Exchange. Don't yawn."

"I guess there aren't any wild elephants outside the exchange," I said. Steve looked at me with a slightly pained expression, as if I gave off too much glare. He was drinking black coffee and it smelled bitter on his breath.

"Want to go for a late lunch early dinner?" he asked as I neared the bottom of my glass. Presumably this would be his way of dismissing me for the evening.

"I'm going too," said Neil. "Barnes, Hildebrandt, Berkenshaw press conference, on another thrilling survey of property prices."

"I have to admit," I said to Neil, who seemed a bit more good-humored about everything than Steve was, and not nearly as tired, "for some crazy reason I had a different image of what it was like to be a reporter in Hong Kong."

Neil shrugged. "Well, take a look here." We were in the lobby. He pointed to a gold plaque on the wall. "See these names? See this one?" The plaque was dedicated to members who had been killed in the line of duty. Neil pointed to the inscription for Ian Morrison, of The Times, who died in Korea in 1950. "Know who he was?"

I shook my head.

"The real-life Mark in Han Suyin's novel *A Many Splendored Thing*, or *Love Is A Many Splendored Thing* as the movie bastardized it into," said Neil.

"Sappy shit," Steve mumbled.

"Business is everything now, isn't it?" I said to Neil, who put a hand on my shoulder as if we were old friends.

"Stick with us, love," he said. "Business is dirty and sometimes dangerous."

"Even more so in China, I suppose."

Neil looked at me soberly. "Yeah. In seven short years Hong Kong business and Chinese business will be one and the same, no matter what happens here politically. I covered Tiananmen. The Chinese won't let me in now. Steve doesn't know how cushy he's had it... Oh... excuse me, do enjoy..."

Before I could say anything, Neil was exchanging cheek kisses, on one each side, with a very young Chinese woman who wore a wide patent leather belt on the tiniest waist I'd ever seen. When he glanced in my direction, it was with a look that said don't let on you've been talking to me.

Steve and I strolled down Hollywood Road, looking through antique shops, at furniture and jewelry, Chinese souvenirs. He had his brooding look that I used to think made him look lost in profound thought.

"Tell me what you'd like me to buy for you," he said finally.

"Really, I don't like knickknacks."

"Accept a peace offering," he insisted. So I let him buy me an abacus and a scroll of a landscape with jagged mountains and small figures of peasants stooped over the soil. Then we lingered in a used bookstore. He pulled out a fresh hardback copy of *The Art of War* by Sun Tze.

"Read this?" he asked.

I nodded. I had, after all, been preparing for this trip a while. "Reflections on the art of being macho," I said.

He bought the book for me anyway. "You never know, you might need to understand men and their war games around here."

We strolled a while. "Hungry?" he asked.

"I suppose." We went into a place that was, at that hour, an empty sea of round tables covered with soiled white linens, and smelled of stale soy sauce. An elderly waitress who had rolled her stockings down just below her hemline was gathering up empty dim sum carts. An elderly man brought us tea. Steve and I sat close together at a booth, so close I kissed him on the neck. He smiled sadly.

What was his wife doing while he was touching knees beneath the table with me? I imagined her waiting. If he left and ran around the world with me, would she take him back? My mother, Marian, let Walrus come back after two years. I thought she was actually happier without him. She had friends, she had her job as a high school art teacher, her painting, her political activities — she was demonstrating against the Vietnam War and planning to save the world when Walrus came back, and got her caught up in his farm with the guru and the strangers who came to meditate. I said I was never going to get married then. I was sixteen, and what I really meant was I wasn't going to get married unless some guy came along and wanted to marry me so much he was willing to beg, and promise to be a perfect husband, and have to tear me away from other guys and glamorous places.

I moved an inch away from him. "I think I saw Anne today," I said.

"How would you know if you did?"

"Just a feeling. Is she ever in Central around one o'clock?"

"Actually, I have no idea where she goes during the day," he said.

"She was with an adorable dark-haired boy. She looked unhappy."

He nodded. "Anne is unhappy. She has frown lines instead of laugh lines."

"She's unhappy with you and I'm unhappy without you."

"It should have been different," he said.

I shrugged. " I'm fending for myself. So I'm going..."

"I'll order a few specialties." By the time the waitress had walked off with the order, he was saying that I was smart to come to Hong Kong before China. "It's a beacon to people on the mainland, and if you're coming from the outside world, you should know how to get in and out of it... by train or boat or swimming across the South China Sea. You might want to help someone get here someday..." As if I were here merely to explore the terrain.

"Hong Kong is bizarre," I said. "I don't think the Chinese people look any more at home here than the Westerners. It's like it exists just to produce things and have them consumed, all of these things thrust at us every second so that we won't step back and lie on a beach, which is all anyone should really have to do in heat like this."

I wanted to touch the light stubble along his jaws. He must have made a point of shaving before he met me at the airport; his face hadn't been so smooth since then.

"I produce stories. It's all I have time to think about," he said. He made me feel trivial. I decided not to tell him about my new travel plan right away. I'd spring it upon him tomorrow when I was busy getting ready to move on, and let

him beg me, too late, to change my plans, the same way I'd told him I was marrying Tim.
He served me eggdrop soup and slurped up his own, looking fidgety and conscious of the time. I stirred my porcelain spoon, examining slivers of scallion and lacy bits of egg yolk.
"I hope you'll remember me as the guy who inspired you to go to Asia," Steve said between mouthfuls.
The waitress brought us dumplings and a fish covered with ginger and scallions except for the singed tail and face. "Its mouth is wide open as if it was screaming when they dropped it on the grill," I said.
I toyed with tender fish flesh. I watched Steve eat as if he felt deserving of every mouthful. He saw that I was watching him, and said, "Sorry I'm in such a hurry. I have to get back and do a story tonight on how Hong Kong is still a happening place, business-wise, a year after Tiananmen," he said.
I nodded. I wanted to be the one staying up late to analyze Hong Kong. "Your friend Neil said you don't know how cushy you have it," I told him.
He scoffed. "Gregarious guy, in that come-share-my-prejudices way Brits are. What's he ever done in Asia except watch the Tiananmen demonstrations from a hotel window and chase Asian babes? He's here for the women, like most guys are. Yeah, like your father."
"And you?"
He shrugged. "You know me. I like women I can talk to."
"So what about Asian women?"
"The ones guys like Neil like have a singleness of purpose. They're beautiful and everything they do is to please a Western man, then when they catch him they figure he's their moneybags. You'll see this game everywhere you go, and you'll be strictly an observer. Asian men, by the way, are gonna be playing a game of conquest against the men from the West, for power and money and for their own women, but white women get left out of that too."
He went on. I was thinking as he talked, I guess I have to be out for conquest here and I don't even have anything in mind to conquer. "My mandate here," said Steve, "is tell the readers everything that's going on except of course just how cozy the Chinese government and the Hong Kong companies are, and they're going to get cozier after 1997. The Hong Kong captains of industry know how to pay off the right people with the right favors or secret stashes of equity. Of course if I said that I'd be knocked off, except the editors would pull it out before I got to die as a hero anyway. "
"By the way." He looked at me uneasily. "I have to go to Ho Chih Minh City tomorrow. A business story. Believe me, I'm not pleased, thinking of you

going out with Germans while I'm there... I'll find some way to get to Shanghai and see you..."

"I'm going to China tomorrow," I said, and it was anticlimactic since he'd defused the bomb I was planning to spring.

"So soon?"

"I booked a tour. Then I fly to Shanghai."

He nodded. "You should see some of China before you start the job."

Steve had devoured just enough of the fish to expose its spine. He asked the waitress for the check. "Put that away," he said when I pulled out my wallet. "I'll see you in Shanghai, soon," he said. "I promise. I know a promise from me isn't worth much, but... Do you have to look at me as if I'm such a schmuck?"

Since I couldn't change him, I wondered if I could steal something important from him. "So..." I asked, "what is making Hong Kong such a happening place business-wise these days?"

I tried to remember all the names he rattled off, Chinese, British and otherwise, all of them hesitant now to say they'd given money to the demonstrators in Tiananmen and eager to do anything to expand their empires into China. Most of them in the property business, he said. They might have widgets made in China, but what they really wanted was to build buildings and keep property prices rising, never believing that property could be a finite bubble because the virgin territory in China was so vast it would take more than a lifetime to develop.

"Are you really interested in this?" he asked.

"I like mining your brain."

I felt, in fact, like some kind of explorer, searching dark crevices for something I could use someday.

"Well," he said, "for a while I thought you were going to shoot me, but this is certainly preferable."

How presumptuous of him, I was thinking as we left the restaurant, strolling out to face a sun that seemed to have no intention of going down.

"Why don't we walk down to my office," he suggested. We walked down cement staircases, past storefronts selling porcelain and cheap clothes, carpentry shops, a few merchants pulling steel gates down over their doors but the city still abuzz with activity.

"See all the commercial buildings, and how they face the north shore?" he said as we descended. "The Brits started it because there's a natural harbor there. Facing north isn't the best direction according to feng shui, but it's lucky there's plenty of room to reclaim land here, so that when the Chinese started businesses here they could make the land flat. You know, every one who builds here consults a feng shui master. The Chinese believe that nature is a living organism. You're not really supposed to tamper with nature, and you're not supposed to build on a hill because dragons live beneath the hills and will get mad if they're disturbed. Not that it stops anyone... it's just created a big business for geomancers who make sure a new business or a new building uses auspicious shapes and numbers, like the number of stories and the date it opens."

"Look at that one." He pointed to a skyscraper with a triangular facade at the top. "A triangle is supposed to be bad feng shui, because sharp points connote fire," he said. "But some people say this guy knew just what he was doing. All the buildings around it are tall and thin, like tree trunks, but wood can feed fire. The guy who owns this building is a property developer who'd happily devour all around him, so presumably it's either that or his empire goes up in flames.

"I interviewed that guy — his name's Oscar Wong — a few weeks ago," Steve continued. "I was trying to do a story pointing out how these guys ride with the prevailing wind. Last year Oscar Wong made a great public display of giving money to the Tiananmen demonstrators, but when I talked to him he said Deng Xiaoping's decision to, quote 'stop the havoc' unquote, brought a much-needed stabilizing force to the whole region. Opinions bend with the wind here just like in China."

"In China they do it to survive..."

"Yeah, here too," he said. "To survive as a CEO you now have to suck up to the Chinese government. Not just because China's going to be in charge soon, but because China is where all the business is."

I felt as if there was something glowing between us as he taught and I listened. Then he looked at his watch and broke the spell.

"I really wish you could come back with me," I said on a foolish impulse.

"Don't pressure me," he said. By then we had paused at the skyscraper that housed his office.

"I was expressing a wish. Fuck you."

"That's not cute," he said.

We parted with Steve flagging down a cab for me, thrusting the two bags of souvenirs in my hand, and saying, "I suppose you're going to go back and plot my death after all... I'm sorry, really."

I slammed the car door.

What was happening? I used to have men all over me partly because I could act indifferent about sleeping with them. Of course it was all part of a game; I was indifferent to most of them, knowing they had no use for what I might be beneath my looks, but it was infinitely easier to become occupied with a battle against unwanted attention than it was to go out and do something monumental.

I made a great show back then of being the pretty young woman who longed to be appreciated for my brain. I'd been occupied with the game while Steve was becoming a serious journalist.

In my room, I sat on a hard-backed chair and flipped through Sun Tze, idly wondering about the ways that men might match wits against men. The room seemed darker when I was alone, with the noises from the motor in the air conditioner and the pipes in the bathroom growing shrill with no conversation to drown them out. I wondered if Anne would be phoning her husband at his office tonight, checking to be sure he wasn't in some hotel room with some other woman, and feeling only half-reassured when he answered. Who was to say he'd be there, anyway? Maybe he was on his way right now to yet another rendezvous.

My mother used to paint on nights like this. She'd have a beer — "I've learned to like proletarian drink, but your father can't stand the stuff," she told me once — and she'd set up a bowl of fruit and paint it on canvas in splashes of color that didn't exist in nature. She'd tell me about how in China they were even trying to make men better husbands, while everyone sacrificed material gain to make the country a better place in the long run, and sixteen year olds didn't ever ask their parents to buy them a Corvette Stingray because everyone rode a bicycle, thus combining physical fitness with equality. But she never went to China, even after it opened up. She hated flying so much she hardly ever traveled.

Sun Tze said war was an art. To subdue your opponent without fighting is the pinnacle of skill. Make him come to you of his own accord. Pretend inferiority and encourage his arrogance. Await his moment of vulnerability.

And inhabit his territory until it becomes your own.

Chapter 2

In a dream I rushed, sloshing through wet and fertile soil. Jagged green hills rose out above rice shoots, wispy against a blue sky with cheerful clouds encircling the peaks, the countryside sloping down with a mind of its own, oblivious to peasants, motionless in pointed straw hats, stooped for eternity over the earth. I was wearing old-fashioned clothes, a long dress over corsets, and high-buttoned shoes. It was difficult maneuvering through rice paddies dressed that way, but I was running for my life, clutching at my own wide-brimmed straw hat, knowing that a secret document was hidden beneath the satin band. Something to do with microfilm, and someone without a face stalking me for it.

I crossed a border, to a room with fine silk carpets and decorated lacquer chests. A huge window overlooked the sea, with no glass to separate the outside. Steve was reclining seductively on an ornate lacquer kang, but I was rising from the bed to attend to some important business.

"What is this?" I asked lifting, from the floor, a filmy white negligee.

"Oh... she left it here this afternoon. I see her every afternoon," he said casually.

My head swarmed. "I won't let it happen. Stop seeing her!" I stomped, wild with fury. I threw the gossamer lingerie out the window and let the sea devour it.

The man who lay beside me snorted in his sleep. I woke with a jolt. We were joined like spoons in a single bed. The hotel in Guilin was full of twin beds.

"Must be their attempt to discourage population growth," I'd joked to Gerhard the night before. He was another German, curiously enough, but he was short and stocky with a brown beard and gentle brown eyes. His arm, which was wrapped around my waist, was plump, and his hands were smoother than mine. All of his skin was soft, I'd discovered that night, and smelled clean even when he began to sweat on top of me. He was a gynecologist, of all things.

I watched Gerhard's face, pressed into a pillow, sleeping with a half-smile that curled in the same direction as his beard. I tossed around and sat up in bed, trying to shed the dream. A pale light shone through the window and made the room and all its unfamiliar objects as billowy as a state of sleep. If I had begun to change form myself I wouldn't have been surprised.

I was traveling, on a ten-days-in-China package, with a group of seven Americans and Europeans, mostly around my age. My first sight of China was from a train window. Past the green and white buildings rising out of the New Territories and the long expanses of neon were the factories of Shenzhen, bellowing out black smoke. Then villages. On the left I looked at red brick houses and water buffalo strolling through the streets as if it were a holiday. On the other side were factories and smokestacks. Peasants in coolie hats bent over rice paddies in the distance, the size of crickets against the landscape. I had a biography of Sun Yat Sen in my lap. He said China's obsession with cannons and ships, instead of human materials, would backfire. He said leaders should be chosen through an examination system much like the one China had used for centuries to choose civil servants, but not through elections American-style. Certainly not by peasants seizing power, proclaiming they would make a utopia just by having right on their side, turning revolution into cult worship.

Our first night in Guangzhou, we drank at the hotel bar and sorted out one another's faces. There was a professor of business administration from UCLA, a man, traveling alone. Two lawyers from Washington, a husband and wife. A young guy with beautiful eyes, possibly gay, who was some kind of computer troubleshooter and had been in Hong Kong on business. A porcine German Swiss man who made animated films, and his French wife, who was taking a vacation from their three children.

"This is the luck of the draw," said the man from Washington. "We were afraid we'd be traveling with newly-weds and nearly-deads."

I smiled smugly, at everyone, especially the German with the beard.
"China is such a mess," I said to Gerhard at a massive round table at lunch the next day. A dozen lunch dishes revolved past us on a tray in the center, with little bowls of sauce and peppers. Everyone was drinking a warm beer, the local brew. There were food stains all over the linen tablecloth. I noticed people at the next table spitting chicken bones onto the floor.

"I like the perfume you are wearink," Gerhard said to me.
"I'm Jewish," I told him while we were still in Guangzhou.
"So?"

The trip was like a checklist. The Temple of the Six Banyan Trees, the Sun Yat Sen monument, and our guide grew misty-eyed, telling us about how Sun founded the modern republic. The Sculpture of the Five Rams, the Pearl River, the luxurious White Swan Hotel, the walkway where young lovers strolled, clerks at the Friendship Store yelling to us like hawkers, selling cloisonné and jade souvenirs. The streets of Guangzhou were grim and polluted, at least twice as congested as Hong Kong. No one looked chic or happy as they grazed bare arms against the bodies of strangers, fighting human obstacles just to get from one spot to another. When we walked, we kicked cigarette butts and melon rinds out of the way. Men smoked down to the stubs and had tobacco-stained teeth. People spat on the ground as they rode their bicycles. In my mother's version of China, nothing was dirty like this. And what would she have thought of the billboards everywhere, advertising watches, kitchen appliances, even cars, exhorting the masses to aspire?

In Guilin, the caves and the trip down the Li River. The business professor made a joke about building time-share condos along the shore.

Not through these mountains, surely. They swelled out of the ground, as supple as if they could keep growing. The mountains surrounded the river, covens of mountains parted through the middle to allow a valley and river between them, a place where farmers could drive their water buffalo and fishermen could drift along on flatboats. From the foot of these mountains, men might invent a myth called heaven just to imagine they could protect themselves from the whims of earth.

"You see? That is a camel," said our guide, pointing to a mountain peak coming up on the left. It had a vague hump and head shape. "And there is a bird." I snapped photos like an obedient tourist.

"I will take your peecture and you take me," Gerhard said. He asked the French woman to take a snapshot of the two of us, and we stood against the railing of the boat, arms around each other. He bought me a set of jade chopsticks at the market in Yangshuo while I was taking photos, and he came to my room that night. Our conversations were all about discovery — how things were in his country, in my country, in the broad expanse of China. We'd probably have nothing else to talk about. Gerhard slept. I couldn't. I wanted someone to talk to.

I had friends in New York who would spend hours dissecting the visit with Steve ("What did you expect from a married man, silly?") and the fling with a German gynecologist who wasn't particularly versed in what the female body wants. We were cruel to men behind their backs, my women friends and I. We'd all been through therapy and consciousness raising, and knew our personal struggles with men were political, brought on by society's expectations. We knew how to live without men and we wished we could live with them. We had our secret codes; make fun of them, make jokes that "perfect man" is an oxymoron, all as a sacrifice to some divine goddess to keep the worst thing — growing old without love — from happening.

The tour group flew to Beijing. At the Summer Palace I shot a roll of two old men, looking obsolete in blue Mao jackets, who sat playing music that sounded like nightingale chirps, one with a flute, the other waving a bow over an erhu, a small bamboo instrument with a base the size of a can and a few strings stretched out on a thin pole. They laughed when I started shooting, acting flattered. Behind them was the marble boat, the Empress Cixi's ultimate frivolity, the boat that didn't carry passengers or cargo, the boat that looked like a pavilion for hosting party games on a summer night, built with funds that the imperial ministers had earmarked for the Chinese navy. The dynasty, decadent and blind even to its own need for military defense, lost the mandate of heaven. Nowadays people were saying the same thing about the Deng regime.

Our tour guide took us to Tiananmen Square, to see the mausoleum where Mao Zedong lay in a pickled state under glass, dressed in his fatigues and red-starred cap. We strolled beneath Mao's giant portrait outside. "This is an important place," was all our guide said.

"I feel like I shouldn't be here, supporting the regime," I said to Gerhard. There was more I wanted to tell someone. "My mother had high hopes for the revolution here at one time," I added, tentatively.

"Seeing the outside world is the best thing for China," he said. He put his arm around my shoulders and smiled down at my breasts.

No notes or photos, I thought. I couldn't do justice to the spirit that haunted Tiananmen. Besides, the police were paranoid these days and might stop me for writing in a notebook.

"Hello." A thin young man in a white polyester shirt sidled up to us. He had brown teeth and wore thin socks under open-toed sandals that clicked like tapshoes against the pavement, and had elevated, tortuous-looking heels.

"*Ni hao*," I said.

"Spik-a Engrish?" the young man asked.

"*Nein*," said Gerhard.

"I plastic my Engrish?" the man persisted.

"Huh? Oh... you practice? *Ni xuexi Ying Yue*?" I said.

"You have cigarette?" The young man grazed my elbow. Gerhard glared at him as if willing him to go away. I wondered why he didn't appreciate the opportunity to talk to a local.

"No," I said.

"You know this, Tiananmen?" the man asked.

I nodded eagerly. "We saw it, all over the world."

"How are you? Are you from America? Have cigarette?"

"Here," said Gerhard. He reached into the pocket of his khaki shorts and pulled out a pack of Marlboros. He didn't smoke, but carried cigarettes to give out as tips and bribes. Awful, that a physician would hand out cigarettes. He gave the man what was left of the pack.

"Let us go now," said Gerhard.

"Goodbye," said the man.

The next morning we were all in a good mood, riding out to the Great Wall, filled with the fuzzy exuberance of having drunk together half the night. Maybe we were celebrating our status as voyeurs in this country, breathing foul air and kicking melon rinds out of our path and knowing that it was just a lark. To all of this I succumbed.

"Coca Cola?" A pimply girl stood in my path at the entrance at Badaling. "*Bu yao.*" I was getting tired of the high-pressure sales tactics.

Gerhard grabbed my hand. "Look at China," he said. Rolling green hills stretched out all the way to the Mongol plain, so vast they seemed to reach the edge of the earth. And through the hills, the crumbling wall of bricks went on forever, a series of sagging walkways that led up to watchtowers with arched windows and parapet roofs.

Men and their wars. Men built long border walls to protect their rival kingdoms, starting around 770 B.C. — that was what the sign outside the entrance said. The Great Wall was many walls, joined together when China was unified in the third century B.C. Slaves dropped dead in the heat, putting it together brick by brick. Yet here it was, almost three thousand years old, stretching across land that had barely changed in all that time.

"You are smiling," Gerhard said. We trudged up rickety steps. The hills were lopsided from the angle we climbed. Just beyond the wall a white dromedary stood posing, with a Chinese couple between its two humps. Gerhard's polo shirt was soaked in sweat.

The grasses in the distance were a green I'd never seen before, the color of something found after years of searching. I could spend the rest of my life inhaling exotic scenery. My shattered fantasies of the week before didn't really matter, any more than the heat and sweat did. I was air, and grass and hills, and the pilgrimage of tourists speaking many languages. I had actually succeeded in escaping from myself, here on the Great Wall.

"This is euphoric, no?" I said to Gerhard. We breathed heavily as we climbed stairs to the next tower.

"It is good, how do you say, aerobic exercise."

Ahead of us, a young Chinese woman teetered up the stairs on cheap, battered high heels, baby blue to almost-match her slacks. Band-Aids stuck out beneath the straps that crossed her ankles and arches. The young man with her wore the same stack-heeled sandals I'd seen all over China.

"Buy coins? One hundred years old!" Another hawker, a gangly teenage boy, held a Chinese coin up between his thumb and forefinger. The coin had a hole in the center and was greenish with age.

"They make them look old," said Gerhard.

We stopped, gasping, on the flat roof. We were about halfway between the entrance area and the highest tower within this range. I'd make it up there if it killed me. I got a quick shot of a little girl who was sitting between parapets, wearing scarlet rouge and lipstick, and a pipe cleaner and sequin tiara on her head. The little girl caught sight of my camera right after I clicked the shutter. She said something to her mother, who was holding her up, and the mother turned around, glaring, scanning the crowd for the culprit. I pretended I was shooting the horizon.

"Come?" said Gerhard. I nodded. He was patient with my picture-taking. We trudged, not talking. It took all of my strength to climb in the heat. But when we made it at last to the top tower, a breeze swept across. It was crowded at the top with tourists who'd made it. Most of our group was already there.

"I kees you on the Great Wall," said Gerhard, pulling me up off the ground. After that the man from Washington threw his arms around me and kissed me on the mouth. Then his wife and I embraced stiffly.

"Tee-shirts!" exclaimed a hawker. The tee shirts said, "I climbed the Great Wall." Some guy came up and put a red and white cotton hat on my head, with earflaps and bells and colorful embroidery.

"One dollar," he said.

"*Bu yao.*" But I let Gerhard take my picture with the silly hat on.

I parted from the group at the Beijing airport the next day.

"Don't cry. We will write. I will see you someday again," said Gerhard.

But I wasn't crying, and he didn't look particularly sad either. I'd felt so close to these people who'd been strangers only a week ago, yet everything that had happened so far was simply a prelude. A man built a house that looked complete, but he saw that there was one brick left over, so he hurled it up into the air. That was where I was going.

On the plane to Shanghai, I still felt the clean taste of Gerhard's lips. It washed away with the orange soda pop that the flight attendants served. Looking down over the clouds, I wondered what important stories Steve had been digging up in Vietnam while I'd roamed through China as a tourist. I'd had fun this week, but I wasn't the victor. I'll know I'm over him, I thought, when I don't care about keeping score.

I arrived in Shanghai late at night. A plump young woman was holding up a cardboard sign with my name on it at the airport. She was the teachers' sponsor, she said, and loaded my bags onto a van.

The university where I would be teaching was on the southwestern edge of town. The air smelled like nightsoil.

The guesthouse where foreign teachers and students lived was a gray cement block. The lobby had no decoration except for the patterns of the cracks in the walls. On the right, as you entered, was a reception desk. There were five administrative people sitting around chatting, but they all looked up and inspected me when I entered the lobby.

"Hello," I said to the woman with short permed hair, who was seated at the desk looking somewhat official.

She eyed me suspiciously.

"You are a teacher?" she asked me in Mandarin. Her "shhrrs and "zhhhrrs" ended abruptly. It was different from the way people talked in Beijing, with sounds that rose into crescendos and echoed like a tuning fork as they fell. I had a room to myself with two flat twin beds. I scattered my camera equipment on the shelves, put my computer on the desk, and hung up the abacus and scroll that Steve had given me. I arranged Gerhard's jade chopsticks in a criss-cross on top of the chest. I dove into one of the thin beds, exhausted.

I had a bad dream that night. I was in the dark, in a movie theater, and I turned to my father, who was sitting next to me. I unzipped his trousers. I thought I might vomit. But he pulled my head down into his lap and I obeyed him. He told me this was my gift. He would have loved me all my life if I'd done this earlier, he said. I couldn't seem to stop, performing the job as though I were on an assembly line. Bright lights down the aisle blinked "Exit."

The dawn light made me shiver. I looked around the stark room, at my things already arranged there, and suddenly I couldn't wait to shake off the night. I dressed and raced downstairs. I scanned the dining hall. It had long tables and a sea of faces. I spotted an empty chair and moved toward it.

"Anyone sitting here?" I asked the young Chinese woman who smiled at me expectantly. She was short and built in rectangular shapes, her arms chubby and squared off, her face boxy and her hair bobbed into bangs that ended in sharp corners. Although the rest of her reminded me of a bear cub, her dark eyes blinked at me like a cat about to strike, behind glasses that were, in fact, shaped like cat eyes. The smell of new clothes hung over her blue jeans and red striped shirt.

"Oh, please sit," she said, and pulled out the chair. Plates of scrambled eggs had been set down. My eggs were cold, and full of big black peppercorns.

"You look normal," said the young woman. "I'm Laurie Wong." She talked like an American fresh out of boarding school, her jaws locked together as she let out a whiny trill, like the lightest touch of a silver spoon on crystal. "Coffee's there," she said, pointing to a large thermos, with flowers lacquered onto it, at the end of the dining hall near the kitchen. "It's not too bad. The eggs are disgusting." She rolled out the word eagerly, so that it came out "diiz-guust-eeeng."

Our other companions at the table were a peculiar collection of young pimply-faced boys, a handful of spinsterly-looking older women, and a couple of frightfully overweight people. The white linen cloth was full of stains and fresh spills.

"Weirdos, huh?" Laurie whispered to me. "Don't worry," she added. "There are a few okay people here."

She told me she'd arrived two days before, and had sussed out the other teachers right away. She was from Hong Kong, but had gone to school in the U.S., and had just graduated from Barnard.

"There's a big developer named Wong in Hong Kong," I noted. "Of course, I know it's a common name..."

"That's my dad." Laurie looked at me curiously, seeming eager to change the subject. "I should tell you something about this dorm. Don't drink from the teacups that they provide in your room. I saw a maid cleaning out the teacup with the same cloth she'd just used to scrub the toilet seat."

"Gross!" I laughed the way I would have in high school.

She smiled approvingly.

I had coffee, black since Laurie told me the milk sat out on the table all day, and some cold white toast with chemically-colored red jam but no butter. Laurie waited for me.

"You have to meet Jeannette," she said.

We knocked on a door down the hall from mine. A beautiful woman with chin-length auburn hair who, to my relief, looked to be around my age, answered the door. She rubbed sleep out of her eyes but said for us to come in. She had on a tee shirt, and she reached for a pale pink bathrobe. Jeannette Hardaway was petite, with a supple dancer's body. She had very round eyes, brown with long eyelashes that seemed too heavy for her heart-shaped face. I wanted her to like me, which made me nervous, until she said, "Oh, I look awful before I put my makeup on." Her face was milky white, with blue veins below her eyes. She probably covered all of that up with makeup. She played with the ends of her hair and had a sort of squeaky, little-girl voice. She was hardly interested in sizing me up, I realized; she was one of those women who turned shy when she felt she didn't look good.

I used to wonder if I could be happy with just the company of women. There was that time with my roommate in New York, Sandy, when we were both just out of college, when I watched her pour down a beer, her eyes sparkling, her legs and arms rangy. Sandy never put on makeup and never worried about the way she looked. I wanted to brush my lips against her flawless cheeks. Most of the women I knew had made love with another woman at least once, including Sandy.

"Forget it," she'd said. "You'd just be experimenting. If you're going to be a philanderer like your father, pick on men."

I wanted to look at Jeannette and the way her tee-shirt draped around her erect nipples, but it was a funny kind of lust, more curiosity than anything else. I imagined telling her about Steve and Gerhard and laughing with her years from now. I wanted her to be my best friend, even if it would mean hours of counseling her on the merits of a new hairstyle. I fussed in the mirror, too; after all, checking up on some part of me that I wanted to make sure was still there...

"I came to get away from a lot of problems at home," Jeannette said. She told me that she'd owned a boutique in Boston that had gone belly-up, and that she had a younger boyfriend at home, with whom she'd tried to have a baby, but had miscarried in the final trimester. He was now engaged to someone else.

"I'm going to look into adopting a Chinese baby while I'm here. They're all girls — people abandon girls — and the Chinese don't mind if you're a single parent," she continued. "What brought you here?"

"A long time ago, I was going out with someone who got me intrigued with Asia," I said. "Then I got married, but I left my husband. I thought it was about time I did this."

"Come in here and listen to my tapes any time," she said. Jeannette's room looked lived-in already. She had brought a portable stereo and a stack of cassettes that stretched just the length of one of the long shelves. She had John Lennon, John Coltrane, mid-career Dylan, Janis Joplin, Springsteen, Tina Turner, Eric Clapton, some Mozart and Tchaikovsky, Gershwin, Edith Piaf, and newer stuff like Simply Red and REM. She had snapshots of her family in little gilt frames on her desk and above it a shelf full of current paperbacks. A New England patchwork quilt covered one of the beds.

Jeannette had taught ballet, designed dresses, sold real estate, owned an eclectic little store, toyed with the thought of teaching English abroad for a long time before she got around to doing it. We'd both gone to college with no concrete plans, only the vague ambition to be available for an epic life. I thought we were made for each other as best friends, but it turned out that I had competition.

We'd been talking for almost an hour when a young Eurasian woman about Laurie's age bounded into the room. The door was open and she didn't bother to knock.

"Jeejee, I've got a deal for us on bikes," she said to Jeannette. She had a voice that reminded me of a soft drink bubbling over.

"This is Alison Marker," said my new almost-friend. "This is Madeleine Fox... she's from New York."

"Cool," said Alison.

This one had long chestnut hair that gave off a waft of spring dew when she swept it off her shoulders, as she did frequently while she talked, twisting it into a fat coil over her shoulder, pulling it into a knot and fastening it with a pencil from Jeannette's desk. Everything about her, in fact, was dewy, from her honey-colored skin down to her bare feet, which she planted gracefully across Jeannette's desk when she sat down, curling her long toes. Her face was too round and unformed to be exactly pretty, but she positively glowed with a kind of confidence that said I'm young and was a star in college and I know how to cultivate success. I hated her for being so confident, especially when she wasn't even articulate enough to say anything other than "cool."

Alison tugged at the pencil in her hair, which cascaded back down to her shoulders. She pulled her hair up and secured it with a flowered chiffon band that had been around her wrist while she told me all about herself. She came from Winetka, Illinois, by way of Germany and the Philippines; an Army brat. Her mother came from Shanghai, and Alison had majored in Mandarin in college, and had spent her junior year at Beijing University, a year that had been interrupted by Tiananmen. This she said gravely, pausing as if to see if I looked impressed. She was going to teach here for a year, then go to law school. She was torn between Harvard and Stanford, where the boyfriend who wanted to marry her was studying now.

"My other boyfriend's in med school in Colorado, and he keeps calling me out here," she said, looking from Jeannette to me. She pulled the flowered band out of her hair. "I don't even want to get married yet, and he said he wants to work in Asia for a while..." She looked at me. "Do you speak Mandarin?" she asked me, in Mandarin.

"A little. Wo xue li yi nian le," I said.

"*Wo yijing xue li yi nian le.* You should use *yijing* to make it clear, since your tones aren't good."

I threw my hair back and lowered my eyelids at Alison. "It took more zan one man to change my name to Shanghai Lilly," I said in a throaty voice. She looked back at me as if I'd lost my mind.

"Do you know who Marlene Dietrich was?" I asked her. "She was way before your time."

"Nope." She looked annoyed. "I've gotta' go look at these bikes."

"She's so cute, isn't she?" Jeannette said after Alison left the room.

Our campus was in a part of town that had once been all farmland. Chinese peasants with gnarled bare feet sold watermelons and wilted onions along the street outside our school. Down a long road filled with construction, a highway intersected. Some sort of beautification project had been enacted to plant flowers along the shoulder, but the flowers gave off no aroma except the smell of nightsoil. Everywhere buildings were going up, and Guilin Road, the street outside our campus, was a mass of rubble and construction cranes. The local government planned to turn this part of the city into zone for computer chip factories.

Laurie, Jeannette, Alison and I bought bicycles together. We taught classes in the morning. Lunch was served promptly between 12:20 and 1:30. The mail always arrived in late morning, and by one o'clock the desk clerks would have it sitting on an untidy pile, so that whoever was on duty could sift through it and attempt to identify names.

I found a Mandarin tutor, Xia Xiao Hua, who drilled me on Mondays, Wednesdays and Fridays right after lunch, in exchange for a small fee paid in much-coveted foreign exchange certificates. She was a tough young graduate student.

"Fu Mei Lan," she said in our first class. "That will be your Chinese name."

It meant Blue Plum Blossom. With disdain, she said it fit me. In old Chinese painting and poetry, thin women were called plum blossoms while bosomy women were peonies, she explained folding her arms, smugly, to cradle her own ripe breasts.

Xiao Hua and I had to work in the television room just off the lobby. The Chinese students weren't allowed past the lobby in the Foreign Guest House, nor were we supposed to go to their rooms. But we all visited our students. They slept eight to a room, with a shower down the corridor. At their dining hall they stood in line three times a day for a portion of watery, sour smelling soup, and they had to provide their own cups. In our guesthouse, maids changed our sheets and mopped our floors once a week, albeit with filthy mops. From time to time a rat did a meter dash down the hall. But we had private rooms with thermostats that we could set to either too hot or too cold, a black-and-white television in each room, and private bathrooms with plenty of hot, brownish water. We had a large, noisy dining hall of our own, with a head chef, a tall young woman named Miss Wu, who was always eager to please us. The vegetarian dumplings were delicious, not too doughy and filled with fresh spinach and onions. The stir-fried fish was bony, but had a nice ginger garnish, and if the meat was gristly and inedible, we could always fill up on stir-fried cabbage or string beans, mixed up with rice and plenty of mild red chili sauce.

The receptionists all knew our names. I didn't know any of theirs, except for Mrs. Ting, the portly housemother who was always yelling at the receptionists, the janitors, and the cheerful hump-backed woman who did our laundry, hauling it back and forth each morning in a big wheelbarrow. Alison told me that just about everyone in the dorm knew where we all were at any moment. "The walls have ears here," she said.

One of the men knocked on my door the first Tuesday, right after lunch. "Mad A Rin. *Dian hua*," he said, making dialing motions with his index finger and holding his hand to his ear. He pointed to a stop sign yellow phone sitting on a long wooden counter in the middle of the hallway.

"Hi." The voice was a jolt.

"Steve?"

"I just got back."

"Oh?" I wished my hands wouldn't shake. "So...how was Vietnam?"

"The Korean companies are there, the Japanese companies are there. And can you believe the Vietnamese are eagerly waiting for the Americans to come and invest? It's a wonderful place... I'll have to take you there before it gets developed like China."

"I was free to go this time," I said.

I could practically hear him searching for an answer. "This was a quick trip. Not to the nice parts."

"I had a grand adventure," I said.

"A romantic adventure?"

"That was the least of it."

He didn't answer right away. "I wish I could be there with you."

"Guess who's teaching here. Your pal Oscar Wong's daughter," I said.

"Oh yeah? Does she take after him?"

"I like her. She's young but she seems grounded"

"I was a jerk, wasn't I? Can I plead temporary insanity from overwork? Can I come and see you sometime?"

"You're my only old friend in Asia. If we keep it to that I won't lose my head." I figured I might be in a transformed state by the time he came to Shanghai anyway. Every morning I looked in the mirror and was surprised to find that I looked the same.

"Okay, I'll be there. I don't know when. I'll call you again, okay?"

Afterward, I knocked on Jeannette's door. What a relief — Laurie was in her room and Alison wasn't.

"Easy for him to come on strong now, with you here," said Jeannette.

I nodded sadly. "He was always promising to show me around China."

Laurie looked at me like a wise cat behind her glasses. "The trouble with the Chinese is they expect their leaders to be wise and benevolent, like good Confucian emperors," she said. "Now they've lost faith in this regime, but they're hoping a better one will come along."

This from the daughter of the sleazy Oscar Wong? Maybe I would get along without Steve just fine.

"Yeah," I agreed. "They need a Marxist revolution."

Chapter 3

We were caught in a storm.
"I'm going to burn my clothes if they get wet. Do you know how polluted the rain is?" Laurie turned around and whined out to me, grinning through tight jaws.

We had stayed at the Jinjiang shopping arcade too long. Now we crept down Huai Hai Road on our bicycles, in axle-to-axle traffic, as a smoky twilight began to descend over the sky. A bicyclist veered to the right and miles behind him, patterns mutated. Chaos and harmony all at once. I was happiest in the thick of it. I wasn't taking many pictures yet; I wanted to be sure I wasn't shooting deceptions.

My new red Phoenix had begun to squeak, already. It was supposed to be the best brand in China, and after less than three weeks it needed oiling. The rain became heavier.

"This is dis-gust-ing," said Laurie. She turned away and pedaled determinedly, her head sinking behind her squared shoulders. Her arms were bare and it was getting colder.

Many of the bicyclists hauled hand-rigged contraptions alongside their back wheels. Some were filled with metal machine parts. Others carried flocks of live chickens with white feathers that had turned gray. Radios blared tinny music, truck horns wheezed, bicycle bells trilled. Young boys wore tee shirts with pictures of almost-super human warrior characters out of movie studios in Hollywood or Hong Kong. Young women cycling home from work wore knee-high hose, and cheap, battered high-heels in pastel colors.

Shanghai was a fetid place where people once died of overcrowding, where students and writers once brewed the fervor of revolt in smoky coffeehouses. You could feel ancient toil in the air, you could imagine the kind of men who'd ruled and been conquered in the grime on the old, cracked French colonial houses with bay windows almost hidden under laundry that hung from poles beneath the eaves. But Shanghai was a place where you could never trust the sights before you, unlike Hong Kong, where no amount of greed and privilege seemed sheltered from sight.

Shanghai was once paneled interiors heavy with cigar smoke and the swirl of sherry, champagne, beef and bacon, seared ham, puddings, pastries, oranges, figs, and port and claret on the palate. It was back alleys where people still washed their faces in sewer water, it was Confucian bluster and servility to authority. It was a revolution that was more of the same, mass submission to a false god, death to those who even thought of anarchy.

The name means "above the sea" and even though the waterfront was on the Huangpo River, the sea was everything. Men had arrived by boat to play there with no mercy, building and making money, admiring the little dolls that were live women with bound minds and feet. Men bound the masses to hard labor in the revolution, then they said wear the cheap versions of Western fashion we produce. The young women of Shanghai now rode bicycles, hobbled over slippery cement, worked in jobs, all the time blistering their feet in those painful high-heels, Band-Aids poking out beneath. The boulevards in Shanghai had stores with dingy windows showing dummies in elaborate white bridal gowns, Western-style, with a thousand petticoats. Dummies waiting for the world to bring in consumerism, beckoning women to come in, become a bride and learn to want things, buy things and make your country better.

The bicyclists ahead of us were nearly at a standstill. A truck, painted flat turquoise, lumbered into my path, then crept up right beside me on my left. I found a narrow strip of space ahead of me and maneuvered away. Behind me, it wheezed like an asthmatic and weaved a little to the left, then lurched forward, back in my path, so close that I could feel its hot metal.

"Watch out... better move out of the way of that maniac..." Laurie shouted. She was on my right, inching forward. I pedaled fast, till I was just ahead of the truck. But someone else crept up, almost touching handlebars with me. A boy hunched over, his head covered by a rain poncho. He stared at me and shouted, "Look out," in Mandarin. Then he jingled his rusty bicycle bell, pulled out full speed ahead, into a minuscule gap of space ahead of me. I slowed down to keep out of his way.

"Would you look at..." I started to say.

The truck lunged again. I heard a wheeze, then a screech. Metal against metal. It seemed to keep coming, out of control. I felt my wheels give way. The truck kept moving. I was hurling forward. My right elbow crashed against the street, right into a pothole, filled with filthy rainwater. My hands skidded, raw and stinging against cold tar. My bicycle entangled, back wheel on top of my throbbing right arm, my right foot sticking out of bent spokes on the front wheel. My right leg scraped against something. My skin burned, my limbs ached. Hitting farther down against hard ground, I strained to keep my head up, imagining it might crack like an eggshell. I could feel my whole body trembling.

I might be about to die.

Above me, a circle of faces with dark slanted eyes stared down.

"Can you move your leg?" Laurie asked in a different voice, calm and not whiny. She was trying to grab me by the armpits.

I wiggled my right leg under my bicycle. It didn't hurt, except for the searing pain where my skin had been scraped and the throbbing of my elbow.

"Yeah," I said. I tried to breathe in. The air was thick, too hot, with a stench of tar. I peered at the crowd, scanning in vain for a hole to break through, free, unsurrounded. "Where's my bike?"

A wizened man stepped forward and lifted the bike while someone else, a young man, helped me sit up.

The young man touched my elbow very gently. "Oooow!" I screeched as my whole arm jumped.

"I am sorry," he said calmly, in good English.

He pulled at the torn cloth of my stretch pants and peered at the wound on my leg. The rain washed my blood down in rivulets, onto my sock and shoe, but it looked like no more than a nasty scrape.

The gnarled man set my bike upright. The handlebars and front wheel were mangled. He grinned at me, revealing a mouth of tobacco-stained stumps.

"I have a repair shop," he said, speaking Mandarin slowly and loudly. "I will fix it for you."

"*Xie, xie,*" I said.

"Where do you live?" he asked.

"Shanghai Teachers University," said Laurie.

"I will bring it to you tomorrow," he said.

The young man asked me if I could move my leg. I wiggled it again.

"I think you have nothing broken," he said.

Laurie looked up and shouted, "Hey!"

The gnarled man was pushing his way out of the crowd, with my bike. He turned around and waved to us and shouted, "*Ming tian.*"

"I wonder if you'll ever see your bike again," said Laurie.

"I think honest," the young man said. He had a gentle, confident voice. I looked up at him. Through the rain, I saw that he was quite handsome. Gaunt, in that brittle way that so many mainlanders are, but with broad, confident shoulders. He had flawless skin, the color of roasted butter, with intelligent, brooding dark-chestnut eyes and an unusual long Roman nose with a delicate little bump where sunglasses could rest, although he wasn't wearing any in the rain. He talked with his whole face, grimacing over the English words, animating his lips and even his perfectly aligned white teeth. As if experimenting with the pronunciation. He still had his hand on my wounded leg, a hand with manly square knuckles but long fingers that moved like fine brushpens.

Mild lust is a simple emotion. I wanted nothing more than to feel the cool touch of his hand and inhale his faint smell of sweet butter.

"I can stand up," I said. He and Laurie helped me up.
"I will welcome you at my apartment," the young man said. "I study for medical doctor and my mother also is a nurse."
"You sit on my bicycle," he added "You also come," he directed Laurie. Maybe this was a good idea, since I had no idea how clean or accommodating our school infirmary would be. I wasn't even sure that it was open in the evening. I squirmed my rear end onto the bar over his back wheel, and contorted my legs so that my feet were wedged against the minuscule piece of metal that sticks out in the center of the wheel. He sat on the bike and waited patiently.
"Put your arms on me," he commanded.
I grabbed onto his waist. My legs felt cramped, and the scrapes still stung as we rode. He felt firm in spite of being so thin.
Raindrops were still trickling down, fat but not as determined as before.
"What is your name?" he asked me before we got started, articulating each syllable and sounding pleased with the way he said it, probably mimicking a recording in a language lab.
"Fu Mei Lan."
"That is pretty. Your English name is what?"
"Madeleine Fox."
"Also prettier. Does it mean something?"
"Fox means *huli*." I was showing off something I'd learned from my tutor. He laughed lightly. "A good luck fox." He drew out the word, baring his nice teeth and making it sound like "faacasa."
I knew what the young Chinese meant when they said good luck. If we got to know each other, he would very likely ask me if I'd be willing to sponsor him, so that he could emigrate to America.
"What is your name?" I asked.
"David."
"Your real name."
"Li Tian He."
He climbed into the seat and we began riding. I jostled on my slippery perch.Tian He/David waved jauntily, defiantly even, to people who crept alongside us on their bicycles to stare. A foreign woman riding on the back of a Chinese man's bicycle is something to gossip about. If I'd been a Chinese woman and he a foreign man, the police might have stopped us and asked me questions. It happened just last week, when a young American guy who taught English at our school went out with a Chinese girl.
I pressed my head against his slender back to keep from falling. Laurie was ahead of us, and kept looking back to make sure we were still there. She looked at me with a smirk on her face.

We headed toward the southwestern part of the city, the same general vicinity as our school, although Shanghai is so vast that "near" is always a relative term. We passed an infinite sea of dirty pale gray and pale yellow apartment buildings. The rain had finally stopped and people were in the streets playing mah jong and cards, sipping hot tea and munching cold brown tea eggs.
At last, he pulled into a courtyard surrounded by a compound of dreary three and four-story buildings. Lights had begun to flicker against the night. Laurie and David and I dismounted and surveyed one another. We were filthy.
"We're going to frighten your mother," said Laurie.
"She does not frighten so much" he said.
David would have been born during the Cultural Revolution, and most likely his mother had been through unspeakable horrors.
He led us up three flights of stairs, each one darker and mustier than the previous one. He walked fast even though his shoes looked like beds of nails. They were made of a cheap brown leather, with stacked heels and rough soles that clattered like tap shoes against cement, with nothing but thin greenish socks to protect his feet. I'd seen the same shoes on men all over China; there was some kind of equality in uncomfortable footgear. Cooking odors mixed with bathroom smells all the way up. Garbage on one landing, laundry hung in the hallway on the next level. Laurie gave me one of her bemused looks that said "disguuusting."
Politely, Laurie said to David, "You look a lot like my brother. He lives in Hong Kong." Her brother, whom she worshipped, had an MBA from Wharton and was working for his father's property development empire in Hong Kong. Though the light was dim I could see that David looked pleased.
My legs ached from the climb. At last, David stopped at a door and opened it. A slight woman with curly gray-streaked hair rushed up to greet him. She was wearing a colorful silk dress, strikingly stylish for China. She had been sitting a long time, waiting for her son, I could tell by the way she smoothed out the folds in her dress and pushed at her hairdo, to pouf it up.
She surveyed the three of us. She had a face that hid a zillion feelings. Not serene, just perpetually unrevealing, though from her shrill voice, scolding David in the rapid-fire tones of Shanghainese, and glancing at us from time to time, it was clear that she was mad at him for keeping dinner waiting and bringing home two motley-looking foreigners. I watched her as she peered at me through squinting eyes. Her skin was smooth, no laugh or frown lines. If memories haunted David's mother they showed in her lack of expression, as though she'd taught herself not to feel too readily. She had stooped shoulders, in spite of the obvious strength in her arm muscles. A prominent blood vessel wound its way up her forehead on the right side, palpitating a little faster when

she first started lighting into her son. When she turned to Laurie and me and gestured her arm hospitably, satisfied with his explanation of who we were, the blood vessel pumped slower.

"This is my mother, Wang Ming," said David in English. She squeezed my hand so hard it hurt.

"Welcome, welcome, Engrish teacher," she said. She laughed a little, expecting me to be surprised at her knowledge of English, but still her eyes squinted and looked resigned. Laurie and I might be, in her estimation, just another passing trend the political winds had blown in. Indeed, she might be right.

She squeezed Laurie's hand after mine and said, "Come in please, Engrish teachers." That turned out to be the full extent of her English vocabulary. She pointed to the well-worn rubber flip-flops lined up beside the doorway. We took off our shoes and found flip-flops that more or less fit.

The apartment was standard Shanghai fare. Two rooms, each with a kang with a straw mat over it to make it appropriate for sitting during the day and sleeping at night. There were assorted chairs and tables, including a Formica dining table and a refrigerator in the larger front room. Sliding doors behind the dining table led to a bare terrace. The floor was linoleum, with a few cheap throw rugs, and a couch and easy chair covered in mismatched naugahyde. The walls were covered in hideous orange-flowered wallpaper. On the wall opposite the kang in the front room was an elaborate set of shelves, containing a stereo, a vast array of bootlegged tapes, and large state-of-the art Sony television, with a VCR beside it. There were salty cooking aromas in the front room.

"I am sorry. Our apartment is very small," said David. We were also accustomed to Shanghai people being apologetic about their living quarters.

"Come," Wang Ming said to me in Mandarin. She pointed to my wound.

"Where is the bathroom?" I asked her, showing off my command of simple questions. She led me out of the apartment, into the hallway, through a door that led to a room the size of a broom closet, with cement floors and walls. It was a good thing this room wasn't attached to the apartment — it smelled as if the toilet had backfired. There was a toilet with a seat the color of chlorine, and a tank, with the top gone, that flushed slowly with rust-colored water, getting everything down after a few tries, and even a plump roll of scratchy pink toilet paper, the kind that begins to disintegrate when it gets wet, hanging on a wire nailed into the wall. A shower hose and gas water heater were mounted on the wall beside the toilet. I looked for soap, but found nothing except a slight film on the floor beside the drain, so I rinsed my hands with cold water from the hose, and shook them dry. It was a pretty luxurious bathroom, compared to the squatters and community showers in the dorms for the Chinese students at our school.

When I opened the door, Wang Ming was standing on the other side, waiting for me with her arms folded. We went down the dark hallway, into a bigger concrete room. Two woks sizzled on an old black stove. A mop stood upside down beside the stove. A cleaver lay neglected on a long, ancient wooden table. She pulled me over to a huge sink. Over the sink was a shelf that had a box of gauze and an assortment of bottles, some with red crosses, some with skull and crossbones on the labels.

Wang Ming was small. I was a full head taller, but she was far more commanding. She put a hand on my thigh, tugging at my ruined pants.

"Take off," she demanded.

I understood elementary commands, but I looked at her quizzically.

"I am going to bandage your leg," she explained.

I nodded. Under her watchful eye I removed my pants clumsily, taking off the flip-flops, feeling something slippery on the floor that almost made me lose my balance in my socks. It hurt when the fabric brushed against my wound. She watched. I tugged at my tee shirt, trying to pull it down over my faded purple panties. Her expression gave away nothing.

With my leg straddling the sink, she began washing the wound with a clean cloth and a big cake of tan-colored soap. She worked meticulously and didn't say anything. She kept glancing at my purple crotch.

She pulled down a small bottle of iodine, and touched the dropper to my wound. I screeched, and felt my leg flinch.

"You are not brave," she said. I yelled out again when she dabbed my palms. She pulled down the gauze box and conjured up yards of sterile cotton, which she secured to my leg with adhesive tape.

"You must come back the day after tomorrow. Then I change this," she said to me in elementary Mandarin.

Then she surveyed me, half dressed, with an iodine stain seeping through the gauze.

"Come," she said.

She ushered me into the small back room. Through the doorway, I saw David and Laurie drinking tea and talking in the larger room. Wang Ming gestured to Laurie to come in. She opened a closet door and pulled out a pile of folded clothes.

"Put on dry clothes," she directed us. "I will leave you. Then you come eat." She went back into the kitchen.

"What did she do to you?" Laurie quizzed me. She inspected my bandage.

"Well, at least it's clean."

I rummaged through the clothes as best as I could with my palms stiff from the pain, and tried not to get iodine rust on anything. There were two tee shirts, probably David's, an ugly blue polyester skirt, and a shapeless green polyester dress.

"This is crazy, isn't it?" I said.

"Yeah, but David's a nice guy. He was just trying to do a good deed," she said.

"I suppose he figures it's good to cultivate *guanxi* with foreigners," I said and I pulled off my shirt. It smelled like sweat and rain.

Laurie was examining the clothes, lifting up each garment one by one and inspecting it meticulously. She wrinkled her nose at me.

She giggled. "I think he likes you. You'll get stuck with him asking you to sponsor him."

I picked out a clean tee shirt with a kung-fu master stenciled on it. I wriggled into the skirt, which felt like thick plastic casing around my hips. Laurie was sniffing the underarms of the dress. I wished she'd hurry up.

"What makes you think he likes me?" I hated myself for smiling inwardly, as if it should matter what this young impoverished boy thought of me.

Laurie was examining a dress. At last, with her tee-shirt pulled over her head, muffling her words, she said, "Oh, nothing really. He just asked me a bunch of questions, like how old you are."

"Did you tell him?"

"Yeah. He was amazed. He said he thought you were about his age." The dress was tight on Laurie. Wang Ming was raw-boned, filled out only a little by age and childbearing.

I wondered how old David was. Probably under twenty-five.

We went into the bigger room. Platters upon platters of food were arrayed upon the Formica table. Wang Ming had gone all out for her son's visit.

"Bet you'll love those," Laurie whispered to me, her eye on the oblong plate piled high with steamed whole frogs, their outer skins removed to show slick, milky-white membrane and bluish blood vessels.

"Please sit," Wang Ming ordered us.

Our hosts thrust the platters at us. Pallid green balls of winter melon, a tasteless vegetable even when stir-fried. Chicken broth with bits of tofu in it. Wilted stir-fried green beans, beef chunks in a rich soy sauce, steamed pork dumplings. I took a minuscule bit of everything but the frogs.

David ate a frog with relish, holding it in his chopsticks and sinking his teeth into the springy flesh. He smiled at me. His lips were greasy. I smiled back while biting off half of a dumpling, holding the chopsticks shakily in my sore hand. I felt soy sauce slide down my chin.

Laurie told Wang Ming and David about her Shanghainese roots. Her father had been born in Shanghai, where his father had been a tea merchant. Her grandfather fought with the Kuomintang, and right after the war, he knew his family would be doomed if they stayed, so they took a boat to Hong Kong, pretended it was just a holiday trip, so they couldn't take much with them.

"Some of my relatives were persecuted later for having a KMT agent in the family," she added.

"Did they then get killed?" David asked sympathetically.

"They never heard from them again so we thought probably," she said. In English she told David and me that in the past few years her father had arranged for fake passports to smuggle two cousins out and they'd started a branch of his property business in Macau.

Wang Ming squinted at her intently, and the blood vessel on her forehead palpitated. But all she said was, "Eat more. You are not eating." She shoved the platter of frogs in my direction. I accepted one gingerly. It slipped from my chopsticks and landed on my plate.

Wang Ming turned back to Laurie. "And is your mother from Shanghai?"

Laurie nodded. "Her parents were, but she was born in California. My parents met when my father was going to university in America, and my brother and I were born there."

"You like meat?" Wang Ming asked her, spooning a mammoth helping of beef chunks onto Laurie's plate.

While Wang Ming was concentrating on loading her plate up, Laurie reached for my frog. She grabbed it quickly, and tickled my arm with it. I forced myself not to shriek.

David smiled at both of us, apparently unoffended.

"Where do you come from in America?" he asked.

"New York."

He smiled. "I would like to go there. Are you in America a teacher?"

I shook my head. "I'm an editor at a travel magazine." It would be too complicated to use past tense; then they'd think I was going to be a teacher permanently.

Wang Ming looked at me with casual interest.

"Eat more dumplings," she said, pushing the platter at me again. "Does your family live in New York?"

I said yes.

"Do you have brothers and sisters?"

"Yes, an older sister."

"What does your father do?"

"He ran a company but now he is retired," I said. Fortunately she seemed satisfied with that. We had no common language in which I could say he used to be a partner in a firm that did fund-raising and public relations for non-profit organizations, but since his grandly-staged suicide attempt after his partner in the farm sued him for mismanagement of funds, he's been writing short stories and a novel in which he attempts to get into the heads of everyone but himself.

"What does your mother do?"

"She taught art at a high school." I concentrated on spearing up a single shriveled green bean slowly with my chopsticks. "But she died this winter."

Wang Ming's blood vessel popped out a bit momentarily, but she just nodded.

"You are... no, you *have* a exciting life," David said to me in English.

I shrugged. "And you are in medical school?" I asked him.

He nodded. "I wanted to study in America. I was accepted at UCLA. That is not near New York, is it?"

"No. California. Other side."

He nodded. "I like California also to live. But I think they will give me trouble to go. Hello-o?" He smiled and looked at me expectantly when he said "hello?" the way that means "wake up, space cadet."

"What sort of trouble?"

"They lost my application twice at the office. I think they aren't going to let me out. Last year I demonstrated... you know... Beijing." He lingered over the name.

Wang Ming stared at him, silent, her blood vessel popping.

"I'm glad you're okay," I said.

"Many of us went gone early morning. You know? Later the tanks. It is bad now."

"What is bad for you?" I asked.

"I know at the time I go for jobs. We may fight, you know. Like, hello-o-o? The Communists are violent."

"Hello-o-o? You talk like an American teenager," I said. That made him laugh, a quick little laugh, just self-deprecating enough to show that he was pleased with the impression he'd made.

"Have a frog," Wang Ming said to me. I picked up the smallest one I could find, shuddering at the veins that I could swear were still pumping blood. I had successfully mauled and shredded the other one, so that it looked as though I'd nibbled at it.

"Do you have a boyfriend?" Wang Ming asked, her squint intent upon me as I tried to pry off a minuscule sliver of frog foot.

"No special boyfriend," I said.

She seemed to want to see the conversation lighten up, so I asked David if he had a girlfriend.

He looked pensive. "No special girlfriend. You know, in Shanghai we do not have many apartments in Shanghai. I have no apartment, a girl will not marry me."

David rode us home. I shifted around for a comfortable position on the back wheel of his bicycle, with my arms contorted awkwardly around his waist, my hands eagle-spread backward because it hurt to touch anything. We flew against the chilly, grimy night. The buildings looked like sleeping factories. There is nothing picturesque in this part of Shanghai in the dark. But it was quiet enough that we could talk to each other as we rode if we spoke loudly.

"I liked your mother's cooking," I said.

"Frogs you do not like."

"Oh, well, everything else." We laughed. I hugged him a little tighter.

"It is okay. We will welcome you again and no frogs for foreign guests."

"Do you have foreign guests very often?" There was a teasing tone in my voice, mild lust speaking up.

"Only American girls on accident." I was gratified to hear him tease back. And to hear him call me a girl, even though in other contexts it might have made me bristle.

"My sister in America says there are no accidents," I said.

"Does she mean there is a reason always?"

"Exactly."

"I agree."

"You don't believe in superstitions, do you?" I said.

"Communism I don't believe. All capitalism I don't believe."

"I don't either. I believe in certain elements of each one, even superstitions."

"You are a smart girl," he said.

It occurred to me that he might be well versed in the art of flattery. He could probably get to America if he had a sponsor, after all. I cringed. To sponsor someone you had to put aside about twenty thousand dollars into a fund for them. I had the money. My money would be gone in no time if I helped out all the people who'd already talked about needing sponsors, just in the three weeks that I'd been there. I tried to imagine what my mother would have done in such a situation. No doubt she'd have written at least one check by now.

He pedaled silently for a while. I listened to his rhythmic breathing against the silent sprawl of city.

"Do you still want to come to America?" I asked.

"Of course," he said. "But it is hard."

We were getting close to Guilin Road. Laurie was a few feet ahead of us. She kept looking back, to make sure we were still following.
"You need a sponsor, don't you?" There. I'd said it.
"I need you know a sponsor?" He mimicked my pronunciation. With utterly guileless good humor, or so it seemed, he added, "Maybe you. Maybe next year you are rich."
He turned onto Guilin Road, onto gravel. I got off the back of his bike, and walked alongside him as he pedaled haltingly. Up ahead, Laurie had stopped to wait for us.
David looked at me quizzically. I could see him clearly in the lights coming from the strobe on the second floor of the industrial looking building on the corner, with its big sign, in English, that said Shanghai Agricultural Mansions Disco. Inside, a crowd of people were dancing.
"I think you will be my American friend to be good luck," he said. "You see, I am su-per-stit, you say? "
"Hurry up, guys!" Laurie said. She seemed to be fairly bursting to say something. She probably couldn't wait to get back to the dorm and tell Jeannette and Alison about everything, from the man with the disgusting teeth who took my bike on up to the frogs. She was going to tease me about David too. I could tell by the way she was grinning at me.
Even at this late hour, a few men were working on the street. Two cranes sat idly on the sidelines. On the sidewalks, people were still strolling about. I told David there was no need for him to walk us all the way to our dorm, but he insisted that we were his foreign guests and should be escorted all the way home.
At last we arrived at our front door. The lobby was still lit. A few of the administrators, two men and a woman, were chatting at the desk, and keeping a watch on us.
"Goodnight, Wong. Goodnight, Mei Lan," said David. He stood there stiffly, his hands in his pockets. "How do you say your English name?"
"Ma-de-leine."
"Too long. I call you just Fox maybe?"
Laurie was standing beside the door, waiting to open it, but not about to miss a word. She wrinkled her nose at me.
I wondered if I should tell David that in America calling someone of the opposite sex a fox can be a compliment. I decided it was best not to. He might feel compelled to respond. Or maybe he would be embarrassed and not respond, but never call me Fox again, leaving me wondering if I'd completely misread him.
I laughed a little. Laurie made a face at me.

"Sure," I said. "Hello-o-o?" I had never felt so sly before, and I wondered, knowing how the winds can blow back and forth, if he was going to outwit me someday.

Chapter 4

Just a few weeks into the semester and I already knew I didn't like teaching. I was still a bundle of knots when I looked at the sea of twenty-three faces that sat in warped wooden desks in the cubbyhole that was my classroom. We were down the hall from a bathroom and the whole wing smelled horrible.
    Some of my students never looked up. They were now at the level of such sentences as "Miss Smith's department head is angry because she is late again today," according to the official textbook.
    The morning after my accident, only half the class had done their translations from *People's Daily*. I had them do a translation once a week. In class they read articles from whatever English language magazines I could find and photocopy for them. And I was having them read *Catcher in the Rye*. That was Laurie's suggestion.
    It was her first job, but Laurie seemed to know just what to do. "I tore up the textbook the first day of class," she'd told me. "I did it right in front of the class, and then I dropped it in the wastebasket, right on top of some disgusting ashes and a banana peel and something that looked like vomit. I scared the students to death... they thought I was going to be arrested."
    Laurie shopped at the bookstore in the Jinjiang arcade every week. She picked out magazines and newspaper articles that she photocopied illegally in the library. The head librarian told us that our own country would fine us for copyright violations, but no one really cared. Laurie had her students read aloud from new stories each day, humiliating them into correct pronunciation of L's and R's and other trouble spots while the others laughed, then daring to ask them all to summarize, in English, what had just been read, to make sure they weren't just getting drilled. I tried to do the same thing. I'd made twenty-three copies of the first chapter of Catcher *in the Rye*, and was working on the rest.
    "Anyone want to read aloud from the book?" I asked that morning. My legs and arms were terribly sore from the fall and my wound stung beneath the gauze.
    Xu Chun, a scrawny young man with an oily face and a shock of hair that hovered over his forehead like airplane wings, spat on the floor. Then he raised his hand. "Fu Lao Shi, "he said, holding up his dog-eared photocopy of chapter one, "this is not the way we were taught to speak English."
    "Well, it is sometimes colloquial language. It's the way American teenagers might talk," I said.

"Fu Lao Shi, I think it is a very interesting story," said my most attentive student, Gao Ling. She was very slender, with long sable hair and lips like ripe berries about to burst open. Her cheekbones, very high and perpetually flushed, rose up when she talked so that her eyes became twinkly black slits.

"Really?" A teacher isn't supposed to be eager for praise.

She shrugged and giggled. "He is a funny boy," she said. I was supposed to help them improve their English, but I liked it when the better students started talking about literature and American angst versus Chinese angst.

"Would you like to read the first paragraph?" I asked Gao Ling.

Some of the class dozed. Gao, with her svelte little figure in a skin-tight tee shirt, canary slacks and battered yellow-orange high heels, read two pages, faltering along but doing better when I corrected her. I stopped thinking about my wound. She was so delicate. If I were a man the thought of her lips would keep me awake at night.

"You read very well," I told Gao after class, as we were both walking out.

"Thank you, teacher," she said. She blushed, then giggled. These Chinese women and their shy-little-girl act. I didn't trust it. Men giggled too, when they were about to say no to a request for something.

"But I would like to ask you something," said Gao, shaking off her little laughs and fixing her black eyes on me. "It is about an American boy and his problems. Can we read a book about an American girl too?"

"I'll look for something," I promised.

Gao excused herself and ran in a wobbly gait down the hall to join her friends.

It would have been a nice day except for the way the air always felt so thick with grime. It made your nostrils black when you were out for a long time. An old woman sold anemic melons from an ancient wheelbarrow. Chinese students milled about, some slurping their lunch rations of noodles and gruel from chipped porcelain mugs.

Laurie, Alison and Jeannette were already sitting together at a long table. Carol, the annoying woman from Calgary with the chopped off hair was there too, and a few other teachers.

"Madeleine!" Laurie greeted me when I sat down. "Were your nostrils black this morning?"

"Yeah," I said.

Alison gave us a look that said we were testing her patience.

"Your favorite, Laurie," said Jeannette. "Larvae." She held up a ginger sliver from her plate of stir-fried chicken leg and winter melon.

"The kid was at the acupuncturist this morning," said Alison, to show she wasn't a complete spoilsport, nodding her head to the table at our right.

The retarded boy with the shaved head appeared about once a week with little white bandages arranged in a grid pattern all over his skull. He seemed like a child the way followed his mother everywhere with his head bent sullenly, but he was tall and gawky enough to be thirteen or fourteen. He always sat at a table near the doorway, with his sad-faced mother, who worked in the guesthouse as some kind of assistant manager. She would smack him on the side of his face every time he let food dribble off of his chopsticks. They lived on the floor below us, and kept a big terra cotta pot outside their door, big enough for the boy to get in. Sometimes in the afternoons she would pour boiling water and herbs into it, and submerge his naked body. We would hear him screaming all the way upstairs.

A thin gray-haired man with crutches who was sitting at our table said he was in town just for a few days with a delegation of visiting high school teachers from Minnesota. I hadn't seen him before.

"We went to the Yu Yuen gardens this morning," he told us. "We were kind of horrified. How do they let it get so full of trash?"

"Wouldn't be if they hadn't turned it over to the people," said Carol from Calgary. Her voice sounded like razor scraping glass. "They haven't got any respect for property since they've never had any of their own."

I watched Jeannette raise her eyebrows and she watched me. Why was there so much garbage all over China? I didn't understand why people would let a public space get filthy. China was unsanitary and stinking, and people spat on the ground as if it were a ritual to purge their spirits.

"Maybe it's defiance," I said weakly. I wasn't even sure why I felt a need to defend the Chinese masses.

"It's lack of laws. They oughta' be fined for littering," said Carol, making me feel like a dumb fluffy blonde.

As she was putting down my misplaced ideals, I felt a tap on my shoulder, interrupting my effort to hoist up a limp rectangle of wintermelon between my chopsticks.

One of the desk people, the woman with the thick bangs, was standing behind me. "Fu Mei Lan, a man is here to see you," she said.

The bony man with the tobacco-stained gap-mouth was standing in the lobby. Just as he'd promised. My bicycle, as good as new, was propped beside him. He grinned at me open-mouthed, lipless, emanating stale breath.

"I told you I would fix it," he said in Mandarin, enunciating slowly for me. So, David, who'd said he was sure the man would bring my bicycle back, was an apt judge of character.

"Very nice bicycle," he added.

"Wait, I will be right back," I said. I figured he expected anyone who could afford a new Phoenix to reward him for his help. I walked upstairs to my room, pulling my injured leg behind me. It was still faster than the elevator, where the man who seemed to always be on duty would nevertheless be perky enough to make pleasantries before he pushed the button. In my room I opened the drawer where I kept an envelope stuffed with foreign exchange certificates. I ran back downstairs. I held out fifty yuan.

"No, no." He shooed away my money with his hand.

"But you must take it," I said.

He repeated the gesture.

"But this was a very big favor," I insisted.

"No, I did it to help you," he said.

The rule of etiquette was that if someone refuses a third time, he means it.

I thanked him profusely, took down his address, and shook his grease-stained hand. Now we'd sealed an unspoken agreement. Since he wouldn't take my money, I owed the man *guanxi*. Maybe he would ask me to sponsor his child. Favors were worth a great deal more than money. At the very least, I was now obligated to go to the trouble of finding the small side street where he lived and bestowing his family with some kind of present.

Later in the afternoon, another receptionist knocked on my door while I was grading some sentences I'd had my students translate from the textbook. A man this time.

"Dian hua," he said.

I picked up the yellow phone.

"Hello, Fox."

The voice startled me.

"David! How are you?"

David had called to say he would come to pick Laurie and me up at school the next night at 5:30. His mother wanted me to be sure and come so that she could change my bandage, and she was preparing several kinds of dumplings for us.

"Oh no, she doesn't have to make dinner," I protested.

"She invites you."

"That's very nice of her. Really, she shouldn't."

"She wishes you to feel invited. We will not make frogs."

"Okay." I was building up a debt of *guanxi* with David and Wang Ming too.

"On Saturday night, I am going to a disco with my friends to celebrate a birthday. Would you like to come?"

Was he asking me out on a date?

I paused.

"Sure," I said. My social calendar wasn't exactly booked. But I wondered if I would do damage to him by going.

"There is a phone in the office at my school, so I can call you again," he said.

"Oh good. Can I call you there too?"

"It is not a good idea," he said. "We aren't supposed to have foreign friends."

"Well... is it a good idea for me to go to the disco with you?"

"Oh, no worry for you. I am *jinbu*."

"You are what?"

"I don't know in English."

After we hung up, I knocked on Jeannette's door. Alison sat on her bed, her hair in a thick braid. The two of them were cracking sunflower seeds and apparently ignoring two piles of student papers on the bed.

"Oh, Mad!" said Jeannette. "I picked up your mail." She smiled expectantly as she handed me a postcard and an airmail envelope.

The postcard was from Mexico. "We're having a second youth. Drove down from Laredo to San Miguel de Allende and Guanajuato, then the big city. Not exotic by your standards, but just lovely. Much love, Dad and Eleanor." It was in an unfamiliar handwriting that had to be Eleanor's, much neater than my father's, with lean symmetric letters.

"My father is on his honeymoon," I scoffed. Right before I left for China, just five months after my mother died, my father married Eleanor Fayweed, one of my mother's best friends.

I looked at the envelope and grinned in spite of myself at the German stamp and the hard-to-read script.

"The German gynecologist?" Jeannette asked. I nodded.

"Mad had one amazing brief encounter on her way to Shanghai," Jeannette told Alison.

Alison loosened her braid and looked annoyed with me for having done something fun.

"Do you know what *jinbu* means?" I asked her. She brightened, and stopped twisting her hair. I could tell she liked it when people considered her an authority. She reminded me of my sister in that way.

"Sure. That's what they called themselves in the democracy movement." She looked considerably more favorably disposed toward me for allowing her to show off what she knew.

"I have to do a little emergency shopping," I said, trying to sound cheerful. "Anyone want to bike to the Hua Xia?"

Alison and Jeannette looked at each other. "Not particularly," said Jeannette.

I couldn't blame them. It was a depressing hotel.

"What kind of emergency?" Jeannette asked.

"I've got to get something for the man who fixed my bike and for David and his mother by tomorrow."

Alison nodded and held out the purplish paper bag of sunflowers to me.

"No thanks," I said. I'd always found the crackling sound they made annoying.

"Get the bicycle man a tin of cookies," said Alison. "Then go over there and take pictures of his family and blow them up and frame them. Take pictures of David and his mother, too, and sponsor him."

"Very funny." But the rest was a good idea. I didn't say anything about the disco in front of her. She might tell me I shouldn't go.

"By the way, speaking of shopping, I have a news flash," said Alison. "Our obnoxious friend from Calgary said she was in the Friendship Store the other day and they had Tampax!"

Such news was as good as a lottery prize for us. "There's hope for this country yet!" I said.

"Cool," said Alison.

My bicycle pedals spun like wings beneath my feet, hampered only slightly by the pain in my leg. The little squeak was gone. The man had oiled the parts, and turned the screws on the seat so that it was steadier.

I rode over the rubble in the road, not wanting to stop pedaling. A right turn at the makeshift bridge over a narrow ditch filled with sewage. From here a narrow road lead past an arched stone footbridge over a narrow stream, surrounded by willow trees. Little bits of grass sprung up on the banks beside the footbridge. I liked to look at this scene through a small circle made with my thumb and forefinger. Then it appeared to be a Chinese landscape in miniature, a small oasis in the city. In reality, the mottled, motionless stream reeked of factory pollution that had anchored there after winding along for miles, picking up fragments of molding garbage on the way. Two small houseboats were permanently moored there. The household belongings on the boats seemed to consist solely of old tires, scraps of wood, and tin cans.

From there, I passed the street of little shops. In each one there were dusty shelves, with a sparse assortment of wilted fruits and vegetables, bags of noodles, unrefrigerated bottles of soda, a few folded polyester shirts and blouses, small plastic bottles of White Cat laundry detergent, and some screwdrivers and bolts. Past the shops were a few blocks of small dirty-pastel concrete houses. A left turn on to Cao Bao Road. There, gleaming amidst gray factory boxes was the Hua Xia, a lonely mecca for visitors with foreign exchange certificates to spend. A sort of generic luxury hotel that was always much too air-conditioned, even in winter, and always full of good-looking, mildly friendly desk clerks and bellboys with nothing to do. The bulletin board said, "Welcome foreign guests from Tokyo Rotary Clubs." I didn't see any Japanese Rotarians or any other guests wandering about.

I took the stairs up to the second floor, where the gift shops were. So much to affront the eye. They sold new bicycles, and film and candy and bottled water, but mostly it was the standard worthless Chinese souvenirs, vulgar imitations of the fine art that Red Guards exterminated during the Cultural Revolution. Hadn't earlier Marxists meant to bring enlightenment to the masses? The bicycle man might have happily accepted money if there were anything in China worth buying.

I paid for the two tins of English tea biscuits and one burgundy lipstick — for Wang Ming — with foreign exchange certificates and watched the girl behind the counter stroke the fresh bills fondly. A minuscule contribution to the trickly infusion of foreign capital. The popular prophecy was that hard currency would bring in more tasteful and useful goods, and with them a slow evolution toward mass complacency, so that the government would not feel threatened by political rivals and would permit multi-party elections. From decaying watermelon rinds and torn soy-milk boxes planted randomly throughout garden walkways would spring a new and better -ism, with capital to make things sparkle and social welfare to feed babies with the gifts of the learned, all bestowed by a government that would turn benevolent when there was enough wealth to feed every mouth. People still believed in a bright new day. But there is never a perfect revolution when the downtrodden become the rulers and divide the lucre evenly throughout the land. There is only a new portrait in the palace and a new kind of chaos.

Going down the escalator, I scanned the lobby. I gasped. A small gray-haired woman dashed across the lobby. Old clothes, a backpack, like a long-time traveler who doesn't care how she looks.

When people die maybe they go to the Orient. I blinked. She was gone.

* * *

When Alison said sponsor David, I knew the idea was on its way to becoming an issue. Even though she was joking, even though my new friend David might joke about it for the rest of the school year, he would say it with a grain of hope. It was his bad luck that I wasn't my mother. Maybe I wasn't even a daughter who'd keep a promise made on my mother's deathbed. Because my mother was a crusader until the last minute. More than a crusader. She wanted life to be fair across the board, and that meant I shouldn't be happy unless everyone else in the world was.

My mother — I called her by her name, Marian, when I was feeling my most objective — spent the winter of 1989-90 in a hospital bed. Which didn't stop her from reading everything her visitors brought her about the collapse of Marxism in Eastern Europe.

"It's disappointing. They didn't give it a chance," she insisted.

She and Eleanor Fayweed were talking about it one January evening when I arrived. There were always friends in Marian's room, engaged in conversation. She said political discussions kept her feeling alive. The nurses on morning duty would crank her bed up to sitting position, so that she would be ready to receive her stream of visitors, and the nurses on the graveyard shift would turn it back down.

"But Marian, I read that the system lends itself to corruption so easily it's obviously flawed. This article said the whole economy was based on favors," Eleanor was saying. She turned her head. "Hello Madeleine."

I said hello and kissed my mother's hollow cheek, leaving a burst of crimson lipstick there. I found a spot on the floor to put my tote bag, heavy with my Mandarin textbook and morning aerobic class gear, and balled up my coat on top. The mid-winter pall seemed to hang over everything.

"I was editing a story on yet another sumptuous resort on Maui, and I figured it could wait till morning." My voice chattered with a life of its own. The heavy hospital smell always made me feel like escaping into sleep, but I couldn't allow myself to get drowsy, not when I had to use all the life I had churning within, hoping I could transfer some of it to my mother.

"Maui," said Eleanor, smiling. "That sounds much too tame for you."

Eleanor was stout, in her late sixties, with thick silver hair cut short. She wore a gray flannel skirt with a red cardigan and austere pearl earrings. Marian was propped against pillows, her tiny frame barely pressing them. Her arms had become like brittle winter twigs, and her delicate facial bones jutted out of waxen skin like delicate rock sculpture. Her limpid gray hair had been falling out in clumps. She rarely bothered to wear the curly gray wig she'd bought. She was hooked up to two tubes, one dispensing blood and one dispensing nutrients. Bright pink spots blazed on her cheeks now that she was halfway through the transfusion. The blood of some stranger was supposed to restore her calcium supply, and give her an appetite again. But a tray of ground-meat-and-noodle hash, chemical-yellow corn kernels and anemic iceberg lettuce remained untouched, the metal serving cart relegated to a corner.

All of this I could accept as part of the cure. What frightened me was the way her eyes had taken on the leaden colorlessness of storm clouds, and the way she seemed to look way past the room when she was chatting and arguing with her visitors, peering into blank space. I thought it was the cornucopia of pills the nurses brought. All day, all night, just when Marian was beginning to forget her pain, chatting with a visitor, some nurse would come in with a handful of fat round tablets and missile-shaped capsules, and a paper cone of water. Sometimes she would throw up when she tried to drink the water.

"Well, you've got your lovely daughter here now, so I should get going," Eleanor said.

Marian nodded. "Are you going out tonight?" I thought since she'd been sick her Virginia accent had become thicker.

"I'm going to the ballet," said Eleanor. "By the way, I'm having a few people for dinner tomorrow night, so I thought I might invite Walter." She picked up her black shoulder bag and put on her camel-hair coat. "Ta, ta," she said at the door. Everything about Eleanor was solid, even her voice. Alone with Marian, I had a sensation that we might both float away.

How kind of Eleanor to look after Walrus, I thought at the time.

My mother looked at me and past me silently for a few minutes.

"She seems to enjoy being a divorcee," she said finally.

I shrugged. "I don't know. I always get the feeling that she's caught up in being some kind of model for all women, doing all the things she thinks she's supposed to do to be better than ever without a husband, traveling so she can talk about her travels at her dinner parties, and going to lectures on the use of cooking utensils in the Bronze Age and the erotic imagery in mid-fifteenth century Florentine ballads. But don't let that discourage you."

Marian smiled wanly. "Honey, you've got to realize there are some things I'm not going to get to do. But don't be too hard on Walter. You're always so critical of people. I've had an exciting life with him. You loved him, too, when you were little."

"Don't start," I said. She loved to rehash the things that went wrong in my childhood, as well as her own. I could recite my family's curses of the psyche like an epic poem. Grandfather was always giving her money as a substitute for love. So she managed to find Walrus, who was stingy with both money and affection. And when I was a child and he was mean to me she felt comforted on a certain level, to know that a father could say damaging things even to a little girl she considered pretty.

"I know, I was a bad mother. I should never have let him come back. It's my deepest regret, you know, that I lost a daughter that way."

Marian always said that about Katie, even though she came down frequently now, from her house in the Catskills. But she seemed lost to us anyway, now that her life revolved around rituals. Katie had told me privately that she knew this must have something to do with her need to identify with her father, the way she'd let her husband, Mark, talk her into becoming an orthodox Jew. But Walrus was appalled by it. Katie thought it was because he was a wannabe WASP, even though he'd always made it clear that he didn't approve of religion, except the kind practiced by Eastern mystics. Katie had her own quirky nod to mysticism. Her three daughters were always bringing home stray dogs and cats, and she let them all make her backyard their home. She would say there are no accidents, so if the kids found these animals they were meant to keep them.

"You know," I said, "the other day I asked Katie if she was happy with her life, and she just said she didn't want to talk about it, instead of giving me that same old crap about how radiant her spiritual dedication has made her. Maybe she'll still come to her senses. Of course that could be a disaster. What if she decides she's sick of it all and abandons the kids? And the animals?"

Marian looked troubled. "She wouldn't do that. She's levelheaded. Mark's been good for her in some ways."

She didn't really like Mark, you could tell by the irritated undertone when she said his name, the same way she'd had a condescending undertone in her voice when she'd talked to Tim, whom she'd considered a social inferior saved only by becoming an *artiste*. She was as judgmental as I was; she just didn't admit it.

I had a plan. If I could get Marian well enough, I'd convince her to visit me in places where people didn't have the luxury of wallowing in their neuroses.

"Let me show you what I'd like you to do with your hair," she said, in a suddenly cheerful tone. "Give me your brush and I'll get it out of your face."

Dutifully, I reached into my bag, happy to change the subject. I sat on the edge of her bed. No one had tried to tame my hair in years. I threw my head back further and gritted my teeth when the brush hit a tangle. She conquered the hair strand with slow but determined strokes. I could hear her breath getting labored.

Abruptly, she stopped. I turned around. She was holding the brush to her breast. "I can't do anymore," she admitted, staring oddly into space again. Seeming to suddenly remember where she was, she looked at me. "What do you think?"

I stood up and faced the mirror over the ugly Formica bureau. My hair was brushed back to a funny looking crest on top.

"See, it's off your face but still looks as though you've just gotten out of bed with someone. Isn't that the look you want?"
"Mother, you're bad."
She breathed deeply. Closed her eyes for a moment. "Cussed morphine," she said. She licked her dried lips. "Is the Chapstick here?" she asked. I reached for it, on the nighttable, and put it on her lips. She hadn't forgotten where she'd left off.
"Your face is beautiful," she said. "I'm sorry I resented you all your life for being pretty and told you Katie had all the brains. And I'm doubly sorry I taught Katie to think the same thing and lord it over you."
"Don't start again."
"If I stopped arguing with you it would be time to give up. Just let me say something. Remember how when you were a little girl you used to think the most awful things would be entertaining?"
She paused to rest. Speaking was becoming an effort.
"For a while you were always asking me to crash into another car so that you could find out what an accident was like. Can't you see how it would make me worry that you were reckless and lacking in the kind of sense that Katie always displayed, at least back then?"
"I used to imagine that there was some kind of parallel universe, like in the Superman comics that you didn't like me to read, where things made more sense, but that I had to crash through some kind of barrier to get there. You made me worry all the time, you know, saying we were going to be broke and have to move to the slums and all your predictions of doomsday."
"I never thought we were poor. I've always thought I had too much."
"Not so. You always told me we were poor and we might lose the house at any moment when I was in high school."
"I don't remember that."
She looked thoughtful in a pained way. "I've always had a feeling in the back of my mind that it's best to prepare myself for the worst. Then you're not set up for disappointment. Maybe it even wards off disaster, if you pay for reassurance with enough worry." Her voice trailed off. "You know, I don't want to leave you. Or Katie."
"Don't say that."
She ignored me. "Walter is another story."
"You mean, you're willing to die to get away from him?"
She shrugged and nodded faintly.
"You don't have to make excuses for him. You could still leave him," I said.

"Don't be silly, honey. Just learn a lesson from it. I grew up in a time when you had to have a man to prove your worth, and it fell doubly hard on me because my father always told me I wasn't beautiful. But I got something out of this... life with Walter was never dull."

"I think you've convinced yourself of that. It's always possible to fool yourself into thinking you're happy. I did it with Tim."

"You were happy for a while. If you'd been born in a time when you didn't have other options, you'd have had to work harder to make sure he cured his habit and made the marriage work. And you know, maybe he would have. Maybe if you'd had kids he would have had to be more responsible."

"He was a wife abuser. He's still bothering me."

She looked sad. "I know. I'm glad you got away from him, really. Soon, you'll be able to get away... I can't hang on forever."

"Don't say that. Come travel with me."

"Madeleine, don't worry. You'll get to do the things you want to do. But... there is something I've been wanting to talk to you about."

"What?"

"Money."

The word pierced the air between us.

The telephone by the bedside rang.

Marian held the receiver, mostly listening. I could hear my father's booming, resonant voice, always talking louder and faster than anyone in his path.

"That was Walter. He's on his way over."

"I heard."

She looked at me and mulled. "Where were we?"

"Money. Whatever you meant by that."

"Oh, yes... Well... I've had something on my mind. Maybe I shouldn't say this to you."

"But you will."

"It's just..." Mother paused. She stared into space again. "It's something I've been thinking about."

"What?"

"Oh, ... about money."

"Inflation is up and the dollar is down, but you can't solve the problem." She smiled wanly. "I mean, *the* money."

Of course she meant that money, the money that had been sitting in trust since Grandfather died.

"I don't need it," I protested. "I won't need much to live on in China. And you aren't going to die."

"Let's be realistic. You're going to need a lot more than a teacher's salary to do the things you want to do. I will die so that you can go off and be the travel writer and photographer you've been wanting to be. But... .is this what I want?" She paused and stared off into space again. It scared me. "Would I prefer... to give the money to someone who really needs it? Families who are on the street now? I keep thinking... yes, with the money life will be terrific for you... You'll never have to be in a traditional marriage, and you'll probably be happier not married unless you find some man of your dreams... But what if I gave it to a battered women's shelter so that a large number of women could be saved from a life of hell? Shouldn't life be fairer across the board instead of good for just a few?"

"You can't save the whole world." I noticed that panic was rising through my voice. Quite forgetting that Marian had no authority to dispense the money, I reminded myself that I didn't expect to have it any time soon.

A nurse came in, to make her take morphine and something else. A little paper cup of pills, a little paper cup of water.

She sighed and swallowed her pills.

"Don't worry," she said when the nurse was gone. "You'll probably get the money. But if you do I want you to promise me you'll give a third of it to a worthy cause."

"Okay. Let's drop it, please."

Of course I was humoring Marian. And I was doing it because I *could*, because there was a look in her eyes that seemed to reach into another world where she wouldn't be able to call me and remind me I'd made a promise. The moment I said, "Okay," reality hit me, clouded though it was by potions born in test tubes. Liquids, crystals, metallic tones, florescent tones, milky tones, all cavorting throughout her veins, mixing with an unknown donor's blood, turning off pain, holding back cells, just to postpone the only resolution possible.

The money was hardly enough to keep me independent forever. Grandfather hadn't factored in inflation. I was keeping it in moderately safe investments, and I now had just under $90,000, after taxes. Sponsoring David would just about fulfill my obligation.

Chapter 5

The disco was tucked away in a back alley off Huai Hai Road. We parked our bicycles on a side street and wandered past a row of stores, all their doors barred after hours. The video rental window had posters of Rambo and Kung Fu heroes with fiery colors in their eyes. The night seemed painted, like a black-light room from the sixties, a path through the alley carved by machete whips in day-glo green.

David had shown up with two friends, Jennifer and Zhou Feng. They were both medical students. Jennifer had horsy teeth beneath a nose that was long and quivered ever so slightly, as if passing judgment on everything in her path. She could have been the kind of woman people describe as striking, if only she'd thrown her shoulders back and learned to carry herself with a haughty air. Instead of even trying, she was dressed like a little girl, in a pink linen dress with battered high heels and ankle socks in different shades of pink. It was her birthday. She spoke English, but not as well as David. Zhou spoke almost no English. He was tall and handsomer than David, but with such a self-deprecating way of shrugging whenever he said something that I would have turned all my attention to David and ignored him if I'd met the two of them in a crowd. Zhou kept smiling at me with unopened mouth, a smile that was quick and nervous, like the disco music coming down the alleyway.

"These friends are not *jinbu*," David said to me in a soft voice as we strolled in the direction of the music. He strode beside me with his hands stiff at his sides, his cheap white shirt bright in the dark.

"Where are your *jinbu* friends?" My tongue darted behind my lower front teeth to form "jin," and I pressed my lips hard to say "bu." Still, David laughed at me.

"*Jinbu*," he corrected, giving each syllable a falling tone. He did it with a patient voice that made me want to stroll through Shanghai and listen to him pronounce all six thousand characters in the language. "They go out, Paris, America. I see them, no good. Now I dance."

I sighed. So did he. If only I'd studied Mandarin for years, like Alison, then we could have had a real conversation.

A small man with a smarmy pencil mustache stood at the door. He asked us for an admission fee. He was speaking Shanghainese, and I asked David how much it was.

"I will welcome you tonight," he said, handing the host a wad of renminbi. I tried to give David some cash, but he pushed my hand away. I wondered if it was his way of compensating for finding me tedious, with our communication problem, though he smiled with his eyes on my face in a way that suggested other ways of communicating.

The room we entered had garish colored strobe lights and dark walls. It smelled like a dank basement, with cigarette smoke rising through the air and floating past the lights in a rainbow haze. The music was a tinny bootlegged version of the kind of rock-and-roll that is meant to be played so loud all sounds except the beat become muffled. We found a table and sat down at threadbare banquettes. People at tables on either side of us stared at us.

"We have the only foreigner," Jennifer said to me gleefully.

We drank ginger ale, coke, and orange juice. Some people around us were drinking beer, and I thought longingly of the comfortable social buzz it would create, but I didn't want to be the only one drinking alcohol. We all danced. I moved slowly, my leg still sore from my fall. Almost everyone on the floor looked like accomplished ballroom dancers. I danced with David, with Zhou. With Jennifer while Zhou and David danced together.

We sat down for a while. David took a drag on a cigarette. I coughed and moved a few inches away from him. "Do you know this song?" he asked me.

"Yes."

"She is saying what?"

" 'Hold me. Scold me. 'Cause when I'm bad I'm so so bad,' " I said, trying not to flinch.

He giggled. "I think she means about sex?" he asked.

I looked at him and realized I had to smile coyly, or he'd think I was overly bold. "It comes from a time when people went to discos just to find someone to jump into bed with."

David repeated my theory to his friends. They all giggled.

"Now do you want to dance?" David asked me.

We moved to a series of fast tunes. Primitive drumroll pulsed through my feet, my head, my heart. We looked into each other's eyes.

"You are good dancer," he said.

Katie used to tell me I couldn't move to a rhythm. You sing and dance like a WASP, she was always telling me, which was the greatest insult she could bestow. I'd have to write to her and let her know that someone appreciated me on the dancefloor.

A slow tune came on, and girls began dancing cheek-to-cheek with girls.

"Now we sit down?" said David.

When we left, we all bicycled to the end of Huai Hai Road. David stopped pedaling, and pulled up next to me.

"We go this way," he said. "So goodnight."

"Goodnight. It was fun," I said, extending a hand that he ignored. I watched them ride off, three abreast. David was in the middle, and in the moonlight, I could see his profile in a broad, relaxed smile. They were laughing. Zhou and Jennifer were both turned toward him, hanging on to every word of whatever he was saying. I wondered if David was dating Jennifer. Her poufy pink skirt was tucked around her bicycle seat, so that her bare knees rose and fell as she pedaled. The way she turned toward him, she seemed to want him to notice.

David thinks quite highly of himself, I decided.

I rode alone through the inky night, on a long deserted road. At this hour the whole population was sleeping. But there *was* crime in Shanghai, just not as much as in New York. A foreign student at our school was attacked when she went out for a walk late one night, beaten up by a Chinese student who didn't like foreigners. At least that was the way Carol from Calgary had reported it to us. Aeons ago, yet in my lifetime, foreign visitors saw a propaganda machine at work when they came to China, a paradise of workers in dark blue suits, sharing everything equally, keeping the country clean and safe because it belonged to the people. And executing anyone who said it wasn't paradise.

David called again on Monday.

"My mother welcomes you to change the bandage," he said.

Even after Wang Ming took off my bandages and pronounced me healed, Laurie and I visited her. David continued to phone. We went out for coffee and sodas, sometimes for dinner. After his initial hospitality at the disco, he stopped trying to pay my way. In fact, I became a useful source of cash to him. Almost everywhere we went, he would pay the bill in renminbi, and I would pay him back my half and sometimes his in foreign exchange certificates.

Sometimes I thought I heard him sigh when we parted, but he didn't so much as shake my hand. Since other Chinese men did, I wondered if David's aloofness might possible be a sign that he might be having lascivious thoughts and trying to hide them. I had thoughts of my own. It seemed crazy to keep this physical distance while our eyes and voices flirted. Crazy, when he was without a girlfriend and I was without a boyfriend and eager for an adventure. But if I made a move, would I spoil our friendship, which was an adventure in its own right?

One Saturday afternoon, just after the weather had turned brisk and damp, we parked our bicycles and sat on a patch of grass in the Botanical Gardens. We huddled over ourselves in sweaters and windbreakers. I pushed away a dirty straw and crushed lemon tea box. He kicked away a bit of eggshell and scowled.

"China is dirty," he said. "Hello-o?" He looked rosier in the cool weather, his mouth and teeth working even harder to form the English words. His hair was getting longer, curling into slender sideburns, looking jelled. Still, he smelled like sweet butter and sat cross-legged turned toward me, looking fearlessly into my eyes while an inch or two of grass separated our bodies. I'd had that feeling for several weeks, that he really wanted to tell me something, but couldn't communicate. It was as if he kept calling me in anticipation of that moment, when we'd somehow break through this language barrier.

"Hello-o?" I mimicked. "Where did you learn that?"

He shrugged. "American movies. And a teacher taught me 'good heavens' and 'bullshit.'"

"Bullshit? You know what that means?"

"Slang?"

Having just learned the word for shit in Mandarin from Laurie, I told him. He laughed. "China has much bullshit," he said.

He offered me a drink from a thermos of hot jasmine tea he'd brought along, tucked into a deep pocket of his red windbreaker. It seemed to be the only thing keeping him warm; the jacket was a thin layer of nylon, and all he wore under it was a blue and white striped shirt with a synthetic sheen. At least he'd stopped wearing the bed-of-nails sandals, and had on cheap looking black oxfords, probably only a little more comfortable. I sipped some tea and felt warmer.

"You're smiling," I said.

He didn't answer right away. He looked at my heavy-soled black jogging shoes, and the mud and grass caught in the grooves of the rubber, as if all of this was a great curiosity. My mother would be proud of me; I'd taken to wearing jeans and baggy sweaters as if they were a Maoist uniform. I even taught class dressed that way. It was too cold and dirty to wear anything else.

"I can have trouble for you and I are friends. You also are not a teacher, am I not right?"

I nodded, wishing for myself that I could be more dangerous. "I write travel articles," I said.

"Do you not want to understand about the situation in China?"

"Sure."

"You write something? About me," said David. He drew a deep breath and looked at me with eyes that seemed ready to ignite. He came from a culture where people smile and giggle when they don't want to help you, where they speak a language with tones that are fixed, but he had his ways of expressing certain feelings. He sat with tight fists poised on each knee, leaning toward me as if he might deliver a punch. "My father..." he said slowly.

"I don't want to get you in trouble."

He thrust an open palm in my direction, as if to push my concerns away. "My father was a worker. For the revolution. You know? Not good education, work for factory — that was good."

I nodded.

"You know the Cultural Revolution?"

"Of course."

"He made in the factory television sets. He said television is good. For revolution."

"Good for revolution?" I felt a sharp chill in the air as the sky grew cloudier.

"Maybe, " I said, "I bring a tape recorder, and you talk Mandarin and my friends translate?"

He shrugged but kept talking. "Good. Because of information going to people. He had also a short-wave radio. Because of information going – no coming? – to him from other countries. Not good, you know."

"Outside information?"

He nodded.

"Not legal?"

"Legal?"

"Did he go to jail?"

He looked relieved. He leaned closer to me. "Short-wave radio, you go to jail, yes. He wrote, you know, what is it called, a self comment."

"Self-comment... oh, self-criticism?"

"Sometimes you understand me. I'm sorry my English is bad."

"My Chinese is worse." I sighed.

"Crit-i-se-si-sa? You know, *ta si le?*"

"He died?"

"Good, you learn Chinese. He had rope. Like this." David put his hands around his neck.

"I'm so sorry."

"The Party..." he shook his head. "It says you are bad, you are bad. I was six. My father was bad, they said. I believed."

I touched him on the forearm. He didn't move his arm or change his expression. He looked solemn, but beyond grief. I moved my hand, figuring he didn't want to be touched, feeling awkward because I really wanted to throw my arms around him and see what might happen from there. Instead I examined the cracks in my nails and fingers where dirt had edged in, pretending I wanted to keep talking about China.

"A lot of people wanted to believe in Mao. In the West too," I said. David looked scornful. "Mao was Mao Tun. You know, famous Shanghai writer? We say Mao Tun we mean ... contradict. From a famous story. You know? We knew Mao was contradict, so we pretend we believe and make jokes.

Like today, too. You Deng? Xiao Ping means, besides a big name, little bottle. So we throw bottles."
 I nodded. Frivolously, I thought of how my mother and Katie and I used to call the Walter Walrus and it was our way of making fun of the authority in our house. It had started when I was around seven. I looked at the funny pictures with "The Walrus and the Carpenter." "Waal-rus, like Waal-ter. You're Walrus too," I'd said. Katie and I had both giggled. After that, even my mother started calling him "Waa-russ" in her Virginia accent, leaving out the "l" as if she were trying to wash down something that didn't taste good. We all had to obey him, but we all knew that nothing was quite the way he said it was. It used to give me a sense of possibilities when I heard my mother say "Waahhrus."
 "There's not a lot left to believe in now," I said. "I mean, in China, if you don't believe capitalism will save the country."
 "I believe in my life," said David.
 "Do you think what's good for business is good for China?"
 He smiled slyly. "If people make money from business they have some power so they can stop the government. John Dewey. You have read, maybe?"
 "No." But I recalled reading that Dewey had been popular among Chinese intellectuals from the May 4 movement.
 "People alone are not good. Like, maybe criminals. You read Dewey so you know. But I only have it in Chinese, I am sorry, no book for you."
 I stretched my legs out, trying to shake out numbness from sitting. So we couldn't talk about philosophy. "Do you think life is going to get better here?" I asked him.
 He smiled again. "Always going to get better. This thing people believe, or they die. Like rope."
 "Some people starve," I said.
 "You are lucky. And I. Not Chinese peasants."
 "Because not equal anymore. Not here." My mouth felt stiff from speaking my own language in this strange way. Instead of learning Chinese I was going to forget how to speak English.
 He shrugged. "Peasants not equal, not lucky. You make money, do good things with it. Maybe someday they have things too. The country is sick but I am only a doctor."
 "Well???"
 He smiled at me sadly. "I like to talk. I think you also like. Good heavens... a pity, you say? I want go to sea, we say in China. Go to business."
 "So... you can do that." He could, actually, go to work for a private company, surely, or start his own.

"No... not the Chinese way. I learn the right way someday, maybe America, Hong Kong. Then I return and help China."

"Help China as a businessman?"

"At that time I make factories and jobs. Maybe like your father, I have big banquets for rich people, and they give money for *jinbu* and workers."

So my father had a fan in China.

"I looked up *jinbu*," I said, brightly. "It means politically progressive."

"See? You will learn, Fox." It felt odd gazing into his eyes with no idea what to say next. Mild lust leaped to the fore. Sometimes it wasn't mild at all. He shifted a bit, relaxed his hands on his knees, and leaned even closer to me, but with his mouth open, so that we both knew he was going to break the silence. "You and I Fox together will run the world," he said. "We find something not Communist, not capitalist."

"You like Sun Yat Sen, maybe?" I asked.

"Good, Fox. You read about China. We say Sun knew, now. He was Cantonese, not so good. But a Shanghai wife." He laughed.

"He died before he did something wrong. I am afraid to believe one person is perfect, you know, like religious belief? No belief, no person, made things better, all this time."

"I know," he said thoughtfully. "Yes. No utopia.."

* * *

Laurie discovered a darkroom on our campus. When she took me there to sneak a look, I was amazed at the expensive equipment. Thanks to Laurie's ability to outstare improvisational-rule-making administrators, we persuaded the guy who functioned as photographer of educators shaking hands with visiting officials to let me use it. I bought my own paper and chemicals in town, and always had to be out of there by five o'clock. There was no particular reason not to let me use it at night, since it was almost always vacant, but when I grilled the administrators about that, they applied the standard motto of Chinese bureaucrats: When confronted with something out of the ordinary, say it can't be done.

After that, Laurie and I visited Wang Ming, and I took a series of black-and-whites shots of Wang Ming making dumplings and talking, her white floured hands waving like drunken doves. My Chinese improved gradually, and I understood more of her conversation, but with Laurie there to translate, without David around, Wang Ming launched into what she called "woman talk," which meant stories about the nurses she worked with and all the problems they had with men. One of them was living with her boyfriend. The work unit was trying to get her to marry him, but she had been married once and worked hard enough to get permission to divorce her first husband, who had beaten her several times a week, whenever he had problems with his boss or drank after work. Wang Ming, who was a unit assistant supervisor, was on her side, and had just had a talk with the main supervisor, trying to convince her that the woman should be left to do what she wanted. Another nurse was pregnant and her life was being made miserable by her live-in mother-in-law, who had come from the countryside and said if they baby was a girl it would be a disgrace to the family, and she would personally dump the baby outside a foundling home so that the couple could try again and produce a son.

A stroke of good fortune – a pimply-faced boy named Charles, just out of Harvard, who was also an English teacher at our school, had a volume of John Dewey. He spoke Mandarin and was friends with Alison – or rather, I sometimes saw her talking to him in one language or another, bubbling over while Charles gazed at her wistfully. Borrowing the book required spending an hour or so getting to know the lender. Charles was thin, more upper class lock-jawed than Laurie, but had such an eager air of anticipation in the way he asked me "Why do you want to read Dewey? No one in the States does anymore. " His room smelled like pimple medication. I was being impatient, eager to pour through the book and find something relevant. But Charles seemed lonely.

"What is it about Dewey that the *jinbu* of today are interested in?" I asked him.

On one bed Charles had piled up freshly laundered jockey shorts, all white, neatly folded. He'd brought more underwear to China than I had.

"There's the idea that society should seek an ongoing process of perfecting instead of perfection ... " he offered.

"Well, thanks," I said.

"Come and visit anytime," said Charles.

Collectivity is as important to civilization as individual liberty is to creativity and initiative. That was what Dewey said. Yes, vigor is sapped when an individual lacks constructive opportunity. But the mental and moral structure of individuals changes with every great change in the social constitution. Individuals become monstrosities when they are not bound together in associations of some kind, whether economic, religious, political, artistic, or educational. Mass murderers in America are almost always loners. The individual needs to find himself in the new social order. I wondered if that was what David had wanted to tell me about Dewey's affect on him — that he wanted to understand more about capital-oriented societies in order to grow as an individual, and as a member of the social order of China. But how sacred was personal liberty to him? If the social order you inhabit turns out to be oppressive, do you overthrow it for something that takes better care of everyone, or just demand your own rights?

I read some of what the Chinese used to call the sacred Mao Zedong Thought, too. English translations of Mao were somewhat easier to find than Dewey, in a few dusty paperbacks in the Jinjiang arcade, tucked on a back shelf next to some algebra textbooks. I let David come with me to buy the book, so that we could conduct our currency exchange.

I could see how people who had either struggled under the old system or had experienced luxury and found it empty could be seduced by the idea of sacrificing for the good of all. Mao even warned them, the revolution would not be refined, leisurely, gentle, temperate, kind courteous, restrained and magnanimous. A revolution was an act of violence. It would require continuous struggle against conflict. And it was still in progress, in a new experimental stage that was rewarding those loyal to the cause of making money.

On a cold Sunday afternoon with David, I began to sink, imagining China was a bottomless black pit with no escape. Of course this was crazy. My visa would expire someday. But it felt as if I had no past, and time was stuck. We were in a smoky place that passed for a coffeehouse, a place near the Bund called the Dong Hai. It was sweltering inside, warmed by the close contact of bodies packed around tables and blue vapors from several hundred cigarettes. There were families with children drinking luminescent orange sodas, and young men seated in large groups, engaged in heated discussion, with sweat pouring down their faces. We drank coffee that tasted like warm sugar water. We sat on adjacent sides of a small square table, and I shot him up close, with my 50-millimeter lens and flash. All the time I was thinking that I would be choking for eternity on cigarette smoke and the smell of people who don't have the luxury of a daily shower. People stared at us and pointed.

"I don't mind," David said. I got a shot of him with a cigarette hanging out the left side of his mouth. He was leaning against the table, the white tablecloth stained, his white shirt dingy in the smoke. But so much of him glinted — the shellac in his hair, his amused eyes, his face shiny with oil and sweat.

"Don't you worry about attracting too much attention with me anyway?" I asked, behind my camera.

I took a series of him shrugging.

"I think people look at you because you are pretty," he said. Flippant, flirtatious, behind a sculpture of swirling smoke. I got six frames of him that way, then had a coughing fit. I put my camera down on the table.

"Are you OK?" asked David.

"Yeah." I cleared my throat and choked a bit again. "The smoke."

"Sorry," he said. He threw his cigarette, not quite finished, onto the floor and stamped it out. He looked at his hands, at his long graceful fingers, as if wondering what to do with them.

"I read Dewey," I said.

He raised his eyebrows and the skin on his nose stretched almost translucent over the little bump. "John Dewey?" he asked, using his facial aerobics to pronounce the name.

I busied myself with running my fingers over various buttons on the camera.

"Individuals must make themselves be part of a group, he says."

"Something. I understand I think."

I decided I would try. "It is scary to me. Because the group can be wrong."

"Yes." He looked uncomprehending but eager to agree.

"In America, maybe not enough groups," I said.

"Yes. I like that."

"You like? Why?"

He folded his hands on the table and rocked back in his rickety metal folding chair. "I like to know myself in America. Forget a little while about politics. Think about girls, maybe." He laughed and looked at me to see how I'd react.

"I'm surprised you don't have a girlfriend. Or do you have one now?" I said.

He shrugged again. "The time I was in university I had a girlfriend."

"What happened to her?"

"I was young. My mother, her parents said we are young. Things are changes in the country. My mother said I am young, so I will change. Now she is now a design engineer. She married. She says change will come, to wait. She is in the Party, I think because for her job."

"Not so much in common."

"Common? Like share?"

"You didn't think the same."

"Right."

"But what about now?"

He smiled at me, as though my questions amused him.

"I want to go to America."

"But falling in love isn't something you can control," I said.

"Yes." He scratched his chin and took a sip of coffee. "In the Hollywood movies."

"My parents were full of passion about politics when they were young."

"What do you mean?"

I sighed. "My parents were Marxists."

"Yes. I know. Marxists were in West, too."

"My father also, you know, had other women. My mother was unhappy."

"Yes. I understand. So?"

"Politics are politics. But people still need love and to have ... sex." I felt funny, saying that word to David.

"Your mother and father made two mistakes, maybe. Communism and..." he looked even more embarrassed, "sex."

"It's just human," I said. "What about in China, young girls who were concubines."

"I don't know that word."

"Many wives."

"Oh yes. That is gone, of course."

"Of course. But some died, like with rope, because they couldn't have happy love. Your mother has friends who talk about their husbands. They want to be happy with love. I was married too."

I'd never mentioned that to him before. "You were married?"

I nodded. "I married the wrong man and it ended with him doing drugs and drinking too much, but sometimes you just can't help what you do."

"I am sorry you made mistake. It is the problem with America. Too much freedom."

So self-righteous about what was more likely a deficiency, this control he claimed to have over his own yearnings. I toyed with my camera.

"You want to have freedom in America," I pointed out.

"I have education, I know good freedom is this and too much freedom is this." He must have observed that I was close to decking him, because he drew forward, smiled at me indulgently, and said, "You marry me, and take me to America Fox, and teach me how people feel about love."

"You are a terrible flirt," I said. He lit another cigarette. I cleared my throat as silently as I could.

"What is that?"

"Wait." I had learned one thing from hanging out with David. In my leather knapsack, which had once been a nice tan color but was now filthy patches of brown and gray, which was at all times stuffed with my wallet, my passport, packets of tissue, a camera, film, and sometimes a flash or an extra lens, I had also taken to carrying around a thick paperback English-Pinyin and Pinyin-English dictionary. I pulled out the dictionary, which was becoming dog-eared and looked through the English section. David waited patiently. But "flirt" wasn't listed.

"I'll find out," I promised.

"I maybe understand," he said. "Liking girls?"

"You understand more than you tell me, maybe?"

"Maybe. And you too Fox?"

I took a swig of coffee water and coughed. He patted me on the back for a second — timidly, then he pulled away. He sighed just then, leaning back still further, so that I was sure his chair would tip over. It was a strange sigh, of both triumph and resignation, as if he felt we understood each other too well, like a couple thrown together and stuck there forever.

"I do a picture of you, okay?" he asked me. He picked up my camera and clicked one shot, before I'd adjusted myself.

He put my camera back in my bag with an air of finality. He was in charge of the schedule. I knew what he was going to do next, and sure enough, he pulled out a wad of renminbi from his pants pocket. I reached for my wallet.

Chapter 6

"Dear Madlion," began a letter in Katie's forward-slanting script. She'd called me Madlion as far back as I could remember. I assumed she wasn't doing it to make fun of me the way we did with Walrus, because she could do that outright.

"You're so lucky you're a million miles from here," her letter said. "I'm going nuts with school, and Rachel dropped her little troll doll down the kids' toilet yesterday and it backed up and flooded down right onto the dining room floor that we'd just had re-sanded and varnished, and the mail carrier stuffed so much shit in our mail box today that we had to get it out with pliers. But to get to the point...

"I like Eleanor. I really do. But?? Yes, there's a but. Did Walrus tell you he and Eleanor are planning to go off to Trinidad and Tobago for the holidays? (Yes, Christmas, I know that's not a problem for you.) Staying in a five-star resort, too. It's lucky for us he married her, actually — he's obsessing about a blood pressure problem and most likely she's going to outlive him and inherit all his debts. I think he's spending money to get his mind off the dirty deeds he did if you ask me. And he's not inviting me! I asked him — I said I need a break from my screaming husband and kids and he said it's a honeymoon. Can you stand it, at their age? Mark said I'm acting out the classic Oedipal/Electra complex and I wanted to be rid of all the other women in the family so I could have my father to myself, and I told him our mother was the expert at amateur psychoanalysis (I realize this is a contradictory phrase) so leave it alone and concentrate on what he does best, namely making money so the girls can go to good schools and take over the world and rid it of the male mentality.

"Anyway, if you had any crazy ideas about coming home for Chanukah, Christmas, New Year's, whatever, don't do it on your family's account. Mark and I are at each other's jugulars so it won't be very pleasant if you visit. Besides, although Tim hasn't called looking for you lately, who knows where he might be hiding in wait? Here's what you should do. Go live out your identifying-with-Walter fantasies chalking up as many countries as you can. Then when you've had enough, ask Steve, or the young Chinese dissident, or whatever good specimen is around, to be your sperm donor. Then the girls and I will come live with you and start an excellent community of womyn in Asia."

I showed the letter to Jeannette, who paused frequently to ask me to translate Katie's handwriting. At the end, Jeannette said, "She *is* kind of strident."

"I don't exactly want to go home for Christmas anyway," I said. "I feel as if I've just started to build up a shell to shut out the assaults on my senses in China. I don't want to go back to America 'til I've become so un-used to it, I get off the plane and feel like an alien."

"You'd better hope your ex-husband gets abducted by aliens before you go back," Jeannette reminded me. She sighed. "If I go home, I might bump into Ted with his new fiancée." Ted was her former love.

We looked at each other a moment. "Let's go somewhere warm," she said. We decided on Vietnam, because it was cheap and we wanted to see it before it became comfortable, like Thailand and Indonesia. I didn't mention to that I was supposed to see Vietnam with Steve. Jeannette would just tell me to get over him. So be it. Everything I did in Asia without him felt like earning a small badge of honor.

Laurie was thrilled to be going home to Hong Kong. "I can sleep on clean sheets!" she said.

"I'm sure your parents' house is spotless," I teased her.

"Oh, yeah. My mum is a fanatic." I assumed she meant that Mrs. Oscar Wong was a fanatic about keeping after the servants.

I figured Alison would be eager to go home, also, to the parents she called "my dad" and "my mom." She kept framed snapshots of them on her shelves. Her mom was tiny and looked demure, standing outside their house, arm-in-arm with her dad, who was tall and silver-haired. They both wore button-down shirts with multi-colored sweaters draped around their shoulders, and the house was pale tan brick with white trim and a big porch. She had another picture of her dad standing under a tree, with two golden retrievers sniffing at something in his hand while he grinned at the camera, looking like a man who was thinking I have everything I want. But Alison hadn't told me everything.

"It's going to be awful," she said one evening, when she and I were sitting on Jeannette's Yankee quilt. Alison was crunching on sunflower seeds. I dipped into the bag too. The salty sting on my tongue and the crackle of shell against my teeth were false promises of an irresistible flavor in the very next bite. We threw the shells into the wastebasket, where they'd piled up like a miniature landslide.

"Don't you get along with your family?" I asked. Pollyanna-like.

"It's touchy," said Jeannette, who was draped in a desk chair, wearing stretch pants and a kimono that flowed around her limbs. She looked like a dancer at rest, examining her bare feet as she painted her toenails with buff-colored polish.

"My dad'll be partying," said Alison. She had on a dark green sweatshirt and faded jeans. She had a way of wearing the most ordinary clothes and making them look like the only thing anyone should ever wear. She stopped eating sunflower seeds for a minute and pulled her hair out of the bun she'd fashioned around two lacquered chopsticks. She began chewing on one of the chopsticks, managing to look as if she were a model in a pondering pose.

"Military, right?" I asked.

She nodded. "Everybody calls him the colonel."

"I don't get along with my father either," I said, hoping that would encourage her to talk some more. I can't help it. When I was a kid I thought all families were happy except mine, and now other people's family misfortunes are irresistible.

Alison looked at Jeannette, as if for a signal that it was all right to talk to me. Jeanette looked up from her meticulous painting job. "You can come with us," she said to Alison.

"My dad's a boozer," said Alison, the chopstick at her lip. "He can get real mean."

That explained why Alison never drank.

"Yeah, you could come with us," I said. I liked her better at that moment.

"My mom says she needs me there. We have a lot of relatives around for Christmas and we always put on a show of being a happy family."

When a taxi came to take Alison to the airport, she carried her suitcase jauntily, feigning cheer, I assumed.

Jeannette was something of a magician, I decided. She brought one small duffel bag with only two changes of clothes, yet always managed to look crisp in the heat. Every morning she rose half an hour before I did to put on makeup and spray herself with a lemony cologne. In Ho Chi Minh City we stayed in a hotel near the river. The hallway smelled like wet carpets. The hotel dining room, where we had breakfast, was dark and spartan, but with fresh white tablecloths. The waitress poured coffee into each cup through a battered tin filter. It was as rich as cocoa with the buttery sweetened condensed milk they served, and delicious with the crusty baguettes, butter and strawberry jam.

"I've never seen you eat so much," said Jeannette on our second morning at the hotel. I told her the same thing.

"The heat makes me hungry," I said. We'd run out of jam. Jeannette waved to the waitress, who nodded, then forgot about us instantly. She was seating a 40-ish Western man noticeable mostly for his complete lack of a chin.

"How do you like the hotel," the waitress, who was little more than a teenager, was asking the man.

"I just got here last night," he said. He sounded American, or maybe Canadian.

"How do you like the people who work in the hotel?" she asked.

"Wonderful. Especially you," the man said.

"She'll marry him and then find out he's not rich, and he'll wonder how the sensuous little creature turned into such a shrew overnight," said Jeannette. We finished the baguette without jam.

It was the dry season in the south. The heat steamed off buildings and pavement, but still it felt like rebirth after we'd been buried in winter. Even in the heat, the air felt lighter here than in Shanghai. Everything, in fact, seemed lighter; the buildings less massive, the colors of the city bathed in a saffron-tinted light. The women, whether they were young or old, were sprightly and supple, and looked passersby in the eye with a breezy confidence.

"I thought it would be more depressing," said Jeannette. It was a surprise, that in spite of all that had happened in this country, the people seemed so spirited, and the city had a look of expectation.

"My mother didn't buy us Christmas presents during the war years," I told her. "Instead she gave money in our names to aid the people of Vietnam."

Everywhere we walked young guys driving pedicabs tried to stop us, demanding that we ride with them and unfazed when we ignored them. Not that there wasn't a fatalistic side to life. There were almost no traffic lights, and every time we crossed the street we were almost run over by motorcycles. Beggars in the streets had twitching stumps where arms and legs should have been. One had virtually no face, his nose a flat, scarred surface with nostrils and his mouth a mangled hole. Jeannette stopped every time we passed a store. She bought three sets of silver chopsticks, four pairs of jade earrings, an opium pipe and a cigarette lighter inscribed with the name "Joe Schuster, Rochester NY" on one side and "If I die tell my ma this is one helluva bloody rotten war," on the other.

"They're fake," I said.

"Thank God. I'll keep this in my drawer of travel tchotchkas." The rest were presents, she explained to me. Earrings for Alison, chopsticks for Laurie, various items for her family and friends at home. She even bought tiny wooden Buddhas for each of her students. "Aren't you going to buy any presents?"

I bought two small silver opium pipes. "One for David. One for Steve," I said.

"Your mother would be glad you helped a shopkeeper," Jeannette pointed out.

I didn't say anything, but I wondered what my mother would have thought of these shopkeepers who stood beside us as we browsed, demanding, "You buy this. You have money." My mother used to think the world should share everything so that no one would have to be desperate or greedy, and young Asian waitresses wouldn't have to hustle chinless tourists. We went to the

Mekong Delta and chartered a longboat and guide from Mytho. Sputtering down the muddy river, we sipped the juice out of young coconuts. Jeannette, who had a redhead's translucent skin, sat in the shade of the boat's cabin, wearing a bamboo hat. I stretched out in a folding chair, letting sweat and suntan oil melt in rivulets down my face.

"You're crazy," said Jeannette. But I wanted to be tan. I gazed at lush green riverbanks and made some resolutions. I didn't say anything to Jeannette because I was thinking obsessively, about what to do with my life from here, which seemed a fine thing to do on my vacation but not an appropriate topic of conversation on a river that had ferried people in gunboats, on their way to having their lives cut short. I was thinking about not going home any time soon. On an orchard island along the Mekong, our guide took us to a small villa. In the garden a table had been set out for us, with tea and platters of mango, rambutan, lichees, durian, dragonfruit. Then we walked. Children stared at us. They had brown skin and plump cheeks. A little girl offered us fresh roasted corn. She was about five. She smiled at us broadly, but looked down shyly when we thanked her.

"You could get one of your own from China," Jeannette reminded me.

Beneath her hat she looked flushed, and the gray shadow she put on her eyelids had clumped into damp creases, but she gave off a waft of lemon perfume. I felt sticky from all the fruit I'd eaten.

If I had a girl with dark almond eyes, I decided, I'd give her a first name that reflected where she came from, but her middle name would be Marian, and that would probably be the name I'd call her. Child Marian.

* * *

In late January, a million miles from the tropics again, we all felt stir-crazy in our rooms. Outdoors black smoke from a million chimneys overtook the air. It was the dampest, bitterest cold I'd ever felt. People rode their bicycles through treacherous black slush and ice. We did too.

"Can I come and visit?" Steve asked over the yellow phone.

"It's freezing here," I said. "It smells like coal and cabbage."

"I don't expect you to keep me warm. But I'd like to see you."

For several days afterward, I watched Alison with her bubbly confidence. She would probably never have an affair that made her feel like an orphaned lover. If she'd been in my place, she would have asked Steve for some job referrals in Asia a long time ago. I couldn't imagine Alison ever being in love. Or was it that I just couldn't imagine her feeling like a victim of someone else's whims? I tried not to anticipate the weekend that Steve was planning to come, knowing he might cancel at the last minute. But the thought of his visit made me stir inside, simply because I'd been living without sex for six months — a record in my adult life. This wouldn't do. I wondered about David and whether he was protesting too much when he said love wasn't important. We were probably ill-suited for anything serious anyway, but what about a little adventure?

David called on a Sunday afternoon. "You like children, I think?" he asked. "My little niece — she is really my father's sister's daughter — she will play Wednesday night her flute at the Children's Palace. We will welcome you and also your teacher friends."

"Oh... yes, I'd enjoy seeing that." I was more curious about David's extended family than about a children's' recital, but whatever, it would be some kind of experience.

"Do you like hundreds of children? Hello-oo, no? But for you I think many photographs."

"Hundreds? An army?" I said. "You mean, I bring my camera?"

Later that day I showed Jeannette and Alison the glossies I'd made of David in the Dong Hai. I wanted to send a few shots to an editor who was putting together a photo essay on faces of China. The two of them were seated cross-legged on the patchwork quilt with the inevitable bag of sunflower seeds between them. I laid the photos out on the floor.

"He's cute," said Alison. She'd met him a few times, but only in passing in the lobby when she was on her way somewhere else.

"Are you sure you're not having a thing with him?" asked Jeannette.

"The guy with no time for love?" I snickered.

Alison dipped into the seeds. "Chinese guys say things like that," she said. "They just don't go telling everything, especially to foreigners."

Wednesday at dinner Alison surprised me and said she'd like to see the Children's Palace with me, if it was okay.

"It's going to be a hundred screaming little monsters or little soldiers or something like that," I said.

"It's an important part of China."

We both hurried through dinner so that we could get ready. I pulled my hair back with my favorite barrette. On a sudden whim I took off my thin gold hoop earrings and dug out the silver ones with the long teardrops.

Alison came to my room looking cheerful, a whiff of dewy perfume trailing behind her. She had on charcoal trousers and a hot pink sweater. I'd never seen either before. She'd pulled her hair back with a velvet band, very schoolgirlish, but somehow the overall effect made me wish I had such a hairband.

"Wagon train ready to pull out yet?" she drawled, surveying my room and looking slightly uncomfortable.

"Just a minute," I said.

"Is Jeannette going?" Alison asked. She stood with her arms folded and tapped a foot impatiently while I pulled out my eyelash curler. I hadn't put on makeup in months, and I'd never noticed before how much the device looked like a miniature medieval torture weapon.

"Ooowww..." I'd pinched my eyelid. "No... she's got to grade papers." I dabbed on some mascara, barely managing not to jab my eyes. Alison tapped her foot and didn't change her hairstyle.

She was pedaling right behind me when we met David at the corner. He was leaning against his rusty bike, wearing just a thin down jacket against the cold, oblivious to the crowds passing around him in every direction.

"You remember Alison?" I said.

He shook her hand graciously. "*Ni hao,*" he said. When he spoke Mandarin he looked different. His face softened, and his voice was smooth and velvety, his gaze very much focused — focused on Alison.

"*Ni hao,*" she said, and smiled at him as if they shared a secret.

"Shall we go?" I said in Chinese.

We followed David as best we could through heavy traffic. He stopped at every few corners to make sure we were still there.

"I don't know this part of the city," said Alison, thirty minutes into the winding streets. She sounded as if this part of the city had no right to exist.

The houses here were massive, built of cement in European architecture, surely grand in another era, but now full of cracks and graffiti. The current residents had strung clotheslines from their windows to their fences, with sheets and garments hanging frozen in each yard. Many of the houses had no doors or windowpanes. People of every age poked their heads out of doorway and window frame, watching the night descend.

David kept pedaling ahead of us, looking back frequently and waving, shouting apologies for the long ride.

Eventually, he stopped in front of a stately old mansion. Through an iron fence, we saw children everywhere, overflowing the grounds, squealing, shouting, a smell of cherry lollipops in the air and a moving maze of bright little jackets in red, blue, yellow, orange. Expanses of grass, brown and soggy now, originally intended for croquet games and gentlemanly strolls — had been overtaken by spiral slides, see-saws, and mazes. On the swingsets, dozens of small shiny black heads flew back and forth in unrhythmic jumble. We parked our bikes amidst a crowded set of bars.

Little kids flew in every direction, past us, flashes of raw energy brushing our legs and running through.

David caught up with us. "Do you like children?" he asked, looking overwhelmed.

"We were just wondering how many we could take home with us," I said.

"Sorry," he said. "You sometimes speak English too fast."

Alison looked at me quizzically. Then she began to do what she was very good at: speak in rapid-fire Mandarin. I caught that she was telling him that she played the flute when she was little, too. Whether she was telling the truth or not, he didn't seem to care. He seemed to have so much to say to her, and he talked, smiling and frowning and gesturing as he never did when he spoke English. I gathered he was saying he learned mostly revolutionary songs when he was a kid. He sang a few bars from "The East is Red," his voice an octave lower than when he spoke. Both of them laughed uproariously.

"Your friend speaks very good Chinese," David said to me in English.

My Chinese tutor had told me that I had started learning the language too late in life to ever find it easy.

"My family will be happy we have two beautiful American girls," said David, trying to gather us to push through the crowd.

We found Wang Ming, standing in the crowded foyer with David's friendly middle-aged looking cousin and his wife, who were probably about my age, maybe even younger, and their little girl.

The child was an utterly enchanting creature. A long shimmery black bob. Soft, dewy cheeks, with two utterly unnecessary red circles of rouge painted on for the special occasion. Delicate yet utterly mischievous almond eyes. She held her flute in both chubby little hands, and practiced a melody, with her eyes half-closed, intent on breathing life into her metal instrument. The sounds that came out were as crisp and joyous as a pure mountain stream. Her parents beamed at their little treasure.

I took some pictures.

The recital was to begin in about half an hour. A round-faced middle-aged woman in a garish abstract-print dress approached us. In the huge crowd, she had picked out the two foreigners.

"Welcome to the Children's Paris," she said to Alison and me. Alison gave the woman an odd look, as if dying to correct her English pronunciation. Since Alison didn't speak up, I assumed she considered this a person possibly worth cultivating.

"I am Miss Guo," the woman said. "Come, I will show you everything."

We climbed a marble staircase. Upstairs we visited room after room of children engaged in creative play. Painting. Playing instruments. In one room they were dressed in clown costumes, practicing pantomime. Another room was overflowing with little girls in leotards practicing plies at a ballet barre. About five rooms were filled with children playing chess. I took pictures while Alison and our guide waited patiently. I heard them chattering away in Mandarin. On a handsome tiled balcony overlooking the busy grounds, Miss Guo began reciting facts. The building we were in was constructed in 1924. Since 1953 it had been turned over to the people, into a place for children to come and study art after school.

"Do the children have to be accepted?" I asked.

"No. We let them in as we have room. We have three thousand children who belong now. When children get to be teenagers there is room for new ones. I think it is unlike America, because they do not have to pay. But we do have a long waiting list."

"What was it before the revolution?" I asked her.

She looked at me oddly. "Before?"

"Before 1949. Did someone live here?"

"Oh. Before, long time ago. It was a club, for British men."

I imagined the fine rooms filled with pompous, self-satisfied old colonialists, with their brandy and cigars, Chinese servants bowing when they served them. Rich foreign imperialists exploiting resources, pushing opium on the people for fat profits, never imagining that the masses longed for comfort too. A preserve of the privileged, turned over to the people. Three thousand children free to roam and put their energies to creative use. A piece of architectural splendor still intact, survivor of bulldozers and axes, and the children were learning to be artists here rather than being instilled with something nebulous occasionally still known as proletarian values. My mother had gotten something right after all.

I was grateful to Miss Guo for granting me one night to love the revolution, even when, the next day, I found out from a guidebook that the building was actually the home of the Kadoories, the most famous family in the Sephardic Jewish settlement in old Shanghai.

When we were leaving that night, pushing our way through the clamor of children, I told David and Alison it had been terrific to see something in China that worked.

"The Party does this and we must be grateful," David grumbled.

I saw, in the dim streetlamp that he was gazing at Alison as if he never wanted to stop. He apologized to her for subjecting her to all these screaming children.

She giggled and said, "Oh, it was no worse than my flute recitals." He laughed as though she'd said something wildly amusing.

David rode with us to the edge of Huai Hai Road. We pedaled in tandem through a swarm of bicycles, not even trying to catch up with one another.

At the main road, David thanked us for coming. I told him that the Children's Palace was the most memorable place I'd seen in Shanghai and his niece was beautiful. He was looking at Alison.

"My friends Friday night will come to a small party. We will welcome you," he asked. In English, so I assumed I was included.

"It sounds like fun, but I can't because a friend from Hong Kong is coming to visit," I said.

"We will miss you," he said politely.

"I can probably come," said Alison, eager and secure that she was wanted.

Under dim lights from a nearby building, the front wheel of David's bicycle touched the back wheel of hers. In Mandarin, he told her to meet him in the lobby of the Foreign Guest House at seven p.m. He said it just that way, like an order. He nodded a goodnight to her. "Goodnight, Fox," he said, as if throwing a crumb in my direction.

Alison and I said nothing to each other as we pedaled on ice along the treeless road of factories. With everything shut down for the night, it was hard to see anything beyond the frost on our breath.

Chapter 7

The Shangrila Hotel, where Steve had reserved a room, was all that Shanghai hoped to be one day. At the front door two tall guards stood like tin soldiers. They wore silk uniforms the color of vanilla ice cream, decorated with red-and-navy epaulets and gold braid, and high silk hats in the same vanilla color. The lobby was full of Japanese businessmen in dark suits and flawless coiffures. I smoothed my hair self-consciously. It was as if the city had come unsoiled overnight.

I found Steve sitting at a table behind a huge palm plant in the lounge, a hushed place where the walls had massive abstract paintings with nothing jumbled, just soothing blocks and wisps of beige, ivory and gold. The pale lights muted everything. The beefy men in suits at the next table were a chorus of Budweiser fizz and muffled Texas accents saying things like "Huangpo Basin," "747's" and "cattle."

"You came!" Steve said. He squeezed me as if I'd saved him from a shipwreck. I felt stirrings in places that had lain doormat all these months. I had resolved not to go to bed with him, to be smart about this and just be friends, but I let him pull me closer and cover my face with frenzied kisses.

"You came!" he said.

"Did you think I wouldn't?"

"You're a vision," he said.

In fact, we both looked worn down. I'd put on makeup and perfume to try to hide it. He was wearing a new sportcoat and spit-polished loafers, clothes that had not yet adapted to the way he walked and swung his arms, but the circles around his eyes had settled into a permanent brownish-purple hue. I wanted to put my arms around him and let him sleep next to me.

He had a beer; I had a bourbon and water. He stroked my hand on the table. I told him about my class and my friends and my trip to Vietnam. He unwrapped the opium pipe and pretended to smoke it.

Our glasses became empty. A tall waitress in a long slit dress brought refills.

"All people talk about here is the future," I said. "Everything is excusable in the name of building the country... I have a friend, a young guy named David..."

"A *friend*?" His grin teased me.

"Just a friend. I find myself obsessing about his future. I should help him get out of China, maybe... He keeps talking about wanting to go to America, and he's got a point, wanting to see the rest of the world so that he'll understand how to help China better."

"More likely so that he'll understand the principles of investment banking better."

I took a sip of my drink. "Sad how it's turned out here." What if the Chinese were willing to give real revolution another chance, and everyone had to participate in the construction of products and buildings, and serve customers in restaurants, but the workers also served on the boards of corporations, and everyone was also expected to study literature and art and dabble in their own creative expression? Not that I think any master plan is actually going to work."

Steve seemed to be fighting fatigue. "I'd like to see a more perfect country as much as you would, but don't you think a hotel like this would fall apart at the foundation if it had been built by amateurs?" he said, rubbing his eyes. "And there's enough bad art already."

"Hmmm... what about just more equitable value for all contributions?"

"It's too tempting to eat the animals below you on the food chain," he said. He picked up my hand and held it to his face. "So who is this friend, anyway?"

"A young guy, too young for me. He demonstrated at Tiananmen. Should I be saying that?"

"I try not to give in to paranoia," said Steve.

"Well... He jokes about marrying me and going to America. I do wish I could help him get there... "

"Give him time... he can stay right here and still get his BMW. This whole country is starting to run on greed, like Hong Kong, and eventually the government will wise up and just co-opt all the dissidents with material abundance."

"Well... tonight he's taking a younger teacher who speaks Mandarin fluently to a party. Maybe they'll fall in love and he'll be her problem."

"What, are you jealous?"

We had dinner at a restaurant in the hotel "I don't expect you to come to my room," he said when the bill came. He insisted on paying."If you want, though, we can go up there and just keep talking."

"I can defend myself."

He glared at me. "What the hell do you think this thing we have is all about, after all these years?"

"Before I was married, I tried to have friendships with men, but it usually turned into a wrestling match. Including with you."

"Get over it," he said.

We sat in separate chairs. We both drank the little bottles of whiskey from the mini-bar.

"I drink too much sometimes. It sort of flows with conversation," I said.

I thought he was going to say something like conversation is a potent aphrodisiac, and then he caught himself. What he said was, "You're wasting your talent in this teaching job. In Hong Kong lots of people work as freelance writers and travel all over Asia looking for stories."

"It wouldn't be as easy to live there, freelancing, as it's been for you," I said. His eyes narrowed. "I never really tell you what's going on with me."

"I love talking to you," I said. "The rest I'm not sure about."

"Maybe I'm not either. Don't look so surprised." There was something off-balance in the way he looked, his hair rumpled and a stubble of whiskers around his chin and jaws. His shoes were off, his legs stretched out so that his feet were within an inch of nuzzling mine.

"Should I be insulted?" I asked.

He drew his feet back. "You might hate me for this, but I'm going to be honest. You were beautiful and sexy... but I couldn't see being married to you. And you know why, mostly? Because you saw our relationship as a power struggle."

"Welll... ."

"I'm not your father."

"I couldn't forget you were a man who was cheating on his wife."

"I stopped fooling around before you came to Hong Kong," he said.

"So why are you here?"

"To see you. To be your friend, and see if there's still something there. I don't have it so easy, you know."

"I don't know, since you never tell me," I pointed out.

"Why?" he said. " I didn't want to burden you."

Finally he set his glass down and rubbed his toes against mine. "Actually something monumental has happened," he said.

"Another baby?" My heart hit my ribcage like a hammer, bracing me for something I had to know but didn't want to hear.

He looked down at the thick carpet, blush beige, soft beneath our feet. "Don't be flippant... ," he said.

I waited.

"Anne has been back in New Orleans since Christmas. She says she isn't coming back."

I took a long sip of whiskey.

"I don't know what to say. I'm sorry," I said.

He told me about how after they went home for Christmas, she stayed, with Justin, to attend her best friend's second wedding. She met someone at the wedding. Well, not really met him. An old boyfriend who was in the process of getting a divorce. Actually the guy she probably should have married all along, a guy who never strayed from the right track and was now a corporate lawyer, a solid citizen in the world of charity balls and Sundays at the country club. She almost became engaged to him in college, except that Steve distracted her, wrote her a love poem, talked about seeing the Taj Mahal and the Great Wall. She thought that meant a grand tour with a return ticket.

"You did the same thing to me," I pointed out.

"Yeah... I thought of women as a constantly renewable resource. I thought I was supposed to never miss out on a sexual experience. I didn't know that people's feelings were at stake. It's a paradox, when you think about it. I knew I liked sex best when it was with women I loved, but you were all supposed to compartmentalize the experience. As was I. As you saw, I was pretty miserable myself when you got married."

"Did you love Anne... or should I say do you?"

"Well... yes. She seemed so stable and capable of holding me together. She could be critical at times, but I was afraid without that I could just drift off, run away to a desert island without even realizing what I was doing. Anne's not imaginative. She was content right where she was. You were as much of a dreamer as I was, you know. I thought with you I'd never get any work done."

"Maybe she felt neglected?

He poured more whiskey. It made me feel wide-awake, even if it wasn't supposed to. That's it, stay awake I thought. He was looking at me as if I were the only woman he'd ever looked at, which is probably the way he got all of his women into bed.

"I felt like a real asshole, you know, coming home to someone who flitted around looking miserable," he said. "In some ways it's a relief, to come home and no one is there but the amah, who just makes dinner and then disappears."

"Maybe it would get like that with anyone you lived with." I pointed out.

He shrugged. "You should come to Hong Kong for yourself, not for me."

"I was thinking of it. I was thinking about traveling all over Asia for the next few years, and how people do that with Hong Kong as a base." I had, in fact, been thinking a lot about it. If I lived there I'd work and make new friends, and never go into a bar alone.

He moved over to my chair and began to kiss my face, then moved down my neck, planting little kisses, making longing little noises.

I gave a part of myself to this, but giving all had never been necessary. Men have known that for eons. For the time you are locked together the two of you are the center of the world, so closely intertwined that your ecstatic love for him is hardly distinguishable from love for yourself. Lust is easy.

Except that I could tell, as we thrashed about, still half-dressed, that he wasn't hard beneath his pants.
"We could just sleep," I said.
"I don't want to sleep..." he mumbled, his head on my chest. Moments later he was snoring.
I lay there for hours, unable to stop the silent scream that raged through every nerve. Horniness is louder than a battlefield.
In the morning, he started kissing me again, and saying this is my happiest fantasy, waking up with you. His tongue wetting my nipples, I thought melt into this, but he was on top of my thigh and I could tell he wasn't hard.
"Let's order breakfast," I said. The Chinese would call this helping him save face, so to speak.
"Aaawww," he said. But he reached for the room service menu.
We put on the thick white terrycloth robes that were in the closet and ordered Continental breakfast from room service. A pitcher of coffee and two large glasses of fresh squeezed orange juice and a basket overflowing with muffins and the best bread available in Shanghai and a couple of French pastries and a pot of apricot jam. I devoured warm bread and chilled creamy butter. He plunged a knife into the jam, and spread it slowly, in little swirls, on a slice of bread.
I reached my forefinger into the jam pot. A sticky clump, a large piece of fruit in the center. On a horny whim, I reached beneath his robe, spread sweet goo up his thigh, licked it slowly. I felt his muscles tense up, grasping me between his legs, the jam getting warm and runny. Still nothing happened.
"Fuck," he said. I toyed with his hand. Dark, hairy, with strong knuckles and squared-off fingers. A hand that had played symphonies on my bare flesh.
"Do you think this is all there is between us?" I asked.
"Of course not," he said, too quickly for my liking. He pulled me onto his lap. "I've always said I thought you were a great woman in every way, haven't I?"
Then," I said, "we should just see what kind of relationship evolves from here."
He scowled. "It's not as if we have all the time in the world. You can come to Hong Kong, sure, but I probably won't be there."
"What? "
"Like I said, you think I have it so easy. The editors are using my stories less lately. I'm getting the message. I was told over the phone last week that I'm getting too close to the subject. That's a code for we want you closer to New York so we can keep an eye on you." He shrugged. "I'm not going to win a

Pulitzer Prize or write a novel with you as the heroine. You can't imagine the pressure I have on me. You were always a very pleasing diversion from it."

We spent the morning huddled together, occasionally sipping lukewarm coffee that became cold bitter swill, saying almost nothing.

Sometime after the maid had knocked on the door and we told her to try later, he said, "You won't go wherever I go. I might end up in Washington. Cleveland, even. I can feel you cringing."

I twirled around a little Chinese parasol that had been stuck in a muffin. It was true that I was cringing.

"You'd never follow your man wherever he goes," he went on.

Would I? I hadn't realized until now that it could mean following him backward.

We parted on more-or-less friendly terms, with lingering kisses in my room. Steve looked at his watch when we stopped for air. He had a taxi coming.

"Don't worry so much about that guy," he said before he left. "He can take care of himself."

I moved away from him, and sat on my thin bed with the thin lumpy mattress. My room looked even dingier after a weekend in a luxury hotel. The thermostat was blowing out hot dry air, so hot it made me drowsy. I had a strange feeling of being stuck here in China forever. Of course that was crazy. My visa would expire someday.

I shrugged, not wanting to be certain that Steve was right. "Were you really a part of Anne and Justin's lives?" I asked him.

"You can bust my chops," he said. "But I'm going to keep looking out for you."

"Empty promises," I said. "I'll never let a man look out for me again."

"Will you come to Hong Kong and let me be your friend and lover — if I'm still there, that is? Maybe you'll find I'm capable of evolving."

Should I give him a chance, but go in without high expectations? I liked the way his face glowed and smelled like sandalwood. We kissed again, long enough to keep the taxi waiting.

"You have to go, don't you?" I said.

"I could get stuck overnight in Shanghai."

"You could." But he had a job to get to in the morning, and so did I. We walked downstairs with arms around each other. The woman with the curly hair at the front desk and two of the men watched us with eagle eyes as we kissed goodbye. We stepped outside and I caught the thin man staring out from behind the glass.

"We're being watched," I said to Steve.

"Good," he said. "Will you come to Hong Kong?"

"Sometime. Will you be there?"

"Why don't you come and stay with me for a weekend? Think of it as another adventure."

Back upstairs the hot air made my head feel so heavy I crawled into my bed without getting undressed. I'm not going to turn down any chance for adventure, I thought in a semi-conscious state. I saw, in my sleep, an old man, who was David, and Steve, and probably others. He was living on an island, in a temple, wearing robes. I visited him, and he gave me robes too. "You can stay here," he said. I made sacrifices to ancestors with him, laying out oranges, apples, a roasted duck. Then I saw rice fields, and across the fields a dragon, breathing fire and decked out in sequins, prancing across the fields in my direction.

Chapter 8

That Monday after Steve's visit, I could barely stay awake. It felt as if a brick wall were in my path. I skipped lunch and my Mandarin instruction, and slept until the next morning, then stumbled through my class again. He called that evening, just to say hello and he hoped I'd come to visit soon. My hands felt numb and I kept dropping the receiver. I just wanted to sleep.

Gradually, over the next few days, I had little bursts of awakening. It was the end of February, and coal-blackened snow was giving way to chilling drizzles. I discovered that Alison was going somewhere with David almost every night, and realized that I hadn't heard from him since the week before. I stopped feeling exhausted and numb, but I sat on my bed, wrapped in a blanket, hugging my knees, my door locked, just thinking of various things. Steve had called again. He was in pursuit. I'd built a life here at the school that I wasn't ready to interrupt, I thought. In time, in a few weeks, I should face him, see what he was like in Hong Kong, as a man whose wife has just left him. I shivered. What if he wanted to live with me now? What if he wanted to have a harem of girlfriends? I wasn't sure which scared me more.

I wanted, for now, to ignore the loud desire and get on with something else. I thought of David and missed him, and hated Alison, and wished upon her the same fate that seemed to have befallen me — I seemed to have hit some kind of early middle age and lost the dewy allure that once defined me. When I had it I used to pretend I didn't want it. I was kidding myself, really — I'd just wanted to have people idolizing me for some grand accomplishments as well. But, I thought, something else is happening. I ran off to class the next morning feeling like a cloud again, ready to simply be there in this strange new place that had become my home. Gao Ling lingered after class and presented me with a watercolor, of spring lilies and a Chinese poem written the traditional way, in two vertical columns that read from right to left.

"It says 'We will sip the oil of green jade, freshen our mouths in the springs of Flower Lake,' "she said. " This I wrote from an ancient Chinese poem about the top of the mountain, you know, teaching the Tao."

"'The Way made clearly is not the Way,'" I quoted.

"Yes." Gao laughed, looking pleased with me. "But I make this for you, Teacher Fu, because it means also spring will come soon."

"It's beautiful," I said. Her long brushstrokes were feathery at the ends, while her curved ones looked as if they could sway in a spring breeze.

"Would you like me to teach you some characters to use in poetry?" she asked. "I have not much time in the week, but I can come to see you Saturday mornings. Okay? I would like to teach you very much."

I started to protest, but I loved the idea.

We met that Saturday. I bought brushes and ink to practice with between classes. I had travel article assignments with two magazines in New York, including a photo spread of Shanghai portraits. I was too busy to visit Steve for the next few weeks.

Gao told me about her two boyfriends while she taught me calligraphy. Our sessions became about one-third instruction and two-thirds talk about her love life. "Do you have a boyfriend, Teacher Fu?" she asked me. "You are not old and you are still pretty."

"There's someone in Hong Kong," I said. I didn't go into details because I did have a teacherly decorum to live up to after all, even if I wasn't quite old.

"Is he Chinese?"

"No. American."

"Good," said Gao.

"Why good?"

She giggled. "You are not Chinese. I like you very much, Teacher Fu, but I didn't so much like my teacher last year. He was also American."

I gave her a curious look and waited for more. When she didn't volunteer more, I asked, "And did he want to be Chinese?"

"Yes, I think so." She giggled. "He asked me to go on dates with him. Now he is married to my classmate from last year. You see, he liked Chinese girls because I think he believes they have some special secret. Maybe he was a sad man in America, and he thinks Chinese girls will make him happy. Only my classmate pretended to like him because she wanted to move to America, only, and now she is there. I don't like those men, they like me only because they see I am a Chinese girl, not liking me for Ling, as a person. So I have only Chinese boyfriends who understand, and we stay here."

"I once knew a Chinese man who maybe wanted to find an American girlfriend," I confided. The moment I said it, I wondered if I were going too far, jeopardizing David in some way. But surely Gao was no government informer. Still, she giggled more than I'd expected her to. "I know, you are talking about that boy from Fudan University," she said, a teasing tone in her voice. There were no secrets in this country.

I shrugged. Gao grew more serious. "He is with Teacher Ai Li all the time now." She meant, of course, Alison.

"Maybe he wants to marry her," I said, trying to sound dismissive.

"Maybe," Gao agreed. "I don't like Ai Li so much. She thinks she is so beautiful. But maybe that boy marries her to get out of China, yes."

We laughed conspiratorially. I couldn't imagine Alison tying herself down. Still, Alison seemed to be rushing off after dinner every night, if she was there for dinner at all, and she seemed chirpier than ever.

"We're going to a disco," Alison said on a Friday night. "We," as if they were a unit. Did I just imagine her shooting a look of pity in my direction? I watched her bounce out of the dining hall, her hair loose and bouncing with her. I mixed the oily stir-fried cabbage in my bowl up with the rice and stabbed a large limp leaf, keeping my eyes fixed on the operation.

"We should go see Wang Ming," said Laurie, looking at me.

"Good idea."

That Monday, we bicycled through the back streets to her apartment. Wang Ming gave us orange soda floats with vanilla ice cream that foamed over the top like toxic waste. Laurie looked at me with a mirthful glimmer behind her cat glasses. I licked at the foam with the spoon. It tasted like chalk.

"*Hen hao chi,*" I said, feigning enjoyment as I licked at a spoonful of foam. Laurie sipped her soda in slow motion.

"Your Chinese has improved," Wang Ming said to me. "Will you stay and teach next year?"

"I don't think so," I said. "I don't really like teaching. I may go to Hong Kong."

"I think you can get a job teaching English if you want."

I smiled at her politely and took a sip of foam. "How is everything at the hospital?" I asked.

"I might be promoted to supervisor," she said, tilting her head slightly to the left, looking girlishly modest. "If I'm promoted, I think I will use my authority to try to get my friend who lives with a man to leave him," she continued. "Last week he beat her again, and our supervisor now has met with him and asked him to talk with a committee, but he refuses. I don't think a woman should stay with a man when he beats her, do you?"

"No... That's terrible," I said. "Why doesn't she leave him?"

"She says he is frustrated at the factory where he works and so she has to be understanding. Her parents are dead so she has no home to go back to. I've told her she can come and stay with me."

"Won't that be crowded if Tian He is home for the summer?"

I caught Laurie looking at me curiously. Shock waves seemed to reverberate through the blood vessel in Wang Ming's forehead. She squinted at me solemnly, her eyes betraying nothing.

"We must not talk about that."

Orange soda jumped from the glass into my lap as my arm jolted.

"Drink your soda. There is plenty more." Wang Ming squinted at me.

She brought out a big plastic bottle. Laurie politely let her top off her drink, and wrinkled her nose in my direction.

At last Wang Ming said something. "Will you do something for me? Will you help him if you can?" She said "*Nimen*," the plural of "you." Then she kept on talking. The little girl cousin who played the flute was doing very well in school and wanted to be a doctor. Wang Ming's work unit would be taking a vacation to Yellow Mountain next month. The pregnant woman at work had had a boy, so her mother-in-law was thrilled.

"I wish it had been a girl so we could make an issue about it," said Wang Ming.

I nodded. I felt my cheeks getting cramped.

"And what will you do?" she asked Laurie.

"Probably apply to business school." Laurie looked as if she had just bitten into something distasteful. She hadn't sent in her applications yet, as she'd promised her parents she'd do.

"Oh, that is very good. You will get rich."

April came. Steve continued to call, and we'd talk about work and impersonal things, mostly.

Then he issued an invitation. "The foreign editor of *Worldweek* is coming in from New York and we're having a party for him weekend after next," Steve said. "If you want to come work here, you should meet him and talk to him about stringing for us. Of course, I'd love it if you stayed with me, but whatever..."

I would be foolish to turn him down, I realized. The school year would be ending, my Chinese visa would expire, and I'd soon be looking for work. If I wanted to stay in Asia, Hong Kong was the place to be, not only because it was where all the media were, but also because it was the only place where I could get around the immigration department for a while.

"See? All you had to do was start to walk away, and now he's throwing in a bonus," said Jeannette.

I told her I was feeling annoyed with this roller-coaster romance. I was pretty sure I meant it. "Traveling should be an adrenaline rush," I said. "Love should keep you on a sort of even level of contentment." But I didn't know anyone who lived with that kind of contentment.

That week the weather began to grow lukewarm. Local people set up a spring bazaar in the lobby of the foreign guesthouse, and would swarm around us until we brought things. They began appearing every day, and we got to know them. The girl with the flat nose sold fake jade bracelets and *bis*, little disks that sages once used to commune with the heavens. She told Laurie she had a child who needed clothes for school. The round-faced boy sold pink freshwater pearl necklaces and cloisonné owls and pandas. He wanted to open a real store. The skinny guy who shouted like a carnival barker, Wu Tan, sold chops, carved stone stamps personalized with your name or a picture, so that you could dip them in red ink and leave your stamp on letters. He stamped little red pandas and cats on paper all day and night to show off his wares.

Gao Ling and her friends pranced into class each day in new spring clothes that were still too flimsy for the temperatures outside. They preened themselves when they thought no one was looking, taking out wooden combs that they ran through their hair, pulling tiny mirrors from their pockets and dabbing on lipstick.

"Shanghai is now become very fashionable, did you know?" Gao informed me after class one day. Her voice was nasal, and she stifled a sneeze. I offered her a tissue, but she waved her hand to indicate she didn't want it. She was wearing a leopard print bodysuit that was not much thicker than a nylon stocking, with tight red jeans, her feet bare under red high-heeled sandals. I tried not to watch her as she sashayed outside without a jacket. The next day Gao came to class in a deep-plum blazer and matching trousers, polyester but a good cut, and black oxfords with short stacked heels. She stopped to chat with me after class again.

"I think maybe you like this better than what I wore yesterday, Teacher Fu?" she asked.

"Well, it makes you look like a businesswoman. Yesterday you looked like... " I didn't want to offend her and say hooker. "... a rock 'n roll singer."

She tittered. "I want to be dress beautiful." With great eagerness in her voice, she smiled at me and said, "Maybe Sunday we can together shop, Teacher Fu? I think you look young and pretty when you buy new pretty clothes, too. Then you come to my home. My mother and father will welcome you."

That would be the Sunday before my weekend adventure in Hong Kong, so I said fine.

On the day of our clothes-bagging safari, Gao Ling and I shoved our way onto a packed bus, and rode into town gasping for oxygen. On the main avenues, a number of new shops had opened, and lots of young women strolled about in mini-dresses that bore a resemblance to high fashion, sometimes arm-in-arm with young men who wore charcoal blazers with black tweed slacks, or silk ascots under Mandarin jackets. There was a sense of mission in the air; to buy was to hope. We went into the store known as Department Store Number One. Every time I moved I stepped on someone's foot, or someone shoved an elbow into my side. Gao fought her way through the hordes of women that surrounded every clothes rack.

"This for you, Teacher Fu?" Gao yelled out from somewhere in the crowd. She held up a pink polyester blouse. I shook my head. She dived in again and came out with a lime-green pantsuit. To appease her I tried on the pantsuit, a short wraparound peach-colored skirt and a shiny black blazer with red and white piping. I managed to convince her that none of them fit me properly.

"Oh... I am sorry," she said. "We try some more?"

"Let's look for you," I urged. I threw myself into the task, and grabbed a dusky blue-gray pantsuit from a woman who had her hand on it. The woman jammed a heel into my foot in retaliation, but I had the goods.

"That is beautiful. Teacher Fu, I think you have good taste," gushed Gao. She bought the blue-gray suit and a deep olive pinstriped one in the same simple blazer and trouser cut.

"I think people think I am smart when I wear these clothes," she said as we plowed our way out of the store, finally. My back and feet hurt. Gao clutched the plain orange plastic shopping bag tightly to her chest. "You know, Teacher Fu, I also will be a teacher soon. But I think I very more like to go to business."

"You'd be a wonderful teacher!" I protested.

She shrugged. "I want to help China get rich and powerful. For a woman it is good to have an important job. I can help China women much if I am a business woman."

To get to her home, we took three buses to the northwestern edge of town, then walked past a few blocks of shop that sold most of their wares outdoors. From open doorways, television sets blared with Chinese martial arts masters and car chases from America.

Gao's parents lived in a high-rise building with an elevator that swayed back and forth. Her mother, who wasn't much older than I was, had a face very much like Gao's, with the same slender limbs and full lips. But while Gao seemed to warm the room with her wistful glow, her mother looked pale and faded, as if one morning she'd simply squeezed out her youth. Her father was thin and small, with sardonic crinkles around his eyes. He pumped my hand vigorously and said, "We welcome Ling's teacher," with a slight bow.

In the front room, Gao's mother set up a folding table and poured flour all over the top. Gao and her mother showed me how to fold ground pork into slices of dough, sealing them into fat triangular dumplings. We took the raw dumplings to the kitchen, which was across the hall and looked more like a broom closet, with cement walls and floors and a few filthy mops hanging upside down. There her father placed the dumplings into a bamboo steam

basket. A wok sizzled on the old black stove, and over the stench of dirty mops came a waft of sesame oil, garlic, and fish.
"Do you like eels?" Gao asked.
"Sure," I said. I'd learned to appreciate the slithery creatures in a good pungent sauce.
"I am the cook. We are an enlightened family," her father said in Mandarin, smiling and showing the crinkles around his eyes.
"Come," said Gao, pulling me out of the kitchen. In the front room, she showed me to a stiff couch covered in tan Naugahyde, new enough that it still smelled like plastic, and brought me a red plastic glass filled with ginger ale.
"*Kan yi kan,*" said Gao's mother. "You like to see our pictures?" She placed a thick photo album in my lap. Preserved in plastic sheets were enough dog-eared black and white snapshots to keep me occupied all night. I looked politely at pictures of Gao at six months old and as a toddler, when she had a chin-length bob and chubby cheeks.
"Very cute," I said. She was, actually. They were dignified photos: no one had captured her playing with toys or making funny faces. In all of them, at various stages of childhood, she wore a tiny Mao suit and posed against a plain background, with a grave expression on her face and a proud stance in her shoulders. I turned pages, and found pictures of her mother as a teenager, in a Red Guard uniform and long braids, standing as stiffly as if she were made of iron, with a huge tractor behind her. On the same page was a shot of a young teenage boy shooting a rifle, the barrel pointed at the camera.
"Gao's father?" I asked.
Her mother nodded and giggled nervously. "That was a long time ago," she said.
Gao, meanwhile, was digging around in a cabinet. She pulled out a small bundle of newspaper, deftly folded at the top.
"I give you some presents," she said, handing me the package. I unfolded the newspaper. Inside was an array of red Mao buttons, a dozen or so in assorted sizes, and even more Chinese coins of the made-to-look-old variety, with big hollow circles in the center so that they could be strung together.
Gao's mother giggled. "I have a hundred Mao pins," she said. "It's a joke now, you know."
Her father and a man about his age and just as short, but stockier, came in just then, bearing platters of eels and steamed frogs.
"This is my uncle," said Gao. She and her mother set dishes and chopsticks upon the little folding table.
"My father likes to drink beer. You like beer too, I think?" Gao asked me.
"Sure."

I pinned on one of the Mao buttons, which made the whole family laugh. I helped them set out the feast on another folding table. Shopping and chatting had made me hungry. I dipped a dumpling into a little bowl of soy sauce with scallion slivers. It was delicious. I had another. Besides the huge oval platter of eels, there was a huge platter of frogs. I had a medium-sized mound of eels, and stirred some of the sauce into my rice bowl. I nibbled politely at a frog, then had some of the tasty slivers of beef stir-fried with greens, and some large mushrooms with scallions and ginger. Gao's family had a big refrigerator in the living room, and the beer was ice cold and delicious. For desert, we had cold red bean soup.

"*Chi, chi,*" her mother said to me when I tried not to overdo it. They were all eating heartily. How did the family stay so thin, I wondered, but of course they probably ate like this only once in an occasional blue moon.

"Delicious," I said, halfway through the red bean soup. It was just the right creamy texture, and just sweet enough, but so heavy on top of everything else I felt as if it were trickling over the top spout of my stomach. I stifled a belch.

I dragged myself to class the next morning, tasting spicy eels that were trying to slither back up through a sweet red bean ooze.
Halfway down the rank hallway, I jumped and screamed out loud. I screamed even before it registered that something had darted across my path. So close I felt the heat from its plump body, almost too fat to scurry, and saw the glint from its evil eyes and vicious teeth. I heard giggling behind me. I turned and saw Gao and Lu Xia.

"I'm afraid of rats," I said, trying to recover a semblance of teacherly dignity.

"Life is hard in China. I think you are not used to it," said Gao sympathetically. She was wearing the blue-gray suit.

It was a warmer morning than usual. I opened the windows, and we batted at flies. It was time to start reading the papers I'd assigned on *The Color Purple*, the book I'd hit upon to meet Gao's request that we read about an American girl. I'd asked for two paragraphs describing what it made them think about.

"I remember when capitalism was bad," read Ma Lianshu, a plump, shy woman who smiled self-consciously when she read, showing a grotesque overbite that would have been easy to fix with bourgeoisie orthodontics. Ma had hardly ever spoken up in class, and had bent her head down as if to hide her face every time I talked to her.

"This is a book about the poor people in capitalist country," Ma continued. "It is very bad for them. We must always remember that under market reform,"

"Good," I told her before she sat down. "You see, you have expressed thoughts in English." Ma bent her between her shoulders and blushed a deep crimson.

"I want to read," said Gao. She sauntered confidently to the front of the class, as if enjoying the sound of her black stack-heeled oxfords clicking on the worn linoleum. She pushed back her silky hair and stared at the class coolly, waiting as students shuffled, making sure she had the class captivated before she began.

"The girl in this book is poor and black, and her stepfather is like a very cruel ruler," Gao read. "But even for her things get better. She starts a small business. She is independent. It shows that people become happy when they work to help themselves. Maybe when you are rich, like the boy in *Catcher in the Rye*, it is harder to be happy because you do not have to work hard for something you know about, like money."

"Your paper was great," I told Gao after class.

She giggled. "I don't always know the English words. But I like your class, Teacher Fu, because we talk about things."

On the way back to the foreign guesthouse, my head throbbed and the damp air seemed filled with particles that stuck in my sinuses. I found Laurie, Alison, Jeannette and a coterie of other familiar faces already seated at a table.

"We saved a seat for you!" Laurie called out. "Don't eat the chicken," she said, grinning, as I sat down. There were platters of stir-fried chicken parts that looked like mostly wings and skin. I felt bile crawling up from my stomach. I stared at the platter of green beans beside my plate and all I could smell was grease.

"Could you pass the rice?" I asked pimply-faced Charles, who was at my right. I nibbled gingerly at rice and sipped tea, which tasted more like the sulfurous chemicals in the tap water than like a jasmine bouquet.

"There's mold in my bathtub. It's so disgusting!" Laurie announced.

I choked on my tea.

Jeannette put down a little rice bowl that she'd filled with green beans and soy sauce. "Laurie," said Jeannette, "it's time to grow up."

"It'll be time to grow up when I go to business school," she said. She sighed petulantly.

"What do you want to do?" I asked her.

"I like teaching here," Laurie said.

Alison, who had been sipping tea slowly and not eating a thing, looked annoyed. "Oh, really, is this the same Laurie who's grossed out by everything?"

"Don't throw tomatoes," I said to Alison as jovially as I could. Alison had never considered Laurie particularly worth making friends with, but she was crabbier than usual.

Alison looked at me as if I were a tree stump in her way.

"I feel sick. Can I come up to your room and listen to music?" I asked Jeannette as we walked upstairs.

"Sure. I have to grade papers but you won't mind, will you?"

I sat on her bed and snuggled my feet into her warm Yankee quilt.

"What would you like to hear?" she asked.

"Piaf."

A voice from smoky places. I felt so cold inside.

I watched Jeannette at her desk. She had on a gray gunmetal-colored leotard top, the kind of thing Gao had stopped wearing. Jeannette's breasts were firm little cones, a shiny spot on each point. The satin cast a shine at her shoulders too. What if I were a man and I tried to touch her there? My body stirred a little, mostly with curiosity.

"I saw a rat today," I said.

Jeannette looked up from her stack of papers, amused. "They're just little furry animals," she said. The cheap regulation lamp, tan with a short fluorescent bulb, hummed like a cicada, even above the sound of Piaf. In the harsh light Jeannette looked overly made up, as if she were hiding her real character behind doll-like paint. I wished I had the nerve to tell her, stop painting your face and fussing with your hair, just be.

"Look at this." She handed me an official looking letter.

"Oh God," I groaned. The letter was from an adoption agency in China. They knew of babies, but regulations required that Jeannette, as an American resident, go through an agency in the U.S. Before she could obtain approval to adopt, she'd have to go home first, so that a social worker could see how she lived and pronounce judgment as to whether she would be a fit parent.

"I was really hoping," she said "to go home with a baby."

"Are you going to go on with it?"

"Sure. "

I'd had thoughts of doing the same sometime in the future, and the letter jolted me. The future doesn't stick around forever, none of it. You have to unravel your red tape piece by piece. I looked at Jeannette with new admiration, cheerful Jeannette who'd been in love with a younger and self-absorbed man, Jeannette who was determined to give some Chinese peasant girl a chance to have a houseful of things both useful and useless. Her room was full of Chinese ornaments by now; a silk scroll of a fluffy panda sitting in a bamboo grove, a watercolor of a little girl catching a fish, done by one of her students, even a set of the three Taoist immortals in cheap porcelain, another gift from a student. Even in this dorm room, she had created a nest.

Do you think I'm distant? It was a question I formed in my mind but didn't ask out loud. Of course I'd kept a distance from the here and now, all my life. Instead, I found myself asking, "What's going on with Alison?"

Jeannette turned away from her papers again. "Oh, I thought you'd gone to sleep. Listen, do you really want to talk about this now?"

"What... what is it I'm not clued in to?"

She looked at me seriously, leaning forward, her hands between her knees. "You kind of liked David, didn't you?"

"I suppose I did."

"But he was kind of like a project to you. Not a boyfriend."

"Well... ? I know Alison is seeing him all the time. So what?"

"Oh Mad, you're always so defensive."

"So... " I wanted to cry, in a way, but I didn't cry that easily anymore. Eels and bile slithered up to my throat, but I sat back on the bed, swallowed hard, and wished that I could step outside of myself.

"What *is* going on with her and David?" I asked as pleasantly and maturely as I could. "You can tell me."

"Not now... .you're..."

Probably, she was going to tell me I was green. But I was up, running to her toilet, holding my stomach, bending my head down into the bowl that smelled like sewage no matter how clean Jeannette and the maids kept it, thinking I would die from the churning inside until finally, I choked and poured out hideous, slimy liquids that tasted like bile and decaying bowels of eel and sour beer, mixed up with solid particles of red bean and eel tails.

Jeannette came in and put a cold washcloth to my forehead, and stroked my back while the rumblings in my stomach slowed down a bit.

"You'll feel better soon... " she said. I let my head loll toward her thin breasts as she stroked me patiently with soft fingertips.

"Why don't you lie down?" she said. I wondered if she would rather be rid of me. I could go to my room. But I let her lead me, propping me up even though I was the taller one, and helping me crawl beneath her quilt. It felt warm under there, soft and silent except for the warble from the lamp.

With my eyes closed David was in a haze, gazing at Alison the way a lover would. Or was it Jeannette, following me as I tried to cross a bridge? Should I kiss you, a voice asked. I turned around and David was behind me. On the other side of the bridge was a huge beast, and he told me calmly not to be afraid.

"It's not a rat, it's a dragon," he said.

It came closer, a creature with hot pink scales on its side and mirrors for eyes, and when it breathed fire upon me it felt like a warm caress. David jumped on its back and they turned away, into the dusk.

In a sleeping state I heard the door open and a distressed voice that I recognized as Alison. Then it was quiet again. In spite of the foul taste in my mouth and the burning in my throat, I felt calm, enveloped in the laundry-soap smell of the quilt.

At some point I dreamt of walking down stairs until my foot hit air, and I bolted up. It was dark. Where was I? I caught sight of a clockface, and saw that it was 6:40. Everyone would be at dinner. I switched on the lamp and the cicada hum began again.

I focused on a large Chinese silk brocade box on Jeannette's desk. It was oblong, red with dragon designs in gold, black and white threads, a faded spot near the loop that caught a piece of plastic to hold down the top. I hadn't noticed it before?

The door opened, and I saw Alison come in alone. I stirred, a blob under the quilt, and startled her. She had on a rumpled jade green tee shirt and jeans, and her pale face was puffy, as if she'd been crying.

"I left something in here," she said. I nodded. She hovered over me. She twisted her hair and a waft of her dewy perfume hit me. The scent made my stomach churn again. I swallowed, trying not to be sick. She wanted to say something, I could tell.

She picked up the red brocade box in two hands and sat down in the chair, beside the bed, with the box in her lap. She pulled a pair of chops out. They were long, marbleized purplish-black obelisks.

"Nice stone," I observed. They were nice, in fact, although everything I looked at made me queasy. They weren't overly carved and ornate like most chops. "From Wu Tan?"

"Look at the seals," she says. The chop man had tested them for her, and she showed me a piece of tissue paper, with two red seals on it. Three characters in each seal, some of them recognizable.

"Is that your name in Chinese?"

She nodded.

"And isn't that Li Tian He?"

"Mmmhmmm," she murmured. In spite of a note of triumph in her voice, she drew back as though she were afraid I might deck her.

"I think I should tell you and Laurie," she said. "Jeannette already knows but I swore her to secrecy. I was waiting for the right time to tell you something."

"Yes?" I swallowed a renegade gulp of eel-taste.

"I'm scared. They were sitting on Wu Tan's table for a while and Mrs. Ting was looking at them. I never even thought about it... I'm so worried I'll get him in trouble."

"You mean David?" I asked.

She nodded. "We shouldn't even be talking about it in the dorm. You know the walls have ears around here."

"The chops are a present for him, I presume?"

She nodded. "I kind of wanted Jeannette to tell you, but she says it's my responsibility."

She paused, looking guilty. I knew something from the stillness in the air when she paused.

"I'm going to do him a favor," she said.

"What, marry him?" I asked the question teasingly.

I waited for what seemed eternity.

She drew her breath in slowly.

Alison was going to marry him.

Chapter 9

Alison and I stared at each other. The lamp with the cicada hum twitched on and off, illuminating her for seconds at a time.

"I feel weird telling you this," she said in a dark moment. With the light upon her she tossed her hair. "I know you kind of liked him." Her voice was full of triumph and pity.

I figured it was my head that was making me mean. A sharp pain was bouncing around in there like a delirious rat. My throat was raw, parched, yet still full of vile tastes.

"I'm sick," I said. "We can talk about it later."

She stood up to go, but she turned around and stared at the flickering light, then down at me. I sat up in the bed.

"I suppose you haven't even noticed that I like to do nice things for people," she said.

"I would suspect," I said, choking on a bad taste, "that if he's asked you to marry him so quickly he's out for a green card." Immediately, I knew I'd gone too far. What was this dark side, after all, except my mind wrapped tightly around itself?

"You can't expect every man to be in love with you," she said. "I didn't see you offering to help him out. And if you liked him, why didn't you go after him?"

I've never done the pursuing, it occurred to me. I let myself be pursued, but if I had an urge for someone who didn't give me signals, I chalked it up to impulse.

"Is this a love match?" I asked Alison. By then I was sitting up against the wall. I pulled the quilt around me again. I closed my eyes for a moment and waited, hoping something healthier would sprout shoots behind my headache.

"He loves me."

"He might be a con artist," I said.

She tossed her hair and made an annoyed "tcchh" sound. "I know when a guy's in love with me."

"What about your plan to work in China?"

She shrugged. "I don't expect this to hurt my career..."

My stomach rumbled again.

"Jeannette is happy for me," she said.

The door opened slowly. Jeannette came in. Still in her satin leotard, still serene with her makeup on perfectly, even after saving me from the depths of her toilet bowl. She looked only mildly surprised to see us face to face.

"We had ice cream cones tonight," she said. "I brought one up for you, Mad, just in case you feel up to it."

"Thanks," I said. My stomach kicked over at the sight. "But I can't. Why don't you have it, Alison?"

Jeannette held it out to her. Alison was momentarily lost to chocolate and crushed nuts and vanilla ice cream.

"So dark in here." Jeannette rustled about the room, turning on the overhead light and the stereo. "That lamp drives me crazy. I gather you've told Mad."

Alison nodded as she stuffed her mouth.

"I don't know what we're going to do with her," Jeannette said to me cheerfully. She sat down on the foot of her bed, her leg touching my foot under the quilt.

"So did Alison tell you about seeing the guy at the American Consulate?"

"I don't know if I want to talk about it," said Alison.

"Tell Mad," Jeannette said pleasantly. "She might be able to help somehow."

"I'm going to Hong Kong this weekend. Shall I smuggle him in?" I asked.

Alison looked at me sullenly.

"Mr. Briggs at the consulate says I could marry him here and we could wait and go through a lot of official approval for him to get to America, but they might make it harder here because of his being at Tiananmen." Alison threw away the paper that had been wrapped around her ice-cream cone and began toying with her hair again. "He said if David can find a way out on his own — of course he's not gonna say, yeah, sure, let David swim to Hong Kong, or get him a forged American passport — then we get married quickly and he can apply for political asylum in America."

I nodded. "Can you trust people who make passports for profit here?"

She looked at me as if I were stupid. "We shouldn't be talking about it in here, anyway."

"Oh, right." The walls had ears, of course. Where would a microphone be? Behind the mirror? Built within the teacups? In the television?

"Funny," I said. "If there are microphones, wouldn't you think they'd be in the fancy televisions that everyone has?"

Everyone had a television, including Wang Ming. I recalled, suddenly, that the first time I went to Wang Ming's apartment and noticed her television and VCR, Laurie had said something to David. I had a crazy idea, but maybe it would work.

Falling in love was for Hollywood movies, David had said. Maybe he'd said something quite different to Alison. Why should I try to do this for him, an act that might land me in a Chinese dungeon, freezing in rough threadbare cloth, rats nibbling on my bare feet at night? But Jeannette, curled up cross-legged at my feet, looked at me expectantly. Alison scrutinized me.

I had an idea that involved the family of Oscar Wong, a man who could probably get anything he wanted, a man who had helped relatives get out of Shanghai. Because my friend Jeannette expected me to help, and my sort-of friend Alison had challenged me to prove I was capable of helping people. Would my mother have done this? It hardly mattered, because she had never ventured to this side of the world. She would have told me to help victims of oppression, but she was afraid to fly this far. No, I wasn't thinking of oppressed people in general; I was thinking of David. I should have found some way to let him know I lusted after him, and risked the consequences. I should have offered to marry him so that he could come to America. I had one more chance, to be generous. David had come to my aid when a truck knocked me off my bicycle, and surely if he'd found me bleeding to death in the street he would have tried to rescue me. I talked about saving the world but was only gallivanting around as an observer. But I *was* capable of being a friend.

"I just thought of something we could try," I said, reluctantly crawling out of the bed and hitting cold linoleum. "We have to talk to Laurie."

Chapter 10

"Oscar Wong's kids? Well..." Steve grinned deviously. *"Aren't you the Hong Kong socialite?"*

I looked out at red, white and yellow lights through a huge window. I wanted to remember this picture of Friday night, freshly arrived for a weekend tryst in Hong Kong. Undercover. Steve knew my real identity, as the courier, here to fetch a secret document and deliver it to Guangzhou. The White Swan Hotel lobby, by the fountain. David would be spending Sunday beside the fountain, pacing until I got there. If I ended up in a Chinese jail I'd lie on my prickly mattress and remember the colored lights and the taste of wine-soaked kisses. If David went to jail he would, I supposed, imagine Alison.

"What have I gotten into?" I twirled the stem of my wineglass.

"An adventure." Steve looked pleased and stroked my knee.

"How much does ol' Oscar own?"

"Exact percentage? Plenty of Hong Kong and a thief's share of the New Territories. His real estate armies have been creeping into southern Guangdong," Steve said. "You'll hate this part of the Asia for what it is, but it'll get into your blood."

"Do you feel comfortable with me in your apartment?" I asked.

"Why shouldn't I?"

From the quickness of his answer and the smile that played carelessly on his face, I could tell he was more apprehensive than I was.

It was an expansive apartment — Steve had been in Hong Kong so long he'd adopted a number of Briticisms and called it a "flat"— on Kennedy Road, where the city began to rise up into Victoria Peak. He and his family had lived the cushy ex-pat life, with most of the rent paid by the magazine, and a young amah from the Philippines to clean and cook and take care of Justin. Tonight the amah, Lourdes, had brought us salad and pasta, arranged everything neatly upon the glass-top coffee table, then retired to her back room. Anne could have done anything she wanted here. Anything except feel at home, maybe.

The hardwood floors were as smooth as ice, the muted flower print on the upholstery felt stiff and brand new. On one rattan- and- glass end table, five framed photos of Justin stood at meticulous angles. He had Steve's deep amber eyes and tapered profile, but I'd expected an impishness that wasn't there. He gazed into the camera with a strange seriousness of purpose, as if he were worried that he might reveal too much. His hair was light brown. To the best of my recollection, the boy I'd seen with the woman in Central had been darker.

There were no pictures of Anne. It was a place with no visible remorse, as if he'd never lived with the burden of someone else's needs. I supposed we can all be protean shapes, altering to fit the circumstances around us, but this was hard to trust, a place where the past is denied.

"I'm scared shitless," I said.

"A little fear is good for you," Steve said. "I figure we have these reserves of adrenaline left over from when we had to survive in the jungle, and we need to spout out the adrenaline with a challenge from time to time, or else it chokes us and gets turned into neuroses. I'm so glad I got you out of New York, or you got yourself out, whatever." He began to massage my shoulders.

"You've never done anything like this, have you?" I asked.

He talked into my ear and kneaded my muscles. "I've done a lot of things that aren't for outside consumption, not even yours. Be a good reporter and get a look at Oscar's art collection. He always brags about it on the rare occasions when he talks to the press. It could be masterpieces, or it could be clowns on black velvet."

I closed my eyes, and felt his hands on my neck and shoulders; male hands with hard square fingertips, warm and dry, probing the spaces between my muscles, an aroma of sandalwood and male sweat.

"I want to make you happy in a way I didn't last time," he said.

I'd decided on the plane that I might as well sleep with him and get on with this overhaul of our relationship. Reform, revision, redefinition. It was all a blank page. I wasn't sure if we were still in love, but his touch made tiny nerve endings on my neck tingle. And I felt safe with him, compared to what I was about to face tomorrow.

In the bedroom he rubbed up hard against my leg, and I pulled him close to me. He reached into a drawer beside the bed, pulled out a condom, but by the time he opened the package, he had softened.

"Fuck," he said.

"It's not that important," I said. "It's just your state of mind."

"Great. Some state of mind. I won't let you go to sleep unsatisfied." He began kissing me in many places. I kissed him back, all over, but he remained limp.

"It's okay. I'm tired. You're tired," I said.

"Yeah, right, of course I'm tired." He sat up in bed, illuminated by the lamp on the bedtable. He folded his arms. "I might as well tell you what's been happening. The foreign editor asked me if I wanted to go to Sarajevo. It's a maybe... maybe that or maybe they'll send me back to the States or maybe they'll fire me."

"I'd worry about you if you covered a war."

"What else is new? I'm sucked into the vortex of something I don't believe in right here in Hong Kong. You don't still think I'm going to write the great American novel, I hope."

"What do you want to do?"

"I'm happy. Don't I *look* happy?" He laughed weakly.

"Men always think they have to live up to some ideal. Don't go and get yourself killed."

"Yeah, can't do that. I've gotta make sure my son's college education is paid for first."

"Well, I used to think I'd be the happiest person in the world if I had your job." I sunk my head into my pillow. I really did want to go to sleep.

"See? I lived up to your ideal. Shit. I'm so tired." But he was in that run-off-at-the-mouth state of fatigue. "How would you like it if I said I'm tired of having editors send me places to learn all about how greedy and corrupt China is, then tell me the stories I write aren't what they want because we're supposed to be saying capitalism is the thing that will prevent oppression and corruption? And I'm tired of running over people just to get a story that's going to be written anyway into somebody's myth, and I'm going to give it all up and live in a cabin in the woods?"

"Sounds sane."

"You've always had all kinds of ambitions that you haven't fulfilled, although it seems like you're starting to. You'd be bored with me if I just drifted from one day to the next."

I didn't answer.

He leaned back, and suddenly I was listening to his light snore, which came and went depending on the way he turned his head. I watched a yellow light from a crack in the blinds and listened to the bedlam of traffic. I tried not to move but I couldn't get comfortable. Pink dawn stretched through the crack. Maybe I slept a little after that, because the next thing I knew Steve was stroking my cheek and the room was light.

I had a fleeting thought of what it might be like to have a baby in the next room, to wake up on a Saturday in a home where I planned to say a while.

I heard a thundering, shattering boom.

"There goes the pile driver," he said. "The sound of money being made." We both moved slowly, taking showers, having coffee and dry wheat toast with butter and jam. I put on my khaki linen trousers and a white tee shirt, and the necklace I'd made from a black silk string and the old coins Gao Ling had given me.

"You look intrepid," Steve said.

Eventually we went down the elevator, out into the busy street, and kissed goodbye with a taxi waiting.

* * *

I clutched a map and an address, the paper damp in my hands. The driver sat on the right side, British-style, hand-walking the wheel back and forth as we climbed up the curves. On the south side, Hong Kong Island was a jungle. Men had cut scalpel wounds in rock to plant trees on hills that were meant for scrub bush. Like a layer of silicone, rainforest-sized palm leaves made the hills voluptuous. Platinum skyscrapers rose out of the soft folds of green.

The taxi climbed, roaring against gravity. I could live here, I thought. I saw the bay, turquoise on this side of the island and deceptively calm. Men would pave roadways over the water if it was good for business, even though they worshipped a sea goddess. Still, I could live here where metamorphosis was a daily occurrence.

At Deepwater Bay Road, we made a hairpin turn up a steep driveway that ended at a gate. A wizened Chinese woman in a dark blue uniform unfastened the gate, nodded at me, and gestured for me to come in. She looked down at my toes sticking out of my sandals, fixed her eyes on my string of coins, and frowned.

Along the walkway was a small fountain, with a naked cherub spitting water into a round pool. The house was white, made of cement, with a pair of massive white columns on each side of the doorway in front and a tile roof that sloped down into a pagoda shape. Johnny Wong, who was just a year younger than David, still lived with his parents. It was a new house, built last year. There were no trees. The land was full of red soil scars that stretched out to a cliff, with the sea behind it. I shuddered as a huge kite hawk swooped down, close to the roof, wings spread, as if looking for something to devour.

At the doorway were two bisque Chinese lions. I rang a brass bell. A Filipino housemaid answered the door. She smiled at me and spoke good English.

"Mr. John is expecting you, mum."

She touched my elbow gently, and ushered me into the living room. It was full of sleek black lacquer tables and shelves that were cluttered with family photographs and old porcelains. The walls were lined with European landscapes that were little more than pretty, all in ornate gold frames.

"Sit down, mum." The maid gestured toward a plum brocade couch. There were matching brocade drapes over the windows, so that there was only a hint of sunlight in the room.

She brought in a tray of Chinese tea. Behind her appeared a young man in polo shirt, khaki shorts and docksiders.
What had Laurie been thinking? The young man was about the same height as David but broader, squarely built, with youthful solid muscles that would probably turn to flab in a few years. He had flat cheeks, like polished granite, but a broad, soft jawline. His black hair stood on end, as if charged with electricity.
"Hello. Madeleine? I'm Johnny Wong," he said. He offered his hand shyly. He smiled and his eyes looked playful but vacant. Maybe a glimmer of David in the curve of his eyebrows. Maybe he was what David would have looked if he'd grown up eating candy-coated breakfast cereals and hanging around a golf course.
"How are things in Shanghai? Our family is from there you know," Johnny said.
"Interesting city. It's starting to develop like Hong Kong. I hear there's no end to the property market here."
"Business is good," he said, mechanically.
"Are your parents home?"
"No... they've gone on a little holiday to Italy."
A pause descended over us.
"So... What can I do for you?" he asked. No, he wasn't serious, I told myself, trying to stop the flutters inside. He knew what he was supposed to do. Was he was giving me a coded message, maybe?
"Laurie told you about the situation on the phone, right?" Laurie had called her brother from a pay phone at the Hua Ting Hotel, afraid to use the phones in the dorm with the ears all around. She'd raced back to Jeannette, Alison and me in the lobby of the hotel and said he said he'd think about it, there's hope. Laurie had told him as much as she dared — that we needed to borrow his U.S. passport for someone who was in China. Johnny was supposed to figure out that the passport would have to have a Chinese entry visa stamped in it, and an immigration stamp showing when and where he "entered" China. Laurie had said it was easy to get a stamp made. Just go to the outdoor stamp and chop makers who sold their wares in the city lanes. Her father had told her that, after using forged stamps to get the two cousins out of Shanghai. No one asked questions in Hong Kong. Of course it would be a time-consuming favor.
"I'm afraid this is very difficult," Johnny said. He fidgeted in his chair and grinned apologetically.
"I understand," I said.
He let out a nervous little laugh. I knew then he wasn't going to help. He looked away from me, at a large and flowery porcelain vase. When he looked at

me again, he shifted his chubby knees around uncomfortably. I wanted to punch him out.

"My father escaped from Shanghai when he was very young," said Johnny.

"Yes. Laurie told me."

"My American passport is very valuable to me, you must know," he continued.

"Laurie said you had a Hong Kong passport too. Would that be less difficult?"

"Well, I thought about that. But does your friend speak Cantonese?"

"True... he doesn't." He would be found out right away, if he masqueraded as a Hong Kong Chinese person without knowing the language.

"So, do I look like him?"

"Enough for a headshot." Shouldn't there be a law against smugness? "You know, if anything happened to your passport you could go right to the American consulate and report it stolen or missing."

"If your friend was arrested that would look very bad for him, and for me too."

I wanted to say surely your father could fix it for you.

"I think I have to think about it a little more," he said. "Maybe you can call me next week."

"The thing is," I said, "David has gone to Guangzhou and I'm supposed to meet him there with the passport tomorrow."

"Well, I won't be able to do it that soon."

"Did you get the stamp?"

"I'm sorry, I forgot."

There was that infuriating laugh again. "I've been busy, you know, with my dad away."

"Do you think you could do it this week or next? I can come back to Hong Kong."

He shrugged. "My dad is away till next weekend. He'll know what to do. Maybe you can call me after that. I'm sorry, I have to go now."

"Are you working today?" I asked pleasantly. People in Asia routinely worked on Saturdays, I knew.

He smiled foolishly and made a motion of holding his hands around a stick and taking a swing across the floor. "Golf."

"He didn't give a shit," I wailed to Steve. I was back in Central, and we were in a restaurant that had wine spritzers, track lights, and young British waiters bearing salad bowls and fat sandwiches. It could have been New York. I sat with my head in my hands.

"Are you surprised?" asked Steve.

"Laurie's not like that."

"She's the younger child *and* a girl. He's the little emperor of the family. I gather what she asks him to do doesn't carry a hell of a lot of weight," said Steve.

"I never want to be rich and removed from the plight of people in bad circumstances."

"Well, stick with me, babe, and you'll never have to worry," he guffawed.

"You know, I liked David a little when I met him. Maybe I'm doing this to compete with Alison, see who can do more for him. I don't know why I'm telling you all of this."

"I'm your friend, right?"

His eyes danced with mine across the table.

"Here's what you should do," he said. "The kid's a useless wimp. Why doesn't Laurie ask her father to help?"

"That would be a big deal. I mean, I just thought maybe it would be easy if there's a passport already in existence with a picture that looks like David. Stupid idea."

"You tried. Now you need a plan B."

"What?" I stabbed my fork into a pile of Caesar salad with grilled chicken. The restaurant was noisy. Steve picked up his steak sandwich and took a large bite. When he was in a hurry, as he was now to get back to work, he ate too fast. I'd never noticed that before.

"You'll think of something," he said. His eyebrows were slung like dark accent marks meeting in the middle, regarding me with discomfort.

"I was going to buy him American-looking clothes this afternoon. I took his measurements and embarrassed him to death. Why did I think this was going to be so easy?"

Steve nodded and stuffed his mouth with a forkful of cole slaw. "You'd like me to come up with a solution, wouldn't you?" he said, as I winced at his table manners.

"You're not a sage."

"I feel like I got you into this."

He soared his fork downward again, like the kite I'd seen at the Wongs' house. "There are other channels. He can go down to the South China Sea coast and bribe a smuggler to stow him in his boat. Why *don't* you take the afternoon off and go shopping? For yourself. Everybody here shops to ease the blues..."

I did go to a department store at the big mall in Admiralty and look at a few dresses, thinking it would be nice to have something new for the party that night. Nothing appealed to me. I went into the men's boutique, rubbing fabrics, passing through the underwear section and wondering if the young men buying things there thought I was wondering what they wore beneath their pants. I always felt this way in a men's store, like a tourist on an alien planet. Socks with eagle crest patterns that would end up on sinewy feet, shirts with long tails, sweeping down over muscles meant to be like granite. Men's clothes are for changing tires on a bitter night, for flexing muscles in the boardroom. Men wake up to razors, and tame the vestiges of a beast. I wanted to buy something special for Steve, just to show I'd thought of him, but among the vast displays of silver money clips and leather belts and shaving paraphernalia, everything seemed designed for one generic male with rawhide sinews and curly body hairs, someone faceless and known to me only as the other. Near the belts and ties I saw a tall blond man. I shrank back. How could I have picked up that creepy German in a bar? Of course, I'd felt so terribly alone back then.

    I rode a crowded subway back to Central, then stood in a long line outside the Star Ferry terminal, waiting for a taxi in the heat.

    Steve wasn't home yet when I got there. I curled up on the couch. A pile driver sounded in the distance. I closed my eyes and plunged into gloomy sleep.

    "Wake up, sleeping beauty." When Steve shook me awake, the room was dusky, with a few colored lights pouring in through the blinds on the windows and the muted noise of car horns.

    His eyebrows were still slanted, suspicious of me.

    "What time is it?" I mumbled.

    "Time for the mad tea party."

    I pulled him toward me. He smelled like soap and had on a freshly starched shirt. He pulled back.

    "If you want to change you should do it," he said. He sunk into the couch, as if relieved to have it to himself. I realized he had a thin red rim around his eyes and he needed a shave. "Not that you aren't lovely as you are."

    I showered slowly. I put on my black sundress, the only thing I had that was appropriate for a party, and the Chinese coins. I looked ugly, I thought, my eyes bleary and the dent that would be in my cheek forever made me look overly experienced. The Hong Kong humidity had turned my hair into a mass of frizzy little curls. I tried to brush it back from the sides. That was when I first noticed a gray streak, just a thin one, at my left temple. With a mighty yank, I got out three of the offending hairs, but the streak was still there. What was I going to do, start pulling out my hair until I went bald? I sighed and commenced with the eyelash curler torture routine.

    Imperfect and slowly aging, I walked into the living room with deliberate strides. Steve was sitting on the couch looking at a newspaper, staring at the page as if he wasn't really reading it, or at least not taking the words in.

"Hullo," I said.

He looked up, more bleary-eyed than I was. "Black," he said, smiling faintly. "You look awfully tired. We don't have to go, you know."

"I'm fine. For your future in Hong Kong, I'll wake up."

The party was in an apartment on Victoria Peak; an expansive modern apartment, with a fine view of harbor lights, but hardly as grand as the Wong mansion. The hosts were both journalists who'd been in Asia for years, as were most of the guests. A tall young guy, a bit pompous for his age, asked me where I worked. "In Shanghai," I said. I found myself telling him about how David and Gao Ling both wanted to go into business, in their separate ways.

"Don't you find it kind of heartbreaking?" the young guy asked me, sounding more impassioned than pompous. I started to ask him how he felt about revolutionary ambitions, but Steve suddenly appeared, wrapping his arm around my shoulders and pulling me off to meet the foreign editor of Worldweek.

The man who was my reason for being there was named Bill Rudge. He was about fifty, with a leathery tan and an eye that appraised me as if I were a vase that might have cracks.

"Have you done any business reporting?" he asked.

I took a deep breath. "I'm doing a piece on Oscar Wong while I'm here." Just like that, I became a liar.

"We're building up our stringers in the area. We don't pay well for that, I'll warn you. Can you fax me your resume and some samples and maybe we can talk this week?" he said.

"Well... sure... but I'm working in Shanghai and I have to be there Monday morning," I said. I could phone in sick, I was thinking, and pursue a potential golden career opportunity, except that I had to get to David and tell him I hadn't been able to help him. In Bill's appraising eye I saw all of David's opportunities and mine evaporate.

"What do you know about Shanghai?" he asked.

I took another deep breath. "They're trying to turn the farmland around where I'm living into a high-tech manufacturing area," I recited. "And all of the young generation want to go into business." It sounded pretty pointless to me.

But Bill nodded as he took a swig of beer and sized me up. "Send me a file on the young people — can you do it quickly? Two years after Tiananmen, all they're thinking about is getting rich. Do they say it's for the country, or for themselves? And what do they really mean?"

"I don't know how I'm going to do this, but somehow I will... I think I really could live here... Do you think it's okay if I quote David but give him a pseudonym..." I said to Steve in the taxi, around two in the morning. He was stroking the stubble on his chin and barely awake. I felt like bouncing off the roof.

"You're positively effervescent in the wee hours of the night," he said sleepily.

In bed that night — morning, really — I heard him mumble, "I'm going crazy." He kept his arms tightly wrapped around me, but we didn't make love. I'll take the first train, I thought.

But when I woke up, the clock radio at the bedside said 10:33.

"The 12:20 train," I mumbled.

"MMMMhhhmmm." Steve pinned my arms down and began kissing my neck, moving down and nuzzling my breasts. Against my thighs, he was hard and eager.

"No time," I said. But he kept kissing me silently, in places that had lain dormant far too long. I'll rush after this, I decided.

Afterward, we lay intertwined, comfortably silent. I ran my hand across his cheek, feeling the pinpricks of a day's growth.

"Growing a beard?" I asked.

"I don't know what's happening to me," he said.

"I wish I could stay longer."

"My love," he said. "Your crusade awaits you."

Some crusade. David would have arrived in Guangzhou last night. Right about now he'd be checking out of some fleabag hotel, hurrying through the crowded streets in his bed-of-nails sandals, clutching a suitcase with all the possessions he dared take along. Soon he'd be waiting in the lobby of the White Swan. Waiting all day, till I arrived with nothing for him. Probably he'd fly back to Shanghai with me, if he could get a seat. What would I say to him, all the way back?

"Tell David you'll figure out something else," Steve said as he pulled on a black silk kimono. He stood gazing out the window. "I didn't want to start over," he said. "Everything was just right. I don't guess you want to hear this, but I was reasonably happy. If I'd married you it would have been imperfect in different ways. I had my place in the world and I didn't want anything to change. I miss my son."

I was still lying in bed, draped in a cool sheet. "Do you want to go back to the States?" I found myself saying.

"Do you want to stay here with me?" he asked.

I looked at him. "You know we need time," I said finally.

"I dare say you never spoke to Time, said the Mad Hatter. Well, we'd better get you to the station, or off with your head."

We arrived at the train station at a few minutes after twelve. The man behind the ticket booth held his palm up to the glass, as if to push me away.

"Full," he said.

"I'll stand up."

He looked at me disdainfully.

"What about the 2:10?" asked Steve.

The man shook his head.

"It's too late anyway," I moaned.

A skinny teenage boy strolled up to me, his hands in his pockets.

"You want a ticket?" he asked.

"A 12:20?" I said.

"Too late. You want one ticket, 2:10? Only one ticket left."

"How much?" I asked.

"Four hundred dollars."

"Get outta here," said Steve. A one-way ticket was supposed to cost 175 Hong Kong dollars.

I nudged him. The scalper started to walk away.

"Wait," I called after him.

He turned?

"Two hundred?"

"Three hundred," he said. Steve shook his head as I handed out the money.

It was the last train of the day, and it would get to Guangzhou around 5:00, with barely enough time to get to David, then to the airport for my 9:00 flight. Steve waited with me in the long hot line.

"It wasn't..." I started to say. I started to say it wasn't a proposal, I know, but a seed I was planting, for both of us to see if we could start over together.

"Imagine," he interrupted, "what this scene is going to be like when Chinese immigrants start pouring into Hong Kong." He shook his head. "They're going to come here for the opportunities, but all the businesses except maybe the investment banks are going to be moving into China. Hong Kong's going to be an elite preserve of bankers and tycoons who want to keep a home here."

"It wasn't exactly a pro... "

"And Asia's going to be more and more a model for the world, of the business elite in bed with the government, and then all the exploited worker ants. I've begun to think the great majority of people want to be told what to do. It's true; democracy just leads to crime on the streets. Asia's efficient, even if people are miserable, but the masses know they don't count..."

"China's not efficient," I said.

"Think how much worse it would be if 1.1 billion people went wherever they pleased and did whatever they pleased. Yeah, I know it's not real democracy in the West, and it all makes you start to think, in some ways China's old exam system had its merits."

We inched forward. I fanned both of us with a *Worldweek* magazine. I brushed my hand against his deliberately. He reached out and squeezed my arm. I opened my mouth but he kept talking. "Like, why shouldn't there be a regard for the most learned?"

"The most learned men of the ruling ethnic group that is," I said.

"They still had to take exams and prove themselves."

"Which those who went to the best schools had a very good chance of passing..."

The crowd moved forward a few feet.

"It's time, I'm afraid," I said.

He put his arms around me and we kissed. There was no more time to talk about planting seeds. "Good luck," he said.

We held hands and looked at each other a minute. His eyes, I thought, had developed a hollowness behind the purple circles. The train whistle was blowing. Hoarsely over the noise, he said, "We can both learn from our past mistakes, you know. I'd like to try."

Everyone else was scrambling into the cars.

"We'll talk about it... " I shouted. He winked at me as I ran.

I elbowed my way through three cars before I found a seat. Except for the ads for designer briefcases and watches, the train had a quaintness about it, with threadbare upholstery and limp antimacassar doilies on the back of each seat. I managed to squeeze into a window seat, next to a young Cantonese man who was dressed a lot like Johnny Wong. He was studying the racing section of a newspaper and ticking off names with a pencil.

I stared out the window at the concrete skyscrapers plastered over the New Territories. If I could just close my eyes, then wake up and find a passport in my hands. I thought I saw something move on the overhead rack, like a black dog, but it was only a squashed piece of luggage. I blinked. Now I was hallucinating. We steamed past the gray and pale green factories of Shenzhen, chugging on through a village of red clay, and water buffalo and factories.

In China, passengers boarded the train and stood in the aisles. All around, people shouted in their nine-tone Cantonese. It was a loud language, and the Shanghainese considered it ugly.

People pushed through the crowds, looking for toilets or breathing space. A slight figure passed through the car. Short gray hair, in something khaki, like my jumpsuit. A woman with gray hair and a backpack. The train lurched. Black smoke blew outside. Then she was gone.

People pushed and shoved through the immigration booths at Guangzhou. I choked on dust, and pushed against the mob as time ran away. Almost an hour to reach the immigration officer. Another half-hour to plow through the mob and get a taxi.

"White Swan Hotel!" I shouted in Mandarin. People on bicycles again. Trucks and cars honking as if it would help them move. It was nearly seven. I rubbed my arm and flakes of grime appeared.

It was after seven o'clock when I finally got to the hotel. Two smiling doormen bowed to me slightly. I was dirty, while everything in the lobby gleamed. I saw someone who looked like David but wasn't him. I walked around the fountain once before I realized he was there, sitting calmly, almost motionless, pretending to read a book.

He looked up at me, saying nothing, his face glowing with hope. He stood up, and simply said, "Hello Fox," as if we were meeting just to go for a bike ride. I looked him up and down. He had on shiny gray pants that were probably his best, a short sleeved green shirt and a reasonable pair of black oxfords. He'd dressed up but he still looked third world. Slung on his shoulder was a canvas bag, lime green and purple, with an embroidered Donald Duck patch on one side. We didn't touch but I could feel, from an inch away, that he was flushed and dripping with sweat.

"David..." I said. The tone in my voice made him droop all over. "Oh David, I'm so sorry. He didn't do it. He didn't even get the stamp."

David nodded. "Don't cry Fox. You gave a big try."

"I'm sorry... Of course we'll figure out something..."

He looked solemn. "Now I'll come with you," he said.

I gave the doorman 20 yuan FEC to get us a taxi ahead of the crowd. At the airport, David paid a scalper twice the price of a ticket to Shanghai. On the plane, he argued with the plump woman sitting next to me. She finally spewed out a few words and moved to another seat, all the time shaking her head in disgust. David grabbed the seat. We were over a wing.

"Don't worry, Fox," he said. "I will someday do you a big favor."

I took a deep breath. "David, what if I sponsored you?"

"You are not rich."

"Maybe you should just marry Alison here."

He smiled when I said her name. He kept smiling as he looked out the window, daydreaming down at the airstrip and the clouds. When the flight attendant brought around sodas, he turned back to me, still with that dreamy smile. "Is Hong Kong very beautiful?" he asked.

"It's one of the prettiest places and one of the ugliest places I've ever seen."

"How is your Hong Kong boyfriend?"

The plastic cup of orange soda jostled in my hand. "He's not very happy," I said.

"You have a problem? You tell me."

"Don't you have enough to worry about?" He took a long sip of Coke. "I am not worry. I am like reading a book when you tell me stories."

"I'm happy for you and Alison," I said politely because David was looking at me with a patient gaze I'd seen in married or almost-married men before. He looked at me curiously. I'd seen that kind of look before, too. And though I hated to admit it, I wasn't immune, even with Steve's goodbye kisses still fresh in my mouth.

"You know, I was sorry sometimes you wouldn't marry me."

"You didn't ask," I said, lightly.

His tone was teasing, and I recalled some joke the afternoon we went to the Dong Hai when he'd said, "You marry me and take me to America, Fox." I couldn't help but wonder exactly where he and Alison had been, and what his tone was, when he proposed marriage to her. Or did she instigate it? Surely not.

"Let's not joke," I scolded him, and myself.

"Yes, in America I can joke. Not in China." He looked very serious when he said that.

"You'll be married in America," I reminded him.

"So, you were married once, but still you now have another boyfriend and you came here."

I wanted to ask him if he loved Alison, but I realized he probably did, even if he loved her just because to him she represented America, and all that freedom to make irresponsible decisions and be cavalier about other people's feelings. Of course maybe he loved her just because she was beautiful.

Instead I asked him, "What's going to happen to your mother?"

He nodded and looked solemn, but then smiled at me. "I trust my friends, like you, to bring us good luck. Remember, Fox?" He said it flippantly, gazing at me enough to make me stir, but in his voice I detected an undertone of something else; pleading. Even fear. He was flirting for survival — his own and his mother's. They would not be accused of counter-revolutionary activities as his father had in the old days, but if the authorities got wind of his wish to defect, they might stop him and see that he was thrown out of school on some trumped up charge of subversive or criminal activities. Wang Ming might lose her job. How would they get by in China then?

I had taken on an enormous responsibility. So had Alison, but I was also a part of it. Maybe I had taken on the job to show David I could be just as helpful as Alison, but what did it matter at this point? I couldn't let him down.

Chapter 11

"*Maybe,*" Laurie said slowly, "*my dad can do something. Maybe.*" She pulled at a damp blade of grass. She wore brown sandals with two thick straps that showed her plump toes curling up and down.

Jeannette, Alison, Laurie and I sat on a flat strip of ground, a few yards from the college volleyball field. We looked out for passersby as we talked. We pretended we were just absorbing the bits of sunshine that poked through grimy clouds. The campus had a few open-air pagodas, but we didn't want to take any chances. Surely there weren't any hidden microphones on the lawn.

"Why would he?" I asked.

"Come on Laurie. Can't you twist your daddy around your little finger?" said Jeannette. Her face was hidden beneath a huge cone-shaped hat, tied down with a long pink ribbon that was one shade lighter than her tee shirt.

Right, never having experienced it, I often forgot that there were fathers who were ruthless in the world, demanding of their daughters for big things like that they marry well or get MBAs, but ruthless partly so that they could buy their daughters anything they asked for, whether it was a new wardrobe or a forged passport.

Laurie brushed off stray blades of grass from her bare legs. "I don't suppose there's a microphone in there," she said. "My dad expects gratitude from people when he helps them. All of us. All I can expect is that he does it because it's for my friends. But I did hear him talking once, with some strange guy who came to our house, about Yellow Bird."

"What's that?" I asked.

Alison looked at me as if I had the IQ of an insect. But she listened attentively when Laurie explained. "It's a secret operation to get people who were involved in Tiananmen out of China. It's named after an old Chinese proverb — 'The mantis stalks the cicada, unaware of the yellow bird behind.' Some of the people in it are from the triad — you know, the Chinese mafia. Whatever, they get money from Hong Kong businessmen, and my dad might be one. And they get smugglers to pilot boats for them along the south China coast, they even bribe the police and immigration inspectors."

"Of course," Laurie added, "he might have to swim out to a boat, and hope the sharks don't go after him."

"Maybe all of this is crazy," said Alison.

"You're not having second thoughts are you?" asked Jeannette.

"Of course not."

"We've gone this far. We can't leave David in the lurch." Jeannette looked at me. It was the first time I'd ever seen her lose patience with Alison. Jeannette did see through her, I realized then, and the glance at me was an unspoken acknowledgment, like the code between two people of a certain social strata that says this person over here is not our kind. I could never say anything outright to Jeannette, because that would lower me to Alison's level of shallowness.

Laurie looked at Jeannette, then at me. I felt bad for involving her in this. Laurie who had come to Shanghai to find something of her roots, to avoid going to business school, to practice being a grownup, not to be dragged into a criminal act. She and Alison didn't even like each other.

"What will your dad want from David?" Alison asked.

Laurie shrugged. "Just *guanxi,* someday."

I watched Laurie pack a few meticulously folded blouses and a toiletry kit with five matching plastic bottles. We couldn't say much about her mission in the dorm room. Nor could she spell out the plan to her father on the telephone; she thought they should talk about it at length. She'd told the busybodies at the front desk that she was spending the weekend in Hong Kong because her father was in the hospital, a mild heart attack.

"I wish I hadn't dragged you into this," I said.

The expression behind her cat glasses was serious for a change. "There's a chance," she said, "my dad will want to do it." I started to say something, to tell her I didn't think the marriage would last, something gossipy and unkind, as my flippant way of saying I wished this hadn't gone so far. But in Laurie's serious expression, I saw that she had her own reasons for helping David. Possibly, she had come to Shanghai half-expecting to help someone who wanted to establish a place out in the greater world, the way her parents had.

Silently, Laurie cut an opening in the liner of her purse, and slipped in the envelope with the passport-sized photos of David. Then she sewed it shut. Maybe this was overkill, but we'd all developed a heady dose of paranoia. It was a tense weekend in the foreign guesthouse, waiting for Sunday night. I escaped in my story for *Worldweek.* It's a pretty decent story, I thought at the end. I'd talked to some friends of Gao, and to an American executive in Shanghai who said young Chinese college graduates were eager to be trained, and happy to work for very little money and therefore his best resource for establishing his company as a presence in China. I'd made it sound as if American companies were getting these ambitious kids cheaply, though granted, they were already living better than they'd ever expected. Keeping my fingers crossed that I hadn't missed something, that Bill would be kind in his appraisal, I sent it off to New York by fax modem. Then I tried to grade papers, but I couldn't keep my mind on the task. I found Jeannette in Alison's room. Alison was sitting in a hardback chair, her legs wedged into a lotus position, the skin on her knees stretched and shiny. She was reading a trashy paperback and eating cookies from a cellophane bag. Her hair was in a complicated knot, like a figure eight.

"I'm doing Alison's papers," said Jeannette. "She can't concentrate." The term papers were written on tissue-thin paper. Nothing was ever adequate in China.

Alison grinned at me and looked embarrassed. "Cookie?" She held out the bag. I mumbled no thanks and left.

My head ached. I felt trapped in China. Permeated with the smell of rancid cooking, the grimy heat, as if the week would never end and I'd find myself riding down a road that never reached a border.

About ten o'clock Sunday night, I heard a voice. "Hello??" it called out, from near the elevator. I knew it was Laurie, not just by her whiny pitch, but by some kind of presence that seemed to warm the clamminess in my room. I ran into the hallway. Jeannette and Alison were already there, exclaiming, laughing. Laurie's plump face was flushed.

"My dad is much better," she said. But it so was obvious, from her grin and the glint behind her cat glasses, that she didn't have to utter the code words that meant her father had made some promises.

"Only one thing," Laurie said softly. "We're all in this. We're all going to Hong Kong when we finish exams."

We had two weeks. The next weekend David left Shanghai. He was supposed to make his way south to Guangdong province, close to the Hong Kong border. Oscar had said it was best that he didn't fly and leave a record of his traveling. Some operative with a truck picked him up, and drove him down, stopping overnight at inns where David would pretend to be a truckdriver. If he made it to Hong Kong in the second installment of his escape, he and Alison would get married there. Then they'd have to apply for him to get asylum, with the help of the marriage certificate.

"He could be deported, of course," said Alison. She said it matter-of-factly, as if she were talking about missing a bus.

Laurie eyed her. "Mad and I want to go say goodbye to Wang..."

"Don't say her name in here," said Alison. "I've said my good-byes. I don't like the neighborhood committee over there, they see all."

"But I'm her former patient," I pointed out.

Instead of going to Wang Ming's apartment, Laurie and I bicycled to the hospital, where she usually worked from eight to four. We milled around in the pedestrian traffic outside the entrance, and when she finally emerged at 4:25, we gave a show of surprise at bumping into her.

Wang Ming drew back, startled, at the sight of us. "Oh..." she searched for words. "You have friends near here, yes?"

"Yes... a student, " I said, realizing we needed a cover. Wang's lips looked tight.

"How are things at the hospital?" Laurie asked.

"Very good. I think there might be a wedding soon. But there was also a very bad accident. I'm afraid a young man is dead." She started to move away from us.

"You be well," I said.

"You too," she said, and fled. I looked at Laurie and we nodded at each other, knowing it hadn't been a good idea to see Wang, knowing it would be best for her if we said nothing more about it.

Tuesday night, Laurie came into my room. We were silent for a few minutes, acknowledging the things we had to leave unsaid until we got to Hong Kong. Laurie started talking about not going to business school. She had decided to look for a job, maybe teaching, but first, she and Jeannette were going to go from Hong Kong to Indonesia.

"Don't you want to stay at a beach bungalow in Bali and have mango for breakfast? They make weavings out of fresh flowers and put them on your door," said Laurie. "Then we're going to Lombok and across, all the way to Irian Jaya, after we wash away all the dirt from China."

"The better to be eaten by cannibals when you're tanned and fattened up," I teased her.

"Aaw, come with us," she whined. "The guy can wait a few more weeks."

Combing Asia, seeing jungles. All the things I was supposed to do with Steve as my guide, showing me what he, in all his experience, thought I should see. With Laurie and Jeannette I'd carve the experience for myself. But Steve had called during the week about something that could map out my future. "Bill liked your file," he'd said. They didn't call such a contribution a story, but a file, which would be worked over by a desk person in New York who would get the byline. At the end it would say, in small print, "Reporting by Madeleine Fox in Shanghai." It wasn't a full time job, and it wouldn't pay well, but Steve had said they could use me as a stringer in Hong Kong. "Stay with me for while and we'll see how it goes," he'd said. "It's free rent." Chasing new scenery is easy, too easy, and you can pass through a million landscapes but remain just the same as when you started. If I anchored down in Hong Kong, I might change shapes entirely. I thought of David just then and wished I could witness the changes he was also about to go through.

"Have you told your father what you're going to do?" I asked Laurie.

She ran her hand across my desk a couple of times, examining the dust. "I told him I want to see more of the real world before I go back to school. We talked a lot."

That was when we heard footsteps. Determined steps, the kind that appear in a movie to signal the secret police are about to knock.

When the knock came I bolted up. I glanced crazily out the window, believing for a moment I might fly away. Then the oxygen rushed out of my head. I thought I would faint but I stood there, facing Mrs. Ting, willing myself to wake up from this.

"Some gentlemen would like to have a word with Fu Mei Lan," Mrs. Ting said, glaring at me like a Red Guard about to capture a prize prisoner. And she was not too old to have been part of the youthful brigade who gleefully tortured and killed enemies of the revolution.

"In the library," she ordered me. I walked down the stairs behind her, shaking so it hardly mattered that my wrists weren't bound in handcuffs. She said nothing, but I could tell by the way she hurried that she was enjoying this opportunity to terrify me

As she led me through the door, I saw Alison going out. She was wearing dark blue gym shorts and a baby blue tee shirt, and she looked at me with a helpless face. She twisted her hair savagely as she walked by.

The men were Shanghai police.

Mrs. Ting instructed me to sit, and poured me a cup of tea from a pot that was already sitting on the table. Then she disappeared.

The shorter of the two cops had a mouth that twisted into a permanent sneer.

"Do not worry, I speak English," he said.

I nodded. Alison was on her way upstairs, not in chains, I reminded myself shakily, but what if a police escort was waiting for her somewhere? Did people accused of bourgeoisie thoughts in the Cultural Revolution tremble with a wish to get the trial over with, did they believe it would end even while former friends shoved them into pig sties and barred the gates? I was floating above myself, imagining kissing Steve in Hong Kong and wondering if I would spend the rest of my life escaping into fantasy.

"I hear you are a very good teacher," said the squat cop. The other cop, who was very thin, said nothing, but never took his eyes off of me.

I nodded again. My tea rattled and landed in my lap.

"What will you do at the end of the school year?" asked the talkative one.

"I will go to work for an American bank in Hong Kong in September," I lied. One lesson I'd learned was never mention to Chinese government employees that you ever have been or ever will be a journalist. They'll haul you into court or search your and deport you for being there without a journalist's visa, prying into state matters behind the government's back. Another lesson I'd learned was that Communist government officials loved foreigners who worked for multinational corporations.

"You have learned much Chinese here?" the cop asked.

"Some," I agreed.

"Maybe since you like to speak the language you have made many Chinese friends?"

"Yes, my students, mostly," I said.

"Do you make friends with students at other universities?"

"Some," I admitted.

"What do you talk about?" the cop asked, still polite.

"Well, that isn't difficult," I said. "My friends are curious about America, and I'm curious about China." I squirmed and willed myself not to pee in my pants.

"We hope," the cop said, in a slow voice, "more young people like you will consider coming to China with a foreign company that brings money to build the country. You know, there is sometimes trouble here when young Chinese adults think only of themselves and not of helping the economy grow."

"Of course," I said.

"There is also trouble if foreigners instigate that kind of thinking," the cop said.

"We hope you will come back to Shanghai soon," he continued. Then they stood up.

"We are pleased to make your acquaintance," he said. "You will leave China in several days, I think? Call us if we can help you get a ride to the airport."

And miraculously, they turned and stomped out, leaving me to exit by the door that led to the staircase. I ran, trembling, up to the fourth floor. Laurie, Jeannette and Alison were in my room. Alison was more composed now, sitting in my chair, her hair twisted into a fat roll that hung over her left shoulder.

"Are you okay?" Jeanette asked.

"Oh god," I said. I went into the bathroom and peed for what seemed like eons.

"They want us out of here," Alison said when I was finally seated on my bed, huddled against the cold wall. "I don't think they know where he is or they would have said something, but having to ask outright would be a loss of face."

"And I thought we were being too paranoid." Jeannette shook her head. Alison giggled a little, which seemed an odd thing to do. "Don't say anything to anyone," she said conspiratorially.

We all had to listen to our students give oral presentations the next day. I decided to give everyone a good grade, partly because I couldn't keep my attention focused on them, partly because I didn't dare make an enemy now. At lunchtime, I walked into the dining hall and saw Alison sitting with Carol from Calgary and pimply-faced Charles. I sat down with them.

"So you two had some adventure, eh?" Carol asked me. They all seemed to be having a good laugh.

The others left. "Are you doing okay?" I asked Alison.

She scooped the remains of stir-fried cabbage into her bowl. She seemed ravenous. "We shouldn't talk about it."

"Alison," I said. "Can I ask you a terribly personal question?"

She shrugged and reached for a mouthful of cabbage. "Cool," she said.

"Have you ... well... ?"

"What, slept with him? You should see how embarrassed you are." She giggled.

"Oh... yeah, something like that." I felt my face burning.

" 'Course. What did you think?"

"I wasn't sure how it gets done here... like, where is there a place to do it?"

She looked at me as if I were a raving lunatic. "You're wondering where we did it?"

"Not particularly."

"It happened early on... I wasn't even sure I should be thinking of him as anything but a friend, but we went to his mother's apartment the day after that party that Friday night. She wasn't home, and we went to his room and he said he'd been wanting to kiss me... and we just sort of decided, cool, we really liked each other. I thought it wouldn't be too cool when Wang Ming was home, but we'd close the door... you respect your kids' privacy when you live in tiny spaces."

She was enjoying this. "He was more experienced than I expected." I imagined them standing misty-eyed in front of a judge or minister, and afterward people referring to them as newlyweds and a couple and all those cutesy phrases, and Alison still giving me that look, as if she'd walked off with a medal of honor and I hadn't. Did she imagine him as some kind of prize for an adventurous spirit when she was naked with him on the kang, the rest of the world an inconvenience?

What, I wondered, would Alison talk about afterward? Would she spin tales about her happy childhood? Maybe she'd tell him about the house and car they'd have when they got to America and got rich. And David would believe whatever he wanted to believe.

Alison grinned with her lips sealed tightly, as if she were trying to keep something from bursting out. She mumbled "mmmmm" as a prelude, and when she opened her mouth again to eat a bite of rice, she chewed it up quickly and told me she had a big secret.

"Can you believe it? I got a letter from Webster today." Webster, I vaguely remembered, was the boyfriend in med school at the University of Colorado. She just happened to have the letter in the pocket of her shorts, so she treated me — resumably thanks to this new bond between us, as the two foreign women who'd been seen with David — to three pages of Webster's laments. I concocted a picture of her other boyfriend as she read, imagining him as square-faced and blond, as I learned of how he was struggling through exams and about to begin internship, he missed Alison and had what he called a "glorious idea" that if she wanted to make him part of her future, he would be a doctor in China for a while.

"Of course, he doesn't know about David." Alison giggled and began to nibble on a strand of her hair, which was in a ponytail high atop her crown. "I don't know what I'm going to do-o-o! Web's parents have a private jet, you know... "

"I've *got* to go up and start packing," I said. I caught myself sighing.

"Cool," said Alison.

Chapter 12

That night I woke up sometime in the muted hours when a swirl of dust can sound like a fearsome cry. The Chinese believe your soul departs the material world when you sleep, and needs quiet waking time to return, so I lay in bed waiting fitfully for my defining spirit. If souls travel, had mine encountered David's? Did it know where he was, and if he was safe, and if he had any clue that his flighty bride-to-be might be marrying him strictly as a favor? Did my soul encounter Steve's and weigh the likelihood of our being happy together? Or did my soul and Alison's giggle and preen together, each in search of more than one man?

I went down to the dining hall as dawn began to bathe the walls.
"Never seen you at this hour before," said Carol, one of a few early risers shuffling to the coffee urn. She sat down next to me. "So," she said, her voice gentler with the cushion of early morning, "do you think Alison's going to run off with her rich boyfriend?"

"She told you?"

"I hope she does right by David. You better be prepared to marry him if she doesn't go through with it. Just for convenience, eh? It's okay if you've got another guy somewhere."

I stared into my coffee.

"Lie low the next two days," advised Carol, as if her soul had gossiped with mine. t was Thursday, and we had to wait until Saturday morning for our flight out.

I stayed around the campus, had my last Mandarin lesson, had tea with Gao and some other students, wondered if anyone was reporting on me. I saw Alison with various friends she'd made, beaming like a prom queen with two dates.

"Have you heard from our police escorts?" I kidded with her.

She shook her head. "They've got an eye on us, don't worry."

Saturday morning came, finally. We rode a taxi to the airport. I noticed a black car behind us that never disappeared.

"There were two cockroaches mating in my bathroom just before I left," said Laurie as we rode the taxi to the airport. But her eyes didn't glint behind her cat glasses.

Did I imagine the immigration officer taking an unusually long time to leaf through my passport, to check my data on the computer?

"You are teacher in China?" he asked me in good English, showing teeth the color of old parchment.

I nodded. "Now I go home," I said. I saw Alison beyond the immigration stands, posing like a model for the khaki jeans and red tee shirt she wore. Well, surely if she'd sailed through, I could too. But my hands shook.

Ages later, we were on our way out. I sat next to Jeannette.

"Did you notice a black car?" I asked her.

"They probably wanted to be sure you got out," she said. The plane began to bounce.

"Just an air pocket," Jeannette reassured me.

Then, at last, we tumbled down into the pink and gray skyline. We all tore off the plane, giddy as escapees. "Where is David?" I wondered out loud as we waited for our baggage. No one answered.

"We might have to go out early in the morning," Laurie said. I stopped feeling like an escaped prisoner. The mission had not even begun.

As we made our way through the greeting area, Steve emerged. We kissed as if we were in love.

"We'll call you later," said Laurie. Jeannette and Alison were going to the Wongs' house.

It was mid-afternoon when the phone rang, interrupting my reunion with Steve.

"It might be about some big plan," I said.

"Yeah," he barked into the phone beside the bed. Without a word he handed it to me.

"Have you ever been sailing?" Laurie asked.

"A few times."

"Good. Jeannette's afraid of getting seasick, and Dad says I have to keep out of this 'cause he doesn't want his name getting in it... You and Alison are going sailing tomorrow. You're supposed to be two gweilos on a holiday, with a couple of guys who know where they're going.

"Where?"

"You'll see. Nobody else — it's supposed to look like two couples. They'll pick you up, at seven. They know what David looks like from the pictures I brought before. You're camping overnight."

Steve stroked my back. Maybe we would be happy, I thought fleetingly, and cringed over the strange company I was to be with by this time tomorrow, for God knew how long. Where was David while I lay here naked and feeling loved?

. . "So they do these things by boat?" I asked Steve.

"A lot." He held me against his chest. "Can I come along to protect you?"

"She said no."

He nodded. "I'll worry. You and that ditsy girl and two tough guys. But you could get a great story, you know."

I looked at him, smug against his pillow, and suddenly he didn't feel so warm against me. Was everything just a story for him? "Don't you see, I'm part of it. I'd harm David's mother, and dissidents who try to get out of China after him."

He nodded. "Don't let Oscar Wong push you around. Maybe not this time, but follow it... you've gotta be tough and have good contacts if you're gonna string for *Worldweek.*"

I dressed for sailing the next morning, wondering if I'd fooled myself, wondering if I wasn't tough enough to compete in Steve's world. But I couldn't betray David.

I stumbled down to the entrance of Steve's building that next morning. Alison sat in the front seat of a Land Rover, next to a young Hong Kong Chinese man who looked as if he'd been churned out of a modeling school for gently rugged types. He had the squint and the beginning to be leathery skin of an accomplished sailor.

"Hello," he said politely to me but with no real effort at friendliness. He said it as "hellew," and his English was full of BBC-announcer pronunciations though his accent was still Cantonese. "I am C.K. This is Joe." The man in the back was a little fleshier than C.K., with a glint in his eye that seemed uninterested in anything but getting on with the job. He nodded at me and busied himself with cracking his knuckles. Both Joe and C.K. wore brand-new looking polo shirts and Docksiders. By the way they talked and dressed, by their haircuts that were as manicured as an English garden, I might have mistaken them for a couple of young traders from the Hong Kong Stock Exchange, except that Steve had called them tough guys.

Alison smiled at me with such relief I forgave her for everything. She twisted her hair, pulled a white sun visor on and off.

"Are you a full-time sailor," she asked C.K. cheerily and absurdly. I liked her better for it. The question made even him smile.

"I run a business," he said. "Things people want between here and China." He spoke with good humor, yet with an emphasis on the word "things" that made me shudder.

"Is Joe in your business, too?" I asked.

"I handicap horses and play blackjack in Macau," said Joe, matter-of-factly. His English was quite good, actually. "I studied in America," he went on. "I liked Europe, too. Have you been to the Grand Prix?"

We pulled up outside a marina in Aberdeen, the teeming section on the southern shore filled with tenements and fish markets and yachting clubs. C.K. spoke to a dockhand who left for a few minutes and came back with two huge sacks of sandwiches and an ice chest.

"OK, we are ready," commanded C.K., and led us to a 42-foot cruiser with the name "Empress" on the side. He instructed us to hoist the sails and untie knots, then steered us out toward the harbor with the motor on. In the open water, he shut off the motor.

"Do you know how to steer?" he asked me.

"I've done it before," I said. I'd once done a story for the travel magazine on a sail along the Northeastern shore, from Amagansett to Block Island. I took the helm.

The water was choppy, and I willed myself not to get seasick. At 10am C.K. offered us beer. I took one, deciding it might be better to remain a little drunk throughout this ride. Even Alison took a beer. She sat on the bench close to me, the wind whipping her hair and her face fixed upon the water, her lips in a tight line.

"How're you doing?" I asked her.

She looked toward our escorts, who sat across from her, observing the air and the traffic of container ships and pleasure boats at sea, and the coast of Kowloon along our right, discussing what seemed to be directions and conditions in Cantonese. As the afternoon wore on, Joe's mobile phone rang. He talked for a while, then an hour later it rang again. He spoke in animated Cantonese.

C.K. grinned at us, and said, "He's talking to his bookie."

"Where are we going?" Alison asked.

"We get there by dark," was all C.K. would offer.

My arms were sore. I kept looking at C.K. hoping he'd relieve me. Instead he offered me a sandwich. It was a thin layer of something that tasted vaguely like ham between two slices of white bread, nothing else. I devoured it and still felt shaky.

Finally I told him I had to use the head.

"Okay, Joe will steer. Maybe you are tired?" he said.

I nodded. I crept into a bunk below, and tried lying there, but the cabin rattled inside and I realized if I didn't get some air I'd throw up. My skin felt as if it had grown a layer of brine. I saw that Alison looked deflated, sitting in the same perch she'd been in all day, her hair flying in hard strings. Joe continued to steer. I watched his square hands on the wheel. I was supposed to be posing as his date, if any officials asked. Who would ever believe such a thing? My back felt as if it were made of rubber.

Toward nightfall, we crossed into Chinese waters. C.K. waved to the men in a coast guard boat.

"You know them?" I asked.

"I know everyone I have to know," he said. "You smile and wave too." He put an arm around me, and said, in a captain's command, "We are having fun with our American friends."

C.K. pointed out a few lights of a small port and fishing village. There were factory buildings side by side with lean-to homes. In the water were clusters of fishing boats. "It will be a big port like Hong Kong someday," he said.

"Where are we going?" I asked. I longed to go below, and see if sleep could win out over seasickness.

"We will enjoy some night sailing," said C.K. "All along the coast." He relieved Joe of the helm. As the night grew darker, Joe hung a beacon from the top of the sail. The night and the water were black. How would anyone be able to see us?

"You girls go below now and rest," said C.K.

We sat up in bunks, not sleeping. I looked through a porthole but it was pitch black out there.

"This is insane... I was crazy..." said Alison, choking, crying.

"Quiet," I said. "What do you think they'll do if they hear you?" I tried closing my eyes and thought to sleep would be worse. Where would I wake up?

Alison gradually regained her composure. "I hear him, I'm sure I hear something," she said. But there was no sound but the splashing of the water.

The boat was still moving slowly, cruising the coast. I saw flashes of light, two at a time, then it would stop and flash again.

"Our light," said Alison.

"You know how this underground thing works?" she asked me.

"No. Neither do you."

Ignoring me, she went on. "The Coast Guard patrols were probably in on it. There are fishermen down here who have to be in on it, to hide David. These guys we're with are clean-cut smugglers getting paid well. Oscar Wong probably donated a pile of money already — lots of businessmen did. People think no one in Hong Kong cares about politics, but they know how to do business with China and all the time keep a low profile about giving money to help those who want to get out of China — they all escaped from China themselves, or at least their grandparents did."

It sounded right. Maybe Laurie had told her about the Yellow Bird underground, maybe even David had, but I knew Alison wouldn't want to admit that she'd done any less than been born knowing everything there was to know.

"Courage under the guise of greed," I mused. We waited, huddled under blankets, food in the galley. Where was David waiting, if he was still alive at all?

"He has to find us in the dark, or the wrong Coast Guard patrols will see him," Alison observed.

We sat.

I heard voices, no more than a whisper. C.K. and Joe, of course, but the boat was rocking more, there were more splashes, and the sound of activity. Alison and I jumped out of the bunks. We looked out the doorway. C.K. and Joe were hauling in a line... with someone at the end, grasping a life preserver, but all I could see was a dark shirt. If it was David, I wasn't sure he was alive.

They pulled him on board. I almost shrieked, while Alison stood frozen. It was David, crumpled on the deck. Joe pounded his back and he spat out water. He looked up for a moment, then fell back. His feet were bare and bleeding.

"Towels in the galley," ordered C.K. Alison and I found a stack of towels, and began wiping his feet, while C.K. tore one in half and tied a section around each of David's feet, to bind them.

"He walked over the oyster beds," explained C.K.

We gave him water. He spat out the first gulp, but then drank some, then sank back again. Joe picked him up, ordered us to move aside. We watched as Joe opened the deck hatch. "*Xiang*," he ordered David. Get in. So Joe spoke some Mandarin. It would be useful in his current line of work, of course. Joe helped him shimmy down into the anchor locker.

"It is very dirty in there," C.K. said to us. "But because it's dirty no one will try to look." He began pulling in the anchor. I watched as he unfastened the anchor itself, which he placed on the deck, but then piled the rope and chain into the locker, over David. I could smell brine and seaweed as he packed in the line. David was curled in a heap, huddled against the rope. He looked up at us and nodded weakly. C.K. closed the hatch.

"We turn now. You take the wheel," C.K. ordered me. He and Joe moved the sails, but then, for good measure, he turned on the motor.

"Now, go below. Don't come out," C.K. said. "Go in the fore cabin and don't move."

We huddled on the lower bunk, feeling every bump as the boat chopped through the water. I could have gotten seasick, but I my reflexes were overruled by a strange sensation that felt like lightning bolts running through my head. It must have been the will to survive. If David stayed alive down there, it would have to be this instinct that buoyed him along. So this was how people survived battles, or at least tried until the very end. The lightning bolts in my head almost

split my skull. No, it was a shot, outside. I saw that Alison had tears running down her cheeks. I held her hand.
Another shot seemed to come from our boat. Of course, these guys would have guns. We began speeding faster, faster than I'd ever thought a sailboat could go. We kept going, until the sky began turning rosy.
C.K. stood on deck, his face green. His left arm was wrapped in a towel, and I saw that he was bleeding.
He spoke shakily through clenched jaws. "He can come out," he said, looking down at the hatch. Alison and I rushed out of the bunk, and Joe pulled the door open.
David lay there sideways, his arms around his legs. He opened his eyes and made deep guttural noises. We pulled him out, and I saw how thin he'd become. The rags he wore were full of sea slime.
In the light, I saw Joe talking on his cell phone, and the coast of the New Territories.
We docked at a small marina somewhere near a town of tall buildings rising from the mountains. An ambulance waited. While paramedics took care of C.K. and David, Joe ushered Alison and me to the Land Rover. A shriveled young man who looked like a smuggler to me was driving. Joe let us into the back seat, then got in the front seat.
He turned to us. "You go home now."
"What about our friend?" I asked.
Joe shook his head. "We will bring him when he is ready."
Steve was at work when I got home, but Lourdes, the amah let me in. She looked aghast when she saw me, but only for a split second. Then she laughed a little.
She was a tiny woman, only 25, with long wavy hair and a pretty face except for her smashed-looking chin and nose. She wore flowered stretchpants that showed how thin she was. I realized by the way she recovered her composure, by the way she pulled me into the bathroom and said, "You wash now, and phone the Mister," that she'd no doubt felt the survival jolts herself before.

I tried to sleep, but mostly I sat up in Steve's bed staring out the window, observing Hong Kong. Such a smug place and yet, filled with scarred survivors. From Steve's apartment, the streets wound every which- way like an obstacle course. Somewhere out there was where I belonged for now. The apartment seemed barely inhabited. The bed had a cheap rattan headboard and there were two framed posters from other worlds, one a Toulouse-Lautrec Moulin Rouge painting with the dates of a New York exhibition long past, the other a trumpet player, from the New Orleans Jazz and Heritage Festival. I wondered if Anne had taken everything with her. No, that wouldn't be the case, since she'd called him from New Orleans to say she wasn't coming back. Maybe she'd always considered this a temporary home. The only interesting piece of furniture was an antique red lacquer Chinese chest.

Steve came home around 7:00.

"They shot at our boat," I told him.

"Holy shit... " He sat beside me and I started to tremble. Tears began pouring from my eyes.

Steve brought me food, something Lourdes had stir-fried. It smelled delicious but I couldn't eat much. He insisted I take a sleeping pill after that.

The next thing I knew, the room was light. I reached across the bed and hit Steve's empty pillow. Then I realized the phone was ringing.

"Madeleine!" It was Jeannette's voice, but it seemed to be traveling through a long tunnel. "David's coming over here, any time. Can you come?"

I didn't want to ask more. What if she said he was arriving in a casket? I moved out of bed slowly, reminding myself of each little step. Take a shower. Drink coffee. Lock the door. It was nearly two o'clock when I went outside and flagged down a taxi.

It was a weekday — Tuesday. The traffic flowed in such an immutable stream, the cars new and clean, the people passing all occupied with such a sense of purpose, carrying expensive briefcases and glossy shopping bags and looking as if each day of their lives was a race. I understood it now. They would become part of China in a few years, they had no idea what the future would bring, and every civilian was an emperor of his or her own little fiefdom, racing against some unknown adversary to hang onto power. Their buildings sparkled like amethysts against the sky, the southern hills were a forest of jade, and everyone knew the jewels they possessed were coveted by others. Hong Kong looked like a place made of window dressing, but the sets could crumble and the winding roads would still be there. It was, I saw, a city of survivors. One way or another, you understood the place only after you'd scraped and clawed and earned a medal of your own design.

The Wongs' overdone house, perched so close to the edge of the bay, was a tribute to either greed or fortitude. Maybe both.

The maid let me in and showed me to the dark room again. I thought it was empty, and then I saw David. He was a still, fragile figure in a massive leather chair. He sat under a blanket, a black kimono hanging over his shoulders.

"Hello Fox," he said. He smiled weakly but his eyes glistened in a way I'd never seen before. He looked around the room, and at me, as if he wished to

inhale everything in his presence. I hugged him, saw that he was trembling and breathing heavily like an old man. He started to rise, but I told him not to get up. "I must rest and get better but I am very happy, hello?" he said.
The maid brought a tray of tea, in an English pot, with a plate of sugary English biscuits. "Where are the others?" I asked her.
"Shopping," she said.
"I was not afraid." David said. But his voice was weak.
"I saw you on the boat, do you remember?"
"Yes, I saw you. It was my second night waiting, did you know?"
He paused frequently between words, and wet his lips. "I rode in a truck for a long time, with some machines in the back. I think several days. But you know, I do not see the sun or the dark. And sometimes we stopped. A nice family fed me, but I looked like a truck driver. I am not famous in my face, but I am like a criminal in China now, so I have to be disguise. Then I even get a Chinese identification card with my picture, a new name. I am in the south Guangdong, and I live with the fishermen a while.
"They have little to eat. They fish but the fish are to sell. I fish with them."
"How did you know about our boat?"
He grinned slowly. "A fisherman knows a smuggler. He has a mobile phone, you know? They talk funny there. I don't always understand. They try to speak Mandarin, but you speak Mandarin better than they do. But the smuggler comes in the afternoon and tells me come to the beach. A light high on a boat will flash two times, then off, then two times again. He will take me to the big boat in a little motorboat, if I pay him a thousand yuan. So I pay."
"Did you have money with you?"
He looked sad. "I had Hong Kong dollars, even. I was rich, I think. But the smuggler, he comes about eight o'clock, still not dark, and he takes me near the beach. He said here, you wait here for me. It was a little bar — you know, a karaoke? Near the water. Just a roof on poles. But there are fishermen there, and local officials who run businesses. And there are girls."
"Bar girls?"
"A very young girl. The smuggler says she is his niece and I should wait with her, buy her a drink till he comes back. I think this is a trap. But I am like, this is the man who is helping me now, and he is all I have. So I buy the girl drinks. I even have a beer, because maybe I want to relax. And I feel funny. Maybe, I think, because I have so little food for so long.
"Maybe you think I was foolish. But they are to help me, or else what? I will not die here, I think over and over. The girl wants more drink — I think she has water with color in it only. She gets telephone call, she has a mobile. She says not much, just yes and no, and she hangs up she tells me come down to the

water, her uncle is with the motorboat. We walk and she, you know, likes me. I think I must keep her happy, I know she plays game but I have to play, yes? I know, of course, she will want money. But I do not remember so much about the beach. I think she put a pill in my beer, because I don't know what happens and then I wake up on the beach, with a very bad headache. You know I have no suitcase all this time, just now fisherman clothes. But there was secret belt, with many Hong Kong dollars. I wake up and my dollars are all gone. It is very dark. I think only, did he fool me about the light? So I wait. No light from sailboat. I wait all day, I hide in trees because who do I trust?

"I think only, I must hope this smuggler does know about the rescue, but he thinks more about my money. I can only hope that. Or else I die here, yes? Or I will be a fisherman for all my life maybe. I will try that of course before I die, I have identification as a boy from here, but of course even to fish you must buy boat and fishnets or be in a fisherman family. I try to think can I talk like the people here and convince them, take me as family until I sell some fish myself? But I will wait every night for the light, maybe forever. It is a sad poem, yes?"

I just stared at him, floored.

"I waited all day for the night. Of course, no food because I have no money, and I have to learn who to trust here. I think there will never be night. I look at the leaves and sand, see fishermen come in but I am hiding, and yes I am bored and I sort of forget I am Li Tian He, and maybe I never will be again. I think years pass and maybe I am a hundred years old. I even pull out a hair from my head, to see it is not yet white. And at last night comes. I go to the beach and find some dead fish, and I eat that because I am so very hungry. I am cold, but I can think only the two light flashes. I wait. And you know, I wonder when I see it if I, what is it, see things?"

"Hallucinate?"

"Yes." He stopped and sat back, out of breath. I filled his teacup and handed him a biscuit, which he stuffed into his mouth gratefully.

"Are the Wongs feeding you well?" I asked.

He nodded. "I had American style food already. Bay-con? And eggs."

I tried to laugh. "Good. You need some fattening up."

He sat back. "I will tell you more now."

"C.K. — he was one of the guys in the boat — said you had to walk over oyster beds."

"Yes. I thought something. Some shells, very sharp. And then I swam out."

"They shot at our boat — the Coast Guard, I guess."

"Yes? They shoot at smuggler boats sometimes. But Mr. Wong was here and he saw me this morning himself. He told me they were just some friends with a sailboat, and two beautiful American girls sailing on Sunday, so no one would think they had me there. I think they shot at someone but didn't mean to shoot us."

"Our guys shot back."

He jumped "Yes? I didn't know what I heard real and what, what is it, halloo-simay?"

"They were tough guys. You know what I mean?"

"Yes, I think so. Oh... .you, and Alison..." he smiled a little when he said her name. "You were with tough guys?"

"David," I said. "Why is Oscar Wong taking such an interest in you?"

"I do not know," he said. "But I lose all my money, and he said he is glad he can help a Shanghainese like himself. It is strange, yes, from starving on the beach to this... " He gazed with appreciation at the dark room.

So did I. If a few days of luxury made David think he deserved to live this way forever, could I blame him? Wouldn't anyone who'd spent a day and night prowling like a lone wolf on the South China seacoast be willing to do just about anything to make sure he was never in such a position again? Still, I had a foreboding feeling about Laurie's father. Maybe it was just the gloominess of the living room.

Shortly after that we heard a commotion in the foyer. "Mad!" Laurie shrieked at me as she tore into the room. David's fiancee bounded in behind her, with Jeannette, who hugged me and fussed and said I looked pale and she'd worried about me. The three of them were loaded down with pink and white and soft beige shopping bags. They looked different. They all seemed to be dressed in new clothes, Laurie's hair was in a stylish bob, Jeannette wore more makeup and a new perfume.

But it was Alison I watched with the most curiosity. She wore new white linen slacks, and her hair glistened in a fat twist around two chopsticks. She had some rosy color in her face as testimony to a day at sea, but the way she bounced around, kissing David — which made him light up like neon — hugging me and asking, "Recovered from our big adventure?" made me wonder if her presence on the boat had been a hallucination on my part.

"Tell them," Alison said, gesturing to Laurie and Jeannette. "They didn't believe we got shot at. Can you believe we did that?"

"How is C.K.?" I asked.

Alison shrugged. "He's out of the hospital, too. Probably won't be the last time for him. Here sweetie pie." She began to strew two polo shirts, chino pants, socks and a pair of oxblood loafers about the room. I was supposed to buy David's clothes for his new life, I thought with a twinge of petty resentment.

Laurie's parents came home while we were still sitting around talking. By then David had gotten dressed in the clothes for his new identity. He moved slowly, and the crisp shirt and pants looked heavy over his emaciated frame, but I could envision him gaining some weight and muscle and growing into the clothes of a privileged young man.

I shook hands with the famous Oscar Wong. His palm was as solid as a rock, yet his skin was startlingly smooth.

"Thank you for everything," I effused at him. And what are you really up to that can make my career here, I didn't say. He was as square-chested as a bulldog, his silver hair sprayed and lacquered, comb marks showing a painstaking attempt to keep it from jolting forward in a way that might look youthful. His eyes were twinkly in a way that could no doubt be menacing in a contract negotiation, or merry as they were when Laurie was around, and his mouth set in a firm horizontal line that could look either wry or vicious.

Mrs. Wong — Irene was her first name — was a plump woman with a coiffure carved in shiny black lacquer, perpetually twisting the huge diamond on her wedding ring finger, as if it were uncomfortable. Plump though she was, her jewelry overwhelmed her. She was wearing large round jade earrings surrounded by diamonds and a double strand rope of pearls with a clasp that matched the earrings. She had on a simple deep green dress, and quiet pink nailpolish. Except for the jewels, everything about her was understated, even the way she spoke with a modest schoolgirl giggle, as if nothing should distract from her bedecked earlobes and throat. "My mum is what's known in Hong Kong as a perfect *tai-tai*," Laurie had told us. "She shops, she goes to charity balls, she gets her hair done."

"You will all stay for dinner?" Irene asked.

"Oh, thank you, but I can't," I protested, Chinese style, hoping she'd urge me to stay.

"Oh, but we wanted to get to know the fourth teacher," Irene said graciously.

"Well... may I use the phone?" I knew Steve would say go for it.. I wondered if Steve would, in the same situation, steal off to Oscar's study in the middle of dinner and poke around for evidence of something that might be a clue to his dealings. I felt helpless as a *Worldweek* stringer. But I called Steve's apartment. Lourdes answered. He was not yet home, she informed me.

"Please tell him I will be home after dinner at the Wongs' home," I said.

"Yes, mum."

At a long dining table, a maid served us braised fish, mushrooms in a glutinous sauce, a platter of pork slices, with fried noodles at the end and nothing for dessert but jasmine tea. Johnny Wong arrived just as we were about to sit down, and I watched as his father introduced him to David. I looked for a resemblance. Just a little; they both had the slender, angular noses of the northern Chinese, they both smiled with a deceptive air of effacement, especially as they shook hands with each other.

"Ni hao," said David. "I am pleased to meet the man I'm told I should emulate." His voice was thin, but no matter. He'd said it in Mandarin, the perfect Beijing Mandarin he'd learned as an undergraduate at Beijing University. Johnny shifted his feet, a bit uncomfortably, I thought, seeing that he'd been outdone. Johnny, a speaker of Cantonese, which is nothing but a crude farmer's patois in the minds of the northern Chinese, did not even try to answer in the language of the emperors.

"Oh, you can do much better than that," said Johnny in English. A fallback language in this encounter, as unimpressive as a hand-me-down set of golf clubs.

I watched David captivate the Wong family. Irene glanced at him coyly, and kept saying, "Eat more, Tian He." He ate slowly but ravenously, and she kept urging him on. Oscar said little, concentrating on eating as if the company about him were not truly on his level, but he said, partly I suspected as a way to regain face for the family, "When are you kids getting married?"

"At City Hall. They can do it day after tomorrow," said Alison.

"Very good," he said. "You will all come here for wedding cake afterward." He wasn't talking about a wedding banquet, which would have cost several thousand U.S. dollars for even a small party. Still, I thought this might be his way of demonstrating his ability to bestow kindness. Which he could, of course, just as easily take away.

"And what are your plans in America?" he asked David.

"I... will maybe look into business," David said, looking genuinely shy.

"Weren't you in medical school?" asked Oscar.

"Yes, sir. But I have a dream of business that was not yet possible when I entered university in China."

Oscar nodded his large silver head thoughtfully.

"We can tell you about business," piped in Johnny. His father gave him a stern look, but I saw that Johnny had gained some face of his own. David, sitting across from him, looked flushed, and all too eager to hear more about the Wong empire. Well, wasn't I also eager?

"Are you starting to build in China?" I asked Oscar.

The great tycoon looked at me oddly, probably trying to figure out whether I was spying on him or just being polite. "We have quite a few plans in Guangdong and some of the smaller cities right now," he said. "We have to become part of the city, you see. We go in and build a school, or a hospital. It is quite a new way to do business, but we must, you might say, make friends with the local officials to get permission to build. We built a beautiful school in one small city, very modern."

Oscar had a cold face, but as he spoke his half-smile was like a curtain rising, and I could almost see a cast of Chinese peasants singing praises to their gleaming new temples with hot running water. "Soon the parents of the children who go to the school will be able to work in our office and retail complex, the first tall building they've ever had there, and the first time they can shop in a Western style supermarket with frozen foods so the housewife doesn't have to go out and buy groceries three times a day."

I got home after Steve did. He was in bed reading, but he put the book down and pulled me into bed beside him.

"I was worried about you," he said.

He'll be an adoring lover as long as I'm doing something that intrigues him, I thought in a flash.

"Oscar Wong is a complete charmer," I told Steve. "He was telling all of us, though he was really talking to David, about how exciting it is to be building his luxurious retail-commercial-residential complexes overlooking places where there was once nothing but a view of the shoreline that no one ever saw. He made *me* want to go into property development. The way David was hanging onto every word, I wondered if he was about to be ensnared. I mean, he's here and he's going to have to work on getting to America after he marries Alison. In the meantime, what does he do?"

Steve shook his head. "Take charity from Oscar Wong... become his indentured slave in a pinstriped suit? And you look irresistible." He stroked the outline of my breasts. His breath smelled a bit stale, like bread gone dry. We made love for a long time. We slept nestled with my back to his chest. His head was against my hair and he breathed heavily, with a whistle in his sleep. I jerked my arms and legs through the night to keep from becoming numb.

He crept out while I was still sleeping. He called from the office and woke me up. "I don't know when I'll be home," he said. "I'm busy selling my soul." Had he always been trite, and had I just not noticed before?

"At least you still have a job," I said.

"I have a noose around my neck. But anyway, if it's a job you want I've got good news. New York wants us to come up with more business stories. Think you could do it? I mean, things along the line of your Chinese aspiring yuppies piece. They're only willing to pay the stringer fee, U.S. one hundred and fifty a day... "

"But a foot in the door... "

"If you want to give it a try, you can do something on how expensive property is getting in Asia. There's a press conference you should check out this afternoon, and I'll make sure you get a full day fee for it. Maybe you can even get a quote from your buddy Oscar."

I would have to write something terribly impressive, I thought. As long as Steve was in a position to help me build a career in Hong Kong, as long as he was both my lover and, at least peripherally, my boss, I would have to work like a maniac, just to show him I could dig into corners of this continent that even he hadn't reached. He could always tell me I wasn't measuring up, and if he did, I wanted to be able to turn to some monumental story I'd done and know that I *was* doing a good job, that his judgment was colored by something other than a purely objective evaluation of my skills.

I got to work. I went to the press conference, and learned how quickly property prices were rising all over China and Southeast Asia, and how expensive it was for foreign companies to set up offices in Hong Kong, Shanghai, Beijing, Jakarta, Kuala Lumpur, or any part of the region that could promise a vast untapped market for goods, plus a cheap and abundant labor pool. ("Exploitation!" I exclaimed to Steve, who occupied a corner office while I had a desk behind the secretary. "Find a nice and not over-wrought euphemism," he said.) I made phone calls to get comments from American executives in Asia about how they'd pay almost anything to penetrate this market.

"Can you turn in a file tomorrow?" asked Steve.

"Tomorrow is David and Alison's wedding."

"Better get it in tonight, then."

And so I worked into the evening. I'd planned to spend the afternoon hunting for something chic for the wedding, but my old green sundress and sandals would just have to do. I made phone calls — even at seven o'clock, people were still in their offices — and finally, condensed everything into a 500-word file. I tried to fill this short report with projections and speculations as to how long the property boom could last. "Until there's another political massacre on the scale of Tiananmen or some greedy trader in Asian currencies causes such overvaluation that the bubble bursts," I wrote, and quoted a property analyst and a particularly outspoken banking executive who'd mentioned those scenarios. I waited, my heart thumping, while Steve in boss mode, read my file, his tie loose and his eyes bleary.

"Good start," he mused. "You didn't mention what would happen if some major property barons get caught doing something corrupt."

I had failed. I looked at him squarely. I couldn't let him think I'd neglected something he found so important — and in fact, I hadn't neglected the issue. I'd just let myself be persuaded by my sources that it wasn't relevant. "I asked a couple of people about that," I said. "They asked what I meant. One said corruption has a way of getting swept under the rug, partly because the developers who own companies listed on the stock exchange that have to reveal a certain amount of information about their activities also own very private companies that are hardly known, and they do their real secret dealings there."

"Okay... 'Corruption, even among the very secretive development enterprises in China, is unlikely to bring down the market... '" He punched away at his keyboard. "Don't worry, you did a damn good job for something you never covered 'til today."

Alison's father had sent her some money for the wedding. She'd told her parents not to bother flying out because the ceremony had to be quick, just a formality so that she and David could start petitioning the American consulate to let him stay in the U.S. for a while. She used some of the money to rent a limousine, which we rode to City Hall. I learned that judges there churned out newly minted marriages like fast food, almost 200 couples a day. David and Johnny were already sitting in the back seat of the limo while the bride gathered herself together in a guestroom at the Wong mansion. She ran a wooden comb through her tresses and doused herself with a new bottle of cologne, Laurie and Jeannette and I watching.

"Guess what," announced Alison, halfway out to the car. "My mom called last night and read me another letter from Colorado! What should I do?"

The driver opened the door for her and she climbed into the seat next to the man she was about to marry.

The driver dropped us off on the side street, near Queen's Pier, where I saw that a rainstorm seemed to be brewing. The water was rough, the sky opaque as steel, and the undercurrent of chill in the June air suggested that soon every square inch of the island would be drenched. I'd promised Alison I'd take photos — my wedding present. When the bride and groom looked back on this day, in my photographs, they'd see a murky wash over their wedding — and there was nothing I could do about it.

We hurried inside. A Cantonese couple and their wedding party stood in the courtyard posing for photographs. The bride wore a white train that swept dust along the ground behind her, surrounded by four bridesmaids in pink. Another couple came into the courtyard, the bride in a short veil and long full skirt with three tiers, with two bridesmaids in blue.

"They ought to be shrunk down to two inches high and stuck on top of a wedding cake," said Jeannette.

Alison had bought a simple white silk dress, knee length with long sleeves, and she wore her hair flowing on her shoulders, and held back with a white silk band. Everyone was wearing something new, except me. Jeannette wore a pink dress and jacket made of silk shantung. Laurie had on an ivory suit with embroidery on the lapels. David also wore a new suit, navy and expensive looking, with a red-and-blue striped tie and a gold collar pin. He had put a bit of weight back on in the last two days, though he didn't quite fill out the suit. We waited outside the wedding chambers for half an hour, behind two other parties in full regalia. When the judge told him to kiss the bride David turned red, and kissed her upturned mouth quickly.

The ceremony took no more than fifteen minutes. When we left City Hall, rain was thudding down in sheets. I watched David and Alison sitting together in the car, wearing their wide gold wedding bands, their shoulders touching. She sat looking more contemplative than usual. He was doing most of the talking.

"This is much to celebrate," he was telling us. "Mr. Wong has said I can come work in his company until I can go to America."

He must have noticed my look of horror. "Fox," he said, "you will call me a capitalist for now."

No, no, I wanted to cry out. I fear for you. But what could I say? "I'll report on you if you get too greedy," I joked. I watched him, beaming at Alison and her cheap-champagne effervescence, enjoying the spotlight. He'll do anything to succeed in Hong Kong and so will I, it occurred to me. And what about the bride?

"Are you looking for a job in Hong Kong?" I asked Alison.

"I haven't thought beyond today," she said, and flipped her hair over her right shoulder.

Just when the bride and groom stood posed behind the three-tiered wedding cake, I felt a hand on my shoulder. I turned away from my camera. Steve stood there, rumpled and damp, in a good suit. I hadn't been sure if he was going to make it. I looked at him and felt flushed, remembering our bodies locked together last night. With the camera hanging from my neck, I turned to kiss him, long and lingering.

"Hey... whose wedding is this?" Jeannette called out cheerfully. I could see Alison standing beside the wedding cake, waiting impatiently for me. She made a great show of feeding David a slice of cake, holding her fingers up for him to lick. I focused a frame on him, and took a picture that showed the back of her head. Then I took a shot from behind him, showing Alison's look of triumph, her hair tossed back, her smile full of dazzle.

The candy-striped tent began to sway, and it grew darker inside as the tropical storm gathered force. I put my camera away after the cake ceremony.

Two days later, the same day Jeannette and Laurie departed for Bali, Alison went back to Chicago. The four of us, and Alison's new husband, squeezed into a taxi to the airport, with luggage on our laps.

Alison was chatty again. "My mom and dad can't wait to meet David," she was saying, too loud, as if she wanted the driver to be a witness to a story that the rest of us knew was dubious. "I should be able to get a visa for him before the summer's out... so he can see Chicago before it gets cold." Jeannette was frowning at her. Jeannette had on new white jeans and a pale blue vest of raw silk. I wondered what she was going to do with all of her new clothes while she went to Indonesia. Probably store them at the Wong's house, while Alison stored her husband there.

I watched David kiss Alison goodbye, politely. After that they were talking to each other very seriously.

Jeannette nudged me. "I think they need a private moment," she said. So we walked off, plowed through a family of several generations who were posing for a snapshot. Jeannette and Laurie and I stood outside the gift shop.

"Disgustiiing... I'm sick of getting elbowed," said Laurie. "I want to go somewhere with no civilization. Have you noticed everyone in Hong Kong has bad breath, like soy sauce and garlic?"

"They had a fight last night," Jeannette informed me.

I shouldn't have sounded so amused. "Did it have anything to do with Colorado?"

Jeannette, Alison's faithful confidante to the end, gave me a reprimanding look as she pushed up her bangs and daintily wiped a bead of sweat. "Maybe. She said he wants her to stay in Hong Kong with him and stay home and have babies. She's decided she wants to go back to America and go to law school."

"Babies?" I saw that Jeannette was as doubtful as I was. David would surely have a very different version of the story.

Laurie snickered. "He's got a temper in Mandarin."

"But what will he do here alone?" I asked.

"My dad likes him," said Laurie. She looked up at me with eyes that were earnest this time.

Through the crowd, we saw David coming toward us, striding purposefully, smiling calmly, like Johnny Wong might have.

Keep in touch with him," Jeannette said to me. "He's going to need a friend."

Chapter 13

"Alison will better help me get to America from there. I think in six months, maybe less." In the taxi home from the airport, David pronounced Alison's name slowly, savoring it. If they'd had a fight, he certainly seemed to have forgiven her.

"And are you happy in Hong Kong?" he asked me. "With your boyfriend?"

"Sure," I said. "I'm working for him, you know."

David considered that. "I think you should not do that. Some people work with wife or husband, maybe yes, but not my friend Fox. You will not like when he tells you how to do things."

And how was he going to like having Oscar Wong as boss and mentor? I kept my mouth shut, because I didn't have any options to offer him.

So it was that David and I embarked on our new lives. We scattered in different directions, though our offices were only a few blocks apart. We met for lunch frequently. On weekends, if Steve was busy with work or traveling, I called David and we explored the New Territories and the outlying islands, strolling through the fishing villages of Sai Kung, hiking in the Lantau hills. Sometimes we went to Cantonese movies. He liked romantic comedies and anything with martial arts. I didn't protest that each movie we saw seemed to borrow half of the plot, and most of the actors, from a previous one. He laughed out loud, as if he'd never been free to laugh before. The movies were often corny, as frenetic as the streets of Hong Kong. Loyalties were crucial, unrequited love drove people to acts of madness, like talking to inanimate objects. The little guy — or woman — always triumphed.

David kept telling me I should either live with Steve or work with him, but not both. I asked him gingerly about what he did for Oscar. He admitted, he hadn't been given much to do yet.

"But I learn much," he insisted. "I even am learning Cantonese, so I can be loud crude capitalist. Even capitalists have dreams, you know."

He had learned, for one thing, that Johnny Wong had dreams. David had gone karaoke hopping several times with the junior and not-quite- senior-level executives from the firm, including Johnny. Fortified with beer and a few shots from a bottle of cognac, which was practically *de riguer* at a karaoke table, Johnny had confessed to David how he would like to take off someday and ride a motorcycle across the length of America and sleep beside the Grand Canyon, or meet a Las Vegas showgirl and spend a winter in a ski lodge at Lake Tahoe with her.

"In America, if you're young and poor you can just take off on the road," Johnny had told David.

"Someday, I would like to ride a motorcycle across America," David mused to me. "But first, I make sure I am never left again with no money."

He had, at this point, a minuscule income. His job had something to do with sales, and he was supposed to add commissions to his meager salary once he finished training. Meanwhile, Oscar had played benefactor to a point. Besides helping speed up David's application for a bona fide Hong Kong identification card and passport, Oscar had dispatched his son, Johnny, to take David to their tailor and buy him a wardrobe befitting a young ambitious sales rep. He began to look the part. The clothes helped, but besides that he was growing softer around the jaw as he put on more weight, and he went to a fashionable hair stylist who coaxed his hair to stand up like a well-pruned hedge, glistening and slightly damp.

Oscar had also made an apartment available to David. It was in Wanchai, above a small side street, an alleyway, really, of market stalls selling polyester clothes and produce. Outside the fruit stands sat the little mountains of spiky durian, the Southeast Asian fruit known for its strange bouquet that smelled to the uninitiated — a standing I was just getting over — like garbage rotting on a hot stairwell, and the smell hung over the pavement, hot and wet. The vendors put up red, white and blue plastic awnings on bamboo poles for shelter when it rained. David's apartment was in a narrow building, up three sagging flights of stairs. It consisted of a living room with a shiny hardwood floor and barely room for a couch, a dining table, and a corner with a half-refrigerator and two-burner gas range. There was also a bedroom with a single bed, a wardrobe, and a few square inches of floor space.

"How can you afford this?" I asked the first Sunday that I went to visit. On the one hand, I figured it was better that he live in this gritty part of town and realize how far most people had to claw before they got near Deepwater Bay, but I also knew that any rent in Hong Kong was beyond the salary David was getting. It was late September, and a light shower of rain spattered the city, as if reluctant to make way for the dry season.

"Mr. Wong owns the block, so he does not charge me as much rent as he would charge a ... ."

"Gweilo?"

David also had a tiny office of his own at Grand Harbour Holdings, the building with the triangle top. When I visited him, I had to get past the receptionist, a thin young Chinese woman with a short, perky haircut that looked a bit like an upside-down artichoke.

"I'm looking for David Li."

"Who?" The first time I went there and asked for David, the receptionist looked at me as if I had just said I was going to blow up the building.

"Li Tian He."

"Your namecard?" I'd had cards made that identified me as a freelance writer; you couldn't function in Asia without cards. I handed her one. She eyed it and shrugged.

"You can go," she said, looking toward the right. I walked down a long, narrow corridor with a thick carpet that made everything feel hushed. I poked my head into doorways and found David after several tries, in an office about the size of my cubicle. The door was open. He was seated at a stiff-backed brown swivel chair. His back was turned to me. The office had no windows and nothing on the walls except a poster of a row of Xian's famous terra-cotta soldiers of the third century B.C.

I watched him furtively for a moment. He was hunched over his desk, with a book and a pen.

"*Ngoh che ngoh ge taai taai faan lai uk kei,*" he said out loud, with great effort. He was studying Cantonese. I was making an effort to pick up some Cantonese myself, and I thought that meant "I know my wife is coming back." Then he sensed my presence.

"I didn't want to interrupt," I said as smoothly as I could.

"Fox," he said. He stood up, pumped my hand. I saw his metamorphosis unfolding, in the way he strode in his navy pin-striped suit, the glisten of gel in his hair, the gold tie pin he wore, and the way he looked me in the eye as if he were sure I'd buy a building from him if he wanted me to.

"I cannot say please sit," he said, gesturing to show me that there was no extra chair. There was no room for one. There was nothing on his desk except a Cantonese dictionary, a telephone, a computer and a small framed photograph of Wang Ming. I noticed that he wasn't wearing his wedding ring.

"So... what exactly do you do here?" I asked.

He looked puzzled a moment. "Fox, is it common for people in private companies to not have any work to do?"

"It happens. Where are your business cards?"

He handed me a card, English side up, that gave his title as marketing representative.

"Mr. Wong is building two big office towers in China, one for Guangzhou and one for Shanghai. I have problem not speaking Cantonese. I'm studying it. But I am supposed to sell space to Western companies," he said.

It occurred to me that a truly dedicated sales rep would be showing me the building plans, gushing with such lust for pile carpets and picture windows and ground floor retail complexes that he would start making me want one of the offices in the heart of Guangzhou with a pile driver on every corner. What a relief — David hadn't quite arrived.

We went to lunch that day at a Shanghainese restaurant. "They have everything in Hong Kong," noted David.

"Do you like it here?"

"Very much." The restaurant was noisy, crowds of people shouting in Cantonese at massive round tables. Three middle management types, all men, sat on the other side of our table, packed in, as if we were different tribes inhabiting opposite sides of an island.

David ordered noodles and a large fish. We sipped tea. A heavy silence descended over us. He looked awkward, fidgeting with his hands. "I am trying to stop smoking," he said.

"I'll have to take some pictures of you without smoke. "

He smiled nervously. "I wish we could both stay here," he said. "I know, I am maybe in danger after the handover. But I can make so much money until then."

"You wanted to go to America," I pointed out to him. "And you do have a wife there."

"Will you miss me when I go?" He smiled at me before turning his attention to the fish. He began filleting the fish with his chopsticks. As we adjusted to our new homes, the old flirtateousness had begun to creep back in. I realized I didn't want it to go any further, at least for now. Too many overriding concerns, too many other parties involved. Steve was always teasing me about David, saying such things as "I'll be late tonight, so you can have a quickie with your other boyfriend." I'd assure him nothing was going on, and he'd say he would never stop me from doing what I wanted, but Steve was living proof that giving into every sexual impulse doesn't net you anything but a lot of sex.

"You *are* married," I said to David, firmly.

I filled my mouth with noodles and tasted a bitter melon. David deftly lifted a section from the flank of the fish and served it to me with exaggerated politeness.

"I feel not married." At that moment he looked so puzzled I felt nothing but pity.

"But you *are* married?" I said it like a question.

"Alison's father had a heart attack, you know. She tells me she must stay because she must help him. But also she went to visit a friend... " he stabbed at a bit of fish flesh and said, too casually, "... in Colorado."

He put down his chopsticks and shook his head, mournfully. "I think she wanted to help me but to be not a wife. She loved me a little, but until she got letters from the rich boyfriend."

"What did you want?"

"To take you to lunch in a Shanghai restaurant in Hong Kong. Now I will be happy."

"I feel somewhat responsible since I introduced you."

He toyed with the chopsticks on the table, like a child whose dog has just been hit by a car. He sighed. "You and I could not talk in one language so much. But we agreed, I think. Politics, yes, but we did not agree on how to get there. She... and I could talk in Chinese but very *chao*, you know."

He kept calling her "she," as if it was too painful to say Alison's name.

"You fought?"

He nodded. "She was frightened on the boat. I tell her Hong Kong is so beautiful and she say she hates it here, she is sick for home — no — homesick for America, yes?"

"But you know Hong Kong is a temporary place for all of us. It's going to be different in a few years, for one thing."

"But you see, she promises she will get me a visa, and I am waiting and waiting. So for now, I am lucky to have the job for Mr. Wong."

"Maybe you love Alison." I realized that he did, that he'd loved her prettiness and her mastery of his language, which she was so good at passing off as genuine insight. "But don't be too trusting of anyone."

He looked at me very seriously. "I almost starved on the beach, remember, Fox? I am still like that, but with some clothes and food. I trust you. Because you could come to China only on vacation then go home, but I think you come and stay in Asia for many things, not just your boyfriend, and I think I am to you something you want to understand. The other people I just hope for help."

"Steve, my boyfriend," I confessed, "calls everything here 'a good story.'"

David drained his teacup. The crowd had thinned and we both had to get back to work. "I think he's not a good enough man for you. And I am not just a good story to you."

Together on our sub-tropical island, Steve and I saw each other mostly late at night. We'd talk about politics and stories and even about David. "Are you sure it's just platonic?" Steve asked me, teasingly, fairly often, and got annoyed if I worried about David too much. We'd unwind in bed, making love quickly because we were both tired, sleeping with our bodies locked together, making up for the lack of time we had together otherwise. Even when I did stories for the magazine, I was in the office only to use the phone and write the story and send it off to New York. He stopped bothering to edit me after my property piece ran pretty much as we'd sent it, minus the part about corrupt business leaders in Asia. We were happy, on a certain level.

I remembered an icy January night in New York, when I kissed Steve goodbye on a subway platform, and he whispered, "Run away with me." It was fantasy of course. I went home that night, to an apartment with big windows overlooking a snowfall on West End Avenue. Tim and I sat in our living room drinking with his friends. They all talked about their acting careers. Tim pulled out his crystal vial and the thick slab of mirror. With the delicious sensation of coke taking off from my nostrils, tearing like a race horse through my limbs and spreading a warm glow through my thoughts, I realized I could handle anything, no matter what Tim did. I'm talented and I'm going to do whatever I want, I thought. I thought of the illicit kisses in the hotel room. My limbs felt taut, my skin torrid and sweet, as if I were making love to myself. I watched Tim across the room, his arms rested against his firm thighs, tight faded jeans wrapped around the delicate ripple of his muscles and the bulge between his legs. He didn't wear underwear with jeans. He liked the way his own body felt, too. What if I wanted to go traveling? Tim wouldn't stop me, but he wouldn't go with me either. As quickly as the euphoria had appeared, a bleak wind tore through my skull, knocking over all of the warm thoughts. It occurred to me that we hardly ever talked in terms of "us." He would make me shudder after a technically terrific round of sex, saying we seemed like one unit, but it was just a botched attempt at being romantic and we really did nothing together.

I had come all this way, and Steve and I were just as separate. I began to wonder what it would be like to have my own apartment. I missed the women friends I'd had in China. But I lived, as Steve did, just for today. Like Steve, I became immersed in my work.

I saw that stringing for *Worldweek* wasn't a full time job. Sometimes I'd be very busy for a few days, but then a week would go by and I'd be idle. So I began looking around for other jobs — to make more money of course, but also to keep from feeling like a mere string attached to Steve, waiting to be reeled in and bestowed with a pat on the head and one-fifty a day.

So I found a temporary job but with a magazine that covered business in the region with an emphasis on feature articles from out-of-the-way spots. I was an editor, replacing someone on maternity leave. The other editors were friendly, and no one minded if I spent a day going out on interviews for *Worldweek*, as long as I turned in my edited stories on time. Sometimes I'd spend the day editing stories while making calls for a piece of my own, then turn off my computer at seven or so and go directly to the *Worldweek* office to write and send a file.

Of my two jobs, Worldweek was by far the more prestigious, but the other magazine paid better, and I was higher up the hierarchy, able to pass judgment on other peoples' stories rather than tremble over what the desk writers and Bill in New York might think of mine, and second-guess Steve's opinion of everything I did. I enjoyed having a desk in a console that was mine alone, like a spaceship that I commanded. While Steve rushed off each morning to his plush office, or took off for Bangkok or Jakarta, I took the subway to the end of Victoria Park, then strolled past noisy storefronts selling pink and blue kitchen utensils, the streets heady with the garbage-rotting- on-a-hot-stairwell scent of durian, and further, up, the row of butcher shops displaying bloody carcasses swarming with flies. All of the editors at the magazine had traveled around Asia and had stories to tell. All had come from North America, Britain or Australia, and home was just another set of stories. The editors were mostly in their twenties, a few closer to my age. Some were Western and had come to Asia because they'd heard they could make money while seeing exotic places. Others had Chinese parents or grandparents who'd emigrated in search of opportunity, but the present generation had learned the language of their ancestors in school, then come back to Asia to try and understand it.

Most of the stories were by freelance writers and photographers who contributed on a regular basis, and traveled all over Asia in search of stories. The editors thought that none of the writers could put together a coherent story, and I was encouraged to rewrite leads and grill the writers about the facts, if they were somewhere reachable by phone or fax.

We worked in a modern office on the 30th floor of a building with four elevator banks. In the mornings we made cappuccino from a huge copper machine in the kitchen. The cleaning lady who came in the afternoons was a millionaire. A Chinese-Canadian editor who spoke Cantonese said that was U.S. dollar millions. She told him she'd been socking away money since she started working at fourteen. She owned six apartments, and spent her mornings at a discount brokerage selling her stocks as soon as they started to go up, buying them back when they began to head down. He asked her why she continued to work, and she said it kept her from getting bored.

The editors at the magazine always knew of parties that were happening on Friday and Saturday nights. One editor and her husband, a lawyer, had a sailboat, and invited me out on a Sunday. Steve didn't come with me, except to a couple of Saturday night parties, where he drank beer quietly and was too tired to stay late. On Friday nights, closing night for *Worldweek*, he worked late.

Not everyone in Hong Kong, however, was working at this grinding pace beneath florescent lights and a frigid thermostat. Many of the writers and photographers for the magazine lived here, but touched down in their home base only between assignments. They'd stop by the office looking appropriately scruffy. They'd drink cappuccino from the machine in the kitchen, and sit around talking to the same editors they sent bitter complaints by fax when they saw their stories altered beyond recognition. They tended to write stories that rambled, sounding as if the writer were seeing so much it was hard to hone in on the key point. I was overhauling just such a story about the golden triangle where most of Asia's opium grew, by a writer named Jon Summers, when another editor said, "Knock, knock. Madeleine, just wanted you to meet Jon Summers."

I jumped a little at the name — just a few days ago, he'd sent a fax complaining that I'd been overly surgical, asking so many questions about his story. But all of the editors considered him sloppy with his facts, albeit prolific. He'd hitched rides with truck drivers through the Shan state of Burma, gone into Yunnan province in China, and talked with farmers who grew and smoked opium. I imagined he shared a pipe with them in the evenings. An editor had told me I'd have to question his statistics. I also thought his tale drifted into asides that had too much of a personal stamp for the magazine's formula.

"Hi," the culprit drawled, politely enough, when we met face to face. He filled my doorway. It wasn't so much that he was rangy, tall, a bulky body that could have been muscle-bound if he'd stayed home long enough to go to a gym, as it was his wild look in this white-walled office. Jon was wearing wrinkled khaki pants, an even more wrinkled Hawaiian shirt in faded shades of purple, orange and gold, and rubber tire sandals. He had curly hair, sandy brown, that twirled toward the four winds, and he carried an old khaki knapsack.. Even the scowl on his face looked as if it could have grown there over time, nestled into a face grown leathery by the sun. Not that he was actually old. He was probably around my age.

"So you're the one who's editing my piece," he said. I felt like some kind of philistine in my pumps and tight skirt, pieces of a new office wardrobe.

The editors generally handled writers by telling them how much they loved their stories.

I shook his hand, a large paw. "It's a great story," I said. "Let me get you a chair."

When I sat down again my skirt rode up a bit over my legs.

"I hope you're not going to change everything," he said, a bit more pleasantly. He had an accent I hadn't heard in a while. A Southern gentleman. He had very large sky-blue eyes that looked like beacons against his leathery hide.

"Oh, only for space and style," I said. He sat, one leg folded on top of the other, overtaking the office chair and filling my cubicle with a smell that reminded me of fresh mud, though actually everything about him was clean in a just-scrubbed way, down to his large squared-off fingernails. I pulled my skirt down. He regarded me skeptically all over. Why did I care what men thought of me anyway?

"I guess you give yourself up to the place when you travel, the way you were talking about flopping down for the night with the hill tribe people and all?" I said.

He took a swig of cappuccino. "I grew up in a boring place, and I got out with a vengeance," he said politely. "Ever heard of Virginia Beach, Virginia?"

"How do you do it?" I asked him. "I won't be surrounded by these half-walls forever."

"Well, I keep my overhead low. I live on Lamma Island and never buy clothes. My girlfriend is working in Hanoi right now, so I visit her and look for stories, and then keep traveling. Don't pay rent that ties you down if you want to travel."

I nodded. "I'm living on my boyfriend's housing allowance now but we don't know how long that'll last."

I saw that he looked wounded. Not over my having a boyfriend, but over the housing allowance. Hong Kong had a caste system among ex-pats. Steve was one of the aristocracy, working for the foreign press, with a large share of his living expenses subsidized. The people I worked with made reasonable salaries, but rents were so high on Hong Kong Island they lived in out-of-the-way places, such as Lamma Island or the New Territories, or they lived with two or three friends. I might be in the same situation someday, but I didn't have to tell Jon Summers the self-indulgent writer that, did I?

The editing job gave me a chance to wield a little power of my own, but at a price. When Steve went traveling, chasing stories that would be read around the world, I couldn't take time off to tag along. Of course, I had my own social life. "There's a party on Lamma Sunday... will you be here for that?" I asked him. He was going to Mongolia for the week.

He didn't want to go to the Lamma party. I saw that in his face. "Is it beneath you?" I asked.

"Why do you keep challenging me? I've gotten where I am by working my ass off. No, I don't especially like being around those self-righteous haven't-made-its out there," he said.

"What if I said I'll come with you, wherever you go?" I asked.

"Yeah. That would be good for about six weeks, then you'd hate me for dragging you around."

It wasn't all bad. I met him at the airport when he came back from Mongolia, on a Sunday, unshaven and almost as scruffy as Jon Summers. We kissed long demented kisses, all the way home in the taxi.

"I've got some pasta and salad," I said when we were in the bedroom. He threw his bag down on the floor and crawled onto the bed.

"You cooked?"

I nodded. "And wine. And a video."

"I should take a shower," he yawned. "You smell sweet." He pulled me down on the bed with him. Then he fell asleep until morning. I nibbled on pasta and salad, and tried to watch the Hollywood gangster movie I'd picked out for him, but got bored halfway through it.

I wondered if Anne had left because he'd been so absorbed in his work that he'd neglected her, and maybe Justin too. He complained about the stresses of his job, but it had its exhilarating times too. The trouble was, his life was like a roller coaster. When he was on a high, he was out getting stories. When he was home, he was only resting up for the next adrenaline rush. He kept Justin's pictures on a table in the living room. Small framed photographs of Justin as a baby posing on a blanket wearing nothing but a diaper; as a toddler with his hand outstretched to a temple god, as if trying to feed it; wearing a pitcher's mitt and throwing a baseball; sitting against a plain blue background, a little gentleman in a blazer and tie. The table was like an altar and Lourdes purified it every day with a feather duster. Steve stared at it frequently with a silence that I didn't interrupt.

When morning came, we both had to dash off to work. I took the subway, then walked the familiar route, down hot streets where flies buzzed around the meat and the smell of durian hung like smog. I felt wilted already. I pulled my hair up off my neck and walked that way, with a mass of hair in one hand, balancing my bag with my umbrella and the stories I'd taken home to look at on the other shoulder, listening to horns and drills.

Every shriek from a machine was like a promise of something exciting. I loved it here.

Chapter 14

I loved the uncertainties in Hong Kong as long as I was racing. It was a precipice with a rocky edge. I saw the edge that same afternoon, when I finished editing a story and didn't have something else to start. Idleness sent me plunging, scrambling to keep ahead of the black hole. I made some calls, as Madeleine Fox from *Worldweek*, trying to scrape together some story ideas. Nothing seemed likely to grab Bill in New York. So this is why Steve never dares slow down, I realized. The perpetually 50-degree air conditioning seemed icier than usual. I organized my desk, read other magazines. I considered the postcard from Jeannette and Laurie in Bali held to the pasteboard wall over my desk with a pushpin, alongside office memos and a list of everyone's extension. They were both back in the States now, Laurie in New York pretending to be looking at business schools, Jeannette in Boston selling real estate and being appraised by a social worker to see if she was fit to adopt a Chinese baby. I missed them terribly.

I was home before Steve that night, and Lourdes made me chicken Philippine-style, with coconut and rice. I sat at the glass-topped dining table alone, toying with my food, the room dark except for the pinkish cast from the brass floor lamp that I'd put beside my place so that I could read a couple of letters. There was one from my father, signed "Love, Dad," and in a different hand, "and Eleanor." They were planning to go the Caribbean for Christmas again, they were going to the theater almost every night, or strolling down to the cinema across from Lincoln Center and seeing the latest offerings from France, Italy and even China. Sheets of rain thudded against the windows.

I crawled under the candy-striped sheets in the bedroom. The clock radio said 10:14. I read a book while minutes passed. I tried to fall asleep but kept opening my eyes to see what time it was.

Eventually, the key turned in the front door. It was 11:52.

He stumbled into the bedroom, still not quite tidied up from his trip. His whiskers were thick and his hair needed pruning.

"Hi," he said, and came over to kiss me. He smelled like sweat and stale coffee.

"Long night," I said.

"I'm sick of this," he said.

"Let's take off for Bali and never come back."

"Don't tempt me."

He took a shower and came back in his black kimono and sandalwood scent, with comb tracks in his hair. But his breath was stale beneath a veneer of toothpaste. I shifted when he put his arms around me.

"I missed you tonight," I told Steve.

"Why tonight?"

"I just did. It was raining, I didn't exactly want to be here, I wanted a reason to be here."

He threw his clothes on the floor and curled up next to me.

"It's like," I said out loud, "we've always had a relationship based on stealing time to be in bed. It's still that way."

"C'mon, no analysis tonight... " he mumbled.

We slept curled up together, but I knew there was a wall, built out of the thing we never discussed. I hung my abacus in the living room and kept my cameras and laptop in the room that had been Justin's, along with the chest of forgotten toys, but beyond I never fully unpacked. We both knew that someday, soon, the word would come and Steve would have to leave.

I wondered what he'd do if I told him I'd go anywhere with him — Europe, New York, Cleveland, wherever — and meant it. Partly I didn't want to risk what he might say; what if he didn't want me to come along? But of course I loved Steve partly because of where he was right now. I wanted to be here in Hong Kong, even though the city wasn't exactly throwing out its arms to welcome me. Without Steve around, would I be able to keep stringing for *Worldweek*? I didn't even have legal residence. Each month I had to take the Kowloon-Canton Rail to Lo Wu, the stop just over the Chinese border at Shenzhen, the special economic zone that had sprouted into a mass of foul factories, where I would get out, turn around and go back to Hong Kong with a new thirty-day tourist stamp in my passport. As an American, I wasn't a favored citizen around here. Australians, Canadians and Europeans got three-month tourist stamps.

Some mornings, Steve and I still managed to get up early enough to have coffee together in our kimonos. But it was on mornings such as these that I would watch him open his mouth to speak and feel a flutter in my chest, dreading the moment when I might have to make a crucial decision about him.

"There's something you should know," he said one morning in October, when the sun was starting to shine outside and we had the dining room window open to let in the drier air.

Flutters kicked me from all directions.

"There are rumors," he said, "that the Independent Commission Against Corruption is looking into allegations that several Hong Kong companies are buying parcels of land in China with no intention of actually building... they're just holding the land for the investment value. Grand Harbour is one of them.

I've been hearing that and trying to get the editors in New York to care about businesses building a bubble economy in China... but they're too stuck in the 'gee whiz, you can get a 'burger there' phase. You haven't seen it in the local papers because the commission won't confirm it."

"Would David be involved in that?"

"Hard to tell. Selling offices that aren't going to be built? Maybe Wong'll have him make some initial contacts."

"I'd better talk to him."

"Lesson number twenty-eight hundred about Hong Kong. You better talk to him at home. This is a small town, really, and if you meet him in a public place you never know who might overhear you. Anyway, I'm hoping *you* can get the story that will wow New York."

"I am not just a story to you," David had said. So I was caught between two men. And, I couldn't help but realize, facing an opportunity to raise my profile at *Worldweek*. And maybe even expose some dirty dealings. From the man who'd sent me out on the sailboat to rescue David and taught me, from his safe perch, all about survival.

I went to David's apartment that Sunday. "Don't bring him here," Steve had insisted. "We don't like each other."

A drill was in use, apparently in the apartment next door to David's. I smelled the rain, even inside. We sat on opposite ends of his couch, which had thin cushions and completely impractical all-cream canvas upholstery that had the fishy smell of new fabric. Nothing in the apartment was dirty yet, except the windows and the dishes that were piled up in the tiny sink. It occurred to me that Oscar could have had the apartment bugged. Maybe.

"You look sad," David said. He handed me a can of beer.

I shrugged. "You're the one who's supposed to be sad." With his ever-growing command of English, he was becoming eager to talk about anything that had to do with himself. That included Alison. He brought her name up once or twice every time we got together, just to say, "You know, I was very sad about her but now I am better." He talked about being over her just enough that I knew he wasn't.

"I am not sad with you here," he said that afternoon.

I took a long swig of beer. "Let's finish these and go for a walk," I said. "It's important."

We strolled under umbrellas, pretending to look at the fruits and vegetables the shopkeepers had on display. The rain was delicate, not enough to keep anyone indoors.

"Like these?" I asked idly combing a pile of durians.

"They taste funny, but we will try one."

"Oscar Wong is under investigation," I told him as I picked out a small durian.

David looked at me strangely. "Mr. Wong makes money. Some people don't like it but that is business."

"Do you know what you're supposed to be selling?"

He shook his head. "If it's the wrong thing, it's only because we haven't had the opportunity to make money in China before. I think the same thing could happen in America."

"Why do I believe in you? I wouldn't start a new society with you for anything."

He smiled. He looked awfully smug for someone who could be deported back to China and arrested tomorrow if Oscar Wong chose to turn against him. "Oohh... don't worry Fox. You take care of the good, I take care of the money."

That was as far as I got with him that day.

The next Saturday, I took a train ride to Guangzhou instead of Shenzhen for my monthly border run. I always made these trips on Saturday, because the crowds were so thick the immigration officials would, hopefully, have less time to examine my passport.

I set out in search of the site of Oscar Wong's future development. I rode several public buses, with my cameras, then walked around for a while before I found the intersection, with nothing to guide me but a sketchy map of the area as it was supposed to look after the development. This David had given me begrudgingly.

It was an old residential area, filled with gray cement tenements where people sat out on the streets, selling produce, cassette decks blaring. There were rows of Chinese stores, like in Shanghai and a back alley where dirty children stood in doorways, barefoot but eating candy. I took photographs, found four children tugging at my shirttails, wanting their pictures taken. I took a group shot, while a mother standing behind a cart of apples chuckled. "Buy apples... good, very good," she said in Mandarin. I bought an apple from her.

Just down the street from the apple cart was a massive building, a white cement and glass tower rising miles above the neighborhood. Two others dotted the landscape, one green, one pink. So, real estate had come to the neighborhood. Oscar Wong could bulldoze through if he chose to. There was no sign of land being cleared for the complex with three towers and a courtyard with fountains that he'd had an artist draw. David was selling a dream, so far, if he was actually selling anything at all. But there was no visible proof of something illegal.

I was the one committing an illegal act, once again. I made the late train back to Hong Kong, and stood in a long queue at Kowloon Station. I was always worried I might get caught, and I would if I kept this up too long. The squat man at immigration leafed through my passport, punched some keys on his computer, looked at the photo, looked at me, leafed through the pages again and frowned. Then he stamped my passport. He handed it back to me without a word. Safe for one more month. As usual, I sauntered back into Hong Kong wishing I could grab the thick air and squeeze it, primed for a fresh beginning here as if my life could be measured in thirty-day episodes.

With each new episode came small changes. An editor at the regional magazine left to move to Taiwan, and the one who'd been on maternity leave came back. I stayed on, but there were rumblings of cost-cutting and eliminating jobs by attrition. The dry months had come. Storefronts I passed on the way to work were selling rat snakes, slithering in their cages, because soon it would be winter and people would be needing snake soup to warm the blood.

One night Steve came home late, while I was reading in bed, and I could tell just from the way he avoided looking at me, the way he loosened his tie in slow-motion, staring out the window at nothing in particular, that something had changed.

"What's going on?" I asked. My voice was shaking. I felt as if wild geese were flying out of my mouth.

"I'll tell you about it tomorrow," he said. "Do you mind if I read a while?" I snuggled up to him, in a contorted position, since he was sitting up. I pretended to sleep. I made resolutions. I'll go with him, I thought. No, I can't, even if he asks. I'll stash my things and travel. I'll find a place of my own here, and start looking for travel assignments. I'll live the way Jon Summers and all the other freelancers do. All in hopes that one sleepless night would ward off what I knew was coming — a monumental change.

Steve couldn't sit still the next morning and he had deep violet circles around his eyes. He paced the living room.

"So... " I asked. "Where are you going now?"

He stopped. "You knew?"

I sat, stiff, imagining I might faint, or cry, or something, but I couldn't move. "Washington. Capitol Hill and the cocktail circuit. I'll be a star political writer." There was a sharp edge in his voice. "You can stay here with me 'til the end of the month. I'll help you find a place."

I studied my coffee cup, for a while, then looked up at him. "What if I came with you?"

"We both know you don't want to."

"How do you know our relationship isn't the most important thing to me?"

"Out of the question. I won't take you away from here just when you're so happy."

When he left for work I tried to kiss him goodbye, but he stood stiffly.

"Don't make it harder," he said. How could he turn warm then cold, like a machine?

Lourdes observed us from the kitchen, but turned her head when I saw her watching. When he was gone, she came into the living room and stood facing me. She was wearing her usual flowered stretchpants. On her Sundays off, she played volleyball with her friends on the island of Peng Chau, and sometimes they went out for drinks afterward and kept a lookout for appealing men. She had visions of love and a better life, too.

"He was never happy being at home, mum," she said.

"I'll miss you," I said.

"I have to get another job," she pointed out.

She was right, of course. Steve wanted a home where no one made demands. Maybe he'd be happiest with no one around but an amah who was paid, albeit poorly, to stifle her own wishes.

Oddly enough, I didn't hate him. I missed the conversations we had when I was part of the outside world to him. I wondered if that could be salvaged, if we lived on opposite sides of the globe.

I would move out right away, I decided. Not today, because I had to go to the office, and I had plans for dinner with some friends that evening. But I would start asking around about a couch to sleep on, starting that very night if possible. I packed my tote bag with a toothbrush and extra clothes, just in case. I would start looking for a flat that weekend. I would just have to live with this ache. It was the ache that comes with any kind of death.

.   "Sure, we have a sofa bed. Stay as long as you like," said Suzanne, one of the editors. She was married and lived on Lamma Island. I called Steve's flat around nine, figuring he wouldn't be home yet and Lourdes would have retired to the amah's room. "I'm staying at a friend's tonight, so don't be worried," I said to the answering machine. I took the late ferry with Suzanne. It smelled of gasoline and beer, and echoed with voices, mostly of young ex-pats. The horn blasted as the boat took off, rocking over the inky night sea.

Could I live as a ferry commuter? There was something reassuring about the transition from one island to another, rolling on the waves, catching up with some reading.

The next day I lost my cubicle. "We have to cut costs, so we won't be needing you next month," the managing editor told me. "Keep in touch though. And of course keep coming up with story ideas. Maybe you can do some traveling."

Two more weeks, then they wouldn't need me. I sat in my cubicle doing nothing. No one came by. I heard telephones ringing, but not mine, and cheerful chatter of people who still had their jobs.

I will find something, I reminded myself. Maybe I would run out of money eventually, though... Maybe if I worried about starving enough I wouldn't. There was laughter somewhere in the distance.

Already, I had nothing to do. I left the office before five o'clock. No one noticed. I didn't tell anyone 'bye, have a good evening. It was still light outside, and the streets were full of amahs and housewives. I passed them and didn't remember their faces. The invisible women. Was I one of them now? A little brown terrier sauntered out from a shop. The dog eyed me wistfully and I eyed him back. Something else that wasn't mine to love. A pile driver bammed against tinny music. I didn't know what to do with myself.

I decided to stop at *Worldweek*.

The receptionist there was very young and pale with lips always painted meticulously in a brick-red hue, her hair permed into glossy black curls that bounced along the sides of her face. Even though she knew me, she surveyed me up and down as if I were a two-headed extraterrestrial creature.

"Hi," I said.

She nodded with irritation.

Steve's door was open. I started to peek in. He was on the phone.

He was flushed, chuckling. He held the receiver close to his mouth, saying something about "... sure, you would say that..." in a throaty, tender voice. As if the person on the other end were the only woman in the world. And he jumped, almost tumbling backward in his chair, when he saw me.

"I have to go... we'll speak later," he said into the phone, sounding as if a crisis had erupted.

He looked at me nervously. "Well... *quel surprise,*" he said.

I felt hot. "I think the worst thing that could ever happen to me has happened," I said.

"What do you mean?"

"In a flash, I know why Tim demanded that I choose either him or the things I wanted to do. I know why he read my diary. I wish I could wipe this minute out." Instead I spotted a coffee mug on his desk and threw it in an overhand pass against the wall. He jumped up, closed the door, looked at the shatters, and put his arm around me. I pulled away.

"You'll get a standing ovation," he said, recovering. "But what have I done to deserve this?"

So, he hadn't wanted me to find out. Anne had lived with this for years, knowing what he must be up to, but settling for his being discreet.

"Wait for me? I'll wrap things up and we'll go have a drink." He made it all sound so sensible.

We went to the Captain's Bar at the Mandarin Hotel. A dim lit place with expensive drinks and generous trays of assorted nuts. Full in the early evening of people having affairs or looking for affairs, and just loud enough to have a painful talk without being noticed. I would remember the bar forever after as the place where Steve and I sat facing each other, where he wore an ever-so-slightly rumpled white shirt and beige linen blazer, where he looked at me unhappily, his eyes rimmed with purple but not as much from overwork as I'd thought. I decided I'd burn my gray trousers and printed blouse, otherwise they'd be forever tainted as the clothes I wore that awful day.

"I wasn't going to tell you. Do you really want to know?" he asked.

I thought he enjoyed it a little bit, letting me know that someone else was after him. She was a Hong Kong Chinese woman who worked in a public relations job. Her name was Heidi Lo.

"Is that a joke?" I asked.

She was going to Washington with him.

"She wants to go. You don't," he pointed out.

"How very logical of you. How very practical of her to find a guy who'll get her a green card."

"I don't know if I should tell you this, but she's pregnant. What can I do? If you'd gotten pregnant I would have stood by you."

"Oh, you should have explained to me years ago that all you wanted was a woman who would trap you."

"What you don't like is that if you trap somebody you're right in there with him. I kind of think you'd like a child without the inconvenience of a husband... so do it, have a baby with and then go on your way like you always say you're going to do. I *liked* having a wife and kid."

"And you certainly made Anne happy," I said.

He looked grim. "I know I wasn't a great family man. I guess I couldn't blame her for leaving. But you... .you weren't even trying. You should know I wouldn't take you away from here, when you've only just arrived. You've always been beautiful and smart and fun. But I had big responsibilities and you had no need to be involved in that... hell, I loved the way you managed to sail through life unencumbered, but I couldn't imagine you even being a stepmother to Justin. He's an imperfect kid. I didn't want to tell you, but he's deaf. You didn't need to be burdened with my problems. "

"You haven't seemed very burdened yourself."

"Fine, keep shooting. I loved you most as a free spirit."

"I think you loved me most as your fantasy woman." I sipped vodka and tonic, but I couldn't get a buzz in my head to dull the sense of loss. I would have to find a new home, this time a place that was mine. And I would have to find work, immediately, to fill the hours while I walked around feeling like someone who'd disappeared.

Chapter 15

This is what I got for a life spent, so far, imagining every scene could fall like painted cardboard: a two-bedroom apartment all my own, a 50-minute ferry ride away from Hong Kong's skyscrapers. I looked all over Hong Kong Island town for several weeks, and finally decided the ferry to Lamma Island, rowdy though the passengers might be at times, floated on the sea like a meditation tank that could shut down the pile drivers in my head.

My apartment on Lamma had windows that opened to sunshine, or a soupy sky on cloudy days. I was on the second floor and had a balcony, in a building that looked as if it had been made from a set of shiny yellow Lego blocks, next to a plot of land where other buildings were under construction, buildings identical to mine except that some were pale gray or pink. My flat cost not quite double the rent I'd been paying in New York, but I figured I could let out the second room if necessary and pay less rent than a one-bedroom would cost. Everywhere I went I saw men I thought on first glance were Steve. They had dark hair, or long arms and legs, or they walked with slim shoulders bent in thought. I'd hurry my steps, get closer, and see that they were someone else entirely. I wanted to be happy, but every time I saw someone I thought was him, I imagined him telling Heidi Lo she was the only goddess in the world. Had I loved him? I wasn't sure. I told myself it was only desire. But for so long I'd identified myself as the woman Steve desired most, the woman who traveled with him in spirit if not in reality. Cast off on an outlying island, with Steve erased from my life, I was a blur who'd landed here like plankton. These parts of me, my feet, my voice, my appetites, were strange etchings that operated on reflex alone.

Yet I had not really disappeared. I had a telephone and fax, and a mail carrier who came at noon every day. I sent maps to Katie and friends in New York who thought I'd been shipwrecked somewhere in the far reaches of the South China Sea. Lamma lies just southwest of Hong Kong Island, formed from granite rock before 10,000 B.C. The southern side, craggy like a dragon spine from the water, is shaped on the map like a strange beast with the head of a dodo bird pointing east and the humps of a camel pointing north. On the beast's lower half is the island's highest mountain, Mt. Stenhouse, 353 metres, which is not nearly the mightiest peak in all of Hong Kong. At Sham Wan, the remote bay between the beast's legs, archaeologists have found layer upon layer of sand that they carbon-dated back to the Stone Age, and embedded in the upper layers, coins and pottery from the dawn of civilization.

Just above the beast's back at Lo So Shing Beach, which has clusters of lime kilns dating from the Tang Dynasty, the land formation is squeezed like the center of an hour-glass. Atop that sits the smaller and more developed North Lamma. Along the northern side of the inlet called Sok Kwu Wan are rock quarries. The land up north is filled with floodplains on which Chinese farming families grow vegetables in tiered fields. Some of them are Haklo people, descended from the original settlers. As the families prosper, the children either move away or start building Lego block apartments on their family land. Up in the hills, where banana trees grow, the vegetation is thick and you might stumble across a python or a clump of wild orchids. Blue-tailed magpies whistle like construction workers, and butterflies with wings like blue stained glass flit through pink bougainvillea trees.

The north was where I lived, just off the main strip of Yung Shue Wan, a horseshoe-shaped village along the harbor where the main ferry docks. The harbor has become cloistered since construction crews reclaimed a plot of land to house a massive power station. Before developers came along, the coastline must have had banyan trees, because the name of the village means Banyan Tree Bay. A rather prettified name, I think, although it also connotes a tree that grows sturdy with time, deeply rooted and resilient to almost anything other than bulldozers.

I lived on a hill with a view of the three huge chimneys of the power station. It took me ten minutes to race through the village to the ferry, twenty minutes to stroll through the paved path that curved through jungle bushes to Hung Shing Ye Beach. Along the shore, fishermen brought in hauls to the seafood restaurants on the rattletrap drag called Main Street. The restaurants kept the day's menu swimming in congested holding tanks, the fish blowing morose bubbles. There were plenty of Chinese restaurants, frequented by small-time Chinese gangsters with gold chains and tatoos, and hair dyed orange, along with boutiques selling madras and muslin clothes, houseware stores with pastel dish drainers and crockpots, storefront greengrocers and a closet-sized real estate office. The gweilos gathered at one of the pubs near the harbor every evening. Those who had been there several years complained that the village was being ruined by development, like everything else in Hong Kong. From week to week the construction crews paved over rice paddies and produced new cement blocks to be subdivided into housing.

There were no cars. People visited neighbors on foot and pushed their groceries home on hand trolleys. On the path to the beach bicycle bells would trill behind pedestrians and grab the right of way. Dogs wandered around and followed you as you strolled. The dogs, part chow, part hound, some part shepherd, had evolved into an island breed with dachshund legs paired with big heads, and they looked like cartoons morphed together by cruel computer graphics.

I worked hard, for several magazines, and edited a newsletter for an investment bank that paid so well I could avoid taking in a flatmate. I'd worried, at first, that I'd never be able to master the mindset of finance, but it turned out to make perfect sense; a calculating science, nothing given without a plan to get it back with value added. I began covering more complicated business stories for *Worldweek*. Survival instinct had made me place a call to Bill in New York after Steve left. "I have a couple of ideas for stories, so I hope you can continue to use me," I said, and started firing off ideas.

"Okay. Call me or fax anytime. I think we can use the one about the rising popularity of caviar and cognac in the region," Bill had said. After that I did a piece on the Hong Kong stock market and the forces that kept share prices rising. The main force was real estate. Every major company was getting into property development. I said property and share prices couldn't go up forever. With a couple of experts quoted to back my claim, the *Worldweek* editors in New York kept my file pretty much intact. Then I wrote about venture capital and the unique ways it was used to finance the building of roads and airports in Asia. One of the venture capitalists I interviewed had filled his office with photographs of Asia as it was before his company started providing the capital to build highways.

Without Steve behind me, I had to generate the ideas for *Worldweek*, but I still went into the office when I had an assignment. The bureau chief was still around, when he wasn't traveling. They had not yet filled the correspondent post that Steve had vacated, I used his empty office. I went through the desk, looking for slips of paper that might tell me something about Heidi Lo and whatever else he might have been up to. I looked for old files on his computer, old memos or something, wanting yet not wanting to find something. The hard drive and the desk drawers were empty.

Lamma had a contingent of ex-hippies who'd been roaming so long they had no job skills except selling Indian jewelry, but it had also become a fine island for ex-pats who were in Hong Kong to travel, party, build careers and never reflect on the burdens of solitude. I saw couples who touched each other in public as if they fit together groove by groove, like a jigsaw puzzle.

Everyone seemed to be having a good time. I put on a display of having fun, too. I met ex-pat families who lived in yellow or white houses with swingsets under banana trees outside. The children ran through streams of water from the garden hose, chased puppies, and played games on state-of-the-art computers while the parents had friends over for cocktails and talked about traveling in Nepal or Cambodia.

"Life here is good," David said when he came to visit me on my terrace one Sunday afternoon. "But I think so quiet. Maybe we go to New York?" He laughed, part jokingly and part not, I thought. He sat on one of my folding lawn chairs, wearing ironed blue jeans with perfect creases and shiny loafers. He looked, I thought, as if sitting down with a beer in the sun was the most natural thing to him. There was a tense wrinkle in the center of his forehead, and in the tightness of his lips. But it was, I thought, the tension of too little focus. He was the only friend I had in Hong Kong who never talked about work.

"Have another beer?" I asked.

"No." He pushed his hand out, and stared at a butterfly that swooped down on the railing.

"I am learning to be frank like Americans, Fox," he said finally. "I think you might be happy if you had a baby... ... maybe a baby from China, like Jeannette."

"Wha...at? You've never cared about what's going on with me before." Then again, did I have to open my big mouth? He looked down at his loafers, with the face of a child who's been slapped.

"You think I'm *zisi?*"

He *was* becoming selfish, or at least wrapped up in his new-found materialism. He had a fancy stereo and television in his apartment, and called me every time he bought something new. He would say "Hello, Fox, good news." The first time, I asked "Did Alison come through?" and he said, calmly, "No, I bought a CD player."

"I just said you never ask about my feelings."

He looked genuinely puzzled. "But how can I help you?"

I sighed. "I don't need help."

"Maybe," he said, "I am right. Maybe I can help you get a baby. But I don't know."

"Thanks, but I'm not ready for a sperm donor?"

"Spe-rim doe-nor? That means what?"

"Look it up."

David said he had plans for dinner, so he took the 7:30 ferry home. He had found friends in Hong Kong, a group of young Shanghainese who had also been on the fringes of Tiananmen. He also went club-hopping at night, sometimes, with young financial analysts and middle managers he'd met at the gym. He didn't hang out with Johnny Wong, I gathered because Johnny saw himself as too high up in the pecking order at his father's corporation to be friends with a mere sales trainee.

"A man or woman friend?" I asked him tonight, as we strolled through Yung Shue Wan toward the boat dock.

He smiled in the way that showed his teeth, enjoying my curiosity about him. "Both. I know some girls, but not as important friends as you."

We stampeded through Main Street, along with other villagers and tourists, rushing for the ferry as the shrill bell sounded, announcing that departure was imminent.

"See you later," he said, standing just outside the ticket booth. He kissed me unfrivolously on the cheek, then turned to hand the ticketmaster a ten dollar coin.

I turned toward home, navigating my way into the stream of disembarking passengers. It was not late, a balmy night. I searched the crowd and said hello to a few people I knew, but they were all in groups and didn't try to pull me in. I thought I saw Steve in baggy white pants.

Someone tugged at my pursestrap from behind. My heart jumped; a New York holdover. I looked around and saw Jon Summers, grinning and showing the creases in his leathery face. Weird guy. He had on his tire sandals, as usual, and a faded red tee-shirt. It was a good color on him.

"Sorry, didn't mean to startle you. Butchered any stories today?" he asked pleasantly. Maybe it was the genteel Southern accent that gave him that out-of-place air. Except I couldn't imagine him at a Kentucky Derby or a country club, either.

"Oh... I'm freelancing now."

His high, ever-so-slightly Cro-Magnon forehead shot up. "Well, welcome to the ranks of the riffraff. If you don't have to run off, can I buy you a drink to initiate you?"

The offer was appealing. The times I'd bumped into him previously, we'd always seemed to have plenty to say to each other. So we went to a crowded village cafe.

"Ngoh dei yap m yap choh ngoi bin a?" Jon asked the young Chinese man who greeted us as we walked in. The host nodded, as if it were perfectly natural for a gweilo to speak Cantonese without stumbling over the words. He went off and came back a few minutes later. *"Lai a,"* he said.

"He's setting up a table on the terrace," Jon murmured to me. He said something else to the host in the language that was so full of tinny sounds like "gam" and "yap."

"So you speak Cantonese." I was surprised he'd had the discipline to study it, even if he'd had a girlfriend or two as tutors. Cantonese was harder to learn than Mandarin, and useful only on this minuscule southern tip of the China coast.

He shrugged. "When in Rome... " A busboy came up with a plastic table and chairs and wedged them between other customers on the terrace. We sat beside the railing, watching the dark sea. Fishermen hosed off a trawler. To one side, the power plant glared at the village with bright yellow lights.

"It's only an alien spacecraft," Jon said, nodding in the direction of the power plant. "You don't seem like the type to go through life stoned, so just use your imagination. Do you read Kierkegaard, or are you an annoying Buddhist-vegetarian-yoga-practicer?"

This would go on as long as I stayed alive, no doubt, unless someday I swore off men entirely. I shifted in my chair, looking at Jon's arm resting on the tabletop, a heavy, bear-like arm, all hairiness and leathery hide.

"I'll have whiskey and water," I told the waiter. I turned to Jon and asked, "So how did a nice Southern gentleman like you happen to learn the local language?"

He shrugged again. "I was one of the early gweilos to come to Lamma and I learned it kind of in self-defense... there was a girl who hardly spoke English and all that stuff. You look around and you see the ex-pats in Hong Kong don't feel much like colonialists anymore. It's their place and we don't know if they'll want us here after '97, so what do we do if we've been here so long we think we belong here?"

"Where would you go from here?"

"I ask myself all the time. I'd be unemployable at home. I feel like a Lamma-ite... too bad we can't take this island and secede. Selectively of course. I'm not sure about the new residents who come here because it's the only part of town where you can aspire to be a rock singer and no one laughs at you."

"Guess you don't aspire to be a rock singer."

He took a long swig of beer and shook his head. "I don't aspire. Actually I never knew I had to... that's why I still live light. My father was a second vice president for a big corporation and that was supposed to be security... then he got forced into early retirement. I've got three brothers, and every time I see them all they talk about is how worried they are about hanging onto their jobs. They all got married and two of them are divorced. So, what the hell, I thought America's in decline and the women in Asia are beautiful."

I considered losing control and screaming. "Is your girlfriend Asian? Vietnamese?" I asked, feigning manners.

"No. She's French. And at a distance. I'm not too good at working on a relationship day-to-day."

"Yeah," I agreed. "Relationships take work." I hoped he'd change the subject and tell me a travel adventure story.

He drained his beer and called the waiter over.

"Funny, I don't know why we have to go to such lengths to find meaning in life, but it seems to be human nature," he said. "Also that 'meaning' usually consists of the opposite of what you have. I do sometimes wish I'd been born in an earlier era, though, so that I wouldn't have to be aware of the shortcomings of Buddhism, or Christianity, or Communism or whatever. 'Course then I probably would have been either a cynic or a conservative."

"What about social justice? Or do you just believe in yourself?"

"I'd feed needy people if they followed me home," he said. "I like talking to you."

There was a pause that was not awkward, just dense, like the pause in a poker game when the dealer is shuffling cards and the players await the luck of a draw.

I broke the silence first. "Where are you going next?"

"I was going to go to Malaysia," he said. "But I'm going to Australia instead."

"What's in Malaysia?"

"Birds' nests. Go ahead and steal the idea, 'cause I'm booked solid. Are you traveling around?"

"Not a lot," I said. "I'm getting my bearings."

"Looking for a job?"

"Yeah."

"Well, this is the land of opportunity. It's all been turned around... Westerners coming here for material gain. Who knows how long it'll last; if the handover doesn't get us, the economy isn't going to keep booming forever. I say if you want to work here and make money, do it now. Buy a house if you can and sell it right before the big event. I can't find a real job but maybe you'll have better luck."

Maybe you would too if you'd get some decent clothes, I thought but didn't say.

"Anyway," he continued. "You ought to do some traveling while you can. Everyone wants stories from the field." He was bent over in his chair, his head resting in one of his big paws, regarding me with his intense eyes. I wondered if he was going to try to get cozy. I halfway wished he'd touch my hand or my knee, but he didn't.

We started another round of drinks, and I began picking another man's brain.

Chapter 16

I traveled. Alone, but my objective was to get stories, and in the process I met people. By day, shooting photographs, talking to people, engraving conversations in my memory more often than not because a notebook would have made people clam up, I could almost forget I was Steve's ex-love, X'd out even to myself. I became a part of whatever I observed, wishing to be nothing more. So this, I thought at times, is why people keep roaming. It makes pain easy, because when you grieve for struggling peasants it's their pain you're feeling, not your own.

In January, I followed Jon's suggestion and went to the caves in Sarawak. Two mornings in a row, I groped my way through a black hole down into a netherworld of vermin stench and the shrieking of bats. But bullets were the real danger. Guards stood on duty day and night, watching over birds' nests destined to become soup in the best Chinese restaurants, and black marketeers for the birds' nest soup business sometimes murdered the guards. From there I detoured to Jogjakarta, Bali and Lombok. I hired a tour guide to take me around and rode on the back of his motorcycle. We touched a Buddha inside a large stupa at the Borobudor Temple for luck. I photographed dancers behind the stage, and a shadow puppeteer. I bought a Balinese painting, fed monkeys that hung around the roadside in the north, snorkeled with two sisters from Seattle who were on a vacation, photographed a cremation ceremony where a quarter of the guests were tourists. In Lombok I stayed in a charming hotel with dozens of geckos crawling on my walls, and bought a rice cutter from a woman in a traditional farming village.

Back in Hong Kong, I churned out stories, for *Worldweek* and other magazines, racing against deadlines, preparing for another trip. In February I left for Vietnam, where I interviewed foreign business people about the long-term tactics necessary in this emerging investment market. In Hanoi, a Vietnamese businessman who was also a poet invited me to spend an evening listening to hill tribe music in a Muong hut that an architect friend of his had bought and restored, turning it into a place to host salons where artists met and sipped rice wine. From there I went to Laos, to shoot temples and monks and hill tribe villages for a travel magazine.

I went back to Lamma in March. I was sharing my apartment, temporarily, with a young British woman who had arrived in town right about when I was getting ready to leave, and it was good to come back to a home that looked lived in. I slept for an entire day. It took all of the next day to go through the mail that my flatmate had left piled up on my desk. Some checks. A letter from a bank, saying they were always pleased to invite responsible individuals like me to apply for their credit card. A few letters, the thickest one addressed in Katie's unmistakable handwriting. She'd written on dove gray stationery, wrapped tightly around a folded clipping from a magazine. Katie had finished law school in December, and I'd been out of touch.

"I am at long last a J.D.," she wrote. "I'm going to use the law degree that my husband made possible to defend battered women and children and such.

"Oh lord, Mad, I think he's having an affair. Men who think they're entitled just because they've got money. Or just because they're men. Write and tell me what you think I should do. They're all primitive life forms. You know, I might just take the girls and go back to the city, just the four of us. I've been thinking a lot about that — my inheritance should go toward their education, but isn't that an education in itself, for them to become independent women in New York, at a young age, knowing they can hammer nails in without the aid of a man, and go to museums and theater on their own, and be part of a community of accomplished womynfolk? You think this is idle chatter. Mad — I've given all the cats and dogs to the Humane Society. It was tough on the kids, but I gave the Society a large donation — something Mom would have halfway approved of, although she would have preferred that it go to people in need, I know — and I put my foot down. We have to stop cluttering our lives.

"I've also told Mark no more patriarchal religion in our house. I'm getting more mentally healthy, don't you think? I wanted the rituals because it was my way of identifying with our father — same way your traveling and your noncommittal attitude to relationships was your way. I suppose Mark did it for meaning in life, but now I think he's got some bimbo giving him meaning. He's making me feel so unsisterly. Divide and conquer, you know, that's part of what they do.

"Attached is something very important. No, I don't read this magazine. I found it in the supermarket. Tim won't be bothering you anymore, so you can come home! I don't guess you want to, though. Go traveling. Write ASAP. What am I going to do?"

Katie had enclosed a clipping from a low-brow magazine that had a knack for making celebrities sound like anyone's next door neighbors. It was a story about several actors and actresses who'd kicked cocaine habits, beginning with a mega-star who had disappeared from public view for about five years, finally coming back looking as if he'd aged twenty, judging by the pictures.

Among four others profiled was Tim Donnelly. In a black-and-white photo he stood outside a modest wooden house. His face looked like a balloon that's just been inflated, puffing out beneath hollow eyes. He was wearing a cheap madras shirt, short sleeved, and had his arm around a very blonde woman with apple cheeks and a matronly waistline. Gathered about them were three children. The woman was identified as his wife, Cornelia. One of the children was black, one Vietnamese and one Hispanic. All five of them wore small crosses around their necks.

"Tim Donnelly, 39, says he saw the light and became a born-again Christian after he kicked the habit. 'There were some bad times,' says Donnelly. He was fired from his role on Family Secrets and out of work for over a year. His wife left him.

" 'I wandered around L.A. and pretty much gave up on work and even on staying alive, just crashing with friends and using the last of my money to support my habit. Then one day I thought maybe I need to go to church. That was where I met Cornelia.' "

Cornelia, according to the article, had done drugs and sunk too, years before, but then she and her late husband had realized they had to do something and so they found God. Her first husband died in a small plane wreck when he was traveling with a group of evangelists to spread the word, leaving Cornelia with the three adopted children.

"Christianity does not seem to have hurt Donnelly's acting career a whit," the story continued. "He's back on the daytimes, looking a little older and wiser and playing Dr. Biddle, a man with a mysterious past on Sun and Shadows, and says he's changed a lot of his beliefs.

" 'Cornelia and the kids give me a reason to keep living and working,' says Donnelly. 'I guess you could say God provides the rest. We live comfortably enough now. Cornelia and I talked a lot about her working, and we decided that the most important job a wife can do is be a source of comfort and support to her husband. She's always there for me. I used to admire feminists, and I know they won't like this, but I must tell you, my new wife has made me happy.' "

Katie had scrawled in the margin beside that paragraph: "Gross me out! I'll bet he beats her into submission!"

So sad, I thought, that Tim needed to be happy, when the only route he knew to happiness was detachment. Cocaine was detachment from reality, his religion was detachment from life's complexities. Maybe I was guilty too, of seeking easy explanations for everything. Tim and I both used to feel invincible on our cocaine highs. My women friends and I felt absolved of responsibility when we pronounced all men contemptible. Traveling produced an easy high itself. Was I becoming another kind of addict?

Tim's profile was on the last page of the story. On the other side was the first page of another story that said 4,000 people in the area had volunteered for a search for a 10-year-old girl who'd disappeared from her own bedroom in upstate New York. As many as 4,600 children reported missing each year. Americans were getting mad.

    I could go back to America. It would still be chilly in New York, and I could bundle up in fashionable woolen layers, then peel coats and scarves off in track-lit restaurants, and tell my friends tales of fleeing dissidents and bird nest caves, although they'd probably interrupt to tell me about their past and present relationships. I could lose myself in movies and good red wine, and curl up under a quilt beside a radiator. I could have a child, a girl, and name her Marian and feel a circle of life completed. But what if a killer got to her? I could, on the other hand, stay in Hong Kong a while. I was stuck here a while anyway, churning out stories from my travels.

    That spring I worked seven days a week, often all day until I was too tired to do anything but crawl into bed. I got a credit card. I thought about adopting a baby, a girl who'd been abandoned by Chinese peasant parents, now that I was a solid citizen with my credit restored. One of these days, I decided, as soon as I had time, I'd look into it.

    I could ask Jeannette how to go about looking for a baby. She wrote fairly often. She had sold a house to a couple who decided she had to meet a newly-divorced friend of theirs, and after just a few weeks they became engaged. Her doctor had said she would have trouble carrying a baby to term following the miscarriage of three years ago, but her fiancé liked the idea of adopting a girl from China.

    "Eventually we'll have to go and pick her up. It could take years, but if you're still there we'll come and visit you," Jeannette wrote. "Did you hear from Alison? She's still in touch with Webster, and dating some young lawyer. Guess she wasn't ready for marriage. How is David?"

    Even Alison wrote. She had just started law school at Johns Hopkins. "I met a gorgeous professor who also works for a big international firm," she wrote. "Of course Webster still comes to visit when he can. That was so much fun, our year off in Shanghai."

    At the end, she wrote, "I'm still trying to get permission for David to get to America."

    Laurie was working as an intern at the U.N. and had successfully delayed completing her applications to business school. Her parents were becoming resigned to the idea of her doing something different. She loved her job and had applied for another internship in Asia.

    I wrote to Jeannette and asked about babies. She sent me a list of agencies in the U.S. that handled adoptions in China.

"I warn you, it's nothing but red tape," she wrote. "I've stood in lines for hours only to be told to go to another line. We've both been fingerprinted. And still no sign of a baby. But soon, they keep telling us."

Should I do it? Here on Lamma, a little girl could run free on a path filled with pixie dust. She'd be healthy and smart during those fleeting years when it feels as if youth will never end, instead of growing gnarled at a young age, unwanted in China. She'd have a privileged life by comparison, if I could hang onto Grandfather's largesse, and she'd learn how bleak the soul can feel when you take things like food and education for granted but you're coasting through life alone.

Yet, I didn't have time to fritter away feeling bleak. At work I was often tense, but I was thrilled every time I ferreted out a piece of information and turned it into a story. Late at night, I often had a good laugh with friends over a few beers, and the combination would fill my head with a gentle effervescence. There were Sundays on my island when I listened to the rustling of banana palms through steamy air, and thought this is enough, and all I have to do to feel satisfied is live. But how could I fit a baby into all of this?

In June, I got an assignment that involved going to Shanghai. I went laden with presents — a designer bag for Wang Ming from me, small pearl earrings for her from David, perfume for Gao Ling. Wang Ming told me everything was fine in her job, and she was getting old but not worried about it. She said it so many times, I worried about her. For the first time, I asked her age. She wasn't old. She was fifty-five, but her face had grown translucent in only a year. She gave me a sweater to take back to David, and a heavy jade bi disk that I could display among my artifacts. Gao Ling had managed to get a job as an administrator at the International School but was looking out for positions in foreign companies. She had a boyfriend who had asked her to marry him, but she wasn't ready. I met him, too — a mild-mannered young man who had an office job at a joint venture hotel, and wanted to run his own hotel someday. I was writing a story for an American magazine about the daring new television station in Shanghai that was hovering just over the edge of acceptable foreign programming. I noticed that Gao and her boyfriend both wore expensive-looking Italian shoes, and wrote a short piece for the magazine about the designer fashions and the places that were starting to sell Western gourmet food in China

I was racing. Racing to churn out stories, racing so that I'd be good and tired at night. I did my best to minimize time spent wanting someone next to me, especially time spent thinking of Steve with someone else. This was far worse than being the other woman, this knowledge that he lived with me and had someone else on his mind. I had once hoped he thought of me when he was with Anne. Maybe he did, but I no longer wished that upon her.

I found a circle of friends in Hong Kong, but no one who intrigued me as a potential boyfriend. It was hard to get along without sex, but I did. Living chaste gave me time to consider things. I'd always thought sex was enough to made a relationship, but clearly, I should be looking for a more solid foundation.

At a dinner party, I met Ian Benjamin, and when he walked me to the ferry dock and talked all the way about his work for human rights in Asia, I tried to imagine marrying someone like him — late fifties, recently widowed, two grown children, a Jewish British lawyer and China scholar who'd been in Hong Kong forever, semi-retired and spending most of his time as a consultant of sorts, writing and speaking on why it was important to business in the region to weed out corruption and strive for human rights. He was fairly famous. He kissed me goodnight on the cheek and said he'd let me know if he heard any good story leads, and we should have a drink and talk more sometime anyway. He had a cheerfully crinkly face that melded into a reptilian neck.

Ian had left a message on my answering machine while I was in Shanghai. I called him back and he said, in a voice that sent rumbles through the whole receiver — too much like father with an English accent — "Hellew, my deah. I had hoped to have a drink with you sometime. Would you like to go to a reception at the China Club tomorrow evening? Incidentally, I have some inside information that might interest you. This didn't come from me, mind you, but the Independent Commission Against Corruption is looking into a conspiracy among the big property developers," he said.

"Really? You mean, something new?" My heart was pounding. I could call David, but what then? Was there any more to say this time? And if there was, would I be a traitor in a way, trying to nail the man whose money had rescued David?

"I owe you big time for this," I told Ian, because I knew he thought he was doing me a favor. Would he expect my body in return? It was generous of him, to grant the tip-off before I even accepted his invitation to the reception with a lot of prominent people in Hong Kong politics and business. I went with him, in my best black suit, and Ian looked distinguished, a man everyone was eager to greet. We had dinner afterward.

"You can stay — in my guestroom — anytime you don't want to go all the way back to Lamma," he said at the ferry.

"Thanks, but I have to start making calls early tomorrow," I mumbled feebly. Then he kissed me on the mouth. His lips tasted stale.

"Thank you for everything," I said, and didn't linger.

On the ferry, I felt like an ingrate. If I had returned Ian's kiss with another one, he might reward me with all sorts of story leads, with introductions to movers and shakers in the world, with a career as his mate and colleague in his undoubtedly luxurious flat on Old Peak Road.

But pressed against his stale lips and flaccid chest, I'd felt as if a giant gray tongue had scooped me up and a pair of iron jaws were closing in. I'd fled to the boat a good ten minutes before departure time, gasping for sea air that might shake off a taste that made me feel queasy. Some women liked brainy, chivalrous older men. I tried to imagine how Ian would react if I were to call and tell him, sorry, it isn't you, it's that I have a father-figure phobia and maybe it can be cured if we spend a lot of time talking, no sexual pressure, and I somehow learn to like the way you smell and taste. No doubt he'd say what makes you so presumptuous — and he'd find a woman who was aroused by his fascinating conversation and noble deeds alone.

Calling David at home early the next morning, my limbs murmured with pleasure at the sound of his young voice.

"Fox! " he said cheerily. But I was calling him for reasons that had nothing to do with pleasure. Having seized this opportunity from Ian, I was now about to do something that might make David hate me.

It wasn't that I hadn't wrestled with my decision to pursue the story. I'd thought of Laurie, and wondered if she'd ever speak to me again. Of course, if I got something, Steve might read about it, maybe in *Worldweek*, and I would have won a round against him. If I got something I might expose corrupt business practices — not that I had any power to put an end to such things. If I got something, I would have a great story to show in future job interviews. If I got something, maybe David would see that capitalism wasn't the solution to world's problems.

I invited David to lunch, on me, at our favorite Shanghainese restaurant. I'd bring up the subject there and if he knew anything we'd meet privately, I figured. If he did know something, he might not tell me. But maybe I was being a friend, to warn him that Oscar's empire was being watched.

He was wearing a suit and tie made of fabrics so rich they might have been spun from the hair of a goddess. He was carrying a mobile phone.

"Did you get a raise?" I asked. He looked a bit embarrassed.

"I always planned to make money in Hong Kong," he said.

"I hope you're planning for '97 is all. I got a letter from Alison and she said she's trying."

"I don't know." he said. Gravity pushed the iron will out of his face. He ordered food.

"David, I should tell you, everyone's saying there's another investigation of your company going on."

I interviewed business executives often enough to know that everything in offices was considered some kind of state secret in a stateless territory. It seemed pretty hopeless. Why would someone as low-level as David know the secrets anyway?

"I don't know anything about an investigation," he said.

"The share prices went way down and now they're trading at all-time highs," I said. "You don't have stock in the company, do you?"

He laughed, with a hint of bitterness. "No, I don't make enough money to invest yet. I have to save my money for a ticket to America someday. And to help get my mother out of China."

"How is she?" After my visit, Wang Ming had sent me a letter that was merely a commentary on the weather, but David kept in touch with her through secret channels.

"She is feeling she will be lonely, because it is time for her to retire."

"Can I do anything?"

"There is nothing for you to do."

"Could we bring her here?"

"She could get out if someone helped, I think. They wouldn't refuse an old woman who just wants to visit Hong Kong, maybe to see the nursing schools. But you can not do that."

I wondered if "help" meant sponsoring her, for the usual twenty thousand dollars.

"I want to help," I told David.

"How?"

"Money, maybe."

"I can't take it from you."

"No, really. I have a good job now. It's for her. You can't refuse help for your mother."

I wish I could report that the gray-haired woman with the backpack appeared in a dream and said "What's this — buying David's friendship to atone for what you're about to do to him?" Then I would have known my offer of charity was for me, not for Wang Ming. But I dreamt of other things, predictable things like seeing a man who looked like Steve but then he turned out to look like my father.

I believed that David knew nothing about Grand Harbour's stocks, or even about the investigator's report on several major property companies. I spent the next few days getting quotes from others in the industry. Oscar didn't return my phone calls, nor did his public relations director, whom I tried to reach nine times. I called again and harassed the public relations director's secretary until she put him on the phone. "We are not aware of an investigation," he said. "We do not comment on our investigations," said a spokesman for the ICAC. I was getting somewhere: no one had said there wasn't an investigation going on.

I called Bill Rudge in New York. "Would you be interested in a story about deals that are creating an investment bubble in Hong Kong?" I asked him. "Meaning we're getting so much foreign investment, but what's happening is going to make no one rich except a handful of local developers. And they may be buying property in China that they're selling to American companies based on development plans that are never going to materialize."

"Can you substantiate that?" Bill asked gruffly. "Send us something, but you've gotta prove this."

A property consultant, a Brit, said "Oh, yes. Well, of course, it would come as a surprise if Oscar Wong wasn't doing something crooked. Don't quote me."

"Does it have anything to do with buying parcels of land just to churn over the land bank, but meanwhile selling office space in a development that isn't going to be built?" I asked the consultant.

"I'm sure there's a lot of that going in China," he said. "But no. The investigation, to the best of my knowledge, is about share prices. Don't quote me on any of this."

I asked my source at the Commission about land churning. "Oh, no doubt," he said. "Of course it's for Chinese officials to worry about. It's out of our jurisdiction. Don't say I said that."

I took my files home to write the story. A storm was brewing. There were typhoon alerts, and if I didn't take the 7 o'clock boat home the others might be delayed or canceled. I stared at the sea as waves jolted me back and forth in my seat. The Tao says water is humble and self-effacing but in the end all-powerful.

At home, I closed my windows but the glass panes shuddered like wind chimes. Doors banged back and forth, and the wind pried them open. I turned out most of the lights and remembered the warnings. Don't take a shower in a typhoon. Don't talk on the phone. Don't turn on appliances, especially computers. But my story was due the next day.

What I was able to piece together, from industry analysts and consultants who admitted it wasn't untrue, was that the investigation definitely had to do with plans on the part of a number of property companies to manipulate their own share prices. About a year before, the prices of several major property companies had fallen drastically amidst rumors that the Beijing government had prepared a team of cadres to run Hong Kong after 1997. Such stories always sent the Hong Kong stock exchange plunging, especially property stocks since real estate had become the foundation of the economy. So no one thought too much of it until a few months later, when the prices of a select group of property companies began to soar to all-time highs, fueling speculation that the company heads themselves might have started the rumor about China. Oscar Wong apparently sold a large chunk of his own holdings in his company just before the prices went down. The suspicion was that a number of developers sold off their holdings to phantom buyers, which were really their own privately-held companies. When shares were down they bought into one anothers' companies, so that instead of being competitors, they had formed a secret cartel in which each member had a share in the others' astronomical profits.

Would anyone at *Worldweek* care about this? I tried to emphasize that the Hong Kong stock market was getting more and more Western investment, and that these investments could be in trouble if such secret goings-on took place.

I decided to write just what I'd been told was going on. If *Worldweek* did run it, I could ask, out of deference to David and Laurie, that they use it without my reporter credit. I'd worry about that when they actually accepted it. The editors in New York would quickly forget that it was my story if it appeared without my name. The wind whipped so hard my apartment swayed. Sure, I was exposing a wrong, but would anyone notice? I didn't expect to bring down Grand Harbour Holdings with one little story, but Oscar might put two and two together and blame the expose on David's friendship with me if he needed a scapegoat. My career or David's?

It was almost ten o'clock when the phone rang. I was halfway through the story, and had resolved to turn it in and then worry about the credit. I should let the machine pick it up, I thought, but what if a friend needed shelter from the storm?

"Hello."

"I hope you won't hang up on me."

"Steve!" It was painful to utter his name.

"Can we talk?"

"Why?"

"I can't blame you if you do nothing but answer in monosyllables. Can I talk?"

"I'm really busy with a story."

"I can't expect you to ever forgive me. Couldn't we start over?"

"What about High-Dee-Low?"

"I think it was a mistake. I miss your intellectual stimulation. How is your life?"

"It's okay. I'm working on an important story and I'm tossing around the idea of adopting a Chinese baby. I'm still worried about David." I wanted to say you'll know why soon enough, but if the story had never come out, he'd know I'd tried and failed to carry out the expose he'd once encouraged me to write.
"I want you to be happy. I just wish we could be happy together. We came so close. Are there any new men around? Besides David of course?"
"Friends."
"Seems like a waste of your beauty."
"I have to get back to work. Really." I said goodbye and hung up.
It took a while to get back to work. I called one of my new female friends to dissect the conversation. "He liked me best when I was halfway imaginary," I said.

I made a pot of coffee and worked furiously, until I had nothing more to add to the story, nothing more to rephrase or reconsider. Forgetting David and Laurie, forgetting everything except that I wanted Steve to open *Worldweek* and see my story.

Chapter 17

Surely Oscar Wong never looked at himself in the mirror and thought, "I'm an exploiter and oppressor." We all have excuses. Oscar might think he's helping to fuel an efficient global economy, and take care of his family, not to mention some ambitious individuals in need.

I could make excuses for anything I've ever done. I wanted to be loved. I wanted to shine as a reporter in Asia. I even wanted to stop a bunch of rich, smug crooks from being greedy. I wanted to help David get to the U.S. and find his true calling, whatever that might be — I didn't go sailing with the smugglers to see David bow and scrape to Oscar Wong.

My story came out the next week. The byline went to the New York desk editor, but at the end it said "Reported by Madeleine Fox in Hong Kong." The story ran almost exactly as I'd written it, with just some re-phrasing to fit the space.

The next day the local Hong Kong papers ran similar pieces. I saw Jon Summers on the ferry and he said, "I hear you broke a story."

I smiled thinly and watched Jon move on to sit with a group of scruffy freelance guys. I had tried to call David that afternoon, at the office, and he'd said, "I can't talk to you now." The emphasis was on "you," rather than on "now."

At home, I tried David again. His phone rang and rang. He didn't have an answering machine. Around 10:30 he finally picked up.

"Hello, Fox." He sounded testy.

"How are things at work?"

"We think everyone is talking about us." He paused. "Mr. Wong called me to come to see him today. He was very angry. He ask if I talk to any reporters. I say no because I think of you as friend not reporter. But I know you think I am not belong here so you don't mind writing something. Many people wrote it but you did too. Mr. Wong say if I talk to reporters, any time, he will fire me. So I know you think he is dirty capitalist, but I know what is right for me. I can not talk to a reporter."

"I didn't get anything from you..."

"I am not stupid, Fox. You have a job you do, but this is my job. I am sorry to see this happen."

"Can't we talk..."

"I must go now. It is not good for you to phone me" He hung up.

I lost two male friends. When I phoned Ian to thank him, he said, "Don't mention it. Call me any time you need something." I heard Wagner playing in the background. "I have to run..." he said.

Steve called to congratulate me, however. And Bill Rudge called and said he was in Hong Kong and eager to see me, in the *Worldweek* office, how about Friday morning.

Bill and Paul Scherfield, the bureau chief, ushered me into Paul's office and shut the door. I wondered if someone was trying to sue the magazine because of my story. Paul, who had a scratchy voice and had grown a goatee recently, sat back in his chair. Bill faced me in one of the armchairs.

"As you may know," began Bill, clearing his throat and sizing me up in a way that made me feel like a rooster about to be sent into a cockfight, "we have been considering various candidates for a correspondent position here. We usually bring in someone who's paid dues at home. But we're a leaner, meaner operation than we were just a few years ago. Of course, you've been doing good work for us. If you're willing to work even harder, we're prepared to offer you a post."

"Here? You mean, the job Steve West had?"

Bill cleared his throat and exchanged loaded glances with Paul. "Well, in the sense that you would occupy that office and have many of the same duties. Of course, we're restructuring a bit. Steve is a seasoned reporter, but gets a tad lazy when he's in the field too long."

I wondered if I'd have to work 24 hours a day to prove myself. Or maybe lazy was a code word for too ideological.

"In the sense of getting stories, or the quality of stories?" I asked. Wasn't I supposed to know how to ask questions in the job they were dangling before me? And didn't I have a right to know a few things?

Bill sat back and smiled at me as if we were longtime confidantes. This would last until my next story, I had a feeling. "Oh, some of these guys come to Asia and think they know all the stories already. We'll expect you to look for the unexpected, do a lot more probing than we've had in the past. Now... the bad news is we're taking a chance with someone who hasn't been in the States with us, and we'll have to consider you a local hire. That means we can't offer a housing allowance..." " He named a figure he said they could pay.

They were going to run me ragged and not pay the perks they'd surely offer a man to do the job. I thought sadly of David. Of course, he was being far more exploited than I would be. If I had this job, could I find some way to help him — giving him money to get Wang Ming here, if he'd take it? If they were hiring me on the basis of access to Oscar Wong, I'd lose the job sooner or later. And I'd

probably never get the access to movers and shakers I could have had if I'd been willing to sleep with Ian Benjamin.
 But they were offering me Steve's job.
 I took a deep breath. "I don't think I could work for that salary... without a housing allowance," I said. "Maybe... "
 "We'll see if we can do that much," said Bill. Hopefully I'd earned a sliver of respect by not just accepting a crumb. "And when could you start?"
 He called back that afternoon.
Before I started the job, Steve called and said, with wistfulness in his voice, "I hear congratulations are in order. By the way, make them get you a new computer."
 I decided to stay on Lamma for the time being. *Worldweek* had a corporate apartment in Happy Valley that I was allowed to use on nights that I worked so late I missed the ferry; their concession for not paying my rent.
I became one of Lamma's working-in-the-fast-lane arrivistes who raced for the ferry each morning, wearing trendy versions of office attire and carrying knapsacks loaded down with reading matter for the boat, files from work, gym gear, a change of clothes for the evening. I became one of the ones who sat on the air-conditioned top deck in the mornings, drinking coffee at long wooden tables and talking about work. On the top deck, people cared who you were.
 "This is Madeleine Fox, who works for *Worldweek*," was the way people I knew introduced me to others. We were commuters who took the 7:45 ferry six mornings a week, but all the way there we bobbed above the sea and knew, no matter how much we talked about work, that what we did in some mega-urban skyscraper was a lark, a diversion of sorts from banana groves and tiered fields and conversations in the pub. Most of the people on the top deck somehow managed to write songs or novels, or paint or play with rock bands when they weren't at the office or a party. I started working on short stories again. In another era, we might have fancied ourselves a generation of artists with a label. But the only common conviction among us was that nothing was built to last forever. We were American, Canadian, British, Australian, of European and Asian ancestry, and we expected to scatter after 1997. Along with work we talked about other places to go. Many of us didn't really have a country to call home. I could make Hong Kong my home if I wanted, now that, with a legitimate job, I had a work visa and a resident's identification card.
 Gradually, fewer men looked like Steve at first glance. I began dating others, men close to my age who were in Hong Kong either to make money or to be scornful of the greed. None of them fell in love with me, nor I with them. I bumped into Ian frequently, and he always kissed my hand while his eyes darted elsewhere. I didn't hear from David, but I passed Grand Harbour Holdings

frequently, and sometimes saw him go in or out. He still dressed well, looked more filled out and confident. Once he looked in my direction but if he saw me he didn't let me know. Laurie wrote from time to time, and said she had no interest in her father's business dealings. .
Of course, I worked long hours. I hardly had time to spend the money I made. Paul called me into his office frequently when he was in town, sometimes to point out something I should have done with a story, sometimes with a brainstorm about a story I should pursue. I always went in there with my hands shaking. I wrote a piece about orphanages in China, went to some orphanages posing as a friend of a woman who was adopting, managed by tagging along with a doctor to see a room where the less healthy children were left in squalor. I thought of adopting once again. Jeannette and her new husband were supposed to have a baby waiting for them in China by the end of the year. But I had so little time to take care of a baby.

Time was a matter of minutes ticking away toward a deadline each week, though as weeks passed time was also a lazy rolling of seasons from drizzly to sweltering. In summer, I spent hours under shelter from the rain, but the sogginess seeped through everything. Mold grew in a pair of shoes. A short-legged yellow dog showed up in the alleyway between my building and the next one, cringing from a storm. When I tried to put the dog out on a clear day, he bounded back to my door and howled. Almost everyone on the island had dogs and cats they'd found and taken in. This one had pegged me, it seemed. I named him Sun, as in Sun Yat Sen.

October was when people came back from far-flung travels and the sea was safe for sailing and junk parties. When I couldn't lose myself in work anymore I hiked through the rolling hills past the beach, under a jungle canopy, past clusters of bamboo groves, over the pass between Mt. Stenhouse and Ling Kok Shan, up the short but steep hill from the temple at Sok Kwu Wan. Most of the ex-pats on the island liked to hike on weekends that weren't booked up with work, so I usually had company. "These are wimp hills. Lantau's better," said Jon Summers. I bumped into him hiking in his tire sandals one Sunday, accompanied by a dark-haired woman who wore a tank shirt that exposed a very developed set of muscles. She was small and didn't walk so much as glide, while his big feet sent dirt flying with each step. They were laughing about something when I saw them. His friend with the well-toned body was named Yolanda and she was clearly not French. She said she was visiting from Sydney. Around February, the press began hearing new rumors about a property cartel in Hong Kong. The Commission still wouldn't comment, but I went to lunches with property analysts and consultants, and most of them said to just keep watching out for the release of a report.

I waited outside the sales offices of Grand Harbour Holdings one evening from four-thirty until nearly seven.

David left the office brusquely. I followed him toward the elevators. He was speaking to a slightly older man in Cantonese. I heard condescension in David's tone, the way Ian Benjamin might speak if he took a trip to the American heartland and went into a redneck bar.

A crowd of mostly Chinese office workers waited at the elevator bank. If I let David see me, he'd probably run back to his office and lock me out. I didn't exactly blend in here. And if I talked to him on the elevator, he would be paranoid about being seen by someone who might suspect me of being a reporter. But if he went down without me, I'd lose him.

I took the stairs, down ten flights, hoping against hope that the elevator would be slow, stopping on every floor, and I'd get to the lobby before he did. I flew, annoyed with every door. Downstairs, there was almost no breathing room among the hordes of people leaving their offices. Looking for a young Chinese man in a suit amidst thousands of young Chinese men in suits, I shoved my way to one elevator bank and realized it was only for the eleventh to twentieth floors. David was nowhere in sight.

So I went to Wanchai, and rang his doorbell. No answer. I shivered under my raincoat. Clouds opened, and I pulled out the folding umbrella I always carried in a tote bag. The street was almost deserted, except for a beggar lying in a doorway and a few workmen packing up for the night. I gave the beggar five Hong Kong dollars, and he thanked me in good English. I continued waiting. It occurred to me that he might have a girlfriend; maybe he was spending the night out. Maybe he'd bring a girlfriend home, or a whole group of friends. I had to corner him alone, if there was any hope of regaining his trust.

David came home around nine-thirty. He strode down the street, coatless, umbrella-less, not even a briefcase. He was frowning even before he saw me. When he did reach his front door where I was lurking, he jumped, looking frightened.

"Well, this is a surprise," he said, recovering.

"I'm worried about your job," I said.

"It is not your worry."

"I hear a few people were fired. What will happen to you?"

"Mr. Wong doesn't talk to me anymore."

"I am still your friend."

"Fox, it's cold. I am tired."

"I need to talk to you, just a little."

"About me? Or Mr. Wong's company?"

Both, I thought. I said, "I'm still your friend, no matter what you think."

He sighed. "Come in a little while, from the rain."
We walked up the stairs silently, tensely. As he closed his door, I stood, figuring I wouldn't sit or take off my coat unless he invited me to. "How is Wang Ming?" I asked.
David looked at me suspiciously, but sighed again.
"I have worries. My mother says the old people on her neighborhood committee accuse her of things she hasn't done."
"Like what?"
"I don't know. I think it is dumping trash in the wrong place. Because in the cultural revolution people made up things you did. I think she is afraid they are against her because I left." He paused. "I am try to bring her here. She wants to be with me. I must save my money, not buy so many things."
"How hard is it to get her in?"
"Maybe hard, maybe not. You know the top number of people they will let in Hong Kong from China."
"Quota?"
"Oh, yes, it is quota. Maybe some of my friends can help her come anyway. Of course, that is money."
I wasn't cut out for altruism any more than David was, but I thought I was probably in a better position than he was to make a sacrifice.
"Maybe I can help?" I said.
"It is not your worry."
"How? See if she can come to stay with you and if she needs money."
"I will help her. I can't ask you."
"Remember, I told you my sister says there are no accidents? I feel responsible for your being here. Maybe for her, too."
"No, Fox. Now what do you want?"
That was three times he said no. I felt defeated. "How will you get her here?"
"This is not for a story?"
"Of course not."
He shrugged. "I am borrowing money from many friends. I have friends from Shanghai here now. I can charter a fishing boat at Chao Zhou on the Fujian coast. For more money, she can get a Hong Kong identity card. It is still not so safe if she tries to work in Hong Kong, because it is a card for only a year. So she must retire even though she does not want. But in China they would make her retire soon anyway."
"How much money?"
"I think about one hundred and fifty thousand Hong Kong dollars." That was close to twenty thousand U.S. I nearly choked.
"Really, I could lend you something..."

"You stay out, you leave it to the Shanghai people," he insisted.

"I would like to be friends again," I said. I was still standing. "I will go, but call me if you need anything." I would still have time to make the last ferry to Lamma if I left soon.

He looked at me cryptically. "I will always remember you, Fox. But tonight I am tired. You see I have much on my mind."

In March, on another of those rainy days that sends chills right through the cracks in the windows, I got an unexpected phone call at the office.

"Hello, Mei Lan..." It was the voice of a woman uneasy with speaking by phone. "Do you remember me, *Tian He muqin*?"

"Wang Ming?"

"I am sorry, I study Engrish but too old, not so good. I am in Hong Kong. You come see me? Day, the time when Tian He at work."

I slipped away at lunchtime, battling the subway traffic to Wanchai. Wang Ming hugged me at the door, and I realized tears were running down my eyes.

"I am very happy," she said, her blood vessel pumping at a rapid clip. She looked scrubbed, as if she'd just emerged from a shower, with bright pink spots on her iridescent cheeks. Her hair was grayer and thinner. She was dressed up in navy slacks, a red blazer and navy pumps.

"I am very grateful to you," she said, in English.

"But I haven't done anything."

"You take good care of Tian He. He is healthy and makes much money to help me."

"He is..." I almost said he's mad at me, but Wang Ming looked at me sternly. I was violating Chinese manners, spoiling our reunion with talk of an unpleasant situation.

"You come visit me when he is in office."

"You stay here?" I asked. She nodded. She showed me the foldaway cot that she'd crammed into the corner next to the sofa. I told her she could stay with me if she wanted a room of her own.

"Oh, no." she said. "You eat lunch?"

I shook my head.

She rustled up some stir-fried vegetables, noodles and tea.

"How long have you been here?" I asked her.

She held up two fingers. Two days. She said she thought Hong Kong was beautiful, and she began to cry as she told me how life had been hard in Shanghai after David left, how friends stopped talking to her, how she was happy for him and worried about being a burden, but she was afraid to stay in China.

"Will you go to America if he does?" I had a sudden hope that David's mother might talk some sense into him.
" I wish he to go," she said. "Better after 1997, good to go now. But me, no. I am too old, not such good health."
"No?"
She glared at me and piled more noodles onto my plate. "*Chi, chi.* You come for noon meal any day. We do not tell," she said. "It is like family. Some Chinese families live together but not speak." She laughed sadly. We sat in folding chairs around a pine dining table that stood against the foot of wall space between the tiny bathroom and the even tinier kitchen.
"You must come and I make food for you," she chattered on. "You must eat and sleep more. Drink less, worry less. I am a nurse, I can see from your eyes."
I put down my chopsticks, suddenly exhausted, and found tears pouring out. Wang Ming put her arms around me. Like a mother.
"Yes... " I admitted. "I do... I do." If only I could stay, and be there when David got home, and feel like part of a family.

Chapter 18

I saw Wang Ming as frequently as my crazy schedule allowed.
Sometimes she made lunch for me. One Sunday she even took the ferry to Lamma and came to see my apartment.

"This is the country!" she said, laughing. It was a muggy day with a sky like pea soup, but no rain. We sat on the beach for a while. Wang Ming crossed her legs and sat in the sand, not bothering to take off her pumps or her hose.

She confessed that David was in debt, and worried about his job.

"From my, you know, voyage here, he borrows money," she said.

"I can help," I offered.

"No, no. You wait. When he understands you are friend again, you help. Now do you make much money?"

I gazed at the beach. On days when I could relax I felt as if I were sleepwalking. "Enough," I said. Enough payoff to want to hang onto the job.

"In Hong Kong, I think when you make money you buy house," she said.

The property market was going up, and I was the doomsday reporter out to prove it couldn't boom forever. But anyone who could afford to buy property did. You could buy for only ten percent down, for one thing. Foreigners figured it was a gamble, but if they planned to sell before the handover they had a good chance of making a killing.

Since David hadn't wanted my money, should I pass up a chance to make a killing?

I looked at a few apartments on Hong Kong island. They were all noisy. I checked out the realtor who had an office on Main Street in Yung Shue Wan village. They had houses, not just apartments, off the tiered rice fields. For the price of an apartment on the main island, I could get spacious rooms and yard space.

I moved into a funny, rambling beige stucco house on a hilltop. I had a massive living room with a picture window that looked over the fields. On a clear day I could see the bay peaking out through my wild grove of palm and banana trees. The house had three bedrooms, and an unpaved outdoor patio where I could put a grill and picnic table. The front door was painted red, a lucky color, with a raised entry to keep evil spirits from pouring in.
My house, filled with my photographs and my souvenirs of the places I'd been. I rattled in it. The roof was flat, and at night hard little pods would fall from trees and hit my roof with a loud "pong" that had no rhythm. I would wake up and

squirm in my double bed. I thought again about adopting a baby. But Steve had had little time for his family, and look at what had happened.

What I did do was find Lourdes. It cost so little to hire a live-in amah, and my house had a closet of a maid's room and bath. She was working two part time jobs, but said if I could sign her residency papers when they came up for renewal, she could give notice.

"This is an easy job," she confessed to me after moving in. "No child. I nap in the afternoon." She kept the refrigerator stocked, and even combed Sun the dog once a day.

She was discreet enough to not bring up Steve's name. But I heard from him, and told her, "Steve said to tell you hi. He's not happy with his new wife." Lourdes and I laughed conspiratorially. "Not a surprise," she said.

I decorated the office that had once belonged to Steve with pictures of my dog, my friends, and pictures Katie sent me of my nieces. And I continued to be too busy to spend much time dwelling on what was missing from my life.

In June, we got word on the police wire that the offices of several major property developers were going to be raided.

Paul was in China, and local business stories were usually beneath him anyway. I couldn't be everywhere that a raid was occurring, so I chose to stake out Grand Harbour Holdings. I called a photographer and asked him to meet me there.

A mob of reporters was already waiting outside the executive offices.

"They say there will be arrests. Maybe Mr. Wong himself," a young Cantonese woman from a local Chinese language paper whispered to me.

We waited, and the mob grew.

"Whattaya bet he's counting out bills for the cops right now?" said a British guy.

"Then I oughtta be breaking the door down," complained the *Worldweek* photographer. I looked at him. We exchanged a silent "Why not?" He opened the massive executive door, to the reception room. Two police guards waited in there. They stopped him from going any further. Of course, the other reporters were not about to let someone else go in and take a chance at an exclusive, so the mob soon filled the reception room. The guards started to push at us. The young receptionist ran through a back door as the shouts grew louder. Into the fray stepped the silver-haired Oscar himself, his shoulders squared, his black eyes fixed straight ahead, his mouth grim, with two policemen at either side. He was not handcuffed, but the cops were so close at his side he couldn't possibly get away from them. Two more cops followed close behind.

"What is the charge??" I tried to ask of a cop, who glared through me.

Another reporter, a guy from Australian television, stepped forward and shoved a microphone in Oscar's face. Like he's really going to comment, I thought.

"Mr. Wong, please tell us..." began the Australian.

I felt something snap in the room. Someone tripped backwards over me, and I stumbled, but saw the rage in Oscar's eyes as he swung his fist and punched the Australian reporter in the jaw. Then the police were dragging him out, forcing a byway through the crowd.

I sat on the floor at the police station, surrounded by an ever-growing swarm of reporters, waiting for a statement we'd been promised about exactly who had been arrested and what the charges were. The *Worldweek* photographer, thrilled with his shots of Oscar taking a swing at a reporter, had gone back to his studio to develop the film. The Australian sat in one of the few vacant chairs, his face against an ice pack a station officer had dug up for him.

From a small window, the hazy pewter sky was a warning of heavy rain. More heavy rain. It was the beginning of typhoon season, after all. I shifted around, shaking a foot that had gone to sleep.

Finally, a police officer called us into a small conference room. Photographers wrestled for space to set up. A panel of three British men, two from the Independent Commission Against Corruption, one from the Securities and Futures Commission, which oversaw the stock exchange, sat at a table with microphones.

Oscar Wong and three other chief executives of large property companies were being booked on charges of conspiring to manipulate their share prices. They would most likely be released on bail by late afternoon, and would stand trial in the next few months.

"What is the actual likelihood of a trial?" I shouted out.

"We hesitate to comment on that. There is of course a strong possibility of an out of court settlement," said one of the men.

"Why has Wong been firing people left and right?" shouted a reporter from a wire service.

"You'll have to ask him that," was the retort.

Why hadn't I thought to ask that question? In a panic, I decided I had to get out of that stuffy room and find out what was happening to David.?

It was pouring when I got outside, and every taxi that passed me was occupied. My umbrella was useless in the howling wind, so I walked to the office and let the rain soak me. The crowds in Central were scurrying for shelter. The reception desk was empty at *Worldweek*, and even the business office seemed quiet. The secretary in the news department, in fact, was the only other person about.

"Typhoon coming," she told me. "Everyone has gone home." She was clearly rushing to get home herself. I might be stuck in the office all night, but I had to see what was happening to David. I shivered in Steve's office — my office — and waited for someone to pick up the phone at Grand Harbour. David did not have a direct number — or at least, he hadn't when he was speaking to me. The receptionists there had probably gone home, too, or maybe been fired. The phone rang ten or eleven times before a young sounding woman picked it up.

"David Li, please," I demanded.
"Mavis?"
"David!"
"Your name please?"
"Ms. Fox."
"Fox? We have no one with that name here," said the woman.
"I want to speak to David Li. *Ni shuo Putonghua ma?*"
"Hello?"
"David Li Tian He."
"No one with that name here, I told you."
"Check please. He worked there last week."
"I don't know." She hung up.
I called him at home and he answered.
"Fox! I am surprised." The conviviality in his voice seemed completely false.
"I know. What happened at work?"
"Oh, everything is fine," he said.
"Then what are you doing at home?"
"Mr. Wong sold off the development division and fired everyone..."
"I'm coming over," I said. "I am a friend of your mother, after all."
"Yes... maybe I like to see you too. Be careful, of the typhoon."
I stood crushed by wet bodies on a trolley to Wanchai. Behind me I heard two young British guys saying something about "... a number 7 signal. Party all night, won't we? "

In the alleyway outside David's building, the storefront owners were gathering up cages of live chickens and racks of clothes. White feathers flew in a whirl and an old man was gathering up a pile of mangoes from the ground. Trying to keep an eye on the ground, I stepped over the oddest creatures I'd ever; six giant snails, some poking slugheads out of their white shells. I stopped long enough to watch one move a millimeter with an odd ease, fluid in its hard shell.

Wang Ming was home, busying herself with chopping vegetables. "Don't lie, Tian He," she said.

To me, she said, "There is trouble."

Oscar had sold off the Guangdong development division as a private company, to avoid further investigation into his activities. But first he fired the division's marketing team, on the grounds that they had been trying to sell units under false promises. David had made a few sales, and could conceivably find himself under investigation for having made false claims about the terms of sale. David sat on his sofa, his shoulders slumped. "You were right, Fox, about corruption in the company. I cannot blame you for doing your job. You may write a story about me now if you want, I understand."

"Only if it's about the impact of corruption on employees who can't afford to lose their jobs," I said.

We smiled at each other shyly.

"You must have hot shower and some dry clothes," said David. "And eat. Look outside, how things are flying."

. A stall keeper was trying to salvage strips of his awning that had torn loose and whipped through the wind. He beat at the awning skyward with a broom handle, until he finally reigned in one strip that tumbled down, bamboo pole and all.

Wang Ming gave me a kimono and insisted I wrap myself in a blanket to keep from catching cold. Feeling cozy and fragrant from her lily-scented soap, I had dinner with them. Afterward Wang Ming sat down in front of the television, with her back turned to us while David and I talked. The windows rattled into the night.

"Mr. Wong will pay a fine and be back in business," said David. "But I will still be out of a job."

"You could look for another job."

He looked at me with a confused expression. This was like a different David, shuffling when he walked, his head bent, looking about as if he wasn't quite sure where he was.

"You still have a wife in America," I observed.

"Maybe. But there is my mother. Alison..." her name stuck uneasily in his throat, "said it would be easier to get asylum for me if I'm already in America. As her husband of course. But first I have to get permission to get there. So far I have no luck. Because I am here so long, in America the immigration people don't believe this is a real marriage."

I nodded. "You'd have to go and live with her at least a year, and have an interview to prove it's real."

"I would be happy," he confessed.

"Maybe you tried too hard?"

He looked at me blankly.

"Maybe she wasn't ready to have a baby?"

He looked at me as if I were crazy. "I don't understand. I am not ready myself."

"What would it take to get you a visitor's visa to America?"

"They don't exactly say. They want a letter from your employer in Hong Kong to say you will come back. They give you permission to stay for one month maybe, or maybe ten years, and you have to have enough money for all that time."

"I can give you money. Not for ten years, but some money. Maybe I can write a letter from an employer even. But what would you do if you go? Besides stay with Alison a while, of course. She'll just have to do right by you."

"I want to learn more about business," said David.

"Even after this?"

"It's still good they were investigated and arrested. No one cares about corruption in China."

"But Oscar will probably be making his billions again next month and you're out in the cold."

"I know. I need to have power myself. I knew you wouldn't agree."

"You don't need my approval."

"What else am I going to do?" he asked. "You said your mother had money to do good things. I would need money too."

Wang Ming turned around. "I am tired," she announced.

"She sleeps in here," David pointed out, needlessly. He helped her pull out the cot. I would sleep on the sofa, I figured.

"Sleepy?" he asked me.

I shook my head.

"Come talk more." He gestured toward his little room. We took some beers with us. Wang Ming tucked herself under blankets and said goodnight to us as if all of this was perfectly appropriate.

David sat back at the head of the bed, and I plopped down at the foot. The room had nothing in it but a single bed built under the window, over a frame and a row of drawers, and a formica armoire for clothes, with no more than two feet of space to turn around in. The window rattled. David leaned against the wall and drank a beer quickly. He belched as politely as he could.

"On clear nights I can see the moon over the buildings," he said. "Last night it was new, like a sideways smile."

"The fertile moon."

"Oh yes, you live in the country now." He sighed. "There you know even Oscar Wong cannot stop the weather."

"I never imagined you would notice things like the moon."

He laughed and looked at me flirtatiously, which seemed a rather dangerous thing to do in this cloistered space.

I tried to ignore the thing that stirred in me.

"Do you think Johnny Wong would write an employer letter for you?" I asked.

"I don't think," he said.

"Yeah. We'll figure something."

"Don't worry Fox. Let's talk about it tomorrow," he said.

"Look," I said. "Here's an idea. I've been thinking of adopting a baby. I should go ahead and do it. Then your mother can stay with me, if she is willing to. I'll need someone to help."

"You do want to get a baby?"

I considered what I was saying. "I have the space. I don't want to be a slave to the job and realize in ten years I have nothing else."

"Don't worry now. You work hard, and get tense. Would you like me to give you accupressure? "

We didn't talk much after that, after I succumbed to his heavenly massage, which he started on my feet, and worked up my legs to my spine.

"I never knew you could do this," I said.

"Shhh... You always talk. Once I could help you from your bicycle accident, now here I can help you again, I think." He kneaded my back muscles. "You help me, you help my mother feel at home here. I felt so sad about not seeing you, but I was afraid. And I thought I sometimes felt in love with you, and what did you care for me."

Rain crashed against his window. I started to look up

"Don't talk now," he said. "It will be a big typhoon."

Then I turned over.

It was as if we were acting out an unspoken pact. I had a mild alcohol buzz and I could tell he did too. He was not a great lover, but we pounded frenetically against each other with a mission, as if we had to break rocks and part waters to seal the future.

He moved, faster, moaning, wet heat filling me, the venom of death and the seed that sows life.

Chapter 19

The next morning when we faced each other side by side, naked, we both sort of turned away, as if each of us was giving the other the chance to shrink away without being observed. The windows had stopped rattling. Hong Kong was quiet outside. My cue will determine what happens, I realized. After many awkward seconds, I settled for the obvious. "I need to get to the office."
"Have tea?" he asked.
"No, thank you... really, I have a busy day... "
At the office I scanned the wire stories and the morning papers. By 9:30 I felt armed enough to call Johnny Wong. Amazingly, he picked up his direct line.
"I have no comment about the affairs of the company," he said. He giggled. "I have to go to a meeting now."
I made other calls. An analyst admitted the Commission Against Corruption also suspected a land churning scheme. I wrote a story about the employees who'd already taken the rap. I had some quotes from David but I didn't use his name. Hardly anyone wanted their names used, since they were all looking for new jobs and didn't want to look like whistleblowers.
I saw David frequently in the next few weeks. We said nothing about the night of the storm. I always insisted on leaving before 11:20, when the last ferry departed for Lamma.
We were hatching plans, but the plans pointed us in separate directions. I asked a few people at the magazine what they knew about setting up an incorporated business in Hong Kong, made a few phone calls, and found out that for about twelve hundred U.S. dollars it was possible to set up a shelf company. David and I visited a small accounting office, in a storefront just two doors down from his building, and browsed through a list of names that the tax department had nominated for registry.
David's eyes stopped on the names that started with Gold. There was a whole page of them. Gold Anchor. Gold Apex. Gold Baron. Gold Blaze. Gold Bounty. Gold Camellia.
"Maybe this?" he said. He pointed to Gold Canyon.
I nodded. "It sounds like real estate."
Since the name was on file, it took only a few days to register the company. I became the chief executive officer, David the company secretary. I spent a little more money to have stationery printed. I wrote a letter addressed to the U.S.

Immigration office, saying that David was a senior officer who had been with the company for a year. I said I wanted to let him have a leave of up to six months, and that he had assured me he planned to come back. I lied about his salary. He called Alison and told her what had happened. She said that of course it would be fine if he came to Washington and lived with her.

"An arrangement or a real living together?" I asked.

He sighed. "We will see. I will miss you."

I left an outgoing message on my answering machine at home. "This is Gold Canyon Properties..."

"So you've sold out?" Katie's voice squealed.

"What's the gag?" a friend in town grilled me on the tape. After two weeks of quizzical messages, and more than one friend complaining that there was something wrong with my phone line, a message came from a representative of my country. It was scary, calling back and lying.

The American government let David have a two-month tourist visa.

"You've assumed so many identities," I said to him.

"So many," he laughed, and touched the back of my neck as we walked down the street in Central late one evening.

"You're married," I reminded him.

"I will miss you very much," he said.

"I'll miss you too."

I lent him sixteen thousand dollars to pay off his debts and keep him afloat when he got to America. "I will pay you back someday," he promised, but I told him I knew it was a long-term loan. Jeannette had told me it cost just about sixteen thousand dollars to adopt a baby from China. So perhaps I'd made an even exchange.

Wang Ming agreed that the most practical thing for her to do was move into my house. She couldn't afford to rent her own place, and besides, when her visa ran out in the spring, the immigration office wouldn't be likely to come looking for her on an outlying island. We had until 1997, when all of Hong Kong might be turned upside down, to figure out her next move.

She arrived in August with two big suitcases. The pods that fell upon the roof at night didn't seem so loud after that. A house needs occupants, I decided, or else it has too much room for sounds that might mislead you. Two full moons had passed since the night of the typhoon. The blood vessel in Wang Ming's forehead pumped with suspicious apprehension every time she looked at me. "I am a nurse," she reminded me in Mandarin. "I can tell things about you before anybody else can."

"I have something I'll be happy about. I hope you will be too," I said. She squinted at me, and I was sure that absolutely nothing had escaped her notice.

Chapter 20

Marian Yung Shue Fox was born in March.
Banyan Tree is more a name for a boy, but I think it balances nicely with the name of the grandmother she'll never meet, the grandmother who should have lit up the sky like the power plant in our village. Mari, as we all call her, has round eyes the color of black tea, and golden brown hair as wavy as the sea after a squall. She smiles when she hears voices. The first toy she grasped was a quilted airplane, and she started waving her arms and making it fly when she was only four months old.
"Quite the little Eurasian bombshell," Katie said.
Katie came in February and brought her girls. My house became really full, with our improvised community of womyn. Lourdes hasn't had much time to nap anymore, but she seems to enjoy the company, too. Naturally, I gave her a substantial raise. I put Mari's crib in my room, Katie moved into the third bedroom and her three daughters became fond of sleeping in the living and dining rooms Japanese style, on tatami mats that they rolled away in the morning. The girls learned to ride the ferry to school.
For the baby's sake I let Katie lecture me, with sighs and clucks indicating her infinite patience with my stupidity. I shouldn't be working at a computer and zinging the baby with alpha rays when I was so close to delivery. I was crazy to live on this godforsaken island with no hospital if I went into early labor, and didn't I realize that Wang Ming might kidnap the baby when she realized it was her grandchild? It took me days to get anything out into the breastpump. I woke Katie in the middle of the night when Mari's breathing was irregular. She said I was probably making her nervous, then conceded it was normal. My kitchen cabinets weren't baby-proof, she told me. I moved detergents to the top shelf, tied the handles of the lower cabinets together with string, while Katie supervised.
"The way you hold that baby. You'll drop her on her head," she said.
I was afraid of losing Katie and her daughters, who kept baby Mari from feeling lonely. So I didn't tell her to shut her big fat mouth. I didn't tell her I suspected she'd driven Mark away.
When I started going back to the office, Katie had fights with Wang Ming over feedings and how to hold the baby. It would have been a lot worse if they'd been fluent in each other's language. There were times, I knew, that Wang Ming let Katie rattle on and pretended to understand less than she did.

"You are insane," Katie told me one night. "That woman is a battle axe. You think she isn't going to tell David what's going on? You just couldn't think of the consequences, could you? You think he's not going to want joint custody when he finds out? All those abandoned little girls all over China you could have saved from starving in a miserable orphanage, but no, you had to do this."

"Katie," I sighed. "I think you're bored. Why don't you look for a job?"

"This is a barbaric place," she said after several job interviews. But she found a part-time job as a family dispute resolution counselor at the new mediation center. She even worked with Chinese families, aided by a translator. The husbands beat the wives, the wives beat the kids and the maids, she told me.

"I can't stand it here forever," she said.

Wang Ming, on the other hand, said she'd always dreamed of dying on a tropical island.

"You can visit Tian He if you want," I said. David had moved to New York.

Wang Ming's blood vessel had turned darker. She was a tiny figure with bones of iron, walking to the market each day, bringing home bags and bags of groceries. I could swear Wang Ming came up to my chin when I first met her, but by the time she moved in with me she barely reached my shoulders. She put her hand to her head.

"I am too old to travel now. I will take care of you and Mari," she said. She chuckled. "You like being able to do what men do. You go to work and make money, and I am the housewife."

She was always talking about being old. "You can't stay in Hong Kong forever, I know, but I am old. I will not be here to see 1997," she'd say.

"Don't be silly. You'll be here in the year 2000," I tried to reassure her Of course, everything here is temporary. On the island, there is talk of moving all the seedy little waterfront restaurants into one concrete mall overlooking the harbor.

There are women Wang Ming's age who play mah jong during the day. But they're farm women, and she doesn't speak their language. I keep asking her if she's happy.

"I am with my baby niece," she says.

Mari calls Wang Ming "Lao PoPo", or grandma on father's side. Beyond that, there are things we simply don't discuss.

From the letters I've received from David, however, I gather that she's simply told him I got my Chinese baby, without explaining details. I really would prefer that he not find out.

"He'd want to marry you," said Katie. "Ooooyy! What have you done?"

"You once suggested that I have a baby with him," I pointed out.

"What are you talking about?"

"In a letter."

"I'd never say anything like that."

David hasn't said much about Alison in his letters. They stayed together long enough for him to get a green card. They are still married, but he 's just enrolled at Columbia, where there is a lot of scholarship money for the exiled dissidents. They still talk about an overseas democracy movement, but fewer people come to meetings than did a few years ago. Many of the former activists are working in investment banks. They say they want to help gather all of the overseas Chinese money into worthy investments.

"I am not sure running investment money is for my career," he wrote. "America is amazing. New York especially. So many rich people so many poor people. And people frighten of crime. Fox, we must come up with a better sistem. That's why I study political science. I like to invent a new sistem, like long ago you and I speaked about. Liberty, fredom is not enough, because you have the right to ignore the poor. And you are a collective society. With all fredom you ignore this. You are rich and powerful, I am afraid you do not care, unless government, society make you have responsibility. There is some thing to do. I explore that. I will write someday a proposal for a society insisting we are responsible for some things that do not make profit. Like I think you know. Medical, everyone can have home and food but must work if not sick. First poor people have work to make nayborhod nice, like in China we do some times in the past.

"I am also more proud to be Chinese now. Because America does not do everything right, and it does not care about the Chinese people except to sell them American products. Only some in the university care, but in America the scholar has no power. Maybe business is good for making money and power, but something else should be the heart and learning for society.

"Please Fox, let us write to each other. And you let me know what you think the world should do."

I read David's letter to Katie one night after everyone else had gone to bed. We were on my patio, where I'd rigged up a tin roof, strung some lights and arranged a few chairs with removable cushions. Pods hit the roof, muffled by wind and our voices. Katie was sitting cross legged, framed by the fragrant smoke from two mosquito coils. She was feeling pleased that she'd just talked a woman into leaving her abusive alcoholic husband. We seemed headed for one of our rare nights of deceptive calm, when Katie would come home from work in a mood to talk about the way families force pathological behavior on each member, and we'd have conversations in which we listened to each other and agreed, until we both began to nod off.

"He's starting to come through," I said, after reading her the whole letter, misspellings and all. "He's starting to be the kind of father Mari should have." Katie snorted. I'd said something wrong and I knew this was not going to be an agreeable night after all.

"I've been saying these things for years," she said. "I could start a movement if I wanted to."

"I could see David becoming charismatic."

"Meaning I'm not? People tell me I'm so witty I should be writing, you know."

"So do it."

"Why are you being so touchy? If you want David why don't you just tell him and see if he's an honorable guy or not? "

"I didn't... " I said. "I just wanted a child. Everything was always about him, except that night when we both needed consolation... and I wonder about it. We didn't have very smooth communication, you know. He was kind of spoiled, not realizing the sacrifices women made for him. I mean, he was charming and my friend, and I didn't want him to be toyed with by Alison, but he could have been the one toying with her, as a way out of China, or at least some kind of catalyst like Stee..."

"And you weren't toying with him, with both of them, actually, and with your little girl's life?"

"... Like Steve was for getting me here..." When she interrupted me, the same way we'd both noticed our father interrupting our mother, I really wanted to tell her to go home, although she'd probably just keep talking above me anyway. "Anyway, the rest just sort of happened and it's not like I had a master plan for what he could do for me. If I married him everything would revolve around him... "

"He's not your type at all. What the hell did you think you were doing... ."

"... .for all I know, I had my mind on having a baby and maybe I was just imagining he was trying to help me out. Maybe he just had sex in mind..."

"A one-night stand... ." she said, "I thought you were really getting your shit together when you went off to Asia and said screw it all you were going to do what you wanted to do. "

"Jesus, stop simplifying everything. We were friends... maybe he was just trying to score with me maybe not but don't call it a one-night stand as if I didn't even know him..."

"This is all so irresponsible. Maybe Tim would say you let him down too, you know."

"Whaaaa...? "

"If you'd really loved him and cared about your marriage maybe he wouldn't have resorted to cocaine."

Mari began to cry. I stormed into our room and wheeled her bassinet out of there, trying not to wake Wang Ming but eager to make the floor shake under Katie's feet. I concentrated on changing Mari's diaper but I knew I had to say something, because I couldn't stop shaking with rage. I hurried through the diaper changing and Mari kicked and screamed loud "Aaaahhhhh"'s, as if she were trapped in a burning building. I bundled her up in her quilt with the blue and pink elephants, kissed her and tried to calm myself, but it only made Mari yell louder. She didn't even have tears in her eyes anymore, she was just screaming. I sat down with her in the black-and-gold stenciled rocking chair I'd acquired from a family who had left Lamma. I pumped back and forth in time with my rage.

"Don't rock like you're in an Olympic event. No wonder she keeps screaming."

Mari clutched at my tee-shirt, still screaming, her big eyes demanding.

"Katie," I said, feeling tiny hands close to my throat as if their own future lay on the line. "We've always had an autocratic system. You're free to criticize me and I'm supposed to be disarmed and unable to even fight back, let alone give you constructive suggestions."

"What's with you?"

"From now on I'm going to fight back every time you criticize me, whether you think you're giving me good advice or not. Most of the time you're just doing it to put me in my place. I know that because if I were one of your clients you'd be the first to say I did the right thing in leaving a drug addict who hit me. If you don't take back what you just said about Tim, I want you to go home. I mean home, on the plane."

She looked stunned.

"I happen to be an excellent family mediator," she said.

"Then be one."

She stood up. "I'm going to bed."

She slammed the back door behind her. Mari jolted, startled, looked at me with quizzical eyes, but her screams became calmer. She loosened her grasp.

"What now? Sweetie pie, in the grand tradition of your grandmother the Southern belle, we'll save the world tomorrow, okay???"

Mari let out a soft "aaaaaahhhhh" more like a sleepy sigh. And put her little arms around my neck, limply.

We woke up early on Lamma, with roosters crowing in the distance. I wondered if I'd see Katie on the 7:45 boat supervising her brood of children with their suitcases. If she never speaks to me again, I told myself, I'll manage.

Mari's eyes were questioning me when I leaned over her crib and pulled her out. Wang Ming knocked on my door while I was dressing.

"Drink tea," she said, her blood vessel pumping cheerfully. She handed me a steaming mug.

"Oh... thank you." I took the hot mug gingerly, since it was Chinese style, without a handle. The vapors had the grassy aroma of green tea.

"Tonic for feeling healthy," she pointed out. She didn't usually bring me room service.

Lourdes was making breakfast for the girls. Katie wasn't up yet. I sipped my tea uneasily.

When Katie emerged from her room, she strolled out with her hands on her hips, inspecting the cereal bowls and teacups and Lourdes's flowered pants with one sharp sweeping glance. Then she walked up to me, standing over me with her hands tapping against her hips impatiently. She was dressed for grocery shopping in her drab brown-and-white striped blouse and old khaki pants, full of the just-scrubbed freshness of morning.

"I'm not going in 'til later. I'll take Mari to the village," she offered. I swallowed a mouthful of tea with relief. Wang Ming nodded at her, and bundled the baby into the papoose pouch I'd bought for her.

"Mari, Mari, quite tipperary... how does your gargoyle glow?" Katie cooed as we strolled toward Main Street. Mari gurgled from behind her. We shouted hello to various people who passed by, rushing toward the ferry.

"Such a lucky baby, being brought up on this friendly little island without winter," said Katie. It was November then, and still balmy. "This is the kind of place that legends grow up around."

I was watching her arms. Pale and fleshy arms, like middle-aged mothers had when we were children. Katie was now what she was always going to be. She was frumpy even with her new chin-length layered haircut, with its streaks of gray that bothered me more than they seemed to bother her. She was a bigger, rounded version of what Mother used to be, except Mother used to always look pinched and ready for defeat. Katie fought adversity in her own peculiar way, convincing herself that she always knew just what to do and what everyone around her should do. Somehow it served her, maybe even with me.

"I think he likes you," she said when Jon Summers passed us and said hi.

"He's got women all over the Asian Pacific," I said. "And he always needs a haircut."

Katie wanted to be an authority, but she couldn't risk being contradicted. So after that night, she simply redesigned me in her mind, as some kind of star pupil. To be sure, I had to handle her praise case by case, just as I had her

admonishments, explaining patiently why I wouldn't meet her aspirations. But at least she treated me with respect.
We went walking around the island on a Sunday. I carried Mari in the papoose. Kyle, Rachel and Shana skipped ahead of us through the jungle. Katie and I were talking about serious matters. Paul had just bumped my biggest story of the week, saying he thought it needed more investigation. Sunday was like a deep breath, a chance to whine about the pressures of my job.
"Why don't you apply for that job as regional editor, and be above him?" Katie said. "You did it to Steve, you can do it to him."
"I'd have no time to be with the baby," I said.
"A man wouldn't say that."
"Men miss out on a lot too."
The little girls ran up to us, their arms loaded with green bananas.
"Can we fry these?" asked Kyle.
"Sure, but you don't want to carry bare green bananas," I told her, "because they're full of gooey syrup that doesn't come off your clothes." I showed them how to wrap the bunches in the big banana leaves, bigger than Mari.
"Too many," said Katie. She was tossing the words at Kyle. "Did you leave your brain at home? Now you'll have to I drop some of these and let them go to waste."
Kyle, who was 13 and thin, with doe eyes and crinkly hair, trembled. I recognized the way she twisted her mouth.
"Don't criticize her," I said. Katie gave me a dumbfounded look, shrugged, and pulled down her backpack.
"Load them in here," she ordered her daughter.

In December of the same year, Walrus and Eleanor came.
Their plane was late. I paced the greeting area. We might not make the last ferry to Lamma. They'd probably consider it terribly romantic having to go down to Aberdeen and take a long moonlit ride on a sampan, but I wanted to go home and get some sleep. I watched people trek in from all over the world. Japanese passengers in designer clothes, young Europeans prepared for the tropics in drawstring pants and sandals, an Arabian businessman with four veiled women. I watched them sniff Hong Kong and look around, eyes glazed from flight.
Finally, Eleanor strode toward me, a big woman with long steps, a compact suitcase on wheels, a look of curious delight about her. What if my mother had left my father and gone traveling with her? Walrus strode behind her with a bigger suitcase. He was thinner, his mouth wrinkled and his bald top shiny. He

had the look of a passenger who has left something crucial at home. He had become an old man.

Eleanor hugged me stiffly. Walrus kissed me a moist and sluggish peck on the cheek. He looked me up and down.

"My daughter is a mother," he said, and I felt conscious of the roundness my body had developed. "Where is my granddaughter?"

"You'll see her in the morning," I said. "We have to rush."

We caught the ferry, just barely.

Walrus fell asleep on the boat. He snored.

"You do this every day?" Eleanor asked. I nodded.

"How very exotic!" She sounded as if she was just making polite conversation, but she took a walk down the length of the deck, looking eager for a view. She would be no trouble.

When I got home from work the next day Walrus was playing with the baby. He put his hands over his face and played peek-a-boo, over and over. He tickled her, pulling up her shirt and tickling her bare belly, not stopping when she cried. I pulled her away. Later he sat her on his lap and talked to her in a silly voice.

"When you get big grandpa will take you to China. And to India," he said.

He and Eleanor went off sightseeing and shopping, and he had a couple of suits made by tailors.

"Have you noticed he hasn't bought one little thing for the baby? Or for my kids either," Katie hissed to me.

"They've got Christmas presents, don't worry," I said. "Cheap shit. But what did we expect?"

"Christmas," groaned Katie. "What are we? Don't you wonder what you are? What is Mari, Jewish, or WASP, or Chinese? Buddhist? Market reformist?"

"We're Lamma-ites for now," I said. "Steve ... " I hesitated, "... and I used to talk about starting our own civilization on some island. Starting over."

"Steve couldn't handle you," she said. She made a noise like "aaarggghh."

I stopped myself from feeling smug, realizing that the new, improved Katie was just giving me a gold star to show that she was in charge. I wanted to think the worst of Steve, of course, and if I assassinated his character, it would be a clear-cut case of self defense. But why do we always want to imagine that there's an easy explanation? What if you aren't irresistible, what if you aren't going to win a Nobel prize or find a country where things are perfect, but you still wake up and get on with your job and your place in the world, and that's enough?

One day Walrus met me at my office, alone. He was wearing a somber suit, and he looked distinguished. He was very presentable, I thought, except that he slurped the soup and made loud smacking noises when he ate the shrimp and vegetables.

"The last time I was anywhere near here Chiang Kai-shek had taken charge of China again," he said, his mouth still full of stir-fried greens. "There was going to be harmonious rebuilding after the war. A 25-year-old Chinese woman was shot by a firing squad in Canton because she'd been spying for the Japanese all through the occupation... I think she'd been married to a Japanese."

"Sinister," I said..

"There was a fella' in my unit, a correspondent for the paper, who disappeared when he left to cover the Burma war, on a Jap-hunt with the American-Kachin Rangers. He was either captured, or maybe he was a spy... he spoke Japanese. A Japanese who was captured by OSS said he'd seen a man who looked like him drinking with the Japanese brass and talking about baseball. There was a beautiful Eurasian girl who spoke seven languages who was hanged in Singapore as a Japanese spy."

"Everybody has adventure stories here, but you have real war stories," I said.

"I could have stayed forever."

I stopped feeling enchanted. He could have stayed her forever and fucked young girls who'd been sold into the sex slave trade while villages were being massacred.

"There was a war going on," I noted.

"The whole world was going to see a bright new day after the war. When I met Marian we thought the answer was going to come from the Soviet Union. Then from China..." He slurped up a mound of stir-fried noodles and I seized the moment.

"Do you miss Marian?"

Still slurping, he looked at me strangely. "She was in pain. Those last couple of days I kept screaming at the nurse to give her more morphine. The doctor said there's nothing more painful than bone cancer in those stages..."

I called Katie when I got back to the office. "He liked her best when she was sick," I said.

"You can handle him," she said.

I dreamt that my father took me by the hand and said come down, see what I've built. We wandered past the dry sand and the fishing nets, through a forest of seaweed and coral, breathing brine, a meandering trail along the ocean floor.

"This," he said, "is the city I built."

We passed through a coral gate, and there stood a metropolis of grand opera houses, a sprawling summer palace with red pagoda roofs, a gold Buddha in the center of town, fine stone sculptures and gardens, sleek stores.

"*Atlantis?*" I asked.
"*I built it,*" he repeated.
In my dream, the demon escaped from me and told him, "*I don't believe you. I don't believe in you.*"

I didn't have room for Walrus and Eleanor, so they were staying in the little hotel on Hung Sing Ye beach. He took to sitting on the beach all day. Even though it was too cold to swim or sunbathe, and the water had pieces of white plastic garbage bags floating on the waves like a pernicious weed.

"Let's walk on the beach," he said to me one Sunday. Mari was napping. I shrugged. Cool sea air was a bracer that I needed.

We walked back and forth. It was a small beach and we looked ridiculous. Not that the beach was empty, just that other people were sitting down. Kids played with toys, a young Cantonese guy in well-pressed jeans and windbreaker was talking on his mobile phone.

"Almost an island paradise," Walrus said. "I'm an old man and I'm glad I won't be around to see all the oceans look like this. I guess it fits... I almost found an island paradise, but Marian isn't here anyway."

He looked genuinely sad.

"I miss her," I said.

"She was in pain."

I pivoted around in the sand to face him. Or rather, the demon faced him. Maybe the sea air brought it out.

"You liked her best when she was sick! After all those years with her, you told her you were thinking of some 24 year old secretary all the time and she was so hurt it destroyed her immune system..."

The demon rode the eye of a sand tornado, demanding life.

"... she was willing to die to escape from you..."

"Arrrgggghhhh... ."

From deep inside his throat rose sounds of choking, spluttering, like echoes from inside the storm. Walrus was in the sand, purple. "Aaaaargggghhhhh... " It sounded like a plea.

Mouth-to-mouth? I tried to remember high school first aid. Mouth to his, blow in... keep blowing. A crowd began to gather as I straddled my father. He gasped... and coughed. A strange hand at my back. The young guy in the pressed jeans was calling the Lamma ambulance on his mobile phone. Someone took Walrus in her arms and cradled him with care.

"Is he your father? Don't worry, he will be okay now." The woman who had his head in her arms was talking to me. Eleanor came bounding out of the inn.

"You saved his life!" she said.

No, I wanted to kill him.

Since Lamma had no cars, a tiny emergency vehicle came to pick up people who needed to get to a hospital. It had a red cross painted on the side, and a bell that sounded like toy as it tinkled through Yung Shue Wan village. People passing on the narrow roads stared curiously. Walrus, wrapped in white sheets, stared about himself as if it all made sense. Paramedics loaded onto the police boat. Eleanor and I rode along in the cabin. At the hospital on Hong Kong island, interns rushed him into the emergency room on a gurney. He looked at me and smiled faintly. He was enjoying the attention.

"I always worry about his health," said Eleanor.

I nodded. I was bored with the wait and wished I had a book to read. We sat in the waiting room for almost two hours. Finally, a nurse said to come with her.

He was in a tiny private room. He was sitting up, wearing a starched white hospital gown. His face was shiny, looking just-washed. He kissed us both hello, dry thin lips.

"They said I had palpitations. Almost a mild heart attack. I'm an old man," he said cheerfully. He avoided looking me in the eye.

Eleanor canceled the tour they'd planned of China. "I've been there anyway, and I don't think Walter was that eager to go," she said matter-of-factly. "He's happy just driving out to the country in his new car."

They went home a week later, as soon as my father was able to travel. "I feel great. Better than ever. I'm going to start jogging soon," he told me on the phone, when he was safely far away. But his voice didn't boom the way it used to.

I had another dream about him. He was dying, and trying to pull me close to him, with arms and lips. He was naked under sheets and kept trying to pull me under. I fought him, pounded, not sure if I was stronger than his arms. "I want to live!" I shouted.

"You screamed in your sleep last night," Wang Ming told me.

Oscar Wong's company had record profit growth in the first quarter of this year. He had to pay a fine of ten thousand U.S. dollars, and then he was back in business, as predicted. Laurie still loves her father, but she doesn't want to come back to Hong Kong and see him right now.

"I've decided to join the Peace Corps," Laurie wrote in a letter from Washington, where she's staying with a friend from college. "They have a possibility of teaching English either in Mongolia or Romania next year. Either one sounds good to me, although I'm sure the food will be disgusting either place. I'll let you know if it's going to be two years of yak butter or boiled pig knuckles."

In February, when Mari was eleven months old, Jeannette and her new husband came by with their adopted Chinese daughter, who was just a few months younger.

"We'll have to get together every year, wherever we are, so the girls can be friends," said Jeannette. She was radiant. She brought pictures of their house in Boston. It had a white picket fence. Her husband is an environmental consultant. I wondered if I should go home and find a nice stable father for Mari and a house with a yard. Of course there was the matter of Wang Ming. I have a family to support; I can't take off on a whim.

Steve still calls from time to time. "It's like being on the hot seat every day, in a room with no doors," he said.

He writes about foreign relations policy matters, and travels on the press plane when government officials meet.

"Some people would kill for your job," I pointed out.

"A job isn't everything. I don't guess you're ever coming home."

Maybe, I decided, he wasn't comfortable unless he had something to complain about. He probably complained about me to Heidi, and she seized the opportunity. She is still with him. They have a baby. After she stopped breastfeeding, she got a job as a press aide to a Congress representative who would like to see the U.S. impose sanctions on China for their human rights violations. Anyone watching from the wings would think he'd found the perfect mate. But he says it isn't a happy marriage.

"She's ruthlessly ambitious," he told me. "She sucks up to politicians."

"Well, cheer up, all you have to do is defame someone in her coterie and she'll be gone faster than you can say global superpower," I said. I heard crying. "I have to go."

I held my baby in the rocking chair. I got goosebumps all over, being close to her. Katie was on my case, saying I should find a new man, that I'd only stifle my daughter if I continued loading her with all the affection I had.

"You are my only love," I told Mari. She grinned at me and it was David's grin. Was I depriving him of the joy of a little girl whose satin skin had a sweet-butter scent like his?

Katie began getting restless.

"Should we go back?" she asked me one night.

"I have to stay, you know," I said.

"I didn't mean you. I can't keep the girls away from Mark forever. Shit... I wasn't the easiest person to live with." She bit her lip. "He'd come back if I let him, you know. But I don't want to end up like Mom. You have to repress so much if you go back once your relationship has been corrupted."

"Why don't you find someone new?" I said.

"I hate men."

"When I say that you tell me I'm being defensive."

"But you're beautiful and you know how to flirt," said the new improved Katie.

"I don't flirt."

"Bullshit. You don't even know you're doing it."

"Well so what. I don't trust them so I don't give them any reason to trust me either..."

Katie had started smoking and she flicked ashes restlessly. I stifled a cough.

"You shouldn't smoke," I said.

She glared at me, and I thought I might be in for a lecture on everything I'd ever done wrong. She was stopping herself, I realized.

"I need things," she said. Strange, I thought, studying her. Though her face was growing plumper, fleshy and round in places where it had once been bony, it was a resigned face, with tiny parchment folds around her mouth and a furrowed crease between her eyebrows. She blew out cigarette smoke as if it were a stormcloud, she sucked in her lower lip as if willing herself not to scream. She really had been trying. She must need something from me, to go to such lengths to be kind, even if it wasn't sincere.

I went shopping at lunchtime the next day. I went into a jewelry boutique that was filled with the scent of fine leather and heavily perfumed *tai-tais*. The women who came in looked as if they'd been painted in pearlescense. They held pearl necklaces and diamond bracelets in their hands, stroking each strand tenderly.

A small Chinese man who spoke English in a melodious tenor covered the glass counter with a black velvet tray and a dozen ropes of pearls. His voice tickled the back of my neck pleasantly. I held the pearls in my palms, felt their weight and the way they almost swelled against my touch, like ripe fruit. They are gritty if you run them across your teeth, I remembered, and snuck a strand up to my mouth. Up close, I could swear it gave off a whiff of the sea.

I took a deep breath, after much touching and inhaling.

"These," I said, picking up on a long strand of big baroque pearls with a golden tinge. I held them a moment longer. The man stood watching as if he had all day.

"I will give you a special price," said the man, with a soft whistling sound when he said "special price." He punched some keys on a calculator.

Even with the 20 percent markdown, the number he wrote on a small slip of paper made my face feel hot. I imagined asking my mother if she'd consider this part of the contribution to a worthy cause.

"Not for me!" Katie exclaimed when I handed her the lacquered-paper shopping bag that night.

"I never thanked you for your help," I said.

"Ooooooooyyyyyy," she exclaimed. "What'll I do with them?"

"Put them on, for a start."

"Excessive materialism," she said. But she wore the pearls on the ferry to work the next morning, and smiled mysteriously on the top deck.

A few days later she informed me that Jon had invited us to a barbecue at his house on Sunday. "You'd better come," she said.

"Maybe."

"He said to invite you. He said he never sees you."

"I have a telephone."

She fingered her pearls, then lit a cigarette. "I'm quitting when I get home," she said and had another mysterious look on her face.

Perhaps I shouldn't have been surprised when Jon called me at the office the next day.

"I wanted to invite you to my barbecue Sunday," he said.

"Right. My sister mentioned it."

"I guess it's the only day you have with the baby." How did he know that?

"I'll come for a little while, anyway. What's the occasion? Are you leaving on a trip? "

"The occasion is I'm not going away for a while. "

Jon lived up a hill that ran alongside a narrow ribbon of a stream. Tall grasses and weeds climbed the hill, and a dozen blue stained-glass butterflies hovered around the path. Magpies whistled, but further up their calls were drowned by the strains of Canto-pop coming from a balcony on a cement apartment building. Behind a grove of stubby bush came electric guitar chords and waves of party chatter.

"What, does he live in the woods with a stereo plugged into a tree?" I said.

"Here are stairs. He said stone stairs," said Katie. Her pearls made her dark dress look more like deliberate understatement than something she'd just thrown on. I was wearing khaki pants and my Chinese coins. That was mostly what I wore on weekends.

The stairs, such as they were, had been made of ancient stones stuck in the ground. Some were wobbly. A toad hopped across my path.

"There's my handsome prince," I said.

It was a Chinese style farmhouse, with cement walls, a concrete terrace in front where the party had begun, and behind a knot of guests, two rusted iron doors with posters of temple guards. To the right was a grove of banana trees. Jon, in his usual Hawaiian shirt and tire sandals, was talking to three women and downing a beer.

I peered into the house. The floors were cement, with tatami mats. Two guests were sitting on a Chinese-style kang in the living room, and one at a desk with a computer on it. One wall was entirely bookshelves and a stereo and music library. Stairs led up to a loft bedroom. The place was full of potted plants, a homey touch although superfluous. A gecko crawled across the wall. In the back was a kitchen where a crowd stood around. Someone was talking about getting arrested at a forbidden zone in Tibet. I looked around. A short Chinese woman with permed hair was washing lettuce for a salad, using a hose and getting her feet wet. I'd met her before. She looked up and smiled at me. I moved closer to her, trying to avoid the water at the same time.

"Do you know where the bathroom is?" I asked her.

"I think it's up the hill, that way. Watch out for snakes." She turned off the hose and laughed like a bell caught in a breeze. "Jon needs a girlfriend to civilize him."

Outside the back door was a steep hill. More guests stood around. I knew some of them.

"Looking for the loo?" asked Gordon, a pink-faced guy with a can of stout in his hand. "That-a-way... or we won't look, if you prefer the woods." Several people laughed.

"I have to see this." I laughed too, and headed up the hill, on a dirt path that must have been nothing but mush in a rain storm. The toilet was in a little shack at the top, with nothing but jungle growth beyond. Beside the toilet was a large terra cotta pot, filled with water, and a small plastic bucket, apparently the flushing mechanism. Jon had tacked up two posters, one of the Great Barrier Reef, one of Phuket, and set out candles in the outhouse. Another toad glanced at me with beady eyes before hopping on.

Going back down the dirt path I had to be careful not to slide. I spotted Jon on the side terrace, barbecuing chicken and ribs on an elaborate brick grill. A tangy smell of charred meat filled the air. Katie was sitting on a lawn chair, between two Western men who both had the coifed haircuts of bankers or lawyers. They seemed to find whatever she was talking about terribly amusing. I stood frozen for a minute or two, wondering where to go, searching for a cluster of people who looked as if they had room for someone else. I decided to turn to Jon.

"This is like an enchanted forest," I said to him. "Can I help with anything?"

"Can you hand me the platter with the raw ribs? I kinda' like being in the woods. 'Course it doesn't have an indoor bathroom. "

"It must be rough in the rainy season," I said.

"Not as rough as for a woman," he said, grinning but looking embarrassed.

He turned over a piece of chicken and I admired the deep brown blend of sauce and spices.

"What happens to the posters in the outhouse when it rains?" Next, I thought, I'll be telling him about Mari's diapers. I wondered if I'd lost the art of conversation, or maybe Katie had stolen it from me.

"Can you throw those ribs on that empty spot?" said Jon.

I picked up the ribs with a long fork and tried to dredge up something clever to say. My work, my traveling, my whole life seemed a blur. A hot coal leaped up, brushed my face, made me cry out.

"You okay?" asked Jon. There was something tender in his eyes.

If I were to flee, where would I go?

"Fine," I said. I heard a magpie call.

"Been to Vietnam lately?" I asked him.

"Naw. I think I told you I had a girlfriend there, but we broke up. I'm looking forward to staying home for a while. This is home, for all it's worth. I think there comes a point in your life when you stop where you are and accommodate yourself to your surroundings."

"Are you fatalistic then?"

He laughed. I breathed easier, in spite of the smoke rising.

Two days later he called and asked if I'd like to have a drink after work.

"I may be stuck at the office a while," I said.

"I'll wait."

We met at the FCC. The lounge in front, with the small round tables and upholstered chairs, where you went if you were a local with a busy life to lead, or a visitor with worthy connections and many places to go, meeting a friend at a convenient spot en route. It seemed as if no one was left at the bar these days but the old-timers who looked like beanbags atop their favorite stools, the people who'd traversed the continent in open jeeps and propeller planes, but no longer seemed to be going anywhere.

Jon ordered a lime soda.

"The truth is, I had the barbecue as my last fling before I went on the wagon," he said.

The lounge had a civilized level of noise, the tone of drunks who'd been halfway sober all day and were just starting to have fun.

"It must be tough in a place like this," I said.

He shifted in his chair so that our knees touched. "I could join the Brits and go down with the Union Jack. These are supposed to be the final days of revelry, but here I am wondering what the hell I'm going to do, just when I feel like it's time to close the decadent chapter of my life and find some assignments that keep me closer to home. I started to feel like my life was going to end as a tragicomic adventure, where I end up sinking into some parasite-infested river with a name that most of the world can't pronounce."

"Were you being that decadent?"

"Well," he said, "I drink too much. I always knew that, then I started getting pains in my leg. I went to a doctor who said it was nerve deterioration brought on by excessive drinking. Guess I'm getting old before I even got started."

I took a sip of beer.

"Where will you go if this place stops being *gweilo*-friendly?" he asked.

"New York, maybe. Australia? Maybe I can stay with the magazine and get posted somewhere... anywhere. It'll be sad though. My little girl is a Hong Kong native."

"She's a helluva cute kid," he said. He said that with a longing sigh. He wants to be rescued, I thought. I was supposed to find a man who'd rescue me. But from what? Life as a single mother? I was overtaxed and never had time to put on makeup or buy new clothes, but what would I leave out of my schedule if the perfect man in shining armor came along?

After that Jon called every day.

"I keep calling you even when I have nothing new to say," he observed that weekend, drinking soda water on my balcony. "I really like you."

Is this a good idea, I wondered. There was nothing scruffy or impoverished about the way he kissed. He reigned me in with strong arms and led my tongue in a spirited dance. He stroked my breasts with the lightest touch, like a low note that promised a long buildup to the crescendo.

I held out for another week, then agreed to visit him late Saturday afternoon. At the bushes I paused, trying to remember the way, then climbed the rickety stone steps as though a magnet were pulling me. We didn't talk much at first, but flew instinctively up to the loft. It felt like electronic impulses inside. "Nails. Dig your nails deeper... oh god... you're good," he said.

After, we lay under a canopy of mosquito netting.

"Who is Mari's father?" he asked.

I drew a deep breath and wondered if, technically, he had the right to ask. Then I told him.

"So does this guy know or not?" Jon asked.

"He hasn't said. This is like a reprieve from the inevitable. I know he has a right to know."

"If he really wanted to deal with her, I think he'd ask you more about this baby who mysteriously appeared after he left." There was an edge in Jon's voice. "Of course, I'm saying that. Everything you hear is filtered through the ulterior motives of the speaker."

"I'm not always trustworthy," I warned him.

We made love again, to a recording of Cantonese opera in the distance.

"If you marry him you'll have yet another body to support," said Katie.

"I don't think I'm going to marry him," I said.

"Then it's going to come to a bad end," said Katie. I realized she was probably right. Maybe I was comfortable with Jon because with nothing to give, he had nothing to take away. But I let things go on, simply because for the first time in my life I wanted time to stand still.

Jon didn't like to go to receptions at the American Club or the Mandarin Hotel, or other places where the men wore suits. "Boring people," he said. "I'm not going to buy a suit for them." I had to go to some of these affairs, in the line of duty. Katie went with me sometimes. It was at such an affair — something more fun than usual, for a new exhibition of Ming dynasty treasures at the Hong Kong Museum of Art — that I spotted Ian Benjamin. When I said hello he grabbed my hand and kissed it in his usual fashion, as if I had dangerous claws.

"This is my sister, Katie," I said to him.

He gave her a hearty handshake. "What handsome pearls," he said. I left her talking to him while I went off in search of one of the Legislative Council members who was starting to speak out for a more independent Hong Kong after the handover.

Katie gazed off at the water all the way back to Lamma that night.

"You know that older British man you were talking to?" I said.

She nodded and looked at me strangely.

"I blew it with him," I confessed. "I thought he'd be an old-school sexist swine, but we went out and talked and he seemed interested in what I had to say. But he's so old..."

"He's going to India on vacation, he told me," she said. "You know, I never have been there..."

I worked such long hours I didn't always know what the women in my household were up to. Katie started going out, and giving me mysterious looks that contained a hint of pity. And then one morning, over tea, she announced to me, "I'm taking two weeks off. I've talked about it with the girls and Lourdes. You'll make sure the girls get on the ferry to school, won't you?"

"Where are you going?"

She broke into a smug grin. "India."

Around the time the heavy rains began, Katie sent her daughters back to America to spend the summer with their father.
"I'm moving out, officially," she said.
She is spending the summer on Old Peak Road. The society columnist for the local English language paper had an item the other day about "Human rights impresario Ian Benjamin and his companion Kate Fox, a lawyer, were there... " "We'll have to see how the girls get along with him before we get married," she's told me. How did this happen, exactly, except that she looked at her father and saw a suave raconteur who didn't love her enough to stick around, while I looked at him and saw a monster?

But I am content, for now, enjoying the sound of rain as it hits Jon's roof and drips down from the massive banana leaves outside his door. The stream that runs downhill has overflowed its banks. Jon and I waded up the path barefoot a little while ago, under two golf umbrellas. He carried Mari on his back. "She's getting too big for you to carry," he told me. He dangles hints like that sometimes, and it would probably make me nervous, except that he doesn't follow through.

We are now watching the rain from his living room. We've just finished lunch, and John has made a cup of tea and is sitting down at his computer. There are two geckos on the wall. Mari gets excited when she sees them. "Ek!" she calls them.

"Now you're going to start missing a bathroom," Jon says.

"Probably. Don't you?"

He shrugs. "I can't afford space *and* a bathroom."

He has been writing stories for magazines and newspapers here. I imagine eventually he'll run out of ideas in Hong Kong and go on the road for a while. He gets his stories done, but he doesn't always make his deadlines. He kept Mari at his house a few days ago while Lourdes was back in the Philippines on vacation and Wang Ming went to Hong Kong island to do some shopping. Mari distracted him, he told me, and he missed a deadline. "I thought I'd stop missing deadlines when I stopped drinking. Guess it isn't that easy. Maybe I should be a househusband."

Would he be good for her? He has limited visions, after all. The world, but without an indoor bathroom. He says he will never go back to America because, after spending most of his adult life in Asia, he wouldn't fit in.

But he adores Mari. She says "Za, Za" when he isn't around, and her eyes dart about, searching for him. He comes by to see her when I'm at work. He found a one-eyed kitten and gave it to her, so now my household has one more member.

I take Mari out to the terrace to listen to the rain fall on the tin roof. "Za Za!" she says, and looks longingly inside. I let her go in. He catches me gazing down the hillside, thinking. He steps outside.

"What's the matter?" he asks.

"Sometimes I just stop myself and think what have I done."

"Wouldn't you have liked to have banana trees around you when you were a kid? I saw a picture of furniture in the woods when I was about ten, and I thought wouldn't that be cool, to live in the woods. So I do... Damn... Get away from there." Mari has managed to get into his chair, dribbling her bottle. He grabs her just before formula hits his keyboard.

He might make a good parent, I think, but I don't want to tell him. We're both learning new rhythms. We falter. I will keep trying to find a workable policy, because evenings with him are the happiest time of the day. I want to drink him in when we sit across from each other and ponder life. But I don't know if it will hold up if we leave the island.

I sit on the edge of his desk, while Mari seems safely preoccupied with her toy airplane.

"Are you getting antsy to go traveling?" I ask.

"Realistically... sometimes. I feel like it's the only thing I do well. Except I want to be here with you. There must be some reason I picked a woman with a baby this time."

Mari has begun to cry.

"I should take her home," I say.

"Shall we meet at the Waterfront for dinner?" he says. "I promise I'll finish this so I can stay over."

We kiss for a long time. Then he kisses Mari's cheek.

"See you later sweetheart," he says. She screeches because she doesn't want to leave him.

Mari and I arrive home drenched in spite of the umbrella. Wang Ming has been watching TV. Sun the dog and the one-eyed kitten are curled up beside the television, seeking warmth, and the living room smells like wet fur. Wang Ming looks tired.

"Why don't you lie down?" I ask her.

She says she has things to do.

"Lie down."

She shakes her head.

"Wang Ming... ."

The third time, she agrees she should rest.

I change Mari's clothes and put her in her playpen. She shakes her red rattle — another present from Jon. She looks up at me, happy and dry, although the rain-soaked airplane is next to her. She'll have to see America. And China. She can tell I'm thinking about something and she questions me with solemn eyes. I can tell she wants reassurances, that she'll never lose the shelter that is here. What can I tell her? Jon will be here tonight, the rain will fall throughout the summer. Maybe I won't run out of money. Maybe Wang Ming will be with us for a while. Maybe she won't give away our secret, but maybe I'll have to, if getting Wang Ming into America means telling the authorities she wants to be here with her grandchild.

What have I done, anyway? But here she is, my daughter, and someday we'll look at pictures from her baby years and I'll tell her that I didn't want that time to end, not any part of it. Will she remember this house and this island, and think that's what home is, a place where you wish you could stop time from passing? She sits, cross-legged, and looks rather serene for a baby, I think.

"I promise you we'll go places," I tell her.

About the Author

Jan Alexander worked as a journalist in Hong Kong throughout the 1990s. Her articles, essays and reviews have appeared in *The Wall Street Journal, Far Eastern Economic Review, Newsweek, Money, Worth,* the Philadelphia *Inquirer,* the Chicago *Tribune,* and Frigatezine.com. With Lottie Da she co-authored the book *Bad Girls of the Silver Screen,* a look at Hollywood's depiction of prostitutes. *Getting to Lamma,* her first novel, was first published in Hong Kong by Asia 2000.

Printed in the United States
6577